THE DARKENING FIELD

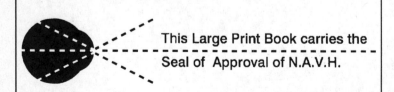

THE DARKENING FIELD

WILLIAM RYAN

THORNDIKE PRESS
A part of Gale, Cengage Learning

GALE
CENGAGE Learning®

Detroit • New York • San Francisco • New Haven, Conn • Waterville, Maine • London

Copyright © 2011 by William Ryan.
First published in Great Britain as *The Bloody Meadow* by Mantle, an imprint of Pan Macmillan, a division of Macmillan Publishers Limited.
Thorndike Press, a part of Gale, Cengage Learning.

LIBRARY OF CONGRESS CATALOGING-IN-PUBLICATION DATA

Ryan, William, 1965–
    The darkening field / by William Ryan.
        pages ; cm. — (Thorndike Press large print thriller)
    ISBN-13: 978-1-4104-4819-4 (hardcover)
    ISBN-10: 1-4104-4819-3 (hardcover)
    1. Detectives—Russia (Federation)—Moscow—Fiction. 2. Young women—Crimes against—Fiction. 3. Murder—Investigation—Soviet Union—Fiction. 4. Conspiracy—Fiction. 5. Soviet Union—Politics and government—1936–1953—Fiction. 6. Mystery fiction. gsafd 7. Historical fiction. gsafd 8. Large type books. I. Title.
    PR6118.Y37D37 2012b
    823'.92—dc23   2012002843

Published in 2012 by arrangement with St. Martin, LLC.

Printed in the United States of America
1 2 3 4 5 6 7 16 15 14 13 12

For Alexander, on his first birthday

CHARACTERS

Efim Andreychuk – caretaker at the Agricultural College

Isaac Babel – famous author, helping with the screenplay for *The Darkening Field,* also Korolev's neighbor

Igor Belakovsky – head of the State Film Board, GUKF

Nikolai Ezhov – People's Commissar of State Security and head of the NKVD

Firtov – a forensics officer from Odessa

Gradov – sergeant in charge of the village Militia station

Count Kolya – Chief Authority of the Moscow Thieves

Alexei Korolev – a detective with the Moscow Criminal Investigation Department

Nadezhda Slivka – a junior detective with the Odessa CID

Maria Lenskaya – production assistant on *The Darkening Field*

Jean Les Pins – a French journalist

Stepan Lomatkin – a well-known journalist

Colonel Marchuk – a senior Militiaman from Odessa

Mishka – a Moscow Thief

Major Mushkin – a senior officer with the Ukrainian NKVD

Elizaveta Mushkina – Major Mushkin's mother and director of the Agricultural College

Papadopoulos – a forensics officer, known as the Greek

Dr. Peskov – a pathologist at the Odessa University School of Anatomy

Pavel Riakov – child star of *The Darkening Field*

Colonel Rodinov – a senior NKVD officer in Moscow

Nikolai Savchenko – director of *The Darkening Field*

Pyotr Shymko – chief production coordinator on *The Darkening Field*

Barikada Sorokina – a famous Soviet film actress

Dmitry Yasimov – Korolev's fellow detective with Moscow CID

CHAPTER ONE

It was snow, or sleet, or something in between — whatever it was, it swirled around them like smoke and seemed to freeze solid as soon as it hit fabric, coating their clothes with a white sheen. It had been snowing, or sleeting, depending on your opinion, for days now and they stepped carefully along the icy path that led to their destination.

Captain Alexei Dmitriyevich Korolev followed the director of the First Mikoyan Agricultural Tooling Trust with a sense of foreboding — the two uniforms and his fellow detective Yasimov trailing behind. Korolev knew this was going to be an awkward job — it just had that feel to it. The director had said as much when they'd told him they were there to question one of his men — at first he'd been all cooperation, but when they'd told him the man's name, Shishkin, and he'd looked to see where they could find him, his attitude had changed.

"Shishkin, Shishkin, Shishkin," he'd said, going through cards in a wooden filing cabinet. "Here we are. Ah. Workers' Hostel Seven. I should have guessed."

Korolev was no mind reader but it was clear that "Workers' Hostel Seven" had a reputation and, now that they were walking toward it, Korolev had a suspicion he knew what kind. The director came to a halt and pointed at a long single-story wooden building, the pitched roof seeming to bend under its thick helmet of winter snow. The hostel had no gutters and melt water had frozen along its length like a curtain that hung down till it touched the snowbank that had drifted halfway up the wall. What few small windows there were lurked high under the eaves, and several panes had been replaced with whatever had come to hand. It was the kind of place where workers, fresh from the country, turned inward, recreating their village in a space the size of a cattle barn.

This bunch wouldn't like outsiders. They wouldn't even like the citizens who lived in the hostels surrounding them. No, this place was a tiny island in the sprawling sea of the city that surrounded it. In fact, the island wasn't really in Moscow, or even in the

Soviet Union — it was somewhere quite different.

"I'm not going in there, Comrade," the director said, stopping, "and I have to tell you, I don't advise you to either. I've shown you where he lays his head. If I were you, I'd wait till he comes out."

Korolev shrugged his shoulders, took a moment to look at Shishkin's photograph, then showed it to the others to refresh their memories. A wide face topped with a mop of blond hair shaved tight at the sides, a rounded, solid-looking jaw, straight lips. He didn't look like a killer — in fact there was something open and fresh about the fellow's face. But apparently Shishkin and his brother had been drinking, and alcohol, as Korolev well knew, could turn a saint into the Devil. The brother had been foreman of a rubber factory in the Frunze district and, it seemed, Shishkin had asked for a job and been refused. Small things became large when vodka coursed through men's veins — he'd had a case once where two men had been hacked to pieces on account of a pickled cucumber.

"How many people in there?" Korolev asked.

"Five hundred souls, give or take," the director said and Korolev knew what that meant — there'd be friends and family who didn't work for the Trust, there'd have been deaths, there'd have been births. A score of rag-footed children were visible around the hostel and a good half of them wouldn't be on any list the director had.

"You see what I mean," the director said, indicating with a nod a clump of sullen men who had appeared at the nearest entrance. "My authority stops here — hell, even the Party activists don't visit this place. They've their own ways of doing things in there, and it works best for everyone if we leave them to it."

Korolev looked at the workers by the door — muscular, work-smudged, tough-standing brutes, and not overly fond of the Militia by the look of them. He took a squint at the snap of Shishkin once again.

"Well, one way or another, we have to go in and talk to him."

He glanced at the two uniforms — they didn't look any happier than the last time he'd looked, but they'd do their duty. Yasimov seemed resigned, and Korolev caught him patting the jacket pocket in which he kept his revolver. They'd all seen hostels like this before — places that followed different rules from the rest of the city around them, and were allowed to by men like the director, desperate for workers to meet the factory's quotas. Korolev started to walk toward the entrance and hoped the uniforms were following. The workers stood aside as they approached, but there was no welcome in their hard eyes, and he could hear them turning and following close behind, cutting off their escape.

He pushed open the door of the hostel and entered.

It was as he'd thought it would be — like the inside of an ants' nest, if ants were humans and lived in the city of Moscow in the year of Our Lord 1937. Everywhere there were people and their possessions. Along one wall small rooms for families had been built, like stables, and from the empty doorframes of which the lucky inhabitants had hung blankets or sheets to give themselves some privacy. Elsewhere, however, every spare inch of floor space had been filled with beds, mattresses and sacking and on them the rest of the hostel's occupants were sleeping, sitting, playing cards, drinking, smoking and doing every other thing that a citizen might do in the comfort of his home — except that here he was sharing his living space with half a thousand others. And above the people hung wet clothing and bedding from washing lines that criss-

13

crossed the room in no apparent order so that the ceiling was invisible. Korolev stood there taking it in, before walking slowly through the room, scanning each face as he did so, and finding himself being examined with the same care in return.

Korolev kept moving forward, pushing gently past the people who stood in the space between the cubicles and the beds, looking for Shishkin. At least it was warm, he thought to himself, even if it was the warmth of a shed full of cattle — the cast-iron stoves that lined the center of the room every seven or eight yards probably gave out less heat than the people crammed in around them. There was no point in asking for the fellow, no one here would tell him anything. Already their presence was like a pebble thrown into a pond — a ripple of silence rolled out from them, till it seemed that the loudest noise in the place was the heavy tread of his hobnailed heels on the wooden floorboards. He cursed the boots, only four months old and things of beauty, but as out of place here as a crystal chandelier. They labeled him as well, and it wasn't a label he much liked to have applied. Still, at least the silent faces turning toward him one after another, grimy white against their work-soiled clothes, made his search for

Shishkin that much easier.

The hostel was split into two main rooms, with a cooking and washing area separating the two, and the farther they advanced toward the center of the building the less the noise of his boots was evident. There were other noises — coughing, the rustle of clothes, the snoring of sleeping workers, dripping water, the cluck of a chicken picking its way between the beds. There was still no sign of Shishkin, but that might be the least of their problems. Women and children were being ushered into the cubicles and young men woken from their sleep to stand and examine the Militiamen with bleary eyes. Korolev could hear people following them through the building, but he didn't look around. If he looked, he'd have to confront them, and that would mean trouble. He squared his shoulders and marched on, feeling the sudden heat from the cooking area, where red-faced women crouched over thermos stoves — the sound of them like the roar of a blast furnace.

The second room was the same as the first and, again, their arrival had a pronounced effect. A youth with tousled hair was playing the accordion but the music came to a sliding halt when he saw the brown pointed *budyenny* caps of the two uniforms. Other

15

gray winter faces turned toward them, watching them, wondering what the four intruders wanted. In the far corner a white-haired man, a thin beard under a hawk's nose, read to a circle of men and women, their heads bowed. It wasn't Korolev's business but he'd wager a month's salary it was a Bible he was reading from and that the man was a former priest. The reader looked up and, without taking his eyes away from the intruders, said a few quiet words which resulted in the silent dispersal of his audience. Korolev watched him place the book in a bag, and sit down on a bed to watch their approach. There was no fear in the man's eyes, but Korolev looked away anyway, trying to make it clear it wasn't him they were after.

It was this turning his gaze away that brought the sleeping Shishkin to his attention. The shock of blond hair was the same, but the face was not so open any more. Moscow hadn't been kind to the smiling youth — someone had hit that nose of his once or twice and left it crooked, and a half-healed scar had replaced most of his left eyebrow. Korolev leaned down to shake Shishkin awake, ignoring the people pushing in behind him, and the gathering of men blocking the only visible exit. He'd deal with

16

those problems when the time came.

"Wake up, Citizen."

The young fellow reeked of alcohol and hadn't shaved for a day or two and, when he turned in his sleep, Korolev couldn't help but notice the dark spatters on the sleeping man's filthy clothing and the black crust of dried blood on his wrist as he lifted a hand to his face. Korolev shook him again and Shishkin's eyes were suddenly wide open — as if he'd been disturbed from a bad dream.

"Shishkin, Ivan Nikolayevich Shishkin — that's you, am I right?"

Shishkin managed to focus and then nodded slowly, even though he seemed unsure of the answer.

"I'm Korolev, Captain Korolev of the Moscow Criminal Investigation Division. From Petrovka Street."

He could hear his words being relayed back through the building. They'd know Petrovka Street — it was famous in its own way. A Soviet Scotland Yard, or so it was said.

"What do you want?" Shishkin said, his voice still slurred from drink.

"Where were you last night, Citizen?"

Something stirred in the young man's

eyes, not quite recollection but certainly unease.

"Here. I was here."

"What's this on your hand, Citizen? Is it blood?"

"I don't know. I had some drink. What of it? Maybe I got into a fight."

"Were you at your brother's? Is that where you were drinking? At Tolya's?"

"No, I was here." But Shishkin wasn't even convincing himself.

"His neighbor saw you go inside at eight o'clock. Then later on he heard you and your brother argue. And then a commotion. And then silence. That was you, wasn't it?"

Shishkin didn't argue. His eyes were focused on the night before, trying to remember, not wanting to.

"He's dead, Citizen," Korolev said, and Shishkin's face drained of color. Perhaps he remembered something — perhaps in his mind's eye he could see his brother's face just before he'd hit him for the first time.

"That blood on your hand — where did it come from?" Korolev asked again.

"Blood?" Shishkin said. "What blood?"

Korolev waited till the boy looked down at the dried blood that ringed his wrist and stained his jacket. Waited till he saw Shiskin swallow hard at the sight of it.

"How did you get back here? Did you walk?"

"I don't know."

"So you were there?"

"No," Shishkin said, his eyes sliding away from Korolev's.

"You'll have to come with us, Citizen. You have some questions to answer."

"It's all a lie. The neighbor is lying. I was here. The neighbor killed him, like as not. He wanted his room — it was a good room. To kill a man for a room — the Devil himself wouldn't do such a thing."

Korolev turned — he saw shock in the nearer faces.

"Can anyone confirm that this man was here last night between eight and eleven? Anyone?"

Korolev looked around and thought there was just a chance this might turn out all right. A small chance.

"Why would I kill my own brother?" Shishkin asked into the silence. "You know what these fellows are like, brothers — they'll make up any lie against you. Don't let me pay for another man's crime."

The workers stayed silent, considering the point, and Korolev could feel the matter going against him.

"There are fingerprints on the hammer,

Citizen. If they aren't yours, you'll be safe enough. You have my word on it."

An older man, with bright blue eyes in a florid, bearded face, made his way through the crowd, followed by a woman. The woman had an oval face, skin roughened from years in the fields and straight gray hair pulled back under a white handkerchief. These would be the leaders of the hostel.

"Vanya, swear to us you'd nothing to do with this," the woman said, her voice almost as deep as a man's. A pleasant voice, but firm as a rock.

"Nothing, I promise you. I was here. No one remembers because I was asleep."

"Why aren't you surprised, Citizen? Your brother is murdered and all you do is deny you killed him. And why no grief for your brother?" Korolev's words hung heavy in the air, and he could see out of the corner of his eye men nodding at the point. It was important he only looked at Shishkin — though he wasn't sure why. Perhaps because his cold gaze was having some effect on the young man.

"You're twisting things — that's what you devils do. He was my own brother, I could never hurt him."

"What about the blood, Citizen?" Korolev

pressed, asking the questions he knew his audience wanted answered.

"What blood? A fight, that's all. This is what you do to men. Wake them up and tell them things. Confuse them. He's alive is all I know."

"He's dead," Korolev said flatly. "He was hit with a hammer. Three times. The first blow shattered his left cheekbone."

Korolev placed his thumb on Shishkin's face where the hammer had struck.

"The next glanced off his right cheek and broke his collarbone."

Again Korolev mimicked the blow, this time hitting the boy a light blow on the shoulder. Then he placed his middle finger on top of the boy's head.

"The last, the order may be wrong, it doesn't matter, but this blow hit him here, punched a two-inch-wide hole and split his skull from back to front. I was with the doctor when he examined him. Your brother's dead all right."

Shishkin flinched each time Korolev touched him and his voice wasn't much more than a whisper when he answered.

"I didn't do anything to Tolya. I swear to you, I loved him."

"Perhaps you were angry with him?"

"This is all lies — I haven't seen him for

weeks. He's still alive, I know he is."

The bearded man glanced up at Korolev. "Tolya's dead, then?"

"Dead as a man with a hammer through his skull."

"It could have been any hooligan from the street. There's no reason it should have been our Vanya."

"Except he was seen entering Tolya's room shortly before he died and seen leaving it soon afterward. If it's some other fellow's fingerprints on the hammer, then we need to do some thinking. But at the moment it looks like your Vanya here is our man. I have to take him with me."

A reaction moved through the crowd as he said this — a squaring of shoulders, a step forward, a scowl — at least some of them would like to stop him taking Shishkin anywhere. He looked at the elders for an answer, wondering what was going through their minds. They'd carved out a little bit of independence for themselves in this hovel of a hostel, it was true, but even they must know that they'd have to give him up sooner or later.

"I give you my word: if the fingerprints don't match then he'll be coming back. But this is murder, Comrades. He has to come with me."

22

The bearded man shook his head slowly. "I can't believe Vanya would do something like this."

The Bible reader with the hooked nose stepped forward. He spoke quietly, but it was clear he had some authority in the hostel and the bearded elder looked relieved by his interruption.

"Vanya, tell us what you remember from last night, and where you were."

"I was here, all night."

"You weren't, Vanya. You didn't come home until after the third shift. Did you visit Tolya?"

The youth's face seemed to crumple in on itself.

"Yes, I was there," the boy sobbed.

"And you drank."

"I did, the Lord forgive me, I did. But I don't remember what happened. I couldn't have killed him, I couldn't have."

Shishkin's hands rubbed at his face, making it difficult to hear what he was saying, but Korolev had heard enough. He put his hand on Shishkin's shoulder and spoke softly.

"Stand up now, Shishkin. Walk with us to the car."

Shishkin did as he was told and Korolev, his hand moving to the man's elbow, guided

23

him. One or two of the workers looked as though they wanted to prevent them leaving but the Bible reader shook his head, and they backed away.

Outside the cold was like a slap in the face and it seemed to unnerve Shishkin, who turned as if to make his way back in, but the Bible reader took his other arm and walked with them. Men and women spilled out of the hostel behind them and followed in silence, ignoring the drifting snowflakes. The only sounds were the wail of a far-off factory whistle and the crunch of feet as they made their way toward the waiting car. Shishkin's head was bowed and Korolev could feel the sobs that spasmed through him.

"What will happen to me, holy father?" he whispered to the Bible reader, who looked at Korolev for his reaction. Korolev was careful to give none.

"Put yourself into the hands of the Lord, Vanya. Pray to him and the Virgin and the saints. Pray for forgiveness and I will pray for you as well. We all will." His voice was very quiet, and Korolev hoped the uniforms couldn't hear.

When they reached the car, the uniforms put Shishkin in the back seat and sat on either side of him — the boy looked small between them. Korolev turned to the priest, maintaining a neutral expression.

"Thank you, Comrade. Your assistance was most useful. We'll commend your actions to the director."

The Bible reader took Korolev's offered hand, perhaps wondering how Korolev could do that if he didn't have his name. But Korolev didn't want to know the priest's name — he just wanted to go home and put this day behind him.

CHAPTER TWO

Maybe the potholes the car had bounced over on the way had shaken the youngster's brain awake, but by the time they brought Shishkin back to Petrovka Street, his memory had returned to him. He'd cursed himself, sobbed, banged his head with his hands, and Korolev had taken the confession that tumbled out of the boy, stopping him every now and then to clarify a point. It was a depressing tale and when it was finished the boy rubbed at his blood-crusted sleeves and asked himself the question Korolev wanted to put to him: "Why?" And the answer eluded them both. Yes, he'd wanted a job at the rubber factory, but not enough to kill his own brother. But he remembered killing him all right, and so Korolev wrote it all down and then handed the confession to him to sign. And Shishkin signed it — tears blurring the ink. Korolev patted the youth's shoulder and then had the uniforms take him down to the cells.

It hadn't been a difficult case, but Korolev felt satisfaction that they'd resolved it so quickly as he began to put the file in order for the procurator's office. But the sense of pleasure at a job well done disappeared when the page he was holding started to rustle loudly. He quickly placed it on the surface of his desk, holding it flat and pushing down, staring at his whitening knuckles, knowing that this was the only way he could stop his hands shaking. It was just that everything was on top of him all of a sudden, he reassured himself, that was all. It had been a long winter, and the Lord knew even the bravest got low during the winter months. And when had he last breathed easily? He remembered a time long before, a summer's day, lying beside a river, his arm around Zhenia, and Yuri sleeping beside them in the shade of the tree. When had that been? The divorce had come through more than two years ago, and they hadn't been happy like that for a good time before it. And his son had been small, very small, and his hair still baby soft. Three years ago, maybe?

"Damn," he breathed, realizing it had been five years at least, and Yasimov looked up in surprise from the report he was writing. Korolev made himself smile, feeling it stretch his mouth taut. Yasimov returned it, giving him a small nod of appreciation.

"For a moment there, Lyoshka, I was wondering how they'd break the news to the family. You handled it well." Yasimov stretched back, releasing a contented sigh. "I tell you what, though — a scrape that close makes the air smell sweet."

"Yes," Korolev agreed, thinking that the air would smell even sweeter if he could get a good night's sleep. It had got to the stage recently when he'd wondered whether there was any point in taking off his clothes at night, so little time did he spend in his bed. But tonight he'd get eight hours, do some washing, eat some hot food.

"To kill your own brother," Yasimov said, shaking his head.

"Alcohol has no family," Korolev replied, reaching for another file he was working on.

"Still, nothing is all bad, you know," Yasimov said, looking as though he was contemplating stopping off somewhere on the way home.

"I can't disagree with that," Korolev said. "The world wasn't made in black and white."

Not at all, he thought to himself; it was mainly gray, the gray of twilight, the gray of the night's beginning.

Korolev's nerves had settled by the time he walked down the wide steps of 38 Petrovka Street and began to make his way home through the still-busy streets of Moscow. He took the longer way, heading toward the Kremlin and through Red Square, passing the recently installed red star that topped the Spassky Tower and glowed like a bright beacon of hope against the black sky above it. It reassured him for a moment, and he felt a surge of pride that he was fortunate enough to be a Soviet citizen, living in the capital of a country that was leading the world by example. But then he remembered the fear throughout the city, particularly among Party members. The works meetings in Petrovka Street were no longer the calm affairs of six months before, but instead had become steadily more and more hysterical. Activists denounced each other for lack of vigilance, for concealing class origins, for having been former Mensheviks or, even worse, supporters of the exiled Trotsky. And every now and then one of his colleagues would disappear.

Korolev kept his head low, sat at the back and was grateful that he'd never joined the Party. But even non-Party members weren't safe — the State expected complete loyalty from all of its citizens and, while he'd fought with the Red Army during the Civil War and had supported the Revolution for twenty years now, Korolev still had allegiances to individuals and beliefs that would put him at risk if they ever came to light.

As it had turned out, however, that icon business he'd been involved with the previous year, the most blatant example of his divided allegiances, had ended up working in his favor in unexpected ways. The matter remained top secret, which was probably just as well from Korolev's point of view, but the injuries he'd suffered in the course of the investigation pointed to it having been a dangerous matter, on top of which Korolev now wore on his chest a mysterious Order of the Red Star that he was forbidden to discuss. According to Yasimov, most people thought he'd uncovered a counter-revolutionary plot and had personally assisted the NKVD, or the Chekists as they were commonly known after an older acronym, in the violent suppression of the conspiracy. It was almost true, after a fashion, but no one in Petrovka Street except for his boss knew the real story, and even Popov didn't know all of it.

Still, for the moment at least, the dark red

enameled star that General Popov had ordered he wear on his chest while on duty, whether in uniform or not, had created a bubble around Korolev, and even around Yasimov. Korolev wasn't complacent, though, far from it. After all, if some of his actions during the icon affair ever became public, they'd result in his immediate re-acquaintance with the interior of a Lubi-anka cell. So for the foreseeable future he wanted to keep well clear of anything con-nected with the Chekists until they forgot he'd ever existed. And, until he was confi-dent they had, he'd carry on keeping a small packed suitcase in his bedroom wardrobe just in case they came for him one night with a one-way ticket for Siberia.

Korolev found himself at the door of the building he lived in on Bolshoi Nikolo-Vorobinsky and began to kick the snow from his boots before opening the heavy front door, light spilling out into the lane as he did so; and as if to remind him that his concerns weren't just groundless paranoia, he caught sight of the red seal that had been applied to Kotov's apartment door by State Security only the previous week and which swung gently in the resulting draft. Poor Kotov had been an administrator with a government ministry until his arrest, but he'd had the nervous stoop and gray pallor of a condemned man for the best part of a month before it. Now he and his wife had disappeared and the only trace of their passing was that damned red seal that would swing there till the apartment was cleared and reallocated. Korolev reminded himself that he was alive, climbing the stairs to an apartment which he shared with the beautiful Valentina Nikolaevna, and by anyone's standards he was a lucky man. He had to remember that. Tomorrow would look after itself.

He could hear Natasha's laugh as he turned the key in the lock, but by the time he entered their shared room Valentina's daughter was sitting grave-faced at the table — her eyes focused on the exercise book in which she was writing. She didn't even look up at him. Valentina Nikolaevna, on the other hand, stood from the battered Chesterfield, putting aside the book she was reading. Every time he saw her he felt his mood lift — a man could dive into those sea-blue eyes of hers and swim to the horizon.

"Are you hungry?" she asked.

They'd come to an arrangement over the last few months — she'd often cook for him, or leave something out for him if he was late and, in exchange, he shared his food parcel with her. It was a domestic arrangement and he was sure there was fondness on her part. For a while, he'd dared to hope a closer relationship might develop, but he wasn't the kind of man she needed. A battered, middle-aged *Ment* with a job that kept him busy most of his waking hours? She could do better, that was for sure. No, a beautiful woman like her deserved a man who could look after her properly, and who she could be proud of. She'd find someone soon enough, he suspected — and then he'd probably be back to cooking for himself.

"We had to arrest a fellow on the outskirts," Korolev said, aware that he'd been looking at her in silence for a moment longer than was polite, and cursing himself. "A murder. It took a while to get the paperwork in order. Anyway, I picked up the parcel from the canteen. Shall we see what we've got?"

He put the package on the table in the small cooking area, feeling that his mouth was not entirely within his control. What was it about her that made him babble like a fourteen-year-old? Sometimes he wished he'd never met the woman, but that was a feeling that never lasted for long. What sort of life would it be if he hadn't?

33

■ ■ ■ ■

Korolev wasn't asleep when the knock at the door came. Thinking about it afterward, he wondered if the car pulling up outside had woken him. It wasn't inconceivable: his bedroom window faced the alleyway and the ZIS would have made a rattle against the snow-swaddled silence of the Moscow night. And, of course, at that time of the morning the streets belonged to the black cars of State Security, and the sound of an engine coming to a halt would have a whole street fearing the worst.

So Korolev was awake, but if it was the car that woke him he'd no memory of it. Instead he was only conscious that he'd been dreaming of that time by the river, only this time it had been Valentina Nikolaevna his arm encircled, and Natasha who'd been sleeping beside them. The memory of the dream was still strong enough for him to feel the weight of the sun on his face and joy rolling up him like a wave. For those two or three moments before the knock came he could have floated up to the ceiling with happiness if his body's weight hadn't kept him fixed to the bed.

Three knocks. One. Two. Three. Not

much noise, after all, but enough to shatter that moment as if it had been a glass hurled against a wall.

Ever since he'd seen poor Kotov being marched away in his pajamas, Korolev had slept ready for an immediate departure and he was pulling on his trousers and boots before he'd even worked out what was happening. The mysterious knuckles battered the door again, louder this time, and more insistent, but Korolev took the time to put on an extra vest, take his warmest jumper and his winter coat and pick up the small bag he'd packed for just such an event, before walking through the shared room. He stopped for a moment and looked around and it occurred to him he might never see this place again. Well, if that was what the Lord intended, then there wasn't much point dwelling on it.

There was another knocking, more insistent now, and Valentina Nikolaevna's outline appeared in the doorway, Natasha's sleepy voice coming from behind her, asking a question that he couldn't quite hear. He shook his head sharply, waving her back in to her daughter, but she didn't move, waiting until he came closer before putting a hand on his chest. He leaned forward, unable to stop himself, and breathed in the scent of her newly washed hair but at the same time remembered himself enough to gently push her back into her bedroom, shutting the door behind her. There was no time to say anything or even to consider what her action might have meant before he turned, inhaling deeply, and opened the door to the hallway.

Korolev blinked, dazzled for a moment by the light on the landing, before managing to focus on the man in front of him. There was only one of them, which was odd, and Korolev leaned forward slightly to see if there were others hiding in the corridor. The young Chekist smiled at his reaction and that irritated Korolev — if he was to be arrested he'd like to be treated with respect.

"Going somewhere?" the lad asked. No more than twenty-five, he'd guess. His deep-set eyes were obscured by shadow, but Korolev had the impression the pup was laughing at him.

"You tell me," Korolev answered, sneaking another look to see where the rest of them were waiting.

"Yes, we have a short trip to make. To the Lubianka."

Again that teasing little smile — it was making Korolev's fist itch.

"Well, I'm ready."

"Good. We must always be prepared. At any time of day or night."

Now the fellow was quoting Party slogans at him. Korolev could feel his confusion creasing his forehead into a frown.

"Look, Comrade, it's half past two in the morning," Korolev began before he ran out of words. *Am I to be arrested?* was what he wanted to ask, but he didn't dare voice the thought.

"And you have your bag packed ready for a trip — that's good." The youngster was grinning now, nodding at the case Korolev had placed beside the door.

Korolev swallowed, feeling his mouth dry as paper, and found he'd taken a great dislike to this unimpressive representative of State Security. But then he had a sudden surge of hope — the fellow wasn't here to arrest him. The rascal was making fun of him because he *wasn't* here to arrest him.

"Look, Comrade," Korolev said, confidence returning to his voice, "either tell me what your business is, or let me go back to my bed."

The Chekist seemed to relent. "You don't need the suitcase, Comrade. Colonel Rodinov wants a few minutes of your time — that's all. The phone system is down so we couldn't call. I've a car outside. My name is

Todorov."

Korolev didn't shake the Chekist's hand, or respond to his introduction. Instead he picked up his overcoat and nodded toward the stairs to indicate he'd follow the fellow. He thought for a moment of going in to re-assure Valentina Nikolaevna, but decided against it. He wasn't out of the woods yet.

Korolev had been waiting in a narrow room, so narrow and so long it was almost a cor-ridor, for the best part of an hour. A stern-looking Dzerzhinsky, the original People's Commissar of State Security, looked down from a poster beside the far door warning him to "Be on your guard!," which Korolev thought was sensible advice, tired though he was.

He was about to look in his pocket for a cigarette when there was a bang that sounded like a door slamming shut and the click of approaching footsteps. Then the young Chekist who'd picked him up at Bolshoi Nikolo-Vorobinsky entered, the uniform he'd changed into crisp against the drab blue walls.

"He's ready, Comrade. He had some mat-ters to attend to."

Rodinov had changed in the short time

since they'd last met. His skin was pale and flabby, whereas before it had been pink and taut, and his round, hairless head no longer seemed to shine with brutal vigor. The eyes that looked up from the file on the table were bloodshot and tired and the greeting he gave Korolev was nothing more than a grunt and a nod of his head toward the single chair in front of the desk at which he sat.

"Korolev," he said after a moment or two, his eyes narrowing as he glared at him, as if willing Korolev to admit his guilt, even if he was guilty of nothing.

"Yes, Comrade Colonel. Korolev. You sent for me."

"I did," the colonel said, and it wasn't immediately clear whether he was questioning the suggestion or agreeing with it. He looked back down at the file in front of him.

"Are you prepared to undertake a confidential mission connected with the security of the State, Captain Korolev?"

Well, there was only one answer to that question.

"Of course, Comrade Colonel."

"Good." Rodinov pushed a photograph across to him. "Then it's settled. Maria Alexandrovna Lenskaya. She was, until last night, a production assistant on Comrade

Savchenko's new film. Now she's dead."

Korolev examined the girl in the photograph.

"Murder?"

The colonel seemed to consider the question, smelling his way around the answer in that fighting-dog way of his.

"Apparently not," he said, seeming to produce the words reluctantly. "She killed herself, or so we're told. But we want to make certain, which is where you come in."

"I see. When did it happen?"

"She was found at ten o'clock this evening."

"Has anyone looked at the body? A pathologist, I mean — I'd recommend Chestnova at the Institute if not."

"No one has examined her and she died in the Ukraine, near Odessa, so I don't think Chestnova will be much use. And we want this matter handled very quietly. At least until we have a better idea of the situation. Comrade Ezhov himself thought of you — he formed a favorable impression from that matter you assisted with last year. He recalled your tenacity, and your discretion." That slight emphasis on the word "discretion" was setting off warning bells. Korolev was wide awake now, that was for sure.

"I'm grateful he recalls me favorably," Korolev said, thinking exactly the opposite.

"A great honor. And, as it turns out, your friend Babel is writing the film's screenplay — a happy coincidence."

"I see," Korolev said, wondering why me? Surely there was someone in Odessa who could handle this.

"We think it best if you go there by chance. I've spoken to Comrade Popov and in recognition of your excellent performance in recent months, you've been awarded a two-week holiday — to be spent where you wish. You wish it to be spent near Odessa. It isn't the summer down there, but it isn't as cold as Moscow — so why wouldn't you visit your good friend and neighbor, Babel? Isaac Emmanuilovich will be made aware of your true purpose and will no doubt do his best to help with your inquiries. One of our more competent Ukrainian operatives, a Major Mushkin, is coincidentally at the location on sick leave but will assist if necessary. If it's suicide, you have two weeks to spend as you please. If it's something else — well, I'm sure the local Militia would be grateful for the assistance of an experienced Moscow detective. You will, however, report to me. The local Militia will be involved only to the extent that you consider necessary. Understood?"

Korolev understood. He looked at the girl's face once again. She seemed an ordinary person — not bad-looking to be sure, but at the same time not visibly worthy of the attention she seemed to be getting.

"A few questions, Comrade Colonel?"

Rodinov opened his hands to signify his agreement.

"Who is she?"

Rodinov paused and considered the question for a moment or two, his gaze dropping to the dead girl's photograph before returning to Korolev. He sighed.

"If I tell you she's a personal friend of Comrade Ezhov's, will that make more sense of the situation for you?"

Korolev felt his left eyebrow rising despite his best efforts to keep his face completely immobile, but the colonel shook his head.

"Don't jump to conclusions, Korolev. As you know, we're surrounded by enemies, both within our borders and beyond them. We have to remain vigilant — careful of even the most innocuous event in case it reveals treachery. The girl was known to Comrade Ezhov — yes. He took an interest in her, as senior Party members often take in younger comrades who promise much for the future. Because of the connection he considers it prudent to make sure there are no suspicious circumstances. The commissar doesn't understand why a young comrade of Lenskaya's prospects and ability would kill herself. He wonders whether there might be more to it."

Korolev didn't for a moment believe that Ezhov's interest in the pretty girl was that of a fatherly older Bolshevik for a young protégée, but he wasn't about to disagree with Rodinov's version of the story. After all, he still had a working brain and a strong instinct for self-preservation. As for the girl, he'd keep an open mind.

"It will take me some time to get there by train," he said.

"There's a plane leaving for Odessa from the Central Airport in two hours and twenty-five minutes. You've just got time to go home and pick up some clothes. Todorov will take you. Someone will meet you at the airport with the information we've pulled together on this matter — you can read it on the way."

Korolev had never been on a plane before and had never expected to be on one either. The prospect took him aback for a moment. The colonel seemed to interpret this as concern about the nature of his mission.

"Look, Korolev. In this case, it's important we act carefully and establish the truth. We could use the local Militia people, but we want to have direct control of this and someone we know working on it. We could send in the local Chekists, but our people can be too enthusiastic. Certainly, if it's murder, we might think again — but for the moment it's your case."

"A few things, then," Korolev said, pulling himself together. "A pathologist should examine her immediately."

"No one will examine her until you're there."

"But, Colonel —" Korolev began, before Rodinov interrupted him.

"You are Comrade Ezhov's eyes and ears. You are to be present at every stage of this investigation."

"But bodies deteriorate, and there are tests that must be done as soon as possible to determine time and means of death."

"Let me remind you, Captain, that as far as the world is concerned this is a suicide, nothing more, and we don't want to do anything that might suggest otherwise. Let me ask you — would the Militia haul a pathologist all the way from Odessa in the middle of the night for a suicide? These days?"

A fair point, Korolev conceded. Self-homicide had become so common recently that it would be rare for a pathologist to see the body at all. Rodinov nodded, seeing that Korolev understood.

"The body has been moved to an ice house so it won't deteriorate, and a pathologist will visit tomorrow at the same time as you arrive. Anything else?"

"If possible, the place where she died should be protected — if it turns out to be murder there's no need to make the forensics men's job any more difficult than it has to be."

"I'll pass that on."

There wasn't much else to be said, so Korolev placed the photograph back on the desk and stood up, ready to go. Rodinov also stood and walked him to the door, placing a hand on Korolev's shoulder.

"This is an opportunity to perform a useful service for Comrade Ezhov — remember that. He doesn't forget his friends."

Korolev nodded, thinking of the dead girl, and wondering whether, these days, it was such a good thing to be Commissar Ezhov's friend.

CHAPTER THREE

The Central Airport's administrative buildings, workshops and hangars were surrounded by a thick white mist and Moscow felt a long way away. Korolev had been driven here at breakneck pace on the icy roads by Todorov, the young Chekist, fog notwithstanding. Now, in contrast, everything was still and silent except for the low murmur of conversation from two mechanics, one of them female, who were refueling the tiny airplane that was taking off for Odessa in less than half an hour.

"A Kalinin K-5," a voice behind him said and Korolev turned to see a burly figure dressed in an ankle-length fur coat. The man's black eyes were the only visible part of him, what with his round fur hat and turned-up collar, but Korolev had the impression of intense watchfulness all the same, as if he were being assessed for some reason. "It's a good plane. Still, best to dress up warm, Comrade — the cabin is heated, but all the same it can get cold up there."

Korolev turned to examine the aircraft once again. It didn't look very solid, but that was surely a good thing if it was meant to fly up to the heavens.

"I don't know much about them," he said, conscious of a certain skittishness in his lower stomach.

"Oh, you don't need to worry. She's a beauty, I fly this route seven or eight times a year. She's always on time, more or less."

The fur hat slapped the aircraft's flank appreciatively as if it were a trusted charger, and its thin metal skin responded with a wobbly boom.

"She has a top speed of nearly one hundred twenty-five miles an hour — can you imagine? And she'll take us all the way to Kursk in one go. We'll be in Odessa in the early afternoon if the wind is behind us and they refuel quickly. There are sometimes delays, of course." The man shrugged his shoulders and Korolev nodded his understanding. There were often delays, but even the possibility of being in Odessa within seven hours was astonishing. It had taken him nearly a month to get back from Odessa when he'd been discharged from the army in 'twenty-two, and that must be more or less the same distance. He put a gloved hand to one of the struts and pulled — it seemed sturdy.

"It doesn't look like much," Korolev said. "I mean — to go so fast and up so high."

"She's reliable," the hat said firmly. "The new planes may be quicker and bigger, but this one's never let us down. Am I right, Antonina Vladimirovna?"

"You are indeed, Comrade Belakovsky." The young mechanic smiled — white teeth flashing in the light from a lantern. It occurred to Korolev that the girl was perhaps too young for such a responsible job.

"You should make a film about her," she continued.

Belakovsky laughed, revealing a pock-marked nose and a scrubby salt and pepper mustache that nestled under widely spaced nostrils. Korolev thought he recognized the fellow from a newspaper, or perhaps a newsreel, and held out his hand in greeting.

"Korolev," Korolev said. "Alexei Dmitriyevich. Moscow CID."

"Nice to meet you, Comrade Korolev. Belakovsky, Igor Zakharovich. And what takes you to Odessa?" Korolev was considering how to respond when an officious-looking woman in a thick padded coat came out of the terminal building.

48

"Comrade Belakovsky? Comrade Korolev? We must weigh you now." She waved them toward the doorway.

"The plane can only carry so much weight, Korolev," Belakovsky explained, seeing his surprise.

Sure enough, inside the terminal a pi lot in a long leather flying coat was standing on some scales with a canvas postal bag in one hand and a half-smoked papirosa in the other.

"Two hundred and thirty-three pounds," said the female clerk, writing it into a ledger. "You're putting on weight, Anton Ivanovich."

"It's the post," the pi lot answered gruffly, sucking on the paper tube of the cigarette, and Korolev was sure his voice was slurred. He certainly looked the worse for wear. At least his colleague, a younger fellow with a clean shirt poking out from his fur collar, had bothered to put a razor to his chin. Unless, of course, he didn't yet have to shave — it was possible, he supposed. The boy *was* very young — but surely there would be exams and so on. They wouldn't let just anyone fly such a valuable piece of machinery, would they?

The passengers lined up and Korolev saw that he was in privileged company. A short, round-chested officer with a general's insignia on his collar and a cluster of medals visible underneath his open greatcoat was next in line. Belakovsky took Korolev's arm.

"Comrade Korolev, you must meet Stepan Pavlovich. You'll have read his articles in *Izvestia.* Lomatkin — the journalist? Comrade Lomatkin, this is Korolev from Petrovka Street. A detective, I'm guessing."

Korolev shook the hand of a thin young man, handsome in a bookish sort of way, who looked slightly nervous. Perhaps it was his first time flying as well.

The next fellow on the scales had Party cadre written all over him — a pale ascetic-looking fellow in a long brown coat that looked even more military than the general's. He stood unsmiling, a small leather suitcase in his hand.

"One hundred sixty-five pounds, Comrade Bagraev," the weigher said. "Captain Korolev, please."

Korolev walked over and took his turn on the scales, sucking in his breath. He hadn't had time to pack anything more than his arrest bag but, still, he wasn't a small man.

"Two hundred pounds," the clerk said, and Korolev could see the Party bigwig's disapproval as he stepped down. It didn't seem to matter that Korolev was a good four inches taller than he, the fellow clearly had him marked down as some sort of speculator, well fed on contraband butter.

"What happens if there's too much weight?" Korolev asked Lomatkin in a quiet voice, so as not to be overheard by the disapproving Bagraev.

"At this time of year they have to be careful with ice building up on the wings."

Korolev looked out through the nearest window at the airplane and imagined it caked with ice.

"What happens then?" he asked and Lomatkin shrugged in a manner that left Korolev in no doubt that too much ice wasn't a recipe for a long life.

When all the passengers had been weighed and their names checked off, the younger pilot and the clerk examined the ledger and the latter flicked balls back and forth on an abacus. Their faces were grave and Korolev felt every one of his two hundred pounds, bag included.

"Captain Korolev?" a voice asked. He looked around to see blue eyes in a pale pudgy face only a fraction of an inch away from his own. Korolev nodded and the man held out a thick envelope.

"Goldberg. Colonel Rodinov sent me with

a package for you. To read on the plane. Please sign this receipt."

Korolev signed with the pen the Chekist handed him and accepted the offering, feeling its weight, thinking someone must have worked like a dog to get it ready.

"Captain Korolev, would you come forward please?" the weighing clerk asked and he caught the tail of a smug glance from the Party bigwig, but Goldberg, assessing the situation in an instant, walked across to the clerk and whispered in her ear. The clerk asked a question, her face seeming to lose a little color, and the Chekist nodded.

"Excuse me, Captain Korolev, I made a mistake," the clerk said, her voice uncertain, and looked down at the list again. "Comrade Bagraev, please — could I ask you come to the desk?"

The Party boss shot Korolev a look of irritation and walked brusquely over to the clerk, his whole demeanor expressing impatience.

"What is the meaning of this? I'm due in Kursk this afternoon on Party business of the highest importance —" Bagraev began, but his protest was interrupted by Goldberg tugging his sleeve. Bagraev looked at him in annoyance but stopped speaking. Goldberg leaned in close and whispered once again.

It was interesting to Korolev to see how quickly the irritation disappeared. Bagraev's mouth opened as though to speak and hung there for a moment, making him look like a beached fish. He darted a look at Korolev, nodded sharply to the Chekist, then turned to walk out of the building without another word.

Goldberg came back. "Is there anything else I can assist with?"

"No," Korolev said, conscious that everyone in the building was looking at him. "You've been more than helpful already, Comrade."

"A pleasure," Goldberg said in his quiet voice. "You'll be met by Major Mushkin at the airport. The colonel asked me to tell you that he expects to hear from you this evening — the major will arrange the call. Enjoy the flight." He touched a finger to his hat in salute and turned to leave.

Outside the fog still lingered as the passengers walked across the packed snow toward the airplane. At first Korolev thought the bone-shuddering noise came from the Kalinin's single engine, but then, through the mist, dark shadows came in a line from the left, accelerating as their propellers struggled to lift them into the sky. The roar of engines felt solid — as though someone were pushing at his chest — and even Korolev recognized that the fuselages belonged to bombers. They came past, one after the other, a chain of fat black silhouettes, their propellers creating a snowstorm that forced Korolev to look through squinted eyes.

"Come on, Comrade," someone shouted in his ear, and pushed him toward the plane. "The imperialists will think twice about attacking us now we have bombers."

It was the young pilot, and Korolev nodded, knowing what terrible weapons such planes could carry, and followed the boy up the steps to the cramped cabin. The pilot turned and gave him a blanket from a pile.

"Here you are, Comrade." He looked at Korolev's well-worn coat and handed him a second.

Korolev settled into his seat and looked out as part of the wing dropped down at the back and the plane juddered forward, turning to the left. He could see burning oil drums marking a way forward across the flattened snow and he made the sign of the cross in his pocket, feeling his stomach squirm as the plane bounced along, slowly picking up pace. Surely only birds and the Lord belonged above — if only he could have taken the damned train instead. The window offered him a distorted reflection that gave him no comfort — his face looked as pale as a choirboy's surplice and as miserable as a bereaved mother.

"Christ protect me," Korolev muttered as the plane lurched into the air before landing again with a solid bump and a worrying slide. He was thankful no one could hear him with all the racket. Finally, with the engine whining like an angry swarm of giant hornets, the plane soared upward and the lights disappeared into the mist.

For a while they flew in a gray world, completely alone, as the plane hauled itself upward, yard by yard, the pressure in Korolev's ears building as he desperately tried to swallow, before, eventually, they left the milky sea beneath them and he saw a splash of blue sky to the left, which slowly grew so that the dawn sun shone into the cabin, bathing the other passengers in gold. Korolev could see the suburbs of Moscow far beneath him, or at least the rooftops, and a frozen curve of the Moskva River where the morning mist had cleared a thousand feet below. He glanced away from the window and caught Lomatkin looking over at him. Korolev nodded back with what he hoped was polite enthusiasm, but he didn't like this flying one bit. Not one tiny little bit.

After a few minutes of gritting his teeth so

hard he thought there was a chance they might crumble to dust, Korolev decided it would be best to occupy his mind. His gaze fell on Goldberg's thick envelope and he opened it.

Whoever had prepared the papers had fixed a photograph of Lenskaya to the first page and he quickly replaced it in the envelope, although not before taking a quick squint at it. She was unsmiling in the picture, looking to the side and downward, her dark hair held back with a ribbon. Pretty, clearly, and there was a certain sexuality about her that was unusual for an official picture. Still, he knew better than to rely on impressions created from a photograph. Whoever had said the camera never lied — well, they'd been lying.

Reading through her Party record he decided that, if nothing else, she must have been tough. An orphan who'd battled her way into the Komsomol, the youth wing of the Party, then the State Film School, and finally the Party itself. Impressive. What was more, her professional career had been exemplary — each teacher, each project leader, each professor, each department head had congratulated her in the most flattering terms. "A comrade of the highest

56

moral integrity and the greatest technical proficiency" was the evaluation of some film director he'd never heard of. He turned a page and came to a sudden stop when Belakovsky's name caught his eye. He looked up, but Igor Zakharovich, hatless now, was paying no attention to him, being more interested in what was passing beneath them. Korolev returned to the papers — praise, of course, this time for her invaluable assistance on a fact-finding mission to the United States of America two years before. Belakovsky had headed a delegation from the Main Directorate of the Cinematic and Photographic Industries — GUKF for short — and now Korolev remembered where he knew the man from. Belakovsky was the GUKF chairman, no less. An interesting coincidence that he should be on the same plane. Korolev looked at Belakovsky once again, curious. Lenskaya had been admitted to the Moscow orphanage in 'twenty-three at the age of twelve. That was her first bit of luck, as back then most orphans had had to take their chances on the streets. The Lord alone knew how many citizens had died in the course of the Civil War and the famines and diseases that had come with it. Twice as many as in the German War, they said. Maybe more still. And the State had struggled to cope with the aftermath. Still, she must already have been able to read and write, as one of her first acts of political usefulness had been to assist in the teaching of the younger children, and perhaps that had given her the roof over her head that many in the same position had struggled to find.

There was no mention of Lenskaya's parents, though, or where she'd come from, or indeed where she'd acquired her education, and no information as to how she'd ended up in a Moscow orphanage, and that bothered him. After all, if she was able to help teach other children how to read and write, she'd surely have been able to tell the orphanage about her past. He made a mental note to ask Yasimov to look into it. Perhaps the Party record had been cleaned up to remove an embarrassing detail. She'd had a powerful friend — and such things were not uncommon. It might be nothing, but it would be worth looking into if this turned out to be more than just another suicide.

He turned to the next document. The author's name and its recipient were blacked out, but it was a report on the film that Lenskaya had been working on when she died. He skipped through the background on the film director Savchenko — he wasn't so uncultured that Savchenko's reputation as a premier artist of Soviet cinema was unfamiliar to him. But here was another interesting thing — Savchenko was one more person who'd recently returned from Hollywood. He checked the dates. More interesting still, they'd all been there at the same time. Savchenko had tried to make some socialist cowboy film, or so Babel had told him once. It had been a failure, and he'd come back to Moscow with his tail between his legs. It was a reasonable assumption therefore that this film, *The Darkening Field,* was an attempt by Savchenko to re-establish his socialist credentials.

Of course, the subject matter of the film was tricky: the murder of the ten-year-old Pioneer Pavlik Morozov by his family when he betrayed them as wreckers was an event that could be looked at in different ways. As far as the Party was concerned, the message was clear — even the youngest citizen owed loyalty not to themselves or their family, but only to the State and the Party — even to the point of death. Some citizens, however, and Korolev was one of them, might just harbor the suspicion that the brat had got what was coming to him. So it would be important for the director of such a film to make sure that the correct message was received by all, and that might be a difficult proposition. It seemed this was also the opinion of the author of the report.

Concerns have been raised at the highest levels which have led to constructive criticism being passed on to Nikolai Sergeevich Savchenko by GUKF Director Belakovsky and others in explicit and forthright terms. Such criticism has resulted in the reshooting of several scenes and the hiring of Isaac Emmanuilovich Babel to assist in rewriting parts of the screenplay to place the political aspects of the case at the heart of the film. However, it would appear that N.S. Savchenko has persisted in his failure to address the Morozov incident correctly and has proved unable to show it as an unequivocal example of selfless socialist heroism. Furthermore the changes made by I.E. Babel have not reflected the direction required by the Party. Instead the story is fragmented, portrays sympathy to the traitors and appears ambivalent about Soviet Power. Comrade Belakovsky has made repeated efforts to persuade N.S. Savchenko of the necessity of developing the film within the bounds of socialist realism rather than bourgeois concepts of dramatic and psychological drama. It is to be feared that, following his visit to the United States, N.S. Savchenko is no longer capable, or willing, to portray the murder of Pavlik Morozov within the correct socialist parameters.

Korolev let out a quiet whistle. He didn't understand exactly what this fellow was going on about, but he understood enough to work out that Savchenko was in trouble up to his neck, as was Korolev's friend Babel. Korolev pulled out his notebook and made some notes, not convinced any of this was relevant to the case, but not prepared to discount it either. If whoever had written the report was of the opinion that Savchenko's approach to the film was causing concern among Party members involved in the production, then that meant there had been tension, and possibly fear, among the cast and crew. If criticism like this was being voiced publicly, it could be as lethal as an aimed bullet. And if the girl had been the subject of criticism, it could be the reason for her suicide.

There was more to be read, including a brief note on Babel, which he took a moment to peruse, pleased to see that Ezhov himself considered the writer politically reliable, if recently unproductive, but by now the aircraft's vibration was beginning to make him feel unwell and so he returned the papers to the envelope and turned to look out of the window, not without a further twinge of nervousness.

They were flying over a forest that seemed to stretch as far as the eye could see but at such low altitude that Korolev was able to make out individual branches, and the snow that weighed them down. The sense of speed was quite terrifying as the long shadow of the airplane raced across the snow-dusted treetops in the flat winter sun. They were following a long straight road which was completely deserted until a cart drawn by two horses appeared beneath them. Korolev caught a glimpse of the terrified face of the peasant as he turned to see what devil was pursuing him, and how the horses seemed to lift in their traces as the plane roared over them. And then they were gone, vanished far behind them.

Soviet Power, Korolev thought to himself. It had a way of coming up on you when you least expected it.

CHAPTER FOUR

Korolev managed something approximating sleep for a good part of the journey, although he joined the other passengers to stretch their legs at Kursk, and by the time they landed in Odessa he was almost used to the strange experience that was flying.

He took his bag from the youth who was emptying the cargo hold and made his way over to the small wooden airport building, the word ODESSA attached to its roof inbetween two obligatory red stars. Several small trucks and a couple of black cars were parked haphazardly in its vicinity and a small crowd of people stood around it, waiting for the passengers, he presumed. It wasn't difficult to spot Major Mushkin.

He was a tall man, just over six feet, and if he wasn't wearing a uniform as such, there wasn't much doubt that he was a Chekist. Certainly every citizen within viewing distance had Mushkin marked, even though no one seemed to be looking in his direction. In fact, that was just it. Everyone was ignoring the burly man from State Security so pointedly that he stood out like a palm tree on an iceberg.

And of course it didn't help that the major's gaze was like a searchlight sweeping the crowd as he flicked the worker's flat cap he carried against his thigh like a whip to the rhythm of a tune only he could hear. Korolev watched him reach for a cigarette case from the pocket of his double-breasted leather trench coat, then bring one of the contents to his mouth. He was about to light it when he became aware of Korolev and, as their eyes met, Korolev felt a shiver run down his spine as every instinct told him that the fellow was bad news. Very bad news.

The strangest thing, he thought as he approached, was that the major was almost good looking. The nicotine-stained blond hair that he'd pushed back from his pale forehead was beginning to whiten around the ears, but was still thick, if a little tangled. His features were regular enough — a broad jaw, high cheekbones and a straight nose — and would have been pleasing on another man. But the major's face had a weary, cynical cast to it that Korolev suspected must be permanent, and it robbed him of any attractiveness or warmth.

"Major Mushkin?" Korolev asked, holding out a hand in greeting.

"Korolev," Mushkin said, ignoring the hand. "My car's over here. We'll talk on the way."

"Comrade Mushkin?" It was Belakovsky's voice. "Are you here to meet us?"

The major turned and looked at Belakovsky for a long moment. "No," he said eventually.

Belakovsky's eyes swiveled toward Korolev, remembering him, before turning back to Mushkin with an apologetic smile.

"Of course, I'm sorry — when I saw you standing here . . ."

"Yes, you jumped to a conclusion." Mushkin spoke the words like a threat.

"Excuse me, Comrade, my mistake. Please forgive me." Belakovsky turned away and, nodding to Lomatkin, walked quickly around the corner of the building in the journalist's company. Mushkin looked at Korolev for a reaction, which Korolev was careful not to provide.

"Well, now you've met Belakovsky. You'll see more of him. Lomatkin, his sidekick, as well, no doubt."

■ ■ ■ ■

The car rattled along a road so straight it could have been laid out with a ruler, although after months of freezing temperatures the surface had nothing of the same regularity. Not that Mushkin allowed that to affect his speed, maneuvering around only the bigger potholes and leaving the car's suspension to deal with the rest — a task that Korolev's bruised body told him was beyond it. It was a good fifteen years since he'd traveled through the Ukraine, but he remembered the steppe all too well and the flat landscape extended unremittingly to the horizon. Rodinov had told him it would be warmer than Moscow, which it was, but only by a couple of degrees and ice still clogged the streams and lakes and scatterings of snow marked each variation in the relentless flatness.

"We found her hanging from a wall bracket in the dining room," Mushkin said, his voice rising to compete with the car's engine.

"So I understand. Anything suspicious?"

"No," Mushkin replied flatly.

Korolev looked out of the window at the passing landscape but after a while of star-

ing at the endless road ahead, the temptation to ask another question got the better
of him.

"Where is this dining room?"

Mushkin sighed and, for a moment, Korolev thought his question wouldn't be answered.

"The dining room is in an old manor
house where the cast and crew are staying
— it was a nobleman's country residence
before the Revolution, now it's part of an
agricultural college. They call it the Orlov
House locally. The College has plenty of
room, is secure and it's near the village
where they're filming. The students and
teachers who would be there otherwise have
been sent to nearby kolkhozes to help them
prepare for the new season's planting, so
it's convenient for everyone."

Korolev was surprised at such a thorough
answer, so surprised that he decided to push
his luck.

"What time did she die?"

Mushkin's lips tightened into a scowl, and
when he answered his voice had acquired
an undercurrent of irritation.

"She was found at just past ten last night.
The last time she was seen alive was after
the evening meal at around seven-thirty. The
caretaker passed through the room where

the body was found at eight o'clock and saw nothing. So between eight and ten is what I would deduce."

"What about the other people staying in the house?"

"A night shoot down at the village. It was a crowd scene, so everyone was involved except for the girl. It seems she was alone in the house after the caretaker left."

"Who found the body?"

"The caretaker — at least he was the one who opened the door when they found her. But he was with Shymko, the chief production coordinator. They'd been down at the shoot — the caretaker was in the crowd for the scene they were filming."

"What's a production coordinator?"

"A fixer. He makes sure everything runs smoothly. He's the adjutant to Savchenko's colonel."

"And this caretaker?"

"He's nearly sixty — he's taken it badly. To me it looks open and shut, no one else involved except for her, but I understand you have orders as to how to proceed." Again that note of irritability.

"I'd like to see the body first."

"As you wish."

"Did you know the girl?" Korolev ventured.

Mushkin nodded, and for the first time Korolev thought he detected a glimmer of sympathy.

"Yes, I knew her — it was a surprise to me." He sighed, and his face took on a gentler, more thoughtful expression. "She didn't strike me as the suicidal type. On the contrary — an able worker, a committed Party activist, well respected by her comrades. Popular. And I'm not aware of any reason why she'd have wanted to kill herself. As I said, I was surprised — but then these things happen."

Mushkin shrugged his shoulders; death obviously didn't impress him any more. And when it came to suicide he had a point. They didn't publish figures, but everyone knew someone who'd ended their own life. It was the nature of the transition they were going through, Korolev supposed: the march from a feudal society to modern socialism exerted pressures on the individual — and not all individuals were made of steel. Sometimes he wished the Party would just give them a few months off. A holiday from change.

"How about personal relationships? A lover perhaps? There's nothing in the file, but young women . . ." Korolev left the sentence hanging.

Mushkin shook his head.

"I'm not in the locality in a professional capacity, Captain, as you've probably been informed. I'm here for a period of rest." The major glanced at him and Korolev felt his reaction to the statement was being assessed. It made him wonder whether the period of rest was voluntary.

"I haven't been monitoring things closely," Mushkin continued, "at least not up until now. It's possible, however. Very possible. She was a popular girl."

By now they'd left Odessa far behind. The villages they were passing through were farther and farther apart, and the landscape was made up almost entirely of enormous fields divided from each other by thin lines of bare-branched trees.

Korolev had heard rumors of what had happened in the Ukraine in 'thirty-two and 'thirty-three — dangerous words heard late at night from soldiers who'd had too much to drink in the Arbat Cellar. How the Red Army and the NKVD had forced the peasants to give up every scrap of food and how, faced with starvation, they had resisted, futilely, and the soldiers and the Chekists had shot them down. The car passed more than one smoke-blackened church, their domes charred black skeletons, and each village was dotted with roofless ruined buildings. Korolev couldn't help but notice that the few hunched peasants he saw seemed older than their probable years, with barely the energy to lift their feet from the ground. They turned their heads to look at the passing car with no interest whatsoever and Korolev had seen that look before, during the war, on the faces of men who'd been fighting too long and had seen too much. On his own face caught in a mirror, not far from here, the day after cavalry had caught his company in the open and he'd hidden underneath his friend Pavel's dead body as the horse men had searched for the living among the dead, the pop of revolver shots marking each discovery. It had taken three days for his hands to stop shaking enough for him to shave. But by the time that had happened he'd been tired, so tired — seven years of fighting and so many dead friends and dead enemies filling his dreams. It wasn't surprising he'd nearly broken. He didn't know where he'd found the strength, perhaps the Lord had answered his prayers, but somehow he'd pulled himself together, shaved, washed his friend's blood from his tunic and marched on with a different group of comrades, thanking the Virgin he still

71

breathed.

Korolev looked across at Mushkin and realized that the Chekist's expression wasn't that dissimilar from the one on the faces of the peasants they'd just passed — a man who'd reached his limit and gone past it. The soldiers in that bar had said that in some places that winter the peasants had organized themselves and taken reprisals against Party officials — even ambushed detachments of Militia and the Red Army — and that the NKVD's retaliation had been savage. Each rebellion had been crushed, no matter how small, and each act of resistance, real or imagined, met with brutal retribution. Mushkin must have been up to his neck in all of that, Korolev thought to himself. He noticed the way the major kept his eyes fixed on the road in front of them as they drove through the battered villages. Was it Korolev's imagination or was the major trying to avoid looking out at the signs of the struggle that had taken place here?

"You said this agricultural college was secure — does it need to be?" Korolev found himself saying, and regretted it almost immediately. Mushkin glanced at him before turning his eyes back to the road ahead.

"The struggle against wreckers and counter-revolutionaries is not yet over in these parts, Korolev."

They passed through another village, not dissimilar to the others — thin, hungry faces and rotting empty houses, the wooden walls gray with age and the damp thatch sagging. The usual signs of Soviet Power were here too — the kolkhoz office, a small Militia post, a collective store. These buildings at least looked as though they were being maintained.

But Mushkin looked neither left nor right, driving through the village as though it didn't exist until, on reaching a large concrete block which announced the Odessa Regional Agricultural College in foot-high letters, he turned off the main road onto a gravel drive. The drive continued into woodland, the first Korolev had seen since he'd landed, and after a minute or so it reached the remains of a small church, burned out long before.

"The family that owned the estate was buried here," Mushkin said, stopping the car and indicating a small graveyard that had suffered as much as the church. "When the Revolution arrived the peasants dug up their graves and scattered their bones over the steppe. Then they burned the church down with the priest inside it."

Korolev kept his face expressionless — he'd heard of worse things happening during the Civil War, and seen things as bad. But he was surprised by the priest. In fact he'd risk a fair amount of money that it wasn't the villagers who'd burned their priest alive. Korolev glanced at Mushkin and something in his expression, the way he looked at the church, made him wonder if Mushkin himself hadn't had something to do with the atrocity. After a few moments of contemplation, Mushkin put the car back into gear and they drove for another hundred yards or so to where the woods opened up and a series of newly built concrete buildings appeared — dormitories, what looked like a gymnasium, classrooms, lecture halls and several large barns. Finally the drive led to a large house built from ochre-colored stone, three stories high and standing in the middle of winter-stripped gardens.

It wasn't a palace as such, but a substantial residence all the same. It didn't look Russian, with its small turrets at each corner and its arched windows, more like a building from North Africa. To the left of the house stood what must have been the stable block, the courtyard of which contained a number of trailers, a bus and a truck, as well as an odd assortment of equipment, some of which was covered with tarpaulins bearing the stencilled logo "Ukrainfilm."

Mushkin stopped the car in front of the ornate entrance to the house. "The local Militia will be arriving soon," he said, looking at his watch. "You're not here in an official capacity, but as Babel's friend. We'll be asking your opinion, seeing as you're here — by complete coincidence."

"So I was informed."

"I'm informing you again," Mushkin said as he pulled himself out of the car. He glanced around at Korolev once, then walked toward the stable yard, his hands deep in his pockets.

Korolev stayed where he was for a moment, looking around him. Apart from Mushkin's departing figure there was no one to be seen. Perhaps Korolev was a little tired, and Mushkin's story about the family graves and the burning priest too fresh in his mind, but he had a sudden image of the porch's black-and-white tiled floor slicked with blood. For a moment the image was so vivid that he couldn't breathe.

Shocked, Korolev sat there, not sure what else to do but open up the packet of cigarettes he had in his pocket, extract one with

75

some difficulty, his fingers rattling a nervous tattoo on the cardboard box, and put it in his mouth. He lit it, wondering if he was cracking up, and feeling so worn that he almost didn't care. Tiredness was all this was, he reassured himself for the second time in twenty-four hours — the previous day's arrest, the Chekist knocking on the door, the Lubianka waiting room, the plane journey, Mushkin. Things like that took it out of a man. He sighed and coughed as he inhaled, savoring the spread of nicotine through his body.

When the bang on the driver's door came, the surprise lifted Korolev out of his seat so high his head touched the roof.

"What the hell?" he shouted, adrenalin shuddering though his body like electricity and his hand instinctively going for his shoulder holster.

"Sorry, Comrade." The smiling face of a small blond boy with a red Pioneer's scarf around his neck was looking in at him through the window, nose flat against the glass. And the strangest thing was that he was the spitting image of Korolev's son Yuri, so much so that Korolev wondered whether he were having another hallucination until he saw the small differences, the slightly darker blue of the eyes, the perfect teeth where Yuri's were a little crooked. But the likeness was uncanny and it was with some difficulty that he pulled himself together.

"Who are you?" he asked, and the question came out a little more gruffly than he'd intended.

"Pavel."

"And do you usually go around scaring the living daylights out of honest citizens, Pavel? And you a Pioneer as well." Which, again, wasn't how he'd intended to speak to the boy and when the boy's smile was replaced with a grave expression he felt a parent's guilt.

"I'm sorry, Comrade," the boy began, but Korolev shook his head.

"Don't be, Pavel. It's me should be apologizing — you caught me by surprise, that's all. Off with you now — we'll meet again, I'm sure, and start from the beginning again."

The boy's smile reappeared and he saluted before disappearing around the corner at a gallop. Korolev hauled himself out of the car, suddenly determined to deal with this affair quickly so he could take what was left of the two weeks to go and see the real Yuri in Zagorsk. He could be there in two days with a bit of luck and Rodinov's help with the journey. Yes, that's what he'd do, he thought to himself, and prayed the girl had indeed killed herself.

He walked into the domed porch, glancing up for a moment at the curved sky-blue roof on which silver stars twinkled, then tried the front doors, which were locked. No one answered when he pulled at a metal chain that rang a distant bell, and there was no one to be seen in the entrance hall when he looked through one of the small windows.

A cobbled path circled the house and Korolev followed it, listening for any sign of human activity and hearing none, only the sound of the wind pushing its way through the garden's trees, and on the opposite side of the building he found a long balustraded terrace that overlooked a frozen lake, ice embracing the withered reeds around its shore. The house was even more impressive from this angle and in front of the terrace there was a large fountain, ice cascading from the mouths of cherubs into a deep, shell-shaped basin, a good twenty feet in diameter. Korolev imagined the Orlovs eating on the terrace in the heat of an August evening, perhaps under an awning, dressed in their summer whites, the windows of the conservatory that ran the length of the house open to let in the slight summer breeze, the fountain's water tinkling beneath them, unaware that their days were numbered.

His thoughts were interrupted by the sound of approaching footsteps. A tall elderly woman with a straight back and almost military bearing appeared around the corner of the house in the company of Major Mushkin. They were talking quietly, the old woman stabbing the path with a walking stick for emphasis as she marched along. She had a thin, angular face and her gray hair had slipped out from under a worn fur hat, before curling around the upturned collar of her greatcoat. If the walking stick was needed, Korolev decided, it wasn't for reasons of speed, as she was maintaining a brisk pace, albeit with a stiff, awkward gait.

He coughed and they looked up, coming to a halt, Mushkin's eyes cold, while the woman seemed to study him as if he were a potential problem that needed brisk and efficient resolution. He raised his hand in greeting.

"This is Korolev, Mother."

"I see," she said. "If you want the film people, they're off somewhere. Ask Andreychuk — he'll be inside. Good morning to you, Comrade Korolev."

She made to move on, but stopped as Korolev opened his mouth to speak.

"Well?" she asked, allowing her stern voice to become a little gentler, making Korolev feel as though he were a child. "What is it?"

"The house seems to be locked, Comrade."

"Locked?" she repeated. "I see."

She pointed her walking stick up at a glass-paned door that offered access to the conservatory.

"That door will be open, or the one at the other end — and Andreychuk is in there somewhere, I assure you. He'll know where they are."

"Thank you, Comrade."

She gave a sharp nod of acknowledgment and proceeded on her way, Mushkin falling into step beside her. Korolev looked after them for a moment, confused. Mushkin's mother? Was that why the major was convalescing here? She certainly behaved as if she belonged here.

He turned back to the house and climbed the chipped steps to the terrace, crossing to the conservatory and knocking on the door Mushkin's mother had indicated, but there was no answer. He looked around him, wondering whether the elderly woman had been mistaken, at the same time thinking the silence was strange. He found himself whistling under his breath, just to keep himself company. Almost reluctantly, he turned the handle and it opened.

The conservatory was a high room, dominated by two elderly vines that looked as if they'd seen better days. He stepped inside and shut the door quietly behind him. For some reason he felt as though he was trespassing, as though the family who'd once lived here might emerge at any moment and discover him tiptoeing through their home.

He paused for a moment, to reassure himself that this was nonsense, that he was here on official business, and, anyway, he was looking for Babel and everything was fine. But still it was undeniable that there was an atmosphere to the place — the girl had died here, of course, perhaps that was the reason for his uneasiness.

He walked through an open door, passing into a large dining room with a ceiling made entirely of glass through which the natural evening light illuminated the room. At any other time he would have paused to examine the roof more closely because it was extraordinary, but at the far end an old man with a bushy white beard stood, head bowed, in front of one of the four large cast-iron candelabras that protruded from the walls

81

and which must have been installed to illuminate the room before the days of electricity. At the sound of Korolev's step the old man turned, and Korolev was surprised to see that the milky blue eyes beneath his thick white brows were wet with tears.

"Are you all right, Comrade?" he asked, walking toward him.

"I'm fine," the man said, turning away to compose himself.

Which was a lie if Korolev had ever heard one. But it wasn't his business to pry — not yet at least.

"Is this where she died?" he asked, surprised to hear his own voice.

"Yes," the old man said, having turned back toward him. "The Lord help me, I was the one who found her."

Korolev nodded his sympathy, surprised that the old man spoke the Lord's name so freely. "Comrade Andreychuk, is it? The caretaker?"

"That's me. Efim Pavlovich Andreychuk. The unlucky Andreychuk. The poor soul who found the dead girl."

"My name is Korolev. Alexei Dmitriyevich. I'm a friend of Babel, the writer. I was sorry to hear the news."

"The film people are out in the fields, if you're looking for them. But they should be back soon." Andreychuk turned back toward the bracket. "She should have stayed in Moscow, you see. This place never brought her anything but sadness."

"What do you mean?" Korolev asked, thinking the words curious. The girl hadn't spent that long on the film — surely not long enough to pack in so much sadness. Andreychuk looked around at him as though he'd forgotten Korolev was there.

"She's dead, that's what I mean," the caretaker said, frowning. "Nothing more than that."

"But you spoke as though she came from around here. I thought she came from Moscow."

Andreychuk's frown deepened, and his voice, when he spoke, was gruff. "She was from these parts a long time ago, or so she told me. She should have stayed in Moscow."

Interesting that she'd been from the area — that information wasn't in the file.

"Was there something underneath?" he asked, looking back at the wall bracket and wondering how she'd done it. "For her to stand on?"

Andreychuk glanced around at him, suspicious but also thinking.

"A chair," he said after a few moments.

"Someone must have moved it."

Korolev looked at the wall fixture and tried to imagine the girl preparing the noose, tying the rope around one of the metal arms — they looked solid enough — and then kicking the chair away.

"A hard way to go," he said, stating the obvious — a skill he'd learned early in his career as a policeman. "There are easier ways to kill yourself."

"I don't know why she did it. All I know is I wish I hadn't been the one to find her. Excuse me, Comrade, I've work to attend to."

The caretaker turned and walked out of the room and Korolev tried to imagine how it must have been for him when he found her — the weight of the corpse swinging, her feet inches from the ground. No wonder the poor fellow was a little taciturn.

He took a deep breath and opened his notebook and by holding his hand above his head estimated the height of the bracket, knowing, as he did, the distance from the ground of his up-stretched index finger. Seven foot two inches, give or take an inch or two. He'd measure it properly later on. He looked around — there was no shortage of chairs, but as to which of them had been underneath the dead girl, it was impossible to tell. He folded his notebook shut and turned to leave the room. If necessary he'd get a forensic team to have a look around, but it was a shame that there'd been no effort to preserve the scene. Perhaps Rodinov had thought it might be indiscreet to do so.

With nothing else to do, Korolev gave himself a tour of the house. At some stage much of the original furniture must have been replaced with more functional pieces, better suited to the house's new role as an educational establishment for Soviet youth, but there was still plenty of the finest marble and gilding in evidence and the walls and ceilings still carried beautiful murals and frescoes.

Eventually Korolev found himself in the large entrance hall, the walls of which were hung with Ottoman weaponry, presumably from when this part of the world had been taken from the Turks. The front door was now mysteriously open and so he walked out through the splendid porch toward the stables, where the Ukrainfilm vehicles stood on the cobblestoned yard.

It had been one of the ironies of the tsarist times that the oppressing classes had looked after their horses better than they had their workers, but now the horses had been kicked out and the stables turned into classrooms. Light yellowed the panes of a window in the far corner of the three-sided yard and he walked toward it and opened the corresponding door marked Production Office without knocking. A bank of three female typists paused, their hands held above the keys like pianists, while behind them a young man with close-cropped brown hair and a pleasant face looked up from whatever it was he was reading.

"Excuse me, Comrades," Korolev said. "I'm looking for Isaac Emmanuilovich. You know, the writer? Babel?"

"Babel," the young man said, rising from his desk. "Of course, but I'm afraid he's out with the crew. They'll be back soon though, the light's gone now. Pyotr Mikhailovich Shymko," he said, advancing with his hand outstretched. "Production coordinator."

"Korolev, Alexei Dmitriyevich. I'm a friend of his."

"Welcome." Shymko looked at the girls as though considering whether to introduce them.

"Larisa." He addressed a pretty blonde after a moment's pause. "Would you take Comrade Korolev over to the house? Make him comfortable while he waits?"

Larisa frowned as she stood to her feet,

but Korolev waved her down.

"Please, Comrades, I can see you're busy. What with the tragedy, you must have your hands full."

"The tragedy?" Shymko echoed, and Korolev noticed that Larisa's eyes had filled with tears.

"The poor girl who killed herself."

Larisa sobbed and ran from the room.

"I apologize," Korolev said, surprised to discover an unlit cigarette had appeared in his mouth. One of these days he'd give up — aside from anything else he wouldn't be able to afford it if he'd reached the stage where his hands were feeding the things into his mouth without conscious thought.

"Excuse me," Shymko said as a telephone began to ring, but Korolev had spotted a black car approaching the house and, deciding it must be the Odessa contingent, made his own excuses and left. When the car stopped, however, it was Belakovsky who climbed out rather than Militiamen and his welcoming committee consisted only of a distraught typist.

"Larisa, is it true?"

"It's true, Comrade Belakovsky, it's true," Larisa wailed, and Korolev, following behind the girl, saw her bury herself in Belakovsky's overcoat.

"Hello again, Comrade Belakovsky," Korolev said and Belakovsky nodded a greeting, before turning his attention back to Larisa.

"Mikhail told me. I didn't believe him." Then he paused, looking back to Korolev, recognizing him yet again, with a look of surprise.

"Comrade Korolev?"

"Yes, a coincidence. I'm a friend of Babel's. I'd no idea we were visiting the same place."

"You have to understand — a colleague has died unexpectedly. She was one in a thousand. A vital part of this production, of course, but more than that. Much more than that."

Behind him stood a sorry-looking man whom Korolev deduced was Mikhail, the bearer of bad news. The other occupant of the car — Lomatkin, the journalist — was leaning against the car door for support, as pale as the dead girl's ghost. It seemed as though Masha Lenskaya had made quite an impression during her short life.

"Korolev," Belakovsky said, as though thinking aloud. "Didn't you say you were a detective — from Petrovka Street?"

"I didn't. You did and I'm on holiday," Korolev replied, perhaps a little too quickly.

Belakovsky glanced at the house, and if it wasn't to see where Mushkin was, Korolev would have been most surprised. The NKVD definitely had a thing or two to learn about secrecy, even if they were always asking it of other people.

"On holiday?" Belakovsky repeated slowly, probably remembering how that fellow Bagraev had been booted off the plane. "What a coincidence. And perhaps fortunate for us. What did you say your specialization was?"

"Petrovka Street normally handles the more serious crimes. And I'm an experienced detective."

"I see — bank robbery, that sort of thing. Murder perhaps?" The fellow was putting two and two together and making four, so Korolev nodded politely, and felt in his overcoat pocket for his cigarettes, pleased that at least this time it was a deliberate rather than instinctive action.

"Yes, I've handled the odd murder or two," he said, lighting the cigarette off the one in his mouth.

Another black car hove into view as they stood there weighing each other up, and when it pulled to a halt disgorged a stocky Militia colonel, who looked at them anxiously. He was followed by a tough-looking young woman in a leather jacket and a bald man carrying a doctor's case. No sooner had the first car been emptied of its occupants than another arrived and three uniforms under a sergeant's command scrambled out. It was turning out to be quite a party, and right on cue the guest of honor arrived.

"Did you hear, Comrade Mushkin?" Belakovsky said. "Korolev here is a Militia detective from Petrovka Street, visiting Babel."

"Indeed," Mushkin said, with a sliver of a smile, and Korolev deduced that the Major wasn't too burned-out to appreciate the humor inherent in the play they were all acting out. But for whose benefit, God alone knew.

CHAPTER FIVE

Korolev had never been in an ice house before. Of course, he was aware that before the Revolution the rich had tried to preserve some of winter's bite to relieve the summer's swelter: he wasn't uncultured after all and he took an interest in the wider world — as any Soviet citizen should. Indeed, in any other circumstances he would have found it interesting to stand in this small, brick-lined cave and to be lectured on its construction and significance. But this was not the time, in his opinion, or the place.

Shymko ran a hand along a line of bricks, his voice barely a whisper but clear in the silence of the artificial cave.

"Two hundred peasants worked for an entire summer under the direction of an Englishman — shifting the earth to build the hill in which we stand. They say he laid each brick himself, the Englishman," Shymko said in his quiet voice. "Look how careful he was, Comrades."

It was true, the brickwork was indeed a curious relic of that previous phase of society's historical evolution, but the dead girl was the reason they were all here and Korolev found it difficult to look at anything other than her white face. They'd laid her out on a trestle table, her head supported on what looked like a sandbag, her skin stretched over the cheekbones where death had pulled it taut. She could have been sleeping, and her features wouldn't have given the lie to it, were it not for the raw marks on her neck where the rope had caught her. As always in the presence of a corpse, he found himself struck by how fragile life was, and amazed that such an intangible thing as consciousness should cause such a change to the physical appearance of a person. The characteristics that had seemed to color the girl's photograph were now absent, as if paint had been rubbed from a picture to reveal the plain canvas underneath.

"Captain Korolev?" Mushkin said and Korolev found himself the center of attention. Major Mushkin, Marchuk the Militia colonel, Peskov the bald Odessa pathologist, Shymko and the thin-lipped young woman in the leather jacket were all waiting for him to do or say something, and he wasn't quite sure what.

"I've seen him work before, Comrades. He spends a lot of time just looking, but the things he sees, the things he sees . . ."

And Babel, of course. How could he have forgotten Babel? How the hell had he managed to wangle his way in here anyway?

"Seeing as we have a comrade from the famous Petrovka Street with us so fortuitously," Mushkin said, pronouncing the last word ironically, "perhaps he might look over the body? I'm sure Dr. Peskov won't mind. Dr. Peskov, you don't mind, do you?"

The bald pathologist shook his head so hard that his round spectacles nearly fell off.

"I'm no pathologist, Major," Korolev began and wasn't surprised to see a muscle in the major's jaw clench with irritation, "although it's true I've seen a few dead bodies. Maybe the Comrade Doctor should carry on with his preliminary examination as he would normally and I can observe over his shoulder. I'm sure his experience in this area is far greater than mine, but an extra pair of eyes is always useful."

Peskov glanced at the colonel, who, in turn, looked toward Mushkin just as a nervous gundog might to his master. Eventually Mushkin nodded his agreement, but not before giving Korolev a long, thoughtful look which the detective was unsure how to interpret. The doctor stepped forward and stood at the end of the table, picking up the dead girl's head in both his hands, leaning forward. His fingers felt underneath her neck as though searching for something. Korolev also approached the body and bent forward to look more closely.

"No saliva," Korolev said quietly, for the doctor's ears as opposed to anyone else's.

"No, but someone may have cleaned her up."

"What was that?" Major Mushkin was interested despite himself.

"Saliva, Major," Peskov said. "With self-asphyxiation, there is invariably a flow of saliva from the mouth, down the chin and straight onto the chest. If the body is hung after death, this doesn't happen, the production of saliva being a living act."

"But it could have been cleaned away, you say?"

"Possibly. There would usually remain some signs on the clothing, however."

"Shymko?" Mushkin turned to the production coordinator.

"She wasn't cleaned up," Shymko answered, his voice hushed at the realization of what this implied.

"What happened to the rope she was found hanging from?" Korolev asked.

"There." Shymko pointed to a coil that sat on the ground beneath the table, about three-quarters of an inch thick. Korolev nodded and leaned down to examine it.

"Doctor?" Korolev said, and the pathologist squatted beside him, feeling the rope's texture.

"Yes, I see what you mean," he said.

"What do you see? What does he mean?" Marchuk asked, glancing at Mushkin for some direction. The Militia colonel sounded panicked — as well he might, thought Korolev.

The doctor pointed to the marks on the girl's neck. "With a suicidal hanging the marks of the rope or ligature are generally above or on the thyroid cartilage, and carried obliquely upward. Do you see?" He mimed a rope holding his own neck up, and ran his finger at an angle from underneath his jaw to the back of his head. "We have such a mark here." He pointed to the girl's neck. "And you see this rope? It's thick enough, yes?"

"Peskov, pull yourself together." Colonel Marchuk's cheeks were reddening as he inclined his head toward Mushkin. "This is no time for blathering."

"My apologies, Comrade Colonel." The doctor's face seemed to become even paler in the solitary light bulb's glow. "But this is an important point. It implies that the rope she was found hanging from was not the cause of death. Do you see here, the long thin bruising, below these other marks? See how it is horizontal rather than oblique? This was caused by something much finer — a cord of some sort, I should think. In short, it seems likely that the girl was dead before she was hung from this rope. In fact it seems most probable she was strangled — from behind if you want an instant view — and that the thicker rope was applied after death. To an extent this is conjecture. I'll have to examine her thoroughly in the proper conditions. There is generally internal damage to the laryngeal cartilage and other bones in the neck. I'll know for certain" — he looked at his watch — "later tonight."

There was silence after the doctor finished speaking. Shymko looked dour, the colonel as though he might be ill and Mushkin grim as a tombstone.

"You're saying she was murdered." The major paused. "You're saying it wasn't suicide but murder."

96

"I'd like to undertake a full autopsy, if that's possible, back at the hospital. I'll call for an ambulance immediately." The doctor looked up at Mushkin. "I understand this is a priority and you'll have my findings as soon as humanly possible — but I will have to examine her properly."

"But that's your initial view?" The major looked at the doctor and then at Korolev. Peskov shrugged, deferring to Korolev.

"I think we should treat her death as suspicious, Comrade Major," Korolev said, feeling about as unhappy at the prospect as Mushkin looked, thinking that the odds on a quick return to Moscow and the chance to visit his son in Zagorsk had just lengthened considerably. "That would seem to be the most sensible approach. And we should not discount murder."

Korolev's last word seemed to echo as first Babel, somewhat enthusiastically, then Peskov, in quiet agreement, and finally Marchuk, in horror, all repeated it. Korolev saw the colonel begin a movement with his right hand that looked suspiciously like the sign of the cross, but he'd remembered where he was by the time his hand touched his forehead, and instead began to rub his eyebrows with his fingers, looking furtively at Major Mushkin out of the corner of his eye.

"Murder?" Shymko said, long after everyone else. "But Citizen Lenskaya was a model worker, an activist of the highest standing."

"Maybe that's why they killed her," Mushkin replied, and for a moment Korolev thought he'd made a very dark joke. "Well, it will be for colonel Marchuk to find out."

Marchuk's drooping head started up as though he'd been half-asleep and someone had kicked his chair.

"Perhaps Captain Korolev . . . ?" the colonel began, his voice dropping to a whisper in the face of Mushkin's impassive stare. "We're short of good men. It's the drive on hooligans and bandits. It's time-consuming."

"And you'd like Korolev to break his holiday to investigate one of your cases because you have too many hooligans and bandits in Odessa." Mushkin folded his arms and gave the colonel a parody of a stern look. "An amazing suggestion."

"My men are stretched thinly," Marchuk said, even more unsure of himself now. "And maybe it would be best for a senior detective to handle a crime like this."

The colonel opened his hands in a gesture

of supplication and Korolev allowed himself the luxury of pretending to consider the request. One sharp glance from Mushkin was enough to speed up his decision-making, however, and he nodded his assent.

"If you think I can be of assistance, Comrade Colonel, then I'm at your service. General Secretary Stalin tells us we should always be ready to sacrifice personal happiness for the greater good. I'm not some petty individualist." Which he managed to say with a straight face, even if a large part of him was wishing he could indeed be a petty individualist — six hundred miles away from this cursed corpse and in the company of his only son.

"You're on holiday and yet you offer it up for the greater good." Mushkin's approval seemed almost genuine. "Your loyalty to the State is an example to us all."

"I'm sure we'd all do the same in a similar situation. Of course I'll need to check with my chief, and I'll need help — as many uniforms as you can spare, a competent junior detective who knows the lay of the land, a forensics team."

"You work for Popov, don't you?" Mushkin asked. "Marchuk and I will call him. What shall we say — initially for a week or so, perhaps? Unless the matter is resolved earlier, or a suitable replacement becomes free. Or, of course, if Dr. Peskov's examination makes it clear that it was suicide after all."

"We'd be grateful, Captain Korolev," Marchuk said. "A crime such as this — I couldn't turn it over to a junior detective. It would be irresponsible."

Mushkin nodded to Shymko, then Babel, and turned to leave. The colonel followed with the doctor, who paused for a moment to smile at Korolev. Shymko was about to follow when Korolev put a hand on his sleeve.

"One moment, Comrade. If I'm to look after this business I've a few questions I need to ask you."

The production coordinator turned back and Korolev wasn't surprised to see concern in his face. The Militia had a reputation for not always being too picky when seeking out the perpetrators of serious crimes.

"Comrade Captain?"

"You found the body?"

"Well, Andreychuk the caretaker was the one who opened the door to the dining room — but, yes, I suppose I did — I was right behind him." Shymko seemed to weigh the words to see if the truth in them could somehow be evaded.

"And you were the first ones to return to the house?"

"Andreychuk had locked up while everyone was down at the night shoot. Except for Lenskaya, of course, although I think she had her own key."

"I see. Tell me what you saw when you found her."

Shymko did as he was told, describing the limp body hanging just inside the dining room, how Andreychuk had dropped to his knees in shock, and how they'd released her from the rope and lowered her to the ground.

"She was cold to the touch. Dead."

Korolev nodded, distracted by a notebook not dissimilar to his own which the leather-jacketed young woman had opened up.

"Comrade?" Korolev looked at her, raising an eyebrow at her notebook.

"Comrade Captain?" she asked in turn, and Korolev could have sworn she gave him the tiniest of mischievous smiles.

"What are you doing?"

"Taking notes."

"I can see that," he said. "Why are you taking notes?"

"I always take notes. A note doesn't get forgotten." She looked down at his hands as if to say he could do with taking a few more notes himself. The worst thing was she'd just quoted his own favorite mantra to junior detectives who didn't yet realize that the brain was an erratic recorder of useful information.

"So, Comrade?" he said, trying to ignore the smirk on Babel's face.

The girl smiled and extended her hand. "Slivka, Comrade. Nadezhda Andreyevna. Sergeant — Odessa CID. Unless the Comrade Colonel just wanted to take me for a drive in the country, my guess is I'm your junior detective. I'll help you track down whoever did this — don't you worry, Comrade Captain."

Korolev shook the offered hand and allowed himself to return the smile. A bit of spirit wasn't such a bad thing in a young detective.

"Well then. Good," he said. "Anything you'd like to ask?"

"Yes," the young female detective said, looking down at her notebook. "Comrade, is Andreychuk the only one with keys to the house? Apart from the deceased, that is."

"Lord no," Shymko began, before collecting himself when Babel tutted at his careless use of the Lord's name — as close to blasphemy as it got these days.

"No," he continued with more care, feeling his way into each word now — apparently having decided that in the kind of company that wrote down everything you said, words could run amok and bite a man where it hurt.

"You'd have to ask Comrade Andreychuk," he continued, "but I have one, and I know the director of the kolkhoz keeps one in his office. Then there's Elizaveta Petrovna, of course."

"Elizaveta Petrovna?"

"Elizaveta Petrovna Mushkina," Shymko clarified, emphasizing the surname.

"Major Mushkin's mother," Babel said, his voice coming from behind Korolev. "She's the director of the Agricultural College. But before that she was a Party boss in Odessa."

"I met her earlier," Korolev said, remembering the elderly lady with her walking stick.

"A hero of the Revolution," Shymko added in a hushed tone.

"And before that," Babel said. "She was in Siberia with Stalin. That's how far she goes back."

"Stalin?" Korolev repeated, not quite believing his ears. Could this get any worse? Now he had to deal with someone who was an old comrade of Stalin's.

"She calls him Koba," Babel said with a significant look.

Korolev swallowed, then decided it was best to get on with the job in hand.

"We'll need a list of who had access to keys and where all the keys were last night. Slivka?"

"I'll see to it."

"And a list of all the cast and crew. Anyone who had contact with Lenskaya. I saw a small Militia post in the village. Can you ask the colonel if the uniforms there can help? We'll want to interview everyone as soon as possible."

Slivka nodded. "They've already been instructed to assist you should you need them. Comrade Shymko, how many people are we talking about? For the cast and crew?"

Shymko ran a hand over his skull, a gesture that seemed to age him considerably.

"Cast — speaking roles we have sixteen. Production and crew? About twenty — small, but Savchenko likes it that way. Extras? Every living soul for five versts. Then there are a few hangers-on. I can get you a list of cast and crew. For the extras you might be better off talking to the kolkhoz people — they assist us with that side of things. I don't even have a list, I just tell them how many we want and when."

Korolev noted Slivka's raised eyebrow. She was right — it could take days to interview that number of people. Perhaps weeks.

"Well, we'll start with the people who had most contact with her," Korolev said, "at least until we have a definite line of inquiry. So who would they be?"

Shymko looked trapped, as though he were considering that question from two different angles. The first being what useful assistance he could give in this regard, and the second being what his colleagues might think of him if he were to point them out to the Militia.

"We'll be interviewing everyone in due course," Korolev said after a few moments, tempted as he was to let the man sweat. "But let me take a guess that she would have had most contact with Comrade Savchenko, yourself and the more senior production members."

"Yes," agreed Shymko, drawing the word out in the face of Korolev's implacable gaze. "But more than them — she was responsible for scheduling the shoot. That meant most people came in contact with her. She made sure the right actors were available for each scene we were shooting and in the right place. This work is normally done in advance, but with Savchenko there's a more" — he chose the next word carefully — "*spontaneous* element. Sometimes we end up rousting actors out of bed when they thought they had a day off and telling makeup artists they have two hours to prepare a hundred extras. It's not easy, I can tell you."

Korolev nodded, but not in sympathy.

"Let's presume she wasn't killed because she woke someone up too early, shall we? This is the Soviet Union, after all, and actors are cultured people not Chicago gangsters. How about we start with you, Comrade Shymko, as soon as you let us have your list? And let's go through it one by one and see if we can't divide it up a little. And, again, I want a list of key-holders and I want each key-holder, and the key, to present themselves to Sergeant Slivka, by the end of the day."

He wrote "keys" and "end of day" in his notebook, so that Shymko would know he was not to be trifled with.

CHAPTER SIX

The dead woman's office was located in the main house, in one of the round turrets. Its three windows gave a panoramic view over the lake and woods, or at least they would have if it hadn't been dark outside. The room was furnished with a table, a stiff-backed wooden chair and a scarred filing cabinet that looked as though it might miss its previous life in the office of some tsarist functionary or other. A prerevolution Underwood typewriter sat on the table, nearly as scratched and dented as the cabinet, but with a new ribbon. A second typewriter with the Latin alphabet sat on the higher of two planks fixed to the wall, which served as shelves and were sagging under the weight of books and paperwork. Korolev didn't want to enter until forensics had done their job, but he ran an eye along Lenskaya's small library from the doorway. Books in English, French, German, Italian. He was impressed — not many girls from an orphanage could speak Russian that well, let alone foreign languages. He turned to Babel.

"We'll need to have translations of these titles. Isaac Emmanuilovich — do you speak any of these languages?"

"My French is good, my German passable, but for the rest . . ." Babel shrugged and Korolev turned to look at him with what he hoped was a Mushkin-like stare.

"I thought you wanted to assist us."

"All right, all right, I'll get you the list," Babel said.

"I speak a little English," Slivka said. "And Italian, if that helps."

"Italian?" Korolev couldn't help but be surprised.

"Well enough, an Italian comrade gave lessons to our Komsomol cell. Nice fellow." Slivka's smile hinted at just how nice she'd found him.

"Good." Korolev spoke a little more brusquely than he'd intended. The idea of the Italian offering her private tuition had distracted him. "If necessary I speak a little English as well. And some German."

Everyone looked at him in surprise. Well, it was a very little English and it had been some time ago, and the German was mainly of the *"Hände hoch, Kamerad"* variety that he'd picked up when a soldier. But if everyone else was bragging about their linguistic talent, he wasn't going to be left behind. Babel raised a skeptical eyebrow.

"Zhenia, my ex-wife, made me go to classes. I can read their script and even understand some of it. Look — *English–Russian Dictionary.*"

"It's written in Russian as well."

"Well, it's not the Russian I'm reading, Comrade Babel," he said, giving the writer another of his best glares. "And we'll need to look through the paperwork, too."

Korolev could feel Belakovsky pressing against his shoulder — the Film Board boss, having been excluded from the ice house, seemed determined to be excluded no longer. Korolev ignored him, turning to one of the uniforms who'd come up from the village. With his rosy cheeks and straw-colored hair, Sharapov looked as though he should be in school rather than wearing a peaked Militia cap one size to big for him. An older, more battered-looking version stood beside him; his superior, Sergeant Gradov. The two other village uniforms, a thin wiry tough from Odessa by the name of Blumkin and a lump of a lad called Olejnik, were already guarding the dining room and the room where the girl had slept.

"So, young Sharapov," Korolev said, and the boy's crystal blue eyes looked up at him eagerly. "No one goes in until the fingerprint team has been over the place. This is where she was last seen alive, so that makes it likely this is where she died."

"Understood, Comrade Captain."

"Sergeant Slivka?"

"Yes?"

"We need to set up an investigation room, then prepare questions for the initial interviews. Where people were last night, who they saw, what they saw, what they know about the deceased, that sort of thing. Gradov?"

The older uniform stood a little straighter.

"You and your boys will be working under our direction for the next few days, asking those questions."

"Of course, Comrade Captain," the sergeant said. Korolev didn't much like the look of him — unless he was wrong, Gradov liked to throw his weight about with ordinary citizens. He just had that look about him — a brute, and not a bright one either.

"Comrade Shymko," Korolev said, "it will be less disruptive if you can find us an office nearby, seeing as this is where the cast and crew are based and we'd like to minimize disruption. We understand the importance of this film politically and bringing the cast and crew backward and forward to the village station isn't going to make your life any easier."

"We're pretty tight for space," Shymko said, looking to Belakovsky for support. The film supremo considered the problem.

"All right," he said after a few moments. "Give Captain Korolev the big room beside the production office. Is there anything else we can do to assist you?"

"But Comrade Belakovsky —" Shymko began.

"Captain Korolev needs to start immediately, Shymko. And he's right — we have to keep disruption to a minimum. This film is far enough behind as it is." Belakovsky turned to Korolev. "If we can work together to reduce disruption to the filming schedule, we'd be grateful, but we understand your investigation takes priority."

"Thank you, Igor Zakharovich," Korolev said. "I'll certainly do my best to keep the disturbance to a minimum. We'll need a telephone line, some desks. A typewriter, probably."

"Shymko will see to it. This has come as a shock to us all, but now we must come to terms with the news and do everything in our power to assist you. There's one thing I'd like to ask, however. Comrade Lenskaya was working on a special project for me. There'll be some papers in her office which I'll need to recover as soon as possible."

"Sergeant Slivka?" Korolev said. "As soon as the forensics men have been in, allow Comrade Belakovsky to look through the papers."

"Willingly."

"And we'll need to interview both of you." Korolev nodded toward Belakovsky and Shymko. "Sergeant Slivka?"

"I'll arrange a time."

"And Sergeant, find the caretaker, Andreychuk. I want to talk to him first. We need to have some lines of investigation to work on by tomorrow morning — all we have at the moment is a dead girl and a lot of questions."

As Slivka set to work, Korolev took Babel's arm and they walked away from Lenskaya's doorway toward the back of the house. Korolev opened the nearer of the French doors and led Babel out onto the terrace.

"What do you make of her?" Korolev asked, walking down the steps that led toward the garden. "Not many female detectives — but she seems bright."

"I wouldn't play cards with her, put it that

way. A good Odessa girl, bright as a button and pretty as a picture, but tough as a miner's boot for all that."

It was true — she was pretty, despite the serious mouth and the shapeless leather jacket. Like so many of the young women whom the Revolution had allowed to pursue traditionally male professions, she'd adopted a mannish mode of dress, but even her leather jacket and her trousers couldn't hide the shape of her body, and it was a pleasant shape. And while at first her mouth had seemed to have a permanent downturn, when she'd smiled he'd seen high cheek-bones, the flash of white teeth and a mischievous twinkle in her eyes. All in all, a much better-looking colleague than his old friend Yasimov.

"Well," he said, as they took a path toward the lake, "as long as she gets the job done."

"Indeed." Babel looked over his shoulder to see if they could be overheard. "And do you mind me asking what that job is?"

"I'd have thought that was clear. We find the fellow who killed Citizen Lenskaya and put him where he belongs."

Babel unstrapped his wrist watch and looked at it absently, his demeanor pensive. "Yes, but why did they send a Moscow detective all the way down here to investigate? And *who* sent you, if you don't mind me asking?"

Korolev considered how to respond for a moment, before deciding to start with a question.

"What did they say when they involved you?"

"The message came from Major Mushkin, who doesn't give explanations."

"I see. Well, I can't tell you much more. The first I knew about it was at two o'clock this morning and since then I've been running to catch up. They wanted me to have a look at the girl — if it was suicide, I was to have a holiday. If not, lead the investigation — under their direction."

"Their?"

"The Chekists." Korolev spoke with a certain amount of reluctance, not least because the conversation was underlining a problem for his upcoming inquiries. If the murder really was to do with the dead girl's relationship with Ezhov, and Ezhov's name couldn't be mentioned, it was going to be difficult.

"Why wouldn't they use their own people?" Babel asked, interrupting his train of thought. "Or leave it to the local Militia?"

"The NKVD doesn't specialize in criminal investigations, I suppose," Korolev said.

"And they remembered me from the icon business."

"It's just that I've heard a rumor that Lenskaya was friendly with a certain Commissar of State Security," Babel continued, "that's all. And if that's really the case — well, I'm wondering if that's why you're here. If it's something to do with him."

"Friendly with Ezhov?" Korolev said with what he hoped sounded like genuine surprise. "I know nothing about that, but even if it were true, what could her death have to do with Ezhov?"

Babel shrugged. "Ezhov is well protected, physically at least. But politically he's as vulnerable as everyone else. More so. Stalin doesn't mind what Ezhov gets up to, so long as his dalliances don't affect his usefulness to the Party. But if this death turned out to be compromising to him, it wouldn't be too difficult to think of people who would benefit from it. Both within the State and outside it."

"Compromising?" Korolev said, not liking the suggestion. "In what way, compromising?"

"I don't know, but why were you sent down here? Ezhov has enemies within the NKVD, you know. Perhaps that's why you were picked — because he doesn't trust his own people. Be careful, Alexei — this could turn out to be a nasty business."

"It's already that."

"Yes," Babel said with a sigh. "You'll have to be careful how you proceed. So — what do you know about Lenskaya? Perhaps I can add something."

Korolev told him what he knew and Babel nodded when he'd finished.

"Well, she was intelligent and lucky with it, that much is certain. And she was ambitious — that much is also true, and flexible in the means she used to get ahead. Ezhov wasn't the only one she was friendly with, if I can put it that way. It wasn't luck and intelligence alone that took her from the orphanage and got her chosen for delegations to Hollywood."

"When you say 'friendly' . . . ?"

"She was a good-looking girl and she didn't want to spend her life queuing for bread. I know she was with Belakovsky. Savchenko as well. As for Ezhov — well, the rumors are they weren't strangers."

"I see," Korolev said. "Others?"

"Probably. They send orphanage children where the labor demand is greatest," Babel continued. "She could have ended up in a factory the other side of the Urals, or at a kolkhoz farm by the Sea of Azov. Who knows who her parents were? Most probably peasants with a couple of cows who woke up one morning and discovered they'd been classified as kulaks and therefore class enemies. What happened to them we may never know, but that she took control of her fate is certain and who can blame her?"

"Are you saying she was the child of a class enemy?" Korolev asked, before cursing himself. Of course that's what Babel was saying. And what's more he was likely right. It made sense.

"All I know is that she had a past before the orphanage, and she kept quiet about it. But if it were the case, it would reflect badly on the People's Commissar of State Security if it came out."

"Not that we know anything for certain," Korolev said.

"Of course not," Babel said, sighing. "By the way, watch out for Mushkin."

"Mushkin?"

"Mushkin. When Soviet Power reached Odessa in 'nineteen, he drove around the city with the corpses of executed enemies dragging behind his car. Just to show everyone who was boss — and he hasn't turned into a priest since then, believe me. You know what happened in these parts a few years back. It wasn't pleasant, and Mushkin has a reputation from then that would scare the Devil. He's here now because even the NKVD thought he'd gone too far and needed a rest."

Korolev remembered the stories that he'd been told about the winter of 'thirty-two. How frozen bodies, skin and bone, had emerged from the snow when the spring came. How the people had boiled any leather they'd had for soup. If the stories he'd heard were true, people had eaten grass until the snow covered it, tree bark, the recently dead, their own children, anything. And still the authorities had come searching for grain, and had found none. And Mushkin had been a part of that.

"Still," Babel said, the smile not quite reaching his eyes, "remember the saying — if you're destined to die at sea, you won't be hanged."

CHAPTER SEVEN

Korolev found Shymko standing in front of the newly designated investigation room, his face yellow in the light that spilled out of it. He raised a hand in greeting.

"I've got you a typewriter, paper and ribbon, and there's a phone line. If you need anything else, let me know."

"Thank you, Comrade."

"And Larisa is typing up those lists you wanted."

Korolev saw that once the man had a job to do, he did it well and efficiently. There weren't so many of his kind around that Korolev didn't appreciate his abilities.

"Excellent," Korolev said, meaning it, and was about to continue when the arrival of Marchuk and Mushkin, along with two forensics men, distracted him. After brief introductions, he sent the forensics men to the dead girl's office, saying he'd catch up with them in a few minutes.

"I see you're settling in, Korolev," Mushkin said, looking around the investigation room.

"I thought it best to take a few practical steps; they'll assist another detective if I'm not released by my chief."

"Or if it turns out to be suicide," Mushkin said in a flat tone. "Anyway, your chief was only too pleased that Moscow CID should be in a position to assist their Odessa colleagues. Isn't that right, Marchuk?"

That same snide undercurrent again, Korolev thought. He found himself hoping that a day would come when the leadership would point out to these arrogant protectors of the State that the People they were meant to be protecting were the same people they spent their time harassing and intimidating.

"Yes," Marchuk agreed, his eyes slipping away from Korolev's with something approaching shame. "Comrade Popov was most impressed that you put the State's needs before your own. We'll do everything we can to assist, of course. Peskov will have a full autopsy report ready by the morning and I'll have the forensics men work through the night if need be."

"Thank you, Comrade Colonel. I take it I'll report to you, then."

The abashed colonel turned to Mushkin, his mouth opening as though he felt he should say something but he wasn't quite sure what.

"No," Mushkin answered instead. "It's been decided you'll report to Moscow. The case has sufficient connections with the capital to justify it. Your investigation will be independent of Odessa CID at this stage, as well as the local procurator's office."

"Unusual," Korolev replied, thinking he'd never heard of a case not involving the procurator's office. After all, it was the procurators' role to take the case to court, so they usually had some oversight of the investigation to ensure the evidence was properly gathered. In theory Militia detectives acted under their direction, although, of course, it didn't always work out that way in practice. Still, it was the way things were done.

"Why? We aren't even certain it's murder yet, are we? Officially you're investigating a suicide: be sure to make that clear to anyone you speak to."

"Of course, Comrade Major."

"I'll leave you and Marchuk to discuss the details. Be quick though, Korolev — you'll be receiving a phone call in the next few minutes."

Korolev looked at the back of Mushkin's leather coat as he marched away, then at the colonel, whose pale face didn't offer any reassurance.

"Comrade Colonel, we may have hundreds of interviews to do so I'll need all the help I can get. Sergeant Slivka? Is she to work with me?"

She was, it seemed, as well as Gradov and the other uniforms from the village. In fact, the colonel gave the impression that he'd have happily given the Moscow detective his first-born child if it would get him done with his involvement in the investigation any faster, and as soon as the conversation had finished, the colonel's car was rattling down the driveway.

Korolev sat behind the desk farthest from the door. The phone rang just as he felt his eyelids begin to close under their own weight and he picked up the receiver tentatively.

"Korolev," he said, his voice sounding much more confident than he felt.

"Well, Korolev, I hear you have a murder on your hands." It was Rodinov, and the colonel listened silently as Korolev brought him up to date on developments. When Korolev had finished he gave a series of instructions — Sergeant Slivka came in to hear Korolev repeat the word "Yes" several times and then thank the Comrade Colonel for his time. She sat down in front of him and waited for him to finish.

Korolev put down the phone with the feeling that things could certainly be a lot worse. Yes, he was under strict instructions to see that Ezhov's name didn't feature in the case in any way, but that he had expected — particularly after his conversation with Babel. On the other hand, he had permission to proceed as he saw fit, except for the proviso that he should try to avoid disruption to the film — and that was something he'd already agreed with Belakovsky.

All well and good, until the colonel had mentioned the foreigner.

"What foreigner?" he'd asked, and so it had emerged that there was a French journalist, a guest of Savchenko. He was to be treated very carefully and if questioning was to be carried out, it was to be discussed with Rodinov first. He could do as he liked with the Soviet citizens, within reason, but this fellow Les Pins was a different story. He was an important supporter of the Soviet Union in the West, and Rodinov wanted it kept that way.

"Did you know about this foreigner?" Korolev said, looking up at Slivka.

"A foreigner?"

"Some Frenchman. He's been fighting on our side in Spain, so he's probably all right. But who knows? Foreigners are always trouble."

"Yes, they can be tricky. Those Ukrainians are the worst."

Slivka's teasing smile was a surprise. She must be a confident young woman if she felt comfortable making fun of a stranger twice her age with the rank to go with it, but Korolev didn't mind. It was more pleasant to work in a comradely atmosphere.

"We're all Soviet citizens here, Slivka," he said, deciding the time had come to drop the "sergeant." "Even you Ukrainians. It's the rest I've my doubts about. They should leave all the foreigners to the diplomats if you ask me. If they have to be dealt with, it's better done by professionals."

Slivka smiled and took a look around her.

"So this is where we'll be working? Will we have to sleep here too, do you think? I wonder: will they give us a couple of mattresses? Maybe a handsome actor as well? Not for you, of course."

Korolev laughed — Marchuk had probably offloaded her onto him, not quite sure

124

what to do with a sparky young female detective, and Korolev couldn't swear he wouldn't have done the same in his shoes.

"Slivka, I'm not sure I introduced myself properly before. My name is Korolev," he said and then, thinking there was no harm in being specific, "Alexei Dmitriyevich, Captain, Moscow Criminal Investigation Division. Petrovka Street."

He stood up and extended his hand, which Slivka took with a surprisingly firm grip.

"Don't ask me why I'm running this case, Slivka, but I am, and I plan to catch whoever killed that poor girl, with your help."

"A sound plan."

"Good, so let's get down to business."

"Agreed," Slivka said, "but before we start, can I ask a question?"

"Of course."

"Don't be offended, Comrade Captain, but is this a Moscow investigation, or an Odessa one?"

Korolev rubbed a hand up the back of his neck, feeling the bristly scrub of his shortcut hair.

"It's a good question — all I can say is that the responsibility for this investigation falls mainly on us, the two of us. We won't be reporting to Colonel Marchuk, and we won't be involving the procurator's office. We'll be reporting to Moscow, but we'll have to make most of the decisions ourselves. I can't tell you any more than that, except that if we mess this up it could go badly. So we'd better not mess it up."

Slivka sucked in the last of the cigarette she was smoking, stubbing it out in the ashtray, shrugged as if the strange circumstances surrounding the investigation were but a minor concern to her, reached into her pockets, extracted another cigarette and lit it by scratching a match along the sole of her boot. She inhaled, cupping her hand around the cigarette the way soldiers and policemen, used to smoking in the open, often did.

"Well, I thought something might be up, Comrade Captain, which is why I asked. I like to know what's what. You can find yourself in trouble if you don't know what's what. And who's who."

She blew out a perfect smoke ring, then took two folded pieces of paper from her pocket and handed them to him.

"One. A list of the cast and the crew, including all the production staff, catering etcetera, etcetera, and the staff of the College who aren't away with the students, which isn't many; and, two, a list of the people who have keys to the house. In other words, people who might have had access to the scene of the crime yesterday evening."

Korolev looked through the longer list. Beside each name was a number from one to three. "And the numbers?"

"I had Comrade Shymko rate each person by the amount of contact they had with Citizen Lenskaya. 1 is daily contact, a 2 means occasional and a 3 means little or none."

"Excellent. We'll start with the people who had daily contact." He looked down the list — his optimism was misplaced. "Most of them, it would seem."

"Yes. More than we'd like, for sure. Thirty-four."

Korolev sighed. He was beginning to feel the dead weight of exhaustion again, as if the last of his energy was being sucked into the floor through the soles of his feet. He rallied himself for one last push.

"Well, the sooner we start — the sooner we finish."

"I agree. Can I suggest we use Shymko's people to arrange the interviews; it will be less disruptive for them if they know what we're up to."

"Good thinking," Korolev said. "Let's try and keep them short — we'll interview them again tomorrow likely as not, but our first objective is to identify potential motives and perpetrators, and anyone who could have been in the house at the time of death."

"And *cherchez l'homme,* right?"

"Possibly," Korolev said, thinking that the most obvious lover to have been responsible for Lenskaya's death was probably Ezhov and that wasn't something he wanted to think about too much. "As it turns out, she may have been romantically inclined, if you take my meaning. Savchenko for one, or so it seems, and probably Comrade Belakovsky as well, although as Savchenko was filming down in the village and Belakovsky was in Moscow, that doesn't take us too much further. Still, there may have been others — let's find out who. It doesn't feel like a crime of passion, though; whoever did this was careful and covered their tracks, or tried to at least. My suspicion is that it was premeditated. Also, whoever did it must have been quite strong. How much did Lenskaya weigh? A hundred thirty pounds or so? It must have been difficult to lift her up to the bracket."

"Indeed," Slivka said, writing in her notebook.

"We need to find out as much as we can about her background as well," he continued. "I have her Party record, but there's a lot missing and not much about her private life. And nothing about her relationships with the people on the film set. Here, you'd better read it."

Slivka took the report and again there was that slight raising of the eyebrows.

"Her Party record? It takes us a bit of time to get them even when they're held in Odessa."

"Perhaps things are different in Moscow."

"I'll go through it. Anything else I should have? Or know?"

Korolev decided to give her the report on the film and the other information Rodinov had provided. He handed her the envelope and Slivka took the documents out, looked through them and whistled.

"Not to be discussed other than with me. And I mean with anyone. For both our sakes."

Slivka nodded her agreement, slipping the papers back into the envelope.

"I have Andreychuk waiting outside for you," she said when she'd finished.

"Good, I'll see him as soon as I've spoken to the forensics men. In the meantime" — Korolev tapped Slivka's lists — "we need to whittle these down — opportunity, ability and motive. That's what we're looking for.

Same as always."

"They filmed the crowd. Maybe we could identify some people from it — rule them out perhaps?"

Korolev considered her proposal: the problem was he didn't know any of the people on the film — not yet anyway — and neither would Slivka.

"It's a good suggestion — look into it. We'll need help, though. I know the writer Babel from Moscow. He's offered to assist — perhaps we should take him up on it."

"Babel?" Slivka said. "I get to work with the author of *Odessa Tales*? My mother might even forgive me for joining the Militia. Tell me he can type as well, and it will be like New Year."

"I suppose he can. He's a writer after all — in fact, I've seen a typewriter in his study."

"Good, because I'm a detective, Captain, not a typist. Just so we're clear about that. It's a point I sometimes have to make."

Korolev smiled — he liked this Slivka.

"Well, I'm no typist either, but I'll pull my weight. Still, it's a good point. I want the interview notes to be typed and clear — if we're to crack this case, it's because we organize the information well. Let's see if any of these uniforms from the village can drive a typewriter. If not, we'll have to see if we can persuade Comrade Shymko to lend us someone. And the uniforms won't have done too much work like this before — let's make sure they know exactly what questions to ask."

"As per your instructions, Chief. Where were they? When did they last see the girl? Who did they see at the film shoot? What did they know about her? Did anyone dislike her? Who was she most friendly with? I'll have it all set out and typed up for them."

Korolev found Andreychuk outside in the cold and told him to wait in the investigation room until he came back, then he started to walk toward the house, allowing himself a little smile as he did so. All right, it was true this case was likely to turn out to be a terrible mess — but at least Slivka seemed as though she'd be useful to have around. Nadezhda. Hope. And not just for the investigation: youngsters like Slivka were the future and, maybe, with citizens like her, a country would emerge from all this turmoil and fear that would shine as an example to the world of how humans could live together, working as one, striving for a common goal. Maybe.

By the time he arrived at Lenskaya's office, the forensics men were packing their equipment while the youngster Sharapov watched them with keen interest.

"Sharapov. Out to the stable block. Sergeant Slivka has plenty of work that needs doing."

The young Militiaman gave a cheerful salute and followed his instructions.

"You were quick. Any luck?" Korolev said to the forensics men.

The older of the two, whom Colonel Marchuk had introduced as Firtov, looked up, a gray-haired man with solid shoulders, silver-gray eyes and a cavalryman's mustache. When he stood, he had the bow-legged stance of a man more comfortable on a horse than on his feet.

"We haven't found much, to be straight, and if you ask me, someone cleaned the place," Firtov said. "There's not a fingerprint in there, and that's not natural. Not even on the keys of the typewriter. A few human hairs and that's it, and no telling when they were left here. Papadopoulos found those."

The other forensics man looked up — he was smaller, rounder, with black hair that swirled in tight curls on his close-cut scalp. When he smiled his teeth were bright in his dark face.

"Papadopoulos? That's not a Ukrainian name, is it?" Korolev asked, thinking he'd end up surrounded by foreigners in this case if he wasn't careful.

"The Greek is as good a citizen as you or I." Firtov's voice had dropped to a growl. "Born and raised in Odessa. As his father was before him. Isn't that right, Greek?"

The Greek nodded, his smile flashing like a lighthouse once again.

"No offense meant," Korolev said, offering his much-depleted packet of cigarettes as a peace offering.

"None taken," Firtov said, helping himself. The Greek didn't seem to smoke. Just as well, thought Korolev, looking at his few remaining cigarettes. Two, after he took one for himself.

"We'll look at the dining room, and wherever else you want, but it's as though a human never stepped into this room."

"What about the books?" Korolev asked, looking up at the shelves.

"Well, we haven't gone through them page by page," Firtov said. "But the covers are clean. It's unusual, as I said."

The forensics men finished packing their equipment and made their way to the dining room, but Korolev remained, examining the office carefully.

The room wasn't that big and books loomed in from the walls to make it that little bit smaller. Savchenko's *Theory of Film* was there, with Lenin and Stalin; Marx — as you might expect — and other writers of the Revolution. But there was something about the way the paper was stacked, and the books lined up spine against spine in a perfect row — it was just a little too tidy. Someone hadn't just cleaned up fingerprints if his hunch was right — they'd carefully re-arranged the entire room. And why would they have done that?

Of course, the most likely reason was that it had been the scene of the crime. After all, this was where she'd last been seen by Andreychuk and the dining room was only a few steps away. He looked at the desk once again, imagining Lenskaya sitting in front of the typewriter, her assailant behind her. Perhaps he'd spoken to her — she might even have answered, not turning around from her typing, recognizing the voice, and then had come the flash of the cord as it passed before her eyes and the bite as it cut into her neck. Korolev had once throttled a German back in the war, not a memory he liked bringing to mind — the fellow had managed to get his hand under the thin rope and had hung on to life with a fervor that had been extraordinary. But the fact was Korolev had been unlucky about the hand. Usually, once a rope was tight around the victim's neck, resistance ceased almost immediately. That was something he'd learned early on as a detective.

"What are you thinking? Your jaw has that hard look to it. And there's a vein pumping in your forehead. You've gone pale and I can hear your teeth grinding."

Babel had appeared, wearing a pair of carpet slippers and a surprisingly vibrant silk dressing gown. Korolev looked at the writer, then turned his attention back to the dead girl's workplace. The killer had to have made a mistake. Babel's appearance had distracted him, but, still, there had to be a mistake.

"This is where she died," he said at last, the words coming out as though he'd been holding his breath, and perhaps he had. "That's what I'm thinking. That this is where he killed her."

CHAPTER EIGHT

When Korolev returned to the investigation room, he found Andreychuk sitting in front of the desk Korolev had appropriated for himself. He nodded to the caretaker, sat down and opened up his notebook.

His first impression was that the fellow didn't look strong enough to have lifted the girl up to the bracket, or even to have strangled her if she'd resisted. But he quickly corrected himself — the old were often stronger than they looked, and Andreychuk clearly led an active life. Indeed, on closer examination the man's shoulders were broad, as was his chest, despite the fact he was no longer young. And, of course, there was always the possibility he'd had assistance, that there had been two involved in the attempted deception, and perhaps the murder itself. Andreychuk seemed to have had the opportunity to commit the crime, but what motive could he have had?

None that Korolev could immediately think of, and then there was his very obvious grief. Not that that could be trusted. And if the office had been cleaned of any forensic evidence, did that point to the perpetrator of the crime having been a simple caretaker? It seemed much more likely that it pointed to someone with connections to the Security Organs.

He thought back to the Shishkin case — the file would probably already be shut and that wasn't unusual. Murder was usually a simple matter, with the victim and the perpetrator well known to each other, and each step of their dance toward death well observed by others. But every now and then a complete mystery came along and then it required patience and time to sift through the facts and decide what was relevant and what could be discarded. Unfortunately for him, the Chekists weren't renowned for their patience.

Andreychuk, his flat cap on his knees, his eyes downcast and his shoulders bent, coughed into his hand. It was a question — when are you going to stop looking at me and when are you going to start questioning me?

"You're the caretaker here, correct?" Korolev said, after a further pause.

"Yes, Comrade Korolev. We met earlier."

"I remember. You were the last known person to see Comrade Lenskaya alive." Korolev gave the caretaker another long, hard look. "And the first known person to see her dead."

"I was," Andreychuk said, not seeming to like the way those two little sentences sounded. Korolev didn't blame him. There were detectives who'd have stopped the investigation at this point, and procurators who'd have felt happy the case was resolved. Everyone had quotas to fill these days, now that administering justice was considered just as quantifiable a task as mining coal.

"Well, Comrade?" Korolev asked, and waited, aware of the value of the open-ended question. Andreychuk lifted his eyes, squinting slightly. He shook his head slowly from side to side. It was true, Korolev thought, the caretaker was in a bad situation.

"I was checking the house," Andreychuk began. "Everyone was down in the village so I was going to shut the place up. But I saw the light on in the young lady comrade's office and so I knocked."

"When was this?"

"At about seven-thirty. I remember because I was due to be down in the village

138

for the film people, but I know my duty, so when I saw the light on I went to find out."

"Find out what?" Korolev said, keeping his voice neutral.

"What she was up to, of course."

"And?"

"She was typing — on a black typewriter." He paused, as if remembering the scene. "She said she wasn't coming down to the village and I wasn't to bother about her. So I left her there, on her own."

"So she was the only person in the house when you left? There was no one else?"

Andreychuk looked at Korolev, and then at his feet. "I couldn't swear to that, Comrade Captain. I didn't check every last room, and I'm not asked to. I was in a rush as well. There might have been someone in one of the upstairs rooms, for example, sleeping perhaps, but there were no other lights on. And if someone wanted to hide themselves — well, I don't check the place that way. It's a big house, and I have to lock up the rest of the College buildings as well. I keep the place running — I'm not a watchman."

"But you saw no one — that's useful. And you locked the house after you?"

"I did." Andreychuk clearly felt more confident about this answer.

"Why did you leave Lenskaya alone in the house?"

"She was like that, Comrade. Always working. It wasn't unusual for her to be working when the rest would be laughing around the place."

"I see, and when you returned later the house was completely secure, is that correct? And no signs of a break-in?"

"Nothing."

"And you were the first person to return to the house?"

"I opened the house for the film people when they'd finished."

"Tell me exactly what you saw when you found her."

The caretaker spoke slowly — as though he were living through the moment of discovery once again so as to describe it the better.

"She was hanging from the bracket in the dining hall, the one you saw. The rope had cut into her neck — it hadn't cut her skin, but it had been pulled into her neck by her weight as far as it could go, almost to her ears, and her head had fallen forward. There was a chair on the ground beside her — I thought she must have stood on it, and kicked it away before" — his voice caught — "before she died. Her arms were hanging

140

straight down. She was wearing the clothes you saw her in, and, well, she was dead all right."

Korolev wrote down the caretaker's words verbatim, then looked up at him. "How high from the ground was she, Citizen? When you found her?"

"Her feet, you mean?"

"Yes."

"Only a few inches off the ground." The caretaker held his hands apart — four inches or so.

"What you did you do?"

"Well." Andreychuk's eyes moved sideways as if wanting to avoid the mental image the question prompted. "I dropped to my knees, if the truth be told. I'd just opened the door, the film comrades had finished in the village and everyone was coming back, and I saw her. Hanging there. And I could see she was dead straight off."

"And then? You cut her down?"

"Yes, we did."

"We?"

"I know Comrade Shymko was one of them. The others — well, I've been trying to remember myself, but the only face I can see now is hers. We stood on a table, and treated her as gently as we could."

"You liked her?"

"She was a good woman. A fine woman. I think everyone liked her."

"Any enemies you know of? Any arguments she might have had, anything at all?"

"She was popular as far as I know. But I'm only the caretaker."

Korolev felt a stab of frustration that clenched his knuckles white around the pen. Only a caretaker, was he? He didn't have eyes in his head? He damned well did if his description of finding her was anything to go by.

"What about particular friends, or lovers?" he said, keeping his voice calm.

"I don't get involved in other people's business," Andreychuk answered, his eyes dropping to his feet once again. Korolev studied him, wondering what he was holding back.

"I'll ask that question again, Citizen. Had she a lover, or a particular friend or friends?"

"She was friendly with most people. I don't know about her having a lover. I'd tell you if I knew something. I know my duty." The words were barely audible.

"Can you write, Citizen?" Korolev asked, allowing his voice to harden.

"Yes, Comrade Captain. I can write all right."

"Well, I want you to write me a list of everyone you thought she was 'friendly' with. When she saw them and so on. Bring it back to me in an hour."

Andreychuk nodded, still not meeting his eyes.

"And another question. The doors to the house — you're certain all of them were locked when you left and when you returned?"

Andreychuk took a bunch of keys from his pocket, as though to remind himself, then nodded slowly.

"I'm certain they were locked when I left, and I know the front door was locked when I returned because I was the one who opened it. As for the others, after we found her . . ." His voice tailed off.

"Everything was in confusion, I'm sure. Do you remember unlocking them though? When things had calmed down."

"No, but others have keys to the house and some of the doors can be opened from the inside without a key. Do you think she might have let him in? The killer?"

Korolev looked up from his notebook.

"I don't think anything at the moment, Comrade," Korolev said. "My job is to establish possibilities and then prove them or disprove them."

But at the moment it seemed there were a lot of possibilities and not much to disprove any of them.

"Will there be anything else?" Andreychuk asked.

"For the moment that's all," Korolev said and then, when the caretaker moved to rise, he looked up at him. "One thing. You said earlier that Lenskaya told you she was from these parts? When was that?"

"I'm not sure I remember it. Perhaps I was mistaken."

"You seemed sure enough earlier. Did she say from where?"

The caretaker seemed to be considering the question. He didn't look comfortable.

"I don't think so. I think I was mistaken."

"You're sure she said nothing, then?"

Andreychuk shrugged.

Korolev didn't say anything, but he was sure the fellow had more to tell them. He'd let Slivka have a go at him in the morning. And perhaps one of the other interviews would shed some light on the matter in the meantime. He made a quick note to himself.

"You can go, but we'll want to talk to you again. And if I were you, Citizen Andreychuk, I'd work on that memory of yours."

The caretaker nodded, bobbed his head in thanks, and quickly left the room. Korolev considered joining one of the Militia-men, already, he hoped, presenting the first interviewees with their menu of questions, but decided against it. It would only confuse them if he deviated from the script. Instead he looked at his list for the next interviewee Slivka had lined up for him — Sorokina, the actress. Well, if nothing else, this case had at least one compensation.

Anyone who'd been to the cinema in the last ten years had almost certainly seen Bar-ikada Sorokina shining in the darkness. She'd grown up on the screen, at first a child and then a young girl and now a beautiful woman. As might be expected, she was often either defending the barricades for which she was named, or storming them. Born to Party members in the tsar's time, her name spoke of the struggle that had preceded the Revolution, and now, twenty-five years later, she was the embodiment of the People's hope for the future, and their determination to defend all that had been achieved. Whenever Barikada stepped before the camera it was to lead them onward, and whether it was to move impossible quanti-ties of earth in order to complete a delayed canal project or to attack a White fortress Barikada always led by example. Of course, it often resulted in her own tragic death, but Soviet citizens knew it was their duty to put the Party and the State's welfare before their own. And if they didn't, Barikada's selfless heroism reminded them.

Korolev looked at his watch — he still had a few minutes before she arrived so he decided to go back over his notes of the Andreychuk interview in case there was something he'd missed. He'd barely started when there was a knock on the door.

"Come in," he called, without looking up, still focused on Andreychuk's notes. The door opened and he waved the person to the desk in front of him. There was no movement, however, and so he lifted his eyes to see who it was.

Barikada Sorokina stood in front of him like a fully limbed and clothed Venus de Milo, a brown fur coat hanging over her shoulders against which her blonde hair shone like gold. For a moment, Korolev was so surprised by the vision before him that it didn't occur to him that she might be waiting for something. Then, to his surprise, he found his body had got to its feet, marched across the floor and given a suspiciously tsarist-like bow to the beautiful actress, who extended her hand, not to be shaken, but to be kissed. Korolev, cheeks burning, found himself complying with her wishes.

"Comrade Captain," the actress breathed, "have we met before?"

Her eyes were a green that was close to emerald, and she seemed well aware of the effect they were having on a bumbling Militia captain. But where else to look? Her breasts stretched against a khaki shirt that seemed to have been tailored so as to make normal breathing difficult for her. He would have to convince his eyes they absolutely did not exist, and hope that she might cover her chest with the fur coat in due course. Her fine white teeth might have made an acceptable alternative except for the slight hint in her smile that her full red lips were his to do with as he wished, should he only ask. He settled at last on her forehead. It was a good forehead, sculpted, uncreased by worry, and it had the advantage that it didn't make his throat constrict with inappropriate desire.

"No, I don't think so," he managed to say. "Although I was fortunate enough to see your last film. So in a way, I've met you, if not the other way around."

"*Appointment at Dawn*?"

"Yes — you were executed by counter-revolutionary brigands. At dawn. It was very moving." It was true, Korolev had found himself wiping his eyes on the back of his overcoat sleeve, grateful for the darkness in the cinema. "You were inspiring."

"Do you remember this?" she asked and pulled her shoulders back and looked at him with utter disdain. "You may shoot me, but the Revolution will never be defeated!"

"Bravo!" Babel said, entering behind her. "I'm surprised the firing squad didn't turn Red immediately."

Which was strange, because Korolev could indeed feel a blush warming his cheeks.

"You've met the beautiful Barikada, then."

"Yes," Korolev said, pleased that his voice seemed to sound relatively normal. "Isaac, we'll need privacy for Comrade Sorokina's interview."

Babel looked a little nonplussed for a moment, then nodded in agreement.

"A shame. I should have liked to see how the best detective in Moscow sets about such an interview. Be careful now, Barikada, don't go giving away your intimate secrets. He's a terrier, this one." And Korolev found himself looking at Babel with a sudden professional curiosity — his words had sounded almost like a warning. But Babel had already turned to leave and Korolev caught only the briefest glimpse of his face in the light before it was gone. Not enough to come to a conclusion, but still — a strange thing to say.

"Will you take a seat, Comrade? I just have a few questions."

"Anything I can do to assist you in your efforts, of course. Poor Masha, how thankful she would have been to know that a detective of your experience is searching for her killer."

"Killer? Who said anything about a killer?"

"Everyone is saying it," Barikada replied, her eyes widening. "Although I must admit I'd my suspicions from the first."

"Well, we'll come to that. But for the moment this is just a routine interview to gather all the facts about Citizen Lenskaya's untimely death." Korolev sat down at the desk to face her, not knowing quite how he was going to go about things.

"Let us begin at the beginning." It was the best place to start, after all. "How long had you known Citizen Lenskaya?"

"Masha? Oh, quite some time. We used to see each other at parties and she was at the State Film School, of course. She was friendly with people I'm friendly with — you know how it is. Moscow is a small town, in many ways."

Yes, Korolev imagined it was — if you were part of the elite. Artists like Sorokina and Babel, senior Party cadres, the technocrats and the Lenin Prize winners, they were no doubt all as thick as thieves.

"Yes, I've heard it said Moscow is surprisingly small," he replied, thinking of the teeming millions of Muscovite workers who queued outside bakeries for bread that there was never enough of and that was often too expensive. "But more to the point, was there anything in Comrade Lenskaya's private life you're aware of that might have a bearing on this investigation?"

"What do you mean?"

"I'm afraid I have to ask about lovers, associates. Whether she drank too much, had enemies — things like that. I'm sorry — it must seem disrespectful to her memory."

"Oh no — you must ask me anything you like. I consider it my duty as a loyal citizen to answer *any* question you may have for me." The actress seemed animated, and Korolev wondered whether she did indeed have something to hide, but then it occurred to him that, as an actress, this was a role she had played several times before.

"Well, shall we consider first whether she had any enemies? Have you any thoughts as to who might have done this?"

"Enemies? Masha? Well, a few of the girls might have been a little jealous of her, but the men all loved her. It was strange, really,

150

because I always thought she was a little mousy. Not that she wasn't pretty, you know — because she was, I don't deny that — but she spent so much of her time reading books, and that makes you squint a little, and then, next thing you know, you begin to look like a mouse."

"A mouse?"

"In my personal opinion, yes — sometimes you can go too far with education. But the men adored her. Perhaps because she was adventurous, if I could express it that way. And didn't restrict herself to one person in particular. She behaved, in many ways, like a man — but still she retained her femininity and charm so that none of them blamed her for it. It was strange how she dealt with them. I admired her for it, I can tell you."

"Any men in particular?"

"Oh. Well, you probably know about Savchenko, and Belakovsky, of course. Everyone knows about them."

Korolev made quick notes. So everyone knew, did they?

"And then that journalist Lomatkin," she continued.

"Lomatkin?" So the fellow from the plane had been her lover — no wonder he'd looked shaken earlier.

"Yes, very much so."

"She had a lot of lovers?"

"I've known her since she was a student, ten years nearly. I might not be acquainted with all of them, but there were certainly a few. I could name several in Moscow off the top of my head, including a very important person indeed."

Sorokina pursed her lips, as though resisting telling him, although at the same time almost begging him to ask. Well, she'd be waiting a lifetime for him to ask that question.

"How about here?"

"Well, there was something, and I want to discuss it with you frankly. I have a small suspicion — I'm not unobservant, you know. In fact in *Red Militia* I played a policewoman myself. You may remember the role."

"Yes, I do," Korolev said — if he remembered rightly she had died a hero's death, not an unusual ending to her films. "You were excellent, as always."

"Thank you, you're very generous in your praise." Sorokina smiled her trademark smile at him, open and warm but at the same time humble. Korolev felt a little like a bear trapped in honey.

"And your suspicion?" he asked, his voice gruff.

"Andreychuk." Her voice became a whisper and she looked at him with a grave expression. "The caretaker. I think he murdered her. I saw them arguing."

"What were they arguing about?"

"I don't know — I didn't hear much of it. I was walking down to the village. I know it's not safe, but you can go stir crazy in this place. It was a clear night and I kept close to the house in case there was any trouble."

"Trouble?" Korolev asked, mystified.

"With the villagers, of course. The kulak class is everywhere around here, and who knows what other counterrevolutionary elements as well. Priests, Makhno's bandits, Petlyurists, White Guards, even Trotskyists they say. The resistance to the kolkhoz collectivization movement is still strong — it's why this film is so important. Some of them are determined to wreck our project, but we'll struggle with all our might to finish it, and show no mercy to the saboteurs as they'll show no mercy to us. *The Darkening Field* will be a dagger into the hearts of the Revolution's enemies — and we mustn't underestimate the lengths to which these brigands will go to stop us."

It was quite a speech, and the feeling behind it seemed genuine. Sorokina paused for effect, placed a hand on the table and leaned forward for emphasis.

"I believe poor Masha may have been a victim of just such an enemy in Andrey-chuk."

"So," Korolev said, deliberately taking things one step at a time, "you think An-dreychuk may have killed her because she was working on the film — because he's against the drive toward collectivization. Have there been other incidents of sabo-tage?"

Sorokina looked thoughtful for a moment.

"Not as yet, but you can see it in the way the villagers look at us. They've been wait-ing for their opportunity, the rats."

"I've met Andreychuk, he didn't strike me that way. What were they arguing about?"

"I couldn't tell exactly. But you're right, I'd always thought Andreychuk a good fel-low, and he seemed to like Masha as well. Well, you know how it is, the way older men treat pretty young girls. They go out of their way for them, bring them little presents — I saw him give her some apples once. And another time I caught him looking at her when he thought no one was watching, and the way he looked at her was more than comradely. Much, much more. And so I was surprised when I found them arguing. And at what I heard him say as well."

"And what was that?"

"He said, 'Go back to Moscow, you don't belong here. It's dangerous here for you. Get away before it's too late.' ' She paused and looked at Korolev with a raised eyebrow. "Well, what do you make of that, Comrade Detective?"

"Interesting, certainly. We'll have to see what his explanation is. Did you hear anything else?"

"Not a word. Masha saw me and came over and took my arm. She looked frightened. As though she'd seen the Devil. And we walked back here as quickly as we could. I asked her what the matter was but she wouldn't answer, just shook her head and looked at her feet. She was a confident, happy soul — that's what men liked about her. But that night she was afraid, I think."

There was an element of the dramatic in Sorokina's recollection, and part of Korolev — the tired to the point of hallucination part — felt as though he'd been transported from reality into a cinematic performance, but the rest of him — the part that was still functioning as a detective — decided the actress was telling the truth, although perhaps with a large measure of embellishment.

"But you said he had seemed affectionate

to her previously."

"Yes, not affectionate, though. More than that." She paused and looked to the ceiling as if for inspiration from God, or perhaps, in her case, Comrade Stalin. "Passionate. That's it. The look he gave her was full of passion. Smoldering. Raw. But it didn't concern me at the time because there was sadness there as well. I can't explain it. It was just an impression."

Korolev looked down at his notes, "smoldering," "raw," "sad." This wasn't like many other interviews he'd undertaken. But what was this about Lomatkin?

"The journalist. Lomatkin. You said he and Lenskaya were lovers?"

The question seemed to come as a surprise to Sorokina. "Lomatkin? But he was in Moscow. I've told you about Andreychuk — shouldn't you arrest him before he gets away?"

"I'll certainly be talking to Citizen Andreychuk again and I'll confront him with your information, you can be sure of it. But please tell me about Lomatkin."

Sorokina seemed to focus on him as an individual rather than as an audience for the first time, and interestingly it was with the wary gaze of someone who thought they were being made fun of. Her lower lip began to harden into the stubborn pout of a spoiled child.

"Babel said you were an unusual Militiaman."

"I'm not unusual at all, Comrade. I just shake the tree till all the apples come down, then work out which one is the rotten one. I don't presume it's the first that falls into my lap."

"I like Andreychuk, I hope you understand that. But I saw what I saw. And I heard what I heard."

"I believe you, and I'm sure your memory of the incident is correct, but there could be an innocent explanation."

Sorokina seemed satisfied with that and gave a brief nod.

"Well, I've done my duty in any event. That's what matters most."

"And Lomatkin?"

"Lomatkin and she, well — I don't know. I think she loved him, perhaps — there was something there. You'll have to ask him. But I've seen them at parties, her big eyes drinking him in like a woman dying of thirst gulping down a glass of cold water. She didn't look at the others that way. He was different. And I'm sure he felt the same way as well."

Korolev nodded, and underlined Lomatkin's name in his notebook. "And what about these others?"

Sorokina shrugged, "They were men, she was a woman. They were helpful to her — and she gave them what they wanted."

"Belakovsky?"

"You won't mention me as the source for any of this," Sorokina said, as though she'd suddenly remembered who she was gossiping about. Korolev couldn't imagine Belakovsky or Savchenko would be grateful — and even such a famous actress as Sorokina had to think about her career.

"You have my word."

"Well, one thing led to another and she went with him on some delegation to America. He was smitten with her. She went as a translator and came back as one of his key assistants. She was bright, better at her job than most others at the Film Board — but, well, conclusions were drawn."

"Is that where she met Savchenko? In America."

"Oh no, Savchenko was a much earlier conquest. She was Nikolai Sergeevich's student at the State Film School. I told you, she was a clever girl. I don't mind saying that I sympathized."

Korolev lifted his gaze to meet Sorokina's and for a moment he caught a glimpse of her own past in those green, green eyes of hers — the compromises, the practical decisions, the unwelcome attentions that had had to be welcomed. There was a tilt to her chin that defied his judgment, not that he was making any. Sometimes you had to do things to survive and he'd done worse things than she ever had, he was sure of it. You didn't fight in wars like the ones he'd been through and come out whiter than white, or redder than red for that matter. He looked at his watch — it was time to finish.

"Thank you, Comrade. We may have some more questions in due course. But you've been very helpful."

She nodded, looking for a moment almost as tired as he felt, and rose to her feet. He walked with her to the door, and wasn't surprised to feel his body resisting each step he tried to take forward. How long had he been without proper sleep? Too long — far too long.

As if on cue, Slivka appeared in the doorway as they approached and held it open for Sorokina with a respectful smile. The actress turned and gave Korolev a small wave, but didn't say farewell. He nodded in return. Slivka watched the actress go and then smiled at him, fondly — the sort

159

of look that a girl her age might reserve for a grandfather.

"You look exhausted, Chief."

"I don't just look it. Listen, roust out Andreychuk, will you? Sorokina says he and Lenskaya argued a couple of days ago." He consulted his notebook. "Apparently he warned her to go back to Moscow, that it would be dangerous for her if she stayed."

"I see."

"I'd like to know what he meant by it."

"Are you sure you're happy for me to talk to him on my own?"

"I've a feeling he'll respond well to you." Korolev's voice sounded slurred with tiredness even to him. He made one more effort. "Any news from the other interviews? Or the forensics man? Firtov, is it?"

"A few things to follow up — Firtov thinks he has a partial fingerprint in the dining room. And Peskov called, the doctor. He asked if we wanted to attend the autopsy. What do you think? He'll do it tonight, if you wanted to go in."

"I'll be honest with you," Korolev said, thinking that his tiredness was making him more open than usual, and being too exhausted to care, "I don't much like watching people poke about inside other people." Which didn't sound like the words of a man prepared to do his duty — he sighed, a long sigh. Children had been born and wrapped in a towel in less time than his sigh took. "How long would it take to drive there?"

She shrugged, "An hour, no more. If I'm driving that is."

"Look at me, Slivka, I can barely stand. Let's tell him to go ahead — speed is important here — but we'll visit him tomorrow morning for his conclusions. We can discuss the case on the way, and the uniforms can carry on with the initial interviews in our absence. Tell him we'll be there at eight o'clock. An early start. Afterward we can go and see Firtov, and find out if this fingerprint of his comes to anything."

"Perhaps I should stay here?"

"No, if I'm assigned to another matter, you'll still be involved in the case, so we should both go." He caught the beginning of a yawn and pushed a fist in front of his open mouth. "Are any of the uniforms from the village able to use a typewriter?"

"No, but Comrade Shymko offered us one of his girls in the end. Larisa."

"I met her. Put the fear of God into her — I don't want her blabbing if she's typing up the interviews of people she knows."

Slivka smirked.

"All right, all right. I know God doesn't

exist." Another lie to be forgiven by that non ex is tent Lord. "Put the fear of a prison cell into her, how about that?"

"With pleasure."

"Has anyone bothered to find us accommodations?"

"They've found a bed for you in the house, but I'm not sure about me, at least so far. Still, if the worst comes to the worst, I'll take the blanket from the car and sleep in the armchair here. I've slept in worse places."

The thought of a bed produced a feeling of intense longing but, on the other hand, he didn't like the idea of his having a bed while his subordinate made do with an armchair.

"We'll toss for it," Korolev said, feeling around in his pocket and producing a ten-kopek coin.

"We won't," Slivka said. "Your bed comes with a good-looking Frenchman in the bed beside it. The girls in the production office think he's safer with you than with me. Or maybe they think you're safer with him — who knows? He's good-looking, that much is certainly true."

"You've met him? This Les Pins character."

"It has been a day of many meetings."

"What did you make of him?"

"A handsome man. Missing part of his ear, though, a clean cut. A knife, I'd say. Or a bullet perhaps. A tough customer, gentle with it and speaks Russian like a grand prince. Anyway, it's been decided. The Frenchman will be 'enchanted' to have your company."

Korolev accepted defeat.

"Fair enough," he said. "And one last thing?"

"Yes?"

"See if you can get me some cigarettes?"

CHAPTER NINE

Before he called it a day, Korolev made one final effort and telephoned Yasimov in Moscow. Because of the late hour he called him at home, explaining the situation to him briefly — Yasimov was smart enough not to ask any questions once he heard where Korolev was calling from. Instead he spoke only to agree to Korolev's requests, which were simple enough. Poke around at the orphanage and see what he could find out about the dead girl's background, ask around at the Film Board and the State Film School about her and, finally, do a little bit of digging into Comrades Lomatkin, Savchenko and Belakovsky and any other lovers who came to light. Korolev knew Yasimov well enough to presume that if Ezhov's name came up in the process, he'd forget he'd ever heard it, which was exactly what he wanted him to do. It was a weary Korolev who put down the telephone and made his way to the main house and the small room he'd been allocated to share with Les Pins.

He was unsurprised to discover that Slivka had been right about the Frenchman — he did indeed speak beautiful Russian, and with a precise yet flowing elegance that for a native would lead to a ten-year stretch in the gold mines of Kolyma, but for Les Pins resulted in a flock of adoring production girls. It was, Korolev thought, not for the first time that day, a very strange world.

Les Pins welcomed him and pronounced himself, as Slivka had also predicted, "enchanted" at the prospect. Korolev decided "enchanted" was not intended to be taken literally, but was just what French people felt obliged to say when they had foisted on them a large Muscovite policeman who looked as though he might snore like a hibernating bear. But then again, with words like that in your repertoire, it must be difficult not to walk on the sunny side of the street, and Les Pins seemed to be a determinedly ebullient character, a firm smile permanently fixed to his face, and a pleasant, melodious laugh that hovered on a hair trigger, ready to tinkle out at the slightest excuse. It was only when Korolev shook hands with him that he felt the missing fingers. Something must have shown in his face because Les Pins looked down with a smile.

"A German bayonet. Verdun. And you?" Les Pins nodded to the saber scar that ran down the side of Korolev's jaw to his chin, so old now that he hardly noticed it any more.

"A saber. A Russian one." Korolev shrugged, thinking back to the Cossack, his horse rearing, leaning down to slash at him for a second time. At such moments a man's life ends or continues. His had continued and the Cossack's had ended. "But the Germans gave me a few scrapes too."

Korolev couldn't help but think of two old dogs meeting in the street, sniffing each other out. For all the Frenchman's smiling suavity, those eyes had stared down the barrel of a gun more than once, and from either end, if he wasn't mistaken.

"So I hear poor Masha was murdered?" The Frenchman turned away and began to undress. His shoulder was bandaged, Korolev noticed, and he moved stiffly, but he was still a relatively fit man. Korolev sat down on the spare bed and pulled off his boots, feeling the stretch in his back as he leaned down and resisting the urge to topple forward and fall asleep right there on the floor, and damn the Frenchman.

"Who said that?" Korolev asked, trying to keep his tone offhand.

"Oh please, Captain Korolev, it really isn't my business — but it's your arrival that tells me it wasn't suicide, not somebody's tittle-tattle. I'm curious, though — who do you think killed her?"

Korolev took his time before answering, constructing his response carefully. It was sensible to be careful with foreigners.

"I don't know how it works in France, Comrade," he said eventually, "but here in the Soviet Union the Militia doesn't discuss such things with citizens, even welcome and honored visitors like you." Korolev reached into a pocket of his coat for his last cigarette and then wondered whether it would offend the Frenchman's sensibilities if he lit up in the man's bedroom.

"Do you mind?" he began and showed a corner of the packet of Belomorkanals.

"Not at all, I'll join you," Les Pins said, producing a blue packet. "So it wasn't murder, then?"

Korolev raised an eyebrow.

"Oh really," the Frenchman said, striking a match, "you're impossible."

Although strangely, the way the French-man said it, it sounded like a compliment.

They focused their attention on the cigarettes for a while, smoke shrouding them, stirred occasionally by an exhalation.

"So you knew her a little bit," Korolev asked, having considered whether asking him the question was a good idea and then finding himself unable to resist. Well, it wasn't really questioning as such, was it? It was more of a conversation. Yes, that sounded about right. Rodinov would understand.

"A little bit." The Frenchman put his finger and thumb about an inch apart. "You mustn't misunderstand me, I'm sympathetic. You know how it is — death isn't unusual in my line of work. I can see you think I'm heartless, but it's not that at all, believe me. My heart is full of tragedies. This is just one more. But I keep smiling, what else is there to do? Tears don't stop bullets — well, not that I've ever seen. Bullets stop bullets and sometimes words."

Korolev remembered that the fellow was some sort of a journalist. A war reporter, Rodinov had said. The Frenchman flicked ash onto a plate that he'd placed beside the bed for the purpose and for a moment looked almost embarrassed.

"At least I hope my words help — help people to understand that we need to

168

struggle for a new kind of world, a world where war is no longer necessary. You would think we'd have learned from the last one, but it seems we learned nothing."

Korolev nodded his agreement.

"Was Comrade Lenskaya upset in recent days?" he asked, after a decent interval. "Is there anything at all that you remember — anything that could be useful?"

Les Pins contemplated the tip of his cigarette, then shook his head.

"I don't think so. She was always in her office, typing away. Masha spoke good French, which was pleasant. But I don't remember anything unusual — nothing at all. You should ask her admirers, you know. Babel, Savchenko, that angry man who is around sometimes. In the leather jacket."

"Mushkin?"

"Yes, he seemed very interested in her. But perhaps it was just professional, because of what he does."

"I don't know what you mean."

"As well for you if you don't, I'd imagine. He has the mark of a serious man. Although I don't believe you for a moment, *mon Capitaine.*" The journalist stubbed out the last of his cigarette. "One of us needs our beauty sleep, and it's probably you, Comrade Korolev. I hope you don't snore."

■ ■ ■ ■

When Korolev awoke, however, just as the first suggestion of dawn was beginning to lighten the edge of the curtain, it was Les Pins who was snoring and Korolev who felt a certain satisfaction as a result. It didn't even matter so much that Les Pins' snores were like the purring of a well-contented cat and, really, almost pleasant to listen to. It didn't matter at all. For a moment, Korolev felt he had the better of the foreigner and, if that wasn't a reason to feel a modicum of pleasure, then he didn't know what was.

After a moment savoring his small victory, Korolev rolled himself out of bed as quietly as he was able and stood up. He could probably have done with more sleep, but it was already six and he was due to meet Slivka in half an hour; and before then he wanted to have a little time to tell himself how to handle the investigation before everyone else started telling him instead. It was, in short, an opportunity to take a hold of the day ahead before it ran away with him.

At least some of the parameters were now a little clearer, he decided, making his way to a bathroom along the corridor. He had

Colonel Rodinov's authority to proceed as he saw fit, so a little arm-twisting could be done if needed, provided he exercised the inevitable discretion. That at least gave him something to work with — if he had to walk around all these actors and Party bigwigs on tiptoes he knew he'd get nowhere.

After a quick wash with his towel, he began to shave at a porcelain sink that looked big enough to be seaworthy. The water was freezing, so cold he could barely work up a lather, but Korolev had shaved in freezing water before and didn't mind too much. He just took it slowly.

He wasn't happy about the situation with Mushkin, if the truth were told — it was as if he'd offended the Chekist in some way. He couldn't put a finger on what he might have done to provoke the man, but perhaps it wasn't something he was responsible for as such. After all, it must be difficult for Mushkin to have someone thrust down his neck by Moscow, and a Militiaman at that. And he doubted Colonel Rodinov had made any effort to sweeten the bitter pill. All the same, you'd have expected the Ukrainian to click his heels and get on with the job, a cheerful smile on his face and a Party song on his lips — not that Korolev could imagine Mushkin singing anything with much

171

joy now he thought about it. In fact, the bitter anger the major radiated reminded Korolev of being in a trench with an unexploded shell, and that, as he remembered all too well, was not a pleasant way to spend your time. If this was the Chekist when he was supposed to be relaxing on leave from his duties, Korolev could only imagine what the man was like when he was pursuing enemies of the State.

Korolev rinsed his face — at least he now had some idea as to how to move the investigation forward. If the Odessa forensics team came up with something pointing to the killer's identity, then all well and good, but it seemed more probable that this was going be a question of gathering information from interviews, analyzing it and then exploring the lines of inquiry it suggested. It would be time-consuming, and there would likely be pressure from Moscow, but he had an able assistant in Slivka and with a bit of luck the interviews would continue to throw up revelations like those offered by Sorokina.

His ablutions finished, Korolev examined himself in the mirror, taking his time about it, thinking that there was more gray than there'd been the last time he'd looked. And perhaps more skin showing through the short hair as well. He liked to think he'd few illusions about what he saw: an average man; not ugly, not good-looking; no genius, but no idiot either. But his eyes seemed to want to evade his gaze, and he wondered about that. He hoped he was an honest man, when the circumstances allowed it, but they didn't always in these times of change. He wondered what the Frenchman made of him. Would he see choices made where all Korolev saw was fate? If Korolev lived in the West, maybe he wouldn't have to shut his eyes sometimes not to see, or put his hands over his ears so as not to hear. But then again, wherever you were in the world, he suspected, you'd find your hands were a little dirty at the end of the day's work. Saints lived only in books so far as he knew, and Korolev lived in the real world, where the road ahead, if there was one, was likely as not pot-holed and spattered with excrement. But you still had to walk it and if he'd learned one thing in the last twenty years, it was to carry on putting one foot in front of the other, and to keep his head down. Which direction he walked in was for the bosses to decide — his duty was just to do as he was told, and to trust that the Party would bring them to a brighter future.

Of course, the Frenchman was a writer,

and he knew what writers were like. At least, Babel, to be fair to him, didn't judge men for what they sometimes had to do. Others of his profession, however, liked to see to the bottom of a man's soul, to judge you as only God should judge, and then to sit in their comfortable studies, with a fine cigarette from an elegant blue packet clenched between their teeth, and clatter out their findings on shiny typewriters, each letter hitting the blank page like a nail in a coffin. Oh, he knew what they were like, those writers. They should look at themselves sometimes and maybe they'd see they were no better than anyone else. And if Korolev had done bad things, it was because he'd had to. The Frenchman would do well to remember that when he looked at Alexei Dmitriyevich Korolev.

Korolev felt an acid rage coursing through his veins — his hands were trembling again, even as he tried to hold them still. Was it the anger, or was it his nerves again, he wondered.

It wasn't just him in the firing line, that was the problem. He knew how things worked these days — if he were to be arrested, it would mean Valentina Nikolaevna would almost certainly also end up in the Zone, then Yasimov, whom he'd worked alongside for so long, and probably Zhenia, even though they hadn't been married for two years now. And what would it mean for young Natasha, if her mother was shipped off to the Zone? Or Yuri for that matter, his own flesh and blood, if Zhenia got ten years? An orphanage, if they were lucky, otherwise the streets. And they probably wouldn't be as lucky as the dead girl — they'd always be children of Enemies of the People and that would bring difficulties that might never be surmounted.

And so he had to remain vigilant, and that meant living on the edge of a blade, and knowing it, and trusting in the good Lord to preserve him and his. Of course, people might tell him the Lord was a superstitious fiction of his imagination, unsuited to the scientific and logical reality of Soviet Power. Well, he'd bet his good boots that half of those same people were praying just as hard as he was to be guided through this valley of shadows. In fact he was sure of it. They might talk like Bolsheviks, but in their hearts Russians would always be Believers. It was just the way they were.

He splashed his face with water cold enough to stop him thinking of anything very much for a moment or two and reminded himself that solving the case was what mattered now and everything else was a distraction.

Five minutes later he was dressed and standing in the dining room where the girl had been found. He considered the height again. Could someone have lifted her on their own if they'd used a table to stand on? Peskov would weigh the girl as part of his autopsy — that might tell them something.

And what about the murder weapon? Some sort of cord, Peskov had said. If the doctor could extract some more evidence from the corpse, that might give him something to follow up. He reached his hand up toward the cast-iron bracket. He'd have to get it measured properly.

"How did the killer do it, do you think?"

The voice came from behind him. He turned to find Slivka, legs apart, standing square, her leather jacket open at the neck. An unlit papirosa hung from the corner of her mouth and she was raising her hands to light it, again cupping them around the cigarette to shield it from a wind that wasn't there.

"Got one of those for me?"

"I forgot. Compliments of Comrade Shymko." She pulled an unopened packet of Our Brand from her pocket and handed it to him.

"Bless the man," Korolev said, opening the packet. He looked back up at the bracket, thinking about her question. "The table perhaps. Did Andreychuk tell you anything interesting last night?"

"Nothing. Denied the conversation had ever taken place."

"And?"

"He's cooling his heels at the Militia station."

"Good. Let's have another go at him when we get back. Whoever cleaned the place after the crime did a thorough job. They must know something about police investigations — and I'm not sure Andreychuk fits the bill."

"I can't decide whether it was planned or not," Slivka said. "Do you know what I mean? Whether whoever did it decided to cover it up before or after the killing. Either way he didn't make too many mistakes. He was calm enough to clean her office of prints, and in here as well. And if you hadn't been sent down here, I doubt a pathologist would have looked too carefully — if one would have even looked at her at all."

There was an implicit question lurking in her words that Korolev decided to ignore.

"You're presuming it's a man," he said after a moment.

"A strong woman — to have got her up there."

"True," he said, turning away. "Come on, let's get to Odessa and see what the sawbones has discovered for us."

CHAPTER TEN

The dawn light was flat across the even flatter steppe as Slivka maneuvered the car, doing her best to avoid the various ridges and trenches that criss-crossed what passed for the road. She didn't drive as fast as Mushkin, or with such disregard for the car's suspension, but she maintained a constant speed and drove with a good deal of skill. Spring might well be on its way, but it was still cold enough to have Korolev burrowing inside his winter coat.

"Have you been to Odessa before?" Slivka asked, her voice rising to compete with the engine.

"Apart from the airport yesterday, no."

"Did the plane fly in over the town?"

"I think so. I wasn't looking."

"Of course," Slivka said, nodding. "You were reading the case material. Admirable."

"There was a lot of it to read," Korolev said, even if what he'd actually been doing was keeping his eyes tight shut and praying to the Virgin.

"A shame, you would have been impressed. From the air you can see what a well-planned city Odessa is."

"Our Soviet planners are the envy of the world," Korolev said automatically.

"They are, although in this case the planning was done long before the Revolution."

"Tsarist planners?"

"A Frenchman." She shrugged. "Wait till you see it — it looks like Paris, they say. Maybe the Frenchman was homesick."

Slivka's smile faded.

"Of course," she added, her words coming out faster than previously, "Soviet Power has transformed the city for the better. In every way."

"I knew what you meant, Slivka," Korolev said. "There's no need to concern yourself."

It was the first time he'd seen her confidence slip, and it saddened him that she should be concerned about such an innocuous comment. Even if, of course, she was right to be.

Maybe Odessa did look like Paris — Korolev had never been there. He'd seen pictures of the place in newspapers, of course, and it seemed to him that, despite the peeling paint, Odessa had a certain *fin de siècle* elegance which might well be similar to that of the French capital. The cold sun twinkled on tram tracks and polished the cobblestones golden as the car roared happily along wide boulevards, scattering the odd pigeon and drawing the occasional glance from pedestrians huddled against the frosty morning chill. Maybe it was also a bit like Petersburg, it occurred to him, before he reminded himself that it had been Leningrad since Lenin's death in 1924 and it was about time he remembered.

"It's a fine town," Korolev said, in response to Slivka's inquiring glance, and wondered if he was the only person who regretted Petersburg's change of name. He was as keen on the Soviet State's forward development as anyone, but Petersburg still conjured up images from before the Revolution, and not all were negative. The old imperial capital might have been built on the bones of serfs, but still it was a city to make a man proud to be Russian. And that was something, even now — when imperial Russia had become the Soviet Union, and was ruled by workers rather than tsars.

"This is Pasteur Street," Slivka said, interrupting Korolev's thoughts. "Just before eight, not bad."

She brought the car to a halt and nodded

181

toward a large building in front of which students in white laboratory coats and round cotton surgical caps stood smoking. This, Korolev presumed, was the university. Like all students the smokers looked hungry, and like all Soviet citizens they looked away when a Black Crow, as police vehicles were known, pulled up beside them.

"This is it? The university?" Korolev asked Slivka as they stepped out of the car.

"Founded in 1865."

Korolev leaned backward to look up at the building.

"In 1865, you say."

She confirmed, "1865," making no effort to keep the pride out of her voice.

Korolev nodded with what he hoped was suitably impressed gravity, then began to walk toward the entrance. Before he'd taken two steps, the nervous white coats had hurriedly stubbed cigarettes against their heels, slipped the butts into their pockets and scurried in through the massive wooden doors like a flock of startled geese pursued by a fox.

"You should visit more often," said Dr. Peskov, appearing at Korolev's shoulder. "I can't remember the last time the lecture hall was full at the start of the eight o'clock lecture."

Korolev shook the man's outstretched hand — it wasn't as if he'd meant to frighten the students.

"Good morning, Doctor."

"Good morning to you — although I haven't had much of a night. We finished your autopsy, though. Follow me, the School of Anatomy is around the corner."

They followed Peskov further along the street and then, when he turned down some steps, into a wide courtyard where Korolev began to realize that the university was made up of a large number of buildings, and not only the one in front of which they'd parked. Peskov indicated an L shaped edifice built from gray stone with large windows, which looked very academically inclined.

"The School of Anatomy," the doctor said, and led them to a door at the side. In the corridor beyond it an elderly man, with the straight back and curled mustache of a former soldier, rose from a chair he'd placed in front of a set of double doors. Seeing Peskov, he unlocked the doors and stood to the side, inclining his head to the pathologist.

"Please," Peskov said, waving them through. "Wait in here and I'll be with you in a moment. As you can see, your instructions as to confidentiality have been followed to the letter."

The room Korolev entered was longer than it was wide with a ceiling that must have been a good twenty feet high. The gaps between the drawn curtains on three tall windows provided streams of light that broke apart the prevailing darkness, and underneath the smell of formaldehyde and the Lord knew what other chemicals, Korolev detected the scent of corruption — of death itself. It was strange: Korolev had the clear sensation that the room was full of people, or their spirits at least. As his vision adjusted to the half light, he had the feeling that eyes were watching him from the glass-fronted cabinet that ran along one entire wall. Confused, he walked closer.

"The Virgin preserve us," he whispered as the contents became apparent.

"What was that?" Slivka said from the window through which she was peering, the sliver of weak sunshine turning her hair golden in the gloom.

"Nothing," Korolev said. "No, not nothing. Have you seen these? It's barbaric. Look what they've done to them, these doctors."

It was true — the cabinet was full of scraps of human beings, skin and muscle stripped back to the bone, fixed forever in

184

some kind of preserving liquid. Here there was a hand, the tendons dyed bright green and numbered, there a foot paused in mid-step, the skin pulled back to display the bones and muscles. There were hearts, and stomachs, arms, legs, heads, jaws, rib cages, spines and parts of the body that Korolev had never seen before, and hoped he'd never see again. It was as if half a dozen men and women had been torn to shreds by some infernal machine, and then the pieces picked up and carefully placed in clear glass jars for reasons that no ordinary man could begin to imagine.

Korolev's attention was caught by a pale face, bleached white as though drowned, with sightless eyes that seemed to be focused forever on the moment of death. It was curious how white the dead man's hair was, and how frail he seemed — although he must have been a young man when he died. And then his lips — they were strange as well, unnaturally thick, as though they'd been stuck on after death like a comic mustache. Korolev had seen corpses before, more than his fair share, but this poor fellow's suffering hadn't ended with his death. Instead his head now floated in a thick round jar, snarling in despair, half of his face peeled back to display its inner workings, his jaw, his teeth and a naked eyeball.

"These doctors are worse than wolves, Slivka, I swear it to you."

Slivka said nothing, just shook her head sadly. There was one thing that interested Korolev about the body parts, though — a large number of them had the tattoos that marked them out as belonging to the tribe of Thieves. He pointed to a blue-inked monastery that graced a deformed knuckle.

"A few blue fingers, I see."

Slivka shrugged. "They have a habit of dying unexpectedly and unclaimed."

"True," Korolev said, looking at the floating head again and wondering who had decided this fellow's life had gone on long enough. He turned back to the room. Eight stainless-steel dissecting tables, in two rows of four, were visible and on one of them a sheet covered most of a human body, except for the blanched feet pointing up at the ceiling.

Despite the weak light, he could see Slivka's cheeks rounding in amusement, and was that a flash of teeth? Was she laughing at him, the scamp? It was all well and good for the likes of her — she probably ticked off the days till the next autopsy she could attend, ghoul that she was. He, on the other hand, hated every aspect of the clinical

186

process that the examination of the dead called for. And he could smell the dead girl, that unforgettable undercurrent of decay in the still air of the room. A place like this was too close to the next world for Korolev. He knew that if he listened hard enough he'd hear voices from the cabinet, begging him to rescue the poor unfortunates imprisoned there and bury them, deep beneath the ground, the way a human being should be buried, in the shadow of an Orthodox cross to mark their passing.

"You may laugh, Sergeant Slivka," he said, "but by the time you get to my age you'll have seen enough death to know it should be treated with respect. It's a precious thing, a life."

If the truth were told half the reason he'd become a homicide detective, and a good one, was to try to make some sense of death.

The door swung open, and Peskov came in, his midriff swathed in a leather apron and his bald head invisible under a surgical cap. He flicked a switch and the room was flooded with a burst of electric light. Korolev turned, his eyes squinting against the glare, and saw that the doctor had been followed into the room by a younger female assistant carrying an enameled tray, on which a number of glass jars were arranged.

"Waiting in the dark? Did no one turn on the lights for you?" Peskov seemed determinedly cheerful, even though his face looked hollow with fatigue.

"No," Korolev snapped, feeling an irrational anger toward the pathologist and his dismembering ways.

"I see," Peskov said quietly, his eyes dropping to the sheeted body of the girl. "Well, we were right. She didn't die from hanging. Strangled first, hung afterward. That's it in a nutshell. From behind. No signs of a struggle, but that's not that unusual as you know."

"Thank you, Doctor," Korolev said and, remembering they were on the same side, nodded his thanks. "No surprise, but good to have it confirmed."

"We did make one new discovery for you, Comrade Captain, that I think will be of interest. Anna?"

The young assistant, at Peskov's nod, stepped forward and placed the tray on the stainless-steel table beside the girl's body.

She seemed to be shy of speaking at first, but when Peskov nodded once again, she began to describe in a low voice the processes that had been undertaken to analyze the girl's blood, the contents of her stomach, her skin, her hair and God alone knew what else.

"While most of the tests were inconclusive or negative — at least so far — it's clear from the analysis of the citizen's blood and her stomach contents that she ingested morphine shortly before her death. The percentage present in her blood could conceivably have been fatal, if another cause had not apparently intervened."

"There," Peskov said, turning unnaturally bright eyes toward them. "What do you make of that?"

CHAPTER ELEVEN

Gray clouds were beginning to roll in from the sea by the time they emerged from the School of Anatomy, in Korolev's case with a feeling of enormous relief.

"Well," he said.

Slivka put her hands in her pockets. "No more beating about the bush, anyway."

"No."

"Who on the film set would have access to morphine, do you think?"

"That I don't know, Slivka. Now, first things first," he said as they began to climb the steps to where the car was parked. "Let's get hold of her medical records. Maybe she'd a good reason for taking it."

"It's possible." Slivka's cigarette tip flared orange. "But if not, well then — our killer gives the girl a possibly fatal dose of morphine, then strangles her and then hangs her. He's nothing if not thorough."

"Or she could have been an addict," Ko-

190

rolev said, following his own train of thought.

"Peskov didn't find any signs of intravenous morphine addiction. No needle marks. Pills perhaps?"

"Maybe. Of course, if it wasn't taken voluntarily by her, then someone could have slipped the drug into her food or drink. We should find out what she ate and drank, if we can. Let's keep an open mind although, if you think about it, it seems likely that two such unusual events are connected."

"You mean the strangulation and the morphine?"

"Yes," Korolev said, catching sight of a wholly unexpected face on the other side of the street. "The likelihood that there's a connection must be higher than that there isn't."

Which was exactly what he was thinking about the appearance of a Moscow Thief on the other side of street, particularly such a nasty specimen of the breed as little Mishka, Count Kolya's sidekick.

"Militia headquarters," Korolev said, his mind made up, "where is it again?"

"Bebel Street. Why?"

"I think I'll take a walk — to clear my head — I can find my own way there. You probably need to fill your boss in on what's been happening anyway. Say I see you in an hour or so?"

"As you wish," Slivka said, her face showing no reaction to his odd behavior, which itself was odd. Well, he'd explain it to her later on. In the meantime, Mishka had given him a come-hither look, rolled the toothpick he was chewing to the other side of his mouth, and sauntered off along the street, the points of his patent leather shoes angling inward as he walked — in a way that marked him out as clearly as if he'd had the word "gangster" tattooed on his forehead.

Korolev crossed the street to follow him, giving his Walther a discreet pat in its shoulder holster as he did so. He'd only met the vermin he was following twice, but one of the encounters had resulted in Korolev waking up in a Lubianka prison cell with a lump on his head the size of an orange, and this time he was taking no chances.

It was a strange performance, Korolev thought, as he shadowed Mishka at a distance of about twenty yards. The Thief clearly wanted to be followed, but he also seemed to want to irritate Korolev as much as possible at the same time. Every now and then he'd stop to tie his shoelace, give Korolev an appraising glance that bordered on the insolent, then turn to admire some pleasing female citizen and let loose a wolf whistle. He wore an immaculate white shirt, open at his neck, the collar spread out on top of a sports jacket, while everyone else was still bundled up in their winter coats. Korolev wasn't close enough to hear what he was saying to the women who were passing, but to judge from the looks he received in return he wasn't making polite conversation. The only thing that stopped Korolev from taking a few quick steps forward, grabbing the Thief by the collar of that crisp cotton shirt of his and throwing him into the gutter was the growing certainty he felt that Mishka's strange performance meant that Kolya was in town. And Korolev was very curious to know why the king of the Moscow Thieves was this far south.

Although Korolev didn't know Odessa that well, he'd the sense that the dance Mishka was leading him in was taking them toward the sea. He kept track of street names as they walked, Red Guard Street, Peter the Great Street, Red Army Street, and when they approached the small square at the end of Karl Marx Street, Mishka turned and there it was — the sea — a rolling gray that extended into the distance.

Mishka looked back at him and winked,

and led Korolev to a wide, tree-lined promenade that overlooked the harbor. He stopped in the shadow of a toga-clad statue, in front of which familiar steps marched down to the docks. Korolev had seen the famous film about the *Potemkin* mutiny, and had flinched back into his seat as the merciless white-jacketed guardsmen had slaughtered the innocent people step by bloody step till they reached the bottom. He knew where he was now, right enough.

"He's waiting for you over there, Comrade Captain." Mishka had turned back to join him, interrupting Korolev's thoughts. "Some view, eh? I'll bet you'd like to get your shorts on and go for a paddle, wouldn't you?"

Mishka's face was smiling, but his eyes glinted like two knives ready to be jammed into your guts if you gave him half a chance.

"A bit cold for me, Mishka, but you go ahead. Maybe take a bit of a swim while you're at it. I've heard Turkey's not far away — a fit lad like you, you never know, you might make it."

Mishka's smile stretched so that his sharp yellow teeth were bared like a fighting dog's. The Party theorists might say Mishka was a victim of the feudal phase of history that the country was struggling to leave behind and therefore capable of reform, but Korolev disagreed. His cop's instinct told him Mishka was only going to have ended up one way — as evil as a snake in a shoe. Nothing would reform a piece of work like Mishka short of a bullet, and whoever gave it to him had better give the rat an extra one just to make sure.

"You're a funny man for a *Ment,* did anyone ever tell you that?" the Thief whispered, coming so close that his breath was warm against Korolev's face. "I'd say you have them laughing all day long in Petrovka Street."

"Brush your teeth next time you come this close, Mishka, or I might just have to brush them for you." Korolev took Mishka's elbow and let the rat feel a little of his strength. Mishka started, his free hand reaching for his pocket, but then he seemed to force himself to relax, and even managed a contemptuous smile. Of course, Korolev could have walked around the Thief, but he wanted the boy to know that wasn't the way this *Ment* did things. He held Mishka's arm for a moment, squeezing it hard and looking into those eyes, seeing nothing but evil, then moved him sideways, giving him a little pat as he let him go.

"We'll meet again, Mishka."

"I'm counting the seconds, *Ment,*" Mishka spat, his expression slipping into a snarl, and Korolev felt a little surge of pleasure. He'd rattled him, he was sure of it, and that Mishka knew he knew it made it all the sweeter.

Count Kolya was standing to the side of the steps, watching the confrontation. The leader of the Moscow Thieves hadn't changed much since the last time Korolev had seen him; his shoulders still stretched the overcoat he was wearing and his broad cheekbones still looked like ridges of solid muscle. His physical presence was one thing, but your attention was drawn to the dark eyes that seemed to weigh a man as surely as any scales.

"Kolya," Korolev said by way of greeting and the Thief nodded in acknowledgment. They stood there, examining each other, like boxers squaring up in a ring. Then Kolya's mouth twitched upward in an unexpected smile.

"Korolev. The steppe is wide, but the road is narrow. No?"

Korolev was struck, not for the first time, by Kolya's cultured voice.

"I suppose so," he said, "at least it is if you have one of your band drag me onto the road when you happen to be passing."

"Mishka being his usual friendly self?"

Korolev ignored the question, inclining his head toward the sea instead.

"So you brought me here for the view, did you?"

"I've a good reason, don't worry."

The Thief pointed a thick thumb, blue with prison ink, behind him. Korolev knew the tattoo — the many-domed monastery that signified an authority among the Thieves. But that only hinted at Kolya's power: the only higher authority among Thieves in Moscow was God, or maybe Comrade Stalin. And even that wasn't certain.

A funicular train made up of a single dark green carriage with the red star of Soviet Power emblazoned on its side stood empty at the top of rails that ran down alongside the steps to the harbor. A rope from which hung a cardboard sign that read "out of order" blocked the approach.

"Why don't we take a little trip? I think the train is working now," Kolya said and then, seeing Korolev's bemusement, "I don't trust walls much these days — people like to put microphones in them and, next thing you know, you're up to your neck in men in uniforms trying to feel the thickness of your collar. No offense, Korolev."

"What's an honest criminal to do?" Korolev said.

As they entered the carriage, they were greeted by the hum of machinery and a small jerk as the train began to move down toward the port at a pace so slow it would have shamed a snail.

"You're right, it's a dilemma. Perhaps I should take a job in a factory, give up my evil ways. Join the Party and live like an honest Bolshevik." There was an emphasis on the word "honest" that indicated all too clearly just how honest Kolya thought "honest" Party members were.

"At least then you'd be contributing something to the welfare of the People."

"The People's welfare, Korolev? You think your precious Bolsheviks care about the People's welfare? They don't — they only care about surviving. And they'd stab their own mother if they thought it would help them survive a little longer. The Lord knows how many people died around these parts for a quota that could never be filled, and all because some fat Party bureaucrat living off canteen food knew he'd be the next one buried if it wasn't."

Kolya's tone was more weary than angry and Korolev wasn't sure how to respond to words that from anyone else would be considered suicidal. He looked out of the window at the port below and decided a change of subject would be best.

"Isn't this a little dramatic? You and me in a tourist train? Just so we can have a quiet chat."

"We're players in a dangerous game, Korolev. It's best to be careful."

"I'm only here on holiday."

Kolya gave a brief bark of laughter and for a moment he seemed genuinely amused.

"A holiday? That's good. I'm here on holiday as well, of course. On the express instructions of the People's Commissar of State Security. How about you?"

Korolev felt fresh air on his tongue as his mouth dropped open in amazement. Kolya waved the detective's surprise away, like a lazy man swatting a fly.

"A little joke — it's just I have men who tell me things, same as you people."

"I don't know what you're talking about," Korolev said, wondering how the hell Kolya had sources that high in the NKVD.

"Of course you don't," Kolya said. "That woman — what was her name? Yes, Lenskaya — she committed suicide. Or maybe not? Come on, Korolev, it's time for us to have a talk."

"The last time we talked, Kolya, you and

that little fiend back there talked me right into a cell in the Lubianka."

Kolya's face hardened. "I'd no choice, Korolev — there was something important at stake and not much time for discussion. I was pleased it worked out all right for you, believe me."

Korolev rubbed at the scar on his scalp that had been left by one of Kolya's men when they'd knocked him cold. It was true, there had been something important at stake, and if Kolya hadn't left him on the floor of the cultist's kitchen for State Security to find, well, strange as it seemed in retrospect, things might well have ended up a lot worse.

"I'm not looking for an apology, Kolya. Tell me what you have to tell me, and then we'll see."

Kolya nodded, then turned to face the sea and gestured down at the port buildings below and the harbor full of ships — everything from square-rigged three-masters to rusting oil tankers, from battleships to fishing boats.

"My mother's people are from this town, Korolev. They're of the Jewish variety. Nothing wrong with that, in my opinion. The best Jews are straight talkers, good to do business with, handy to have around when things get rough and don't squeal to the likes of you when things go wrong. And the worst are no worse than the worst of ours. They came here when the city was founded — they could work at what they wanted, do business as they would and they prospered. Do you know why Odessa is important?"

"Fill me in."

"Look at the sea — no ice. Oh, it's not warm, but this is a port that never freezes over and it's open every day of the year that isn't blowing a hurricane. Goods from all over the world come in, and where there's business like that there's business for a man like me."

Korolev was surprised. He knew Kolya ruled Moscow, at least within the world of the Thieves, but not that his reach stretched as far as Odessa. Perhaps his surprise showed, because Kolya nodded in acknowledgment.

"It's business. Because of my mother's people, I have connections here and responsibilities. The Party may not approve of speculation, but certain people in Moscow want certain products and someone has to supply them. And certain other people in Moscow also want to send certain things abroad, but you know all about that. These products travel through Odessa often as not

— things are more flexible here than where we come from and it helps that there's no winter interruption."

Korolev could imagine what these products were — narcotics, foreign currency, valuables of one sort or another, in short, anything that turned a profit. A thought occurred to him.

"Morphine?"

"As you would expect," Kolya said, scanning Korolev's face for a clue as to the significance of the quesion — a clue which Korolev did his best not to give. After a moment the Thief shrugged. "Listen, Korolev, I do business with people who bring things in from abroad. From Istanbul, Genoa, Marseilles, Alexandria. Even farther away. If someone wanted an elephant and had a thick enough stack of rubles, I could probably get it for them. And if that someone wanted to send the elephant back when he was done with it, I could speed it on its way."

Korolev believed him, despite himself.

"And the border guards, they have nothing to say about this?"

"Everyone has to eat," the Thief replied in a flat tone. "But there are things we don't get involved with, not unless we want to have Chekists and Militia swarming all over us like flies around a honey pot, and we don't. And a shipment of German guns will bring those kind swarming soon enough, you can be sure of it."

Korolev's attention was entirely focused now, and Stalin himself could have been looking in on them from the steps and he wouldn't have noticed.

"German guns? The Germans asked you to bring in guns?"

"Nobody asked me, but that's not the point. The men who did the asking asked people who are under my roof, for family and business reasons, and so when they decided to apply some pressure, it became something I had to deal with. As for who's behind it? I'd be guessing at the answer, and so would you, but I wouldn't be surprised if we'd both be right if it turned out he'd got a toothbrush mustache, a schoolboy's parting in his hair and a way with crowds."

"I don't believe it," Korolev said, believing it.

"Believe what you want but these are tough men, and well organized, and they thought they could get what they wanted by force. But they must never have heard of the ways of Moldovanka is all I can say. Someone got kidnapped, then someone got killed, then another person got killed and I wouldn't take bets someone else again won't get killed soon enough."

"I've heard nothing of this."

"It's in no one's interest for this to come to the attention of the Organs of State Security. I'm telling you because I think you may be of use to us, and we may be of use to you."

"I'm listening."

"Well, when some of this was going on, a man told a story. Why he decided to tell the story, you don't want to know." Kolya's face was grim, and Korolev deduced from it that the storyteller hadn't spoken voluntarily. "But it was a good story, about how someone, a girl — now a dead girl — was bringing information down to Odessa from the capital of this Soviet land of ours, and how that information was as good as gold to whoever was providing these Prussian pea-shooters. In fact that information was paying for these German armaments more or less."

Korolev felt his stomach turn. If Lenskaya had been shipping information down to Odessa, he'd a suspicion he knew where it might have come from. And if it did come from Ezhov — and if Ezhov didn't know — well, then Korolev didn't want to be the one to tell him.

"I see from your face you're working it out. I always said you were smart enough."

"The devil," Korolev said quietly.

"But who knows how this thing worked? Because something went wrong with the arrangement, and while our little songbird didn't know the reason why, he was given the job of rubbing out the girl — except it was him who got rubbed out first. By us, as it happens. That didn't change things for the girl, of course, but you know that already. And then you showed up, hot from Moscow, in an airplane no less."

Korolev tried to make sense of it all — did that mean the girl was part of this bunch of Ukrainian terrorists or not? Had she been killed because she was a traitor or because she wasn't? And what, if any of this, could he tell Rodinov? Kolya's bright eyes watched him as if following his every thought.

"The way I see it, Korolev, both of us have an interest in finding out who's behind this little caper and putting a stop to them."

"I do, but you?"

"I have a reputation, Korolev, and you don't think I'd just stand back and let these people damage it, now do you? Why else do you think I'm down here with my best men? It's too cold for the swimming."

"But why do you need me? It sounds like you're doing all right, so far." It wasn't that Korolev was objecting but he knew it was against the Thieves' code to talk to the Militia.

"We've hit them as hard as they've hit us, true, but we know these people are bringing in these guns some other way, and once that happens things won't be so easy. Much less easy if these fools are successful. This is a weed needs pulling up by the root and it seems to me that if we work together we've more chance of doing the job properly, once and for all."

"Give me names and every one of them will be in a Chekist cell by lunchtime."

Kolya shook his head.

"Think about it, Korolev. If the information was coming from where you and I might dare to think it might have been coming from, or even if it looks like it was coming from that person — well, who would be the ones who'd end up in the cells? Think about it very carefully."

They were almost at the bottom, and the port was now no longer visible past the city's train station, from which large numbers of people were emerging. The funicular juddered to a halt at its small lower platform, where a crowd was waiting to board.

"The morphine, Kolya," Korolev said, before he'd even thought about it. "The girl was drugged."

Kolya looked at him sharply, then nodded. "I'll look into it. Listen, Korolev, be careful — for some reason beyond fathoming our fates seem tied together on this. Your partner's from good stock and she'll watch your back well enough. And whatever's going on — the dead girl is the key. I'll be in touch."

And, with that, he was gone, stepping forward into a group of red-faced sailors, jolly with alcohol, and walking quickly off.

CHAPTER TWELVE

Korolev followed Kolya for a few paces, then stood watching his retreating figure, pushed his hat back, rubbed the scar on his cheek, and tried to make sense of it all. Had Kolya really suggested that Lenskaya had been a spy? And who the hell were these Ukrainian counterrevolutionaries? Not for the first time since the Chekist's knock on the door did he wish he was back in Moscow investigating a nice straightforward homicide. A crime, a motive and a killer — now that's what a murder should be. Spies and gun-smuggling and faked suicides and angry NKVD men and damned airplanes and what sounded like a full-scale gang war, albeit quietly done, well, he'd happily leave all of that to some other detective. Or the angry NKVD men — even better.

He looked at his watch and saw that, on top of everything else, it was a good forty minutes since he'd left Slivka. And what was it that Kolya had said about Slivka being of good stock? What the hell had he meant by that? Korolev glanced up at the steps — there were a lot of them, but they'd be quicker than the funicular. He sighed and started up them two at a time, his mind racing.

The first thing he did was remind himself that, short of a miraculous intervention, there was no obvious way out. He looked up at the sky half-hopefully, but there was no sign of a saint coming to sweep him away in a fiery chariot, more was the pity. Anyway, these people were traitors, so it was his duty to track them down and that was that.

It would be dangerous, that much was certain, and the danger wasn't only from the counterrevolutionaries. If the People's Commissar of State Security, the man supposed to be defending the State from such things, had been having an affair with someone who was slipping secrets to the enemy, then the investigation was a time bomb waiting to blow up in Korolev's face. Particularly if she'd been borrowing the secrets from the said People's Commissar. Duty or not, it would be wise to follow Kolya's advice and keep quiet, for the moment anyway. He took a deep breath as he reached yet another platform — he was already struggling and he wasn't even a quarter of the way up the damned stairs. Anyway, Korolev reasoned to himself as he began to climb again, what had he got to tell? A secondhand story from a Thief who'd never repeat it, even if Korolev managed to produce him for questioning. Which was unlikely. He was practically doing his duty by keeping his mouth shut.

Halfway now, and his legs burned with effort. There were hills in Moscow, it was true. The Sparrow Hills, or the Lenin Hills as they were known now, were definitely hills by any standards, but that didn't mean he went running up them every day. He'd become unfit — too much sitting in cars and at his desk. When he got back to Moscow, he'd get back into training. If he got back to Moscow, of course. He sighed. To look at the investigation from another point of view, though — why had he been sent down in the first place? Rodinov must think something was up, clearly, but wasn't quite sure what it was. After all, if they knew about Lenskaya and wanted to cover it up, it would have been better to have had the local uniforms declare it a suicide and leave it at that. Korolev wasn't the greatest detective in the world, but it hadn't taken too long to work out he was dealing with a murder. Maybe they really did want to find out the truth about the girl's death.

There were still two more flights of steps to go and he wasn't entirely sure he'd make it. Despite his exhaustion, however, it seemed clear to him that he must investigate the case to the best of his ability, and as if he'd never had a conversation with Kolya. He'd put the evidence together, sift it, weigh it and come to conclusions, same as he always did. And if something came up that backed Kolya's story or the Thief contacted him again — well, he'd cross that bridge when he came to it. He reached the top, his lungs raw, his heart thudding in his ears and his legs screaming their surrender. To recover some sort of dignity he turned and looked down at the harbor. A breakwater curved around the bay toward a white and red lighthouse. It was a busy scene, with small boats cutting in and out between the larger vessels, with bustle on the portside and trucks coming and going, but the sea itself was calm and the sun was beginning to break through the cloud once again. And somewhere down there, in one of those ships perhaps, there might well be a stash of German weaponry. Damn it, he was in trouble this time.

■ ■ ■ ■

The Bebel Street Militia station was a substantial building, four stories high and a good fifty yards wide. It wasn't a new construction, looking as if it had been built at the end of the previous century, but its forensic department seemed well equipped, with a filing cabinet that contained the fingerprint cards of all the known criminals in the area, photographic equipment, microscopes, plaster casts of shoeprints and tire-tracks, weighing scales, a small library of reference manuals and an assortment of odds and ends that Firtov had picked up along the way in the hope or expectation that they might come in useful in due course. Firtov gave Korolev and Slivka a guided tour before they got down to business.

"It wasn't an easy crime scene," the tall forensics man said. "As I told you, it's more than likely that someone cleaned the place pretty carefully. We did find a few human hairs, but from their color it seems likely that they belong to the girl, and even if they don't — who's to say how they got there? Not exactly a bloody fingerprint on an axe handle, if you know what I mean. Anyway, the Greek is looking into it."

He nodded over to Papadopoulos, who was sitting bent over a microscope.

"From what we know so far, it seems nearly everyone had good reason to be in Lenskaya's office or the dining room at some stage or another," Korolev said.

"Yes," Firtov replied, "I thought as much." His mustache hung heavy over his mouth so it seemed as if his voice came from behind whiskery curtains. His eyebrows were nearly as thick, but his gaze was sharp and Korolev was confident the fellow knew what he was up to. "I'll tell you one thing, though," Firtov continued, "I've been working in Odessa since 'twenty-one, and the only people who clean up this well after themselves are of the professional ilk. As in they have tattoos or they have identity cards."

"Professional?"

"If it isn't a Militiaman or someone from one of the other Organs, and I'm presuming it isn't, then I'd say it's a Thief. And an experienced one at that."

Korolev put his hands in the pockets of his overcoat and sighed. It could also be a well-trained foreign agent, of course.

"Still, we might have had a bit of luck in the dining room," Firtov said, holding up a

213

photograph. "Seeing as it's a public area we weren't too hopeful — but still, the Greek found a half-print on the bracket. Just enough to be sure that it isn't Andreychuk's or Shymko's — we took their prints last night, seeing as they were the ones that cut her down. Nor does the print match the girl's. So whoever it does belong to should be worth having a conversation with at least."

Korolev leaned in closer. There wasn't much of it — maybe the top third of a digit, but more than that it was difficult to say.

"Anything you can tell from it at the moment?" he asked, squinting at the image once again.

"Not really — my educated guess would be it's a male finger. From its position on the bracket, it might be from a left hand. We're going back out today to fingerprint all the potential owners. I can't guarantee we'll definitely be able to match it, but we should be able to narrow things down for you."

"Excellent — anything else?"

"Perhaps if we'd got to the scene while the body was still in place . . ."

Korolev nodded his understanding.

"Did you look in her bedroom?"

"Yes, and we found quite a few prints

there, but seeing as there were three other girls sharing it, I don't think they'll be much use."

"Did Slivka tell you about the stomach contents? How she was drugged?"

"Yes, we had a think about that, didn't we, Greek?"

Papadopoulos looked over and nodded.

"There was no sign that she was an addict, was there? So Nadezhda Andreyevna said." Firtov looked toward Slivka. "Maybe whoever gave it to her might be, though — we'll keep an eye out when we're taking the prints."

Korolev thanked the two forensics men and then followed Slivka from the room.

"Papadopoulos," Korolev said, as they walked out through the arch that led to the street. "A Greek name, I believe."

"Plenty of Greeks here in Odessa," Slivka replied. "Turks and Armenians, Arabs, Kurds, Poles. Even a few French and Italians from the old days. But the Greek is famous."

Korolev opened the car door and looked over at her. "Why?"

"The Greek can't speak. He can understand you, he can read and write, but he's never spoken a word."

■ ■ ■ ■

The drive back to the Orlov House passed quickly, and they didn't talk much. Korolev suspected that Slivka, like himself, was going over the little they knew and trying to make sense of it. As they turned off to enter the Agricultural College's grounds, Korolev found himself asking one of the questions that had been nagging at him.

"Count Kolya? How does he know you?"

"Kolya," she repeated, smiling wryly as she brought the car to a halt at the side of the driveway. "We're related, that's all."

"Related? You're related to Kolya the Thief?" He'd guessed their paths had crossed professionally at some stage, but to be blood relatives?

"No family is without an ugly member, as the saying goes. Although as far as my people are concerned, I'm the wallflower. That's the way things go sometimes."

"So that's why your mother doesn't approve of the Militia?"

"Not exactly — things aren't always straightforward in a place like Odessa. One hand often washes the other. We share a set of grandparents, but my father was a Party member from before the Revolution, and my mother as well. In the Civil War, and before it, they and my mother's family were often on the same side. My father died in 'twenty-one and since then things are different, as you know. But I know my duty, you don't need to worry about that."

"I'm not worried."

He considered her — young, intelligent and brave as well, he was sure. On top of which, Kolya had as good as told him she was to be trusted, which he was surprised to discover meant something to him.

"I saw Mishka outside the university," Slivka said after a pause.

Korolev nodded.

"Well, I've asked the question before, Chief, and I don't think you gave me a straight answer."

"Stop beating about the bush, Slivka. Let's get to the nut of the matter."

"Well, what's a Moscow detective doing out here in the middle of the steppe? A detective who happens to know Kolya the Thief, so an unusual detective, I'd say — but good at his job, I've observed. Colonel Marchuk warned me to be careful — that the case smelt and that having Mushkin involved made it smell even worse. He told me to keep an eye on you as well, but it seems to me we'll be better off if we're open with each other."

Korolev put his hand in his pocket, found his packet of cigarettes and handed one to Slivka.

"I can't tell you everything, Slivka, but I'll tell you what Kolya told me. And why I don't think we can do anything about it, except keep the information at the back of our minds."

And so Korolev told her what Kolya had told him. He even went so far as to tell her who had sent him.

"Spit on it," she said eventually. "My mother was right all along. Who'd have thought it?"

"Between the hammer and the anvil, that's where we are, Sergeant Slivka."

"Well, I chose to join the Militia and if you're afraid of bears, you shouldn't go picking berries, now should you?"

He gave her a long look. Eventually he nodded his agreement.

"Well, Slivka, we can only do our duty. Come on, let's see how the uniforms got on this morning." And Slivka put the car into gear and drove the last hundred or so yards to the stable block beside the Orlov House, that remnant of a bygone age with its view over a frozen lake and its ghosts — old and more recent.

■ ■ ■ ■

There was the promising clatter of a typewriter being put through its paces as they
entered the investigation room. Larisa,
Shymko's young typist who'd been so upset
the day before, was typing up a storm. Seeing them, she stopped, rose from her chair
and gave them a nervous nod.

"I've been typing, Comrades," she said.
"And I haven't told anyone anything. Even
if some of them have asked."

"Good work. Speech is silver, silence is
golden. How are things progressing?"

"Well, I think. Your men bring me their
notes and I type them up. Here you are."
She handed him an impressively thick
wedge of paper.

"You've been busy," Korolev said.

"Since first thing this morning. But if it
helps you with the . . ." She paused, probably not wanting to describe Lenskaya's
death too specifically, before continuing
". . . with Citizen Lenskaya, then I'm happy.
Comrade Shymko left this for you."

It was a list of key-holders to the Orlov
House. Seven of them. Major Mushkin's
mother, Shymko, Andreychuk, the dead girl
and three names he didn't recognize.

"Slivka? I want one of us to have spoken to all of these people by this evening. Meanwhile I'm going to have a chat with our caretaker friend at the station. Have a look through the notes and see if anything comes up. Work out who we still have to talk to and let's discuss it. Call me down in the village."

He held out his hand and Slivka handed him the car keys.

The Militia station was a two-storied brick building of relatively recent construction, although it looked the worse for the hard winter. He knew the style of place. Upstairs there'd be accommodation for the Militiamen who manned it and downstairs desks and a holding cell for prisoners.

Gradov, the surly sergeant from the night before, nodded to him when he entered. "He's in the cell. Been praying half the night. That girl from Odessa told us we weren't to touch him until you'd spoken to him, but I'll tell you the damned cultist needs a lesson taught, and I'm the man to teach it."

Korolev looked at Gradov coldly, and after a moment the sergeant looked away.

"When you've finished, obviously," Gradov said, "unless you want us to give him a going over before you start."

"That won't be necessary," Korolev replied, thinking a fellow like this could make the local people's life a misery if he put his mind to it. But it wasn't his place to tell the other Militiamen how to do their job, so instead he asked for a chair to be taken into the small room where the caretaker was being kept and, when the sergeant had obliged, asked to be left alone with the prisoner.

Andreychuk looked older than when Korolev had spoken to him the previous night, and a little smaller as well, sitting on the wooden bench with his head bowed. Korolev had visited worse cells in the course of his duties, and at least someone had given the caretaker a dirty blanket which he'd wrapped around his shoulders, but it was chilly enough. Outside in the main room, where the uniforms sat, there was a large tile-faced stove. In this room, however, there was only a much smaller version for which there seemed to be no fuel. The temperature wasn't far off what it was outside, and Andreychuk's face was drawn and pinched with cold.

"Can you get us some heat in here? This place is freezing," Korolev called through the door, and then leaned against the wall looking down at Andreychuk until the sergeant arrived. The caretaker didn't meet Korolev's gaze, which gave Korolev a chance to consider how to approach the task at hand. He'd been tired when he'd questioned him the night before, but today he'd do a better job.

"So, Andreychuk," Korolev said, when the sergeant had left and an orange flame flickered in the grate. Andreychuk didn't look up, but kept his eyes fixed on the floor.

"You weren't honest with me yesterday — were you, Citizen?"

"I was, Comrade Captain."

"Were you? You didn't tell me Lenskaya was sleeping with just about every man on the film set. You must have known, but you chose not to tell me. Why was that?"

"I don't know what you're talking about," Andreychuk answered, his voice barely audible.

"Come on, Andreychuk, she was a friendly girl. Why didn't you tell me?"

Andreychuk's expression wasn't angry, more confused. He shook his head in disagreement.

"She wasn't like that. She was a good worker, a Party member. She didn't behave that way."

"Was that why you argued? Near the village? Comrade Sorokina saw you. She heard you warn Lenskaya to —" Korolev paused to take his notebook from his overcoat pocket and open it to the correct page — "let me see . . . ah yes. 'Go back to Moscow, you don't belong here.' The 'you' being Comrade Lenskaya. And then you said: 'It's dangerous here for you. Get away before it's too late.' Do you remember now?"

Korolev sat down on the chair the sergeant had brought in for him and leaned forward until his head was on the same level as the caretaker's, only a few inches away. Andrey-chuk tried to back away, but there wasn't anywhere to go except through the wall. Korolev was so close he could see the tiny red veins in the whites of the man's eyes.

"I don't need more than that, you know," Korolev said, almost whispering. "I could call up the procurator's office right now, and he'd be happy to go to court with that. Let's see — you were the last person to see her alive, you were the one to find her, and we have you threatening her shortly before her death. I don't doubt that we'll find out the rope came from somewhere in the College buildings, a place that maybe only you had access to. Do you see how it looks?"

"I didn't kill her. And I wasn't threatening her, I was warning her."

"Warning her, you say? Warning her of

what? That you were going to kill her? That sounds like a threat to me." The old man flinched at that and Korolev felt a momentary guilt which he immediately put aside. If the caretaker had been involved in killing the girl, then the questioning was justified. And if not, well, then he had to understand the situation he was in and that his only hope was to be completely honest.

Andreychuk was shaking his head now, and his eyes were wet with tears. Korolev had to admit he didn't look much like a killer.

"You say you liked her?"

"Nothing wrong with liking her, was there?"

"Were you jealous of her admirers?" Korolev asked, keeping his voice dispassionate.

"Jealous? I'm fifty-eight, I won't last many more winters."

"Why not? You're still a vigorous man — there's still powder in your keg, as the saying goes."

Andreychuk's mouth dropped open, an expression of horror on his face.

"You can't believe that. Surely not?" he said.

"Why were you warning her, Citizen? And who were you warning her about? If you didn't kill her, why are you protecting her murderer? Tell me the truth, Citizen. If you've done wrong the punishment will be fair, and if you've done nothing you'll walk free."

"I doubt that," Andreychuk said. "I've seen what you people do. That's what I warned her about."

"What are you talking about?"

"I know what you're like, Comrade Captain — how you oppress the ordinary people. How you trap them and how you deal with them when you have them in your grasp. I knew if she stayed here it would go badly for her, as it's gone badly for me. She was my daughter. There, now you know. I buried her mother not four years past and I didn't want to bury my only daughter as well. But she wouldn't be warned. And now it's come to this."

CHAPTER THIRTEEN

"Her *father?*" Slivka asked, her voice rising in disbelief.

Larisa, who was still typing like the Stakhanovite worker that she was, paused and the carefully neutral expression she'd maintained up until that moment slipped. But after she'd taken a deep breath the pretty blonde typist restarted the clatter that had provided the background music to their conversation.

"More than that," Korolev said, considering young Larisa and wondering whether they should be talking this way in front of her. "He was a father who'd fought with Petlyura's mob during the Civil War and hadn't had the sense to leave the country with the rest of them — an officer, no less."

"A Petlyurist?" Slivka asked. "He doesn't look the type. And he certainly doesn't look like an officer."

Korolev shrugged, wondering what the

young woman thought the officer type was. As far as he remembered, many soldiers back then had been conscripted one way or another — a lot of the Red Army had, certainly. And in a place like the Ukraine, where fortunes had ebbed and flowed, it hadn't been unusual for soldiers to have fought for the Red Army, the Whites, Petlyura's nationalists, and maybe even Makhno's anarchist bandits as well. And as for being an officer, if you could read and write and had a talent for avoiding bullets, well, the odds were in your favor. He himself had ended up commanding a company of infantry at one stage and, for the life of him, he couldn't remember how.

"Well, he's admitted to it, anyway," Korolev said. "After the war he tried to keep his head down, live a normal life. He was happy to support the Revolution, he says. But someone denounced him in 'twenty-four and they made a run for it. Sent the girl to her aunt in Moscow, while he and his wife spent six years working in a factory in Kiev using false papers. Then they came back down this way. In the meantime the aunt died and the girl went to the orphanage and knew enough to keep her mouth shut. They thought they'd lost her — and she thought they were dead. And then she shows up with the film crew."

"But even if her parents were Enemies of the People, that wouldn't apply to the child. Comrade Stalin has said as much."

Korolev looked at her to see if she was joking. Slivka was under a considerable misapprehension if she thought having a Petlyurist officer as a father wouldn't have been a disaster for the girl if it had become known. She wouldn't have been going to America with any delegation, that was for sure. The Gulag more likely.

"Whatever she did or didn't do," Korolev said, deciding to change the subject, "it's Andreychuk who's been concealing himself using false papers for the last twelve years."

"Do you think he killed her?"

He considered the question for a moment or two, organizing his thoughts.

"Not at the moment. First, there's the morphine and then the fact that whoever murdered her cleaned the place thoroughly of any evidence. Where would Andreychuk have got morphine? I don't think it would be easy to obtain around here. And he may have been an officer fifteen years ago, but I'd be surprised if he's familiar with the way an investigation works — and whoever did it probably knows their way around. On top of which I don't see a motive for him to kill his own daughter, and the warning that Sorokina overheard is explained by him thinking Mushkin was on to him, and believing that his arrest might endanger her. If we had a shred of evidence I'd be happy enough to try and fit his face into the frame, but for the moment I don't see it."

"Perhaps he was worried that she might unmask him? If she was a loyal Party member."

"Except that she didn't. And she had several months to do it if she'd wanted."

"We'll have to charge him," Slivka said, and Korolev sensed that she wasn't entirely happy with the idea.

"Yes, false papers if nothing else. I'd better tell Mushkin."

"Still, it tells us something about her — now we know she kept secrets. The question is, was this the only one?"

Larisa's rattling fingers came to another halt.

"Larisa," Korolev said, "you're listening to this because we trust you not to repeat what you hear and don't forget you're temporarily working for an Organ of State Security."

Larisa turned to him, her expression as indignant as a child's.

"Comrade Captain," she said, "my ears

might as well be cut off."

Slivka snorted with amusement before tapping her notebook with her pencil, a more serious expression on her face.

"We also now know that she came from this area. Let's think about it, she comes from here, she comes back for the first time and she dies here. There might be a link, don't you think?"

"He says it was just a coincidence, her showing up," Korolev replied, seeing where Slivka's line of thought was pulling her, like a fish to a barbed hook. Yes, the link could well be the band of terrorists, but he wasn't going to allow the thought to run away with them. It was with some relief he spotted the thin figure of Lomatkin walking toward the house, the journalist's shoulders stooped against the cold. The very man.

"Slivka, I've spotted our journalist friend from Moscow. I think a quick comradely chat would be useful, don't you? In the meantime, arrange interviews for us with Savchenko and Belakovsky." Korolev's hand was already on the door handle, and he didn't wait around for Slivka's acknowledgment of his instructions.

"Comrade Lomatkin, I need to talk to you," Korolev called across the courtyard and Lomatkin stopped, looking gratifyingly anxious.

"Of course, Comrade. May I ask about what?" he said, as Korolev approached.

"What do you think? I'll give you a clue — it's not about the weather."

Lomatkin's eyes opened in surprise and Korolev put his hand on the journalist's arm and steered him back the way he'd come. "Come with me, Comrade Lomatkin, and we'll have ourselves a conversation."

Shymko had come up with the key to one of the Agricultural College's empty classrooms and so Korolev positioned Lomatkin in front of the lecturer's desk, like an errant schoolboy, and himself behind it.

The fellow appeared uncomfortable on the hard wooden seat, but it wasn't just the discomfort of the chair that seemed to be bothering Lomatkin. He looked nervous, like a bird trapped in a cage. Or perhaps a rat. Korolev would find out which soon enough because there was no doubt in his mind that the fellow had something to tell him — the question was whether he'd spill the information voluntarily, or if he'd have to lean on him a bit.

"Well," Lomatkin said, after still more time had passed, and sitting up a little straighter as if gathering his strength. "This seems a strange way to interview someone. I mean to sit there and watch them, and not say anything."

"Citizen Lomatkin," Korolev said, opening his notebook and observing Lomatkin's twitch when he addressed him as Citizen and not Comrade. "I will ask you questions in due course. At the moment, however, I'm waiting for you to tell me about Citizen Lenskaya and the events that led to her death."

Lomatkin's face seemed to lose some color, and his eyes to grow a little larger — a startled bird now. A trapped startled bird. Possibly in a cage.

"What do you want me to tell you, Comrade Captain? I don't know what you mean."

And panicked as well, thought Korolev. Excellent.

"I think you must know it's your obligation to tell me everything. A young comrade is dead, murdered we now know, and I've been assigned to investigate her murder. My duty is to get to the bottom of the matter — yours is to stop wasting my time."

Korolev tapped the wooden surface of the desk with an index finger.

"And. So. I'm. Waiting."

Korolev understood the journalist's dilemma — after all, if Korolev knew things about Lomatkin's relationship with the dead girl that the journalist didn't reveal, then he'd place himself in a difficult situation. On the other hand, what if he revealed information that Korolev didn't know, which might put him in an even more difficult situation? It must be unpleasant, sitting in that chair, knowing that whatever you said might land you in hot water.

Lomatkin exhaled, a barely heard whistle of breath, then looked up at Korolev, his eyes seeming to see the detective for the first time. Korolev nodded encouragingly and Lomatkin half-smiled, as if at the ridiculousness of fate, or perhaps in a plea for sympathy. Korolev remained impassive and the journalist shrugged, then began to speak quietly.

"Well, you must know, I suppose," he said. "About me and her, that is?"

Lomatkin glanced up at Korolev, as if to seek confirmation, and Korolev did his best to keep his face neutral, to give nothing away. The journalist swallowed and looked down at his shoes.

"We were lovers," Lomatkin said, risking another glance up at Korolev. "For a year now — until this, of course."

Korolev nodded and made a quick note,

his pencil's scratch loud in the silence of the empty classroom. He looked up at the journalist and noticed a small bead of sweat roll along Lomatkin's jawline despite the chill.

"Go on," Korolev said.

Lomatkin nervously pushed back a string of hair that had fallen over his forehead.

"I met her through Belakovsky — she'd been seeing him at one stage. I knew about that, in case you're wondering. And I knew she had other lovers as well. I didn't mind, she was her own woman."

Korolev looked up from his notebook, wondering had there been a slight emphasis on the word "other"? Was there no one who didn't know about Ezhov and the girl? But Lomatkin's eyes seemed glazed, as though he were looking at the dead girl, only at some time in the past when she'd still been alive. Perhaps he'd imagined the inference about Ezhov, Korolev reassured himself.

"We had a relationship based on respect, you understand. She didn't have much truck with bourgeois concepts like love. We understood there were complications that made our relationship difficult, but we hoped to overcome them. We felt we were a good match and that we would serve the Revolution better together rather than as individuals. We would form our own collective, she used to say, within the wider collective."

Lomatkin seemed calmer now — he'd tilted his chin upward and some iron revealed itself in his gaze. Korolev thought that the relationship sounded very business-like — not at all like the relationship Barikada Sorokina had described. But if Korolev knew anything, it was that he didn't know much about love.

"I had nothing to do with her death, and if I knew anything about it I would tell you."

Korolev considered the man, conscious that at the same time the journalist was considering him in return. He wasn't bad-looking, this Lomatkin; his clothes were of a good standard and his hair well cut. He looked like what he was, someone who'd been successful under Stalin and whose loyalty had been rewarded. But there'd be people who wanted his position no doubt, or envied his success, and where there was envy, these days, there were denunciations. Yes, to be in the public eye in 1937 was not something for the fainthearted — and now poor Lomatkin had arrived in the Ukraine to find his lover dead and a Militia detective poking around in his private life. Yet the man seemed to be regaining his confidence.

Had Korolev missed something?

"Why are you here, Citizen Lomatkin? Was it to visit Citizen Lenskaya? Or is it just a coincidence?" Korolev gave him his hardest, most quizzical stare.

"I had some business down here. I've been sent to interview the Frenchman, Les Pins, for *Izvestia*. Then I've some pieces to write about our western defenses, and after that I'm off to Sebastopol. A busy week." He hesitated, a thought seeming to occur to him. "I'll admit it was my suggestion that I interview Les Pins, but not from an individualist perspective — he's a renowned fighter for Socialism. I'd never put my personal interest before the Party. Once I discovered he was here with Savchenko, it seemed a good opportunity to come and see him. It was a coincidence that Citizen Lenskaya was here as well."

"Citizen Lenskaya?" Korolev asked, putting an intonation into the question that was intended to remind the journalist that he'd effectively been engaged to the dead girl.

"Masha," Lomatkin said, as though feeling his way around the name.

"Masha?" Korolev repeated and Lomatkin had the good grace to look embarrassed. "Poor dead Masha. And just a coincidence, you say. Do you know I'm all worn out with the number of coincidences that are coming to light today. An astrologer wouldn't believe half of what I've heard."

"I know nothing about that."

"We'll see. You said there were complications with Masha that restricted your relationship. What complications were these?"

"Comrade Korolev, you ask me about complications and you talk to me about coincidences." Lomatkin appeared annoyed for a moment before the annoyance was replaced with a hint of a bitter smile — the kind of smile that would disappear like smoke if you tried to get a hold of it. "Why, if you don't mind me asking for a change, are *you* here, Comrade Captain? Is it just a coincidence that you arrived the day after her death? A coincidence that Major Mushkin was at the airport to pick you up? I think you might know about the complications we faced. It doesn't mean we can discuss them freely."

So the fellow did know about Ezhov. Well, if the cat was out of the bag then it could be chased.

"We'll come to those complications in a moment, Citizen Lomatkin," Korolev said. "But speaking of coincidences, were you aware that the caretaker of this establishment was your lover's father? I think you know him — Andreychuk. Although that's not his original name — being an Enemy of the People, he decided to change it."

Now the fellow's cage was really rattled, thought Korolev. It was one thing having a lover murdered, it was natural that he'd be interviewed, but he had an alibi that was almost indestructible — he'd been six hundred miles away in Moscow, after all. But his lover being the daughter of an Enemy of the People. There was no alibi for that.

"Andreychuk? Masha's father?"

"Yes. He fought with Petlyura, and when those rats were rounded up he changed his name and moved to Kiev and your Masha was sent to live with her aunt in Moscow."

"I knew nothing of this. Masha was a loyal Party member, she'd have given her life for the Party."

"Perhaps she did."

"What are you suggesting?" Lomatkin whispered.

"Perhaps you had her killed to prevent the story coming out."

"This is ridiculous, there were much more important men than me who knew nothing of this, as you well know."

"What do you know about morphine, Citizen?"

"Morphine? It's an anesthetic," Lomatkin said, a little too quickly perhaps.

"And, of course, a poison if taken in sufficient quantity."

"So?"

"So your lover consumed a large quantity prior to being strangled. Would you like to explain *that* to me?"

"Explain what to you? I was in Moscow. How would I know how she ended up taking morphine?"

"It's also a narcotic — perhaps it was self-administered. Perhaps you supplied it to her."

"I was in Moscow, Captain, as I keep telling you. That's all there is to it. You saw me get on the damned plane there, didn't you?"

"Have you ever taken morphine?"

"No. I've never taken morphine. And please stop these questions. Andreychuk is the one with the motive here. I had none. I was devoted to Masha."

"Were you jealous of the relationship Comrade Lenskaya had with the People's Commissar?"

Lomatkin seemed surprised that Ezhov had been mentioned, but he recovered quickly. "Of course not," he said. "Comrade

Ezhov treated her well, assisted her in her career. If you want the truth, she considered it her duty to the Party to comfort the People's Commissar in any way she could. Believe me, that's the truth. The plain truth."

Korolev raised an eyebrow. There wasn't much about a girl's duty to comfort older Party members in Lenin or Marx. But what did he know? "Were others aware of her relationship with Comrade Ezhov?"

"Of course. I'd say half Moscow knew of it. By that I mean within senior Party circles, obviously, and the circles in which she moved. Actors, artists, writers, those kind of people. And she wasn't the only one."

"Who were the others?"

"A ballerina, a couple of actresses you might have heard of — Sorokina for a start. Although that ended a while back."

"Comrade Sorokina was Ezhov's —" he paused, wondering how to put it — "friend?"

Korolev sighed and made a note to himself to haul the beautiful Barikada back in for another grilling, although this time, he thought to himself wryly, it might be better done by Slivka.

"For a year or so, I think. Before he —"

240

now Lomatkin hesitated — "achieved his current position."

It occurred to Korolev that much of a Soviet citizen's conversation these days involved the unsaid, the oblique and euphemistic. Some intellectual would no doubt make a study, in due course, of the ability of Soviet citizens to communicate without saying quite what they meant. And probably what they whispered to each other under the covers late at night as well.

"What I'm looking for here is a motive," Korolev said, returning his attention to the matter in hand. "And one motive might be your jealousy."

Lomatkin opened his mouth to protest, but Korolev held up his hand.

"Don't bother. You're a clever man, a journalist. You know that, despite all you say about free love and respecting Lenskaya's rights as a woman, jealousy is still a good motive. I can tell you we'd have a lot less killings in Moscow if jealousy was eradicated in the next Five Year Plan."

Lomatkin looked glum.

"And all this was general knowledge?" Korolev continued. "I mean, who knew these things about Citizen Lenskaya, and Sorokina for that matter?"

"It was well known."

"What did she tell you about her relationship with the People's Commissar? Did she mention any problems? Not with the Commissar himself, of course, but perhaps other men, other women?"

Lomatkin laughed, a laugh as dry as desert sand.

"There were no problems. The people who knew about the relationship knew other things as well, such as the regard Comrade Stalin has for Ezhov, and the faith he places in his abilities. It changed people's attitudes to her, of course. But it didn't cause her any problems. To the contrary."

It was strange, the man had indeed seemed to relax in the course of the interview.

"When are you visiting these western defenses?" he asked, and saw Lomatkin shift his weight in his chair.

"The day after tomorrow? Tomorrow afternoon I'm meeting a photographer in Odessa. He's arriving by train."

"How far from here?" Korolev asked, wondering what it was that was making him suspicious of the journalist. It was nothing he could put his finger on. And yet . . .

"Odessa?" Lomatkin said.

"Not Odessa," Korolev said, wondering whether the journalist had relaxed so far as to be making fun of him now. "The defenses."

"We're visiting Krasnogorka. The defenses extend all along the Dnester — but Krasnogorka is where we're visiting. Thirty miles from here, as the crow flies."

The River Dnester marked the division between the Soviet Union and Romania. Korolev hadn't known they were so close, but he'd heard of the Stalin Line that defended the southwestern border and seen photographs of sunburned men, their eyes squinting over the sights of heavy machine guns in concrete pillboxes, and been reminded of the German fortifications they'd stormed back in 'sixteen, and the thousands of Russian bodies lying unclaimed on the barbed wire for weeks afterward. The Germans had known a thing or two about building defenses. He hoped Marshal Tukachevsky's military engineers knew as much.

"Can I go now?" Lomatkin said. "I have to call Moscow."

"Yes, but I'll want to talk to you again. When do you plan to leave?"

Again, that slight shift — was it a sign of nervousness, or something else? Once again, Korolev had a feeling he'd missed something.

"As soon as we're finished with the defenses."

Korolev shook his head. There was more to be discovered from the man, and he'd find out what it was. "I'm sorry, Citizen Lomatkin, that won't be possible. I require you to remain here until I'm sure you have assisted us as much as possible with the inquiry. You can't leave here until then."

Lomatkin opened his mouth to protest.

"My authority is absolute in this matter," Korolev continued. "Don't doubt me on this."

Lomatkin considered the statement for a moment, then got to his feet.

"I want to assist you in any way I can, Captain. Masha didn't deserve to die this way, and you have to believe me — I'd never have wanted such a thing to happen to her."

Which was odd, Korolev thought to himself, as that wasn't the same as saying he'd nothing to do with her death.

CHAPTER FOURTEEN

After Lomatkin had left, Korolev sat behind
the teacher's desk, going through his notes.
There were plenty of things to follow up,
certainly, but his thoughts kept coming back
to his conversation with Kolya earlier in the
day, and each time they did he felt his
stomach turn. If this had something to do
with counterrevolutionaries, then everything
else might as well be smoke. These lines of
inquiry looked like they might amount to
something, yes, but perhaps all they were
doing was obscuring the real motive for the
murder — which was this damned conspiracy of Kolya's. Korolev considered passing Kolya's revelations on to Rodinov for
the tenth time, and for the tenth time
decided not to. There was no point in putting his head into the lion's mouth, after all,
even if he sensed it might be there already.

In the end he was relieved to be distracted
by a single sharp knock on the door, and

looked up to see it being pushed open. The elderly lady with the military bearing from the previous day entered, regarded him for a moment, then stepped forward.

"They said you were here. Korolev, isn't it?" Her walking stick thumped across the wooden floorboards toward him.

"Yes," Korolev said, rising to his feet and half-wondering if he should salute her. "We met yesterday, Comrade Mushkina."

"Don't stand. No need for that, we're all comrades here. Now listen, Korolev, I've a favor to ask of you."

Korolev settled uncomfortably back into his seat, while Mushkina stayed standing, leaning sideways onto her stick.

"I've responsibility for the Agricultural College here, you see, and you've arrested Andreychuk, the caretaker. You can't seriously believe the man to be a murderer, can you? He's harmless."

Korolev didn't like to say that murderers often seemed harmless, and that anyone who'd fought through the Civil War knew all about killing and would be lucky not to have blood on their hands — particularly if they'd fought in the Ukraine.

"At this moment," he said, after a short pause, "I remain to be convinced that Citizen Andreychuk killed the girl. I'd like to talk to him again, however, and find out what else he might have to tell me, but that isn't the reason he's being held."

"Why, then? And is there a good reason you can't let him work while you continue your inquiries? Nearly all the rest of the staff are off with the students and these film people need looking after."

"It's a matter for your son, Comrade. It turns out that Citizen Andreychuk was an officer in the Petlyurist army and has concealed his real identity for many years. So it seems to me that he'll have to answer for that to State Security, if nothing else. It's out of my hands."

"A Petlyurist, you say?" She spoke quietly, not showing any of the normal indications of surprise.

"According to his testimony." Korolev flicked through his notebook before coming to the correct page. "His real name is Timoshenko. He comes from Angelinivka, it's about twenty-two miles from here. Near Krasnogorka."

"I know the place."

"I'm sorry to tell you that he's confessed to having fought against the Revolution during the Civil War, possessing false papers and assuming a false identity. All of which are, of course, crimes. And it turns out he was the dead girl's father as well."

"Her father?" Mushkina repeated, surprise finally revealing itself. If she'd known about, or suspected, his assumed identity, she clearly knew nothing about this.

"Yes," Korolev said, closing his notebook.

"Her *father?*" She pronounced the last word with something approaching indignation. "Now that's a surprise to me. His identity's one thing, but that he managed to conceal his relationship to the girl, well, that puts a different perspective on things. And you don't think he had anything to do with her murder? It happens — even in the closest families."

That was true, the large majority of murders were committed by family members or close associates of the deceased.

"Our investigation is not concluded."

"And you intend to charge him?"

"For the false papers? My authority only extends to this specific investigation; what to do about the other matters will be a decision for Major Mushkin."

"I see. I'll talk to him. But you wouldn't have any objection if he's released into my care. I'll take full responsibility, of course."

"If the major is happy, then I am, Comrade Mushkina."

She nodded, giving him a small smile that

seemed intended to represent gratitude, but her face was clearly unused to such a maneuver and the smile seemed more of an expression of pain than civility.

"Very good. Thank you, Captain."

She turned to leave, then paused. "You said he was honest in his response to your inquiries. What does that mean?"

"It means what I said, Comrade Mushkina."

"Does it mean you have an idea who killed the girl?"

"We're still at an early stage of the investigation."

"And you would like to talk to me as part of that investigation, I presume."

"Yes, I would."

Mushkina turned back and sat down in the seat that Lomatkin had so recently vacated.

"Then we should talk immediately," she said.

Korolev hadn't prepared for this interview, but he opened a clean page in his notebook.

"Let me start at the beginning," he said. "When did Andreychuk come to work for the College?"

"In 'thirty-three."

"So you were already here then?"

"Yes," she replied. "I took up the post at

the end of 'thirty-one. My health was failing and I was no longer able to take such an active role in the Party. But I wished still to be of use and so I came here."

She made a graceful gesture with her hand to encompass the room.

"That must have been at the height of the push for collectivization in these parts?"

Korolev wasn't quite sure what he was looking for with his question, but an angry blush appeared on her cheeks and, when she answered, her irritation was clear.

"I'm not sure what you're suggesting, Captain Korolev."

"I was thinking it must have been hard coming out into the countryside at that time. I didn't mean to offend you, I apologize."

She seemed to relax.

"It was hard everywhere. We built this place from nothing, but there was no shortage of citizens who wanted to work for us. The College was a key part of the drive toward collective agriculture in this region and so we were allocated rations for our workers."

"They must have been grateful."

"They were, but we had to turn away a hundred for every one we took." She paused and began to tap the table with one finger, as if considering a problem. "I must appear to have been annoyed just then. I apologize. Some of my Party colleagues thought I shirked my duty by taking this role — but this was the real front line. Here is where the battle for collectivization was fought and won. There's a difference between plans and implementation, Comrade Korolev. And here we transformed theory into reality."

"I'd never suspect a woman like you of shirking her duty, Comrade."

"Thank you."

"And was that when Citizen Andreychuk arrived, during the construction of the College?"

"That's correct. His paperwork seemed in order."

"A good worker?"

"Very good. I kept him on when we finished building. He has worked tirelessly for the College's development — not a Party member, but he participated fully in works meetings and always had the interests of the Collective close to his heart. Or appeared to have."

"You're surprised that he turned out to have a secret past?"

"It's not so uncommon for people to obscure their past these days, Captain." Mushkina spoke flatly, as if stating the obvi-

251

ous. "I was surprised to discover that Lenskaya was his daughter, though."

Yes, who could have told from Andreychuk's craggy, bearded face that he'd have sired a girl like Lenskaya?

"Comrade Shymko told me that you have a key to the house, is that correct?"

"As director I have a key for every building. I walk around the College at least twice a day to see what needs to be done for myself."

"When do you take these walks?"

"In the morning and in the evening, generally. It depends on my responsibilities for the day."

"Maria Lenskaya's office. It was in the closer of the two small turrets to the stable blocks. The ones that overlook the lake."

"I know it."

"I was wondering, did you see her on your walks? As you passed by?"

"Often. She was hardworking. I saw her many times late at night and early in the morning, sitting at her desk. If she saw me passing, she would wave. A productive young comrade was my impression."

"Did you know her personally?"

"I knew her to say hello to, that was all."

"On the night of the murder, did you attend the film shoot?"

Mushkina seemed to hesitate.

"Very briefly. I walked down to see what was going on, but I didn't stay for more than ten minutes."

"And what time was that?"

"Just before eight o'clock I think. They were about to begin filming."

Around the time the girl was last seen alive, in other words.

"What did you do afterward?"

"I walked back here along the road. It was cold, so I walked quite quickly."

"Did you see anyone after you left the village? We're trying to establish people's whereabouts."

"Not on the road, but I met Andreychuk as I passed the house. He was just closing it up."

Korolev looked up from his notes. This was news, and confirmation of the caretaker's statement.

"He never mentioned it when I spoke to him. Seeing you, that is."

"I'm surprised. I spoke to him."

"What did you talk about?"

"Nothing much," she answered, running a knuckle along her chin. "He was in a rush, due to be down at the village, you see. For the film people. I asked him if he'd closed up the other buildings and he said he had."

"And how did you find him? I mean to say, in what kind of mood?"

"A little agitated, perhaps, but I put it down to his being late for the film people."

Korolev hesitated. Why hadn't the caretaker mentioned the meeting?

"So about five past eight?" he asked, trying to puzzle it out.

"Not any later, certainly."

"And did you by any chance walk past Maria Lenskaya's window?"

"Yes."

"And?" he asked, thinking that she was making him work hard for the information.

"The light was on," Mushkina said.

"Did you see Lenskaya?"

"No, I didn't, but I've thought back to that evening more than once, wondering whether I was walking past at the time of her death — and whether I could have done something to prevent it. I don't think so, however."

Korolev studied the old woman, wondering if the ambiguity was deliberate.

"I'm sorry, do you mean you don't think you could have prevented it?"

She considered the question.

"No, if I'd known, I suspect I could have prevented it. But I'm confident she died after I passed her office."

"Why do you think that? Was there something you saw?"

"The typewriter on her desk. It was the American one — the Remington. I noticed it because I used to have a similar one a long time ago. She had two of them, typewriters that is. She also had an old Underwood with Cyrillic keys. When she was discovered, I noticed that the typewriter on her desk, which is visible from the path, was not the same as the one that was there earlier in the evening. So I reassured myself that she must have used the typewriter after I'd walked past her window."

"It would have been very useful for the inquiry to have had this information earlier."

"As far as I was aware, this wasn't a murder inquiry until today, Captain. When I heard it was, I came to see you. And I'm telling you everything I know."

She spoke calmly and she had a point, Korolev had to admit.

"You're sure about the typewriter? You could recognize the difference between the two of them from outside the house?"

"Oh yes. If you look at the back of it, you'll see Remington is written in large white letters. Not our alphabet, of course — but it's quite visible."

"I see," Korolev said, and wondered what

the dead girl had been typing. There hadn't been any paper in the machine when he'd seen it.

For Belakovsky's interview, Korolev found himself back in the same classroom, but this time in the company of Slivka.

"Comrades," Belakovsky said, as he sat down.

"Thank you for sparing us some of your time," Korolev answered.

Belakovsky acknowledged the remark with a grave nod of his head. "When a worker of Maria Lenskaya's caliber falls victim to violence, we must do everything possible to bring her killer to justice."

"And you knew her well, didn't you?"

"Quite well," Belakovsky replied, slanting a calculating glance up toward Korolev. Well, Korolev thought, they could dance around the question for the rest of the day or they could put it on the table and have a good look at it.

"You were having an affair with her, I believe."

Belakovsky looked at Slivka for a moment and Korolev had the impression the Film Board boss would rather not talk about the matter in front of her.

"Sergeant Slivka is an experienced detective," he said, which wasn't entirely true, "and, of course, discreet."

"Very good," Belakovsky said, after a moment's consideration. "Your information is correct. About the affair. But it was in the past. Masha accompanied me on a delegation to America a couple of years back and one thing led to another. It didn't last long but we remained friends. We continued to work closely together and there was no tension — ask anyone."

"And you were, of course, in Moscow at the time of her death."

"Yes," Belakovsky confirmed, his face lightening.

"Excuse me for asking this, Comrade Belakovsky, but you're married — isn't that correct?"

"Yes," Belakovsky said, shifting in his seat and looking at Slivka once again. "My wife isn't aware of the relationship with Lenskaya and I'd like to keep it that way."

"Where's your wife now?"

"In Moscow. She works for the Industrial Procurement Agency. We have a daughter."

"I see. Of course, if your wife were to have known about it, that would have provided her with a motive."

"A motive to kill me, perhaps. Lenskaya wasn't the first." Belakovsky seemed embarrassed. "That was one of the reasons I was glad when it ended. My wife believes in the necessity of a close-knit Soviet family. Who told you?"

"It seems common knowledge," Korolev said.

"Well, not to my wife. I'd have heard about it if she knew, believe me. Anyway, she was also in Moscow, it's easily verifiable."

"We'll check, discreetly of course. Now, tell me about the trip to America."

Belakovsky's thick eyebrows, which had drawn together in a frown while they'd discussed the dead girl, now twitched upward and apart. The shadow of a smile suggested itself at the ends of his down-turned mouth and despite the general gravity of his demeanor, it was clear the memory was a pleasant one.

"America was most interesting. And Lenskaya was an invaluable asset to us in our efforts. She spoke English well — it was what decided us to take her, not anything else, believe me. Without her, we'd have ended up relying on translators with no technical expertise." He paused. "She's a real loss to the industry and the Party."

"And the papers you wanted from her office?"

"There's a project arising from the American trip." For a moment Korolev thought he'd stop there, but Belakovsky after the slightest of hesitations continued. "It's a project of great significance to the State and the Party. You've heard of Hollywood?"

"Hollywood? Of course."

"Then you'll know it's an industrial town, Hollywood. You'll have heard of the factory towns we're building now. Everything devoted to one industry. Magnitogorsk, for example — you've seen all about it on the newsreels, heard about it on the radio. What we're doing for cars, for steel, for armaments — well, we'll soon be doing the same for cinema. Similar to Hollywood, but not a Capitalist film factory — instead it will be built on Marxist-Leninist lines where the People will rule, not American robber barons. It will be a Soviet Hollywood — Kinograd. Two hundred films a year, all year round. And just along the coast from Odessa is the place for it."

"Kinograd?"

"The same. Take my word for it, Korolev — we'll be producing more films than Hollywood in ten years' time. In many languages, not just Russian or even the other languages of the USSR. French, German, English — the workers of the world will demand to see them. Comrade Stalin himself approves. Lenskaya was a vital part of the planning stage — and her latest draft of the report for the Central Committee is missing. I have the previous version, but it's a mystery as to where it could be."

Korolev considered the possibility that a Hollywood gangster had been sent to kill Lenskaya and steal the Kinograd plans, and decided it was unlikely. But then, look at all the old Bolshevik revolutionaries and senior Party members they were uncovering as French and British spies and the like. Nothing could be ruled out these days, it seemed.

"We'll certainly look into it, Comrade Belakovsky," Korolev said, wondering if there was anything about this case that wasn't political in some way or another. "Have you any questions, Slivka?"

"Yes," Slivka said, looking down at the notebook she'd been writing in throughout the conversation. "Did anything unusual happen on the trip to America? Anything connected with Citizen Lenskaya perhaps?"

Belakovsky considered the question.

"There was that rat, Danyluk. He defected in New York — before the boat home. He made life difficult for us on our return, I can tell you."

"A defector — and she knew this fellow?"

Korolev asked, thinking about Kolya.

"Yes, a Ukrainian — the Ukrainfilm delegate, in fact. He defected to the Americans — there are plenty of Ukrainians in America, White Guards, Trotskyists, and Petlyurists. They're all there. We didn't know what he was up to until he disappeared from the hotel, but he turned up soon enough in the American newspapers spreading lies about collectivization. I hope State Security tracks the traitor down and treats him as an enemy should be treated."

Korolev glanced at Slivka, whose face revealed no surprise. Good for her, he thought.

CHAPTER FIFTEEN

Korolev and Slivka sat in silence.

"What do you think?" she asked after a while, her eyes turning to look out of the window. Troubled gray clouds rolled across the steppe toward them. Korolev wouldn't be surprised if they saw snow again before the morning.

"What do I think?" he said, after having considered her question carefully. "I think this Danyluk fellow seems to fit in with Kolya's story. I think Andreychuk being a Petlyurist fits in with his story too. The only question is does Lenskaya fit Kolya's story. I wish I'd met the girl, then I might have a better idea of what kind of person she was — but look at her Party record. She was a loyal citizen and a committed socialist from the moment she entered the orphanage. What age was she then? Twelve? Could she really have just been waiting for an opportunity? She'd no contact with her father for fifteen years and, according to Belakovsky, Danyluk had almost no contact with her. Was she a traitor? I just don't know."

"Kolya thinks she was," Slivka said, reaching into her pocket and producing a packet of cigarettes. "Maybe we should turn this over to Mushkin."

"No, not yet." Korolev considered what Rodinov's reaction was likely to be if he denounced Ezhov's lover as a spy. "We've nothing to back up the theory except a gangster's story and a couple of coincidences. Let's see what else we turn up before we go running to the Chekists."

It was coming toward dusk as he made his way through the woods. Slivka had pointed out a path through the trees to where Savchenko was filming and Korolev followed it as it wound through the winter-stripped trees, their bare branches black against the last of the light. The famous director was expecting him and, after Belakovsky's interview, Korolev wanted to find out what the famous director had to tell him.

Perhaps Korolev was a little distracted, his mind going backward and forward over the case, but at first the movement in the bushes to his left didn't register. It was only when a flurry of snow was dislodged from a branch that he became conscious that this was not the first time he'd heard something from that direction. At first he thought it might be a small animal, a fox perhaps, but it would be odd for a fox to be tracking a human. Korolev stopped for a moment and looked over to where the sound had come from, but the wood was thick with scrub and brush and he could see nothing. He resumed his walk and there was another rustle of leaves, a little ahead of him now, although this time he didn't stop but instead surreptitiously moved his Walther from under his armpit to his coat pocket and placed his thumb on the safety catch. Perhaps he was being paranoid, but after what Kolya had told him and Belakovsky's story about the spy he was taking no chances. He maintained an even speed, conscious now that whoever or whatever had been moving in parallel and was now in front of him, but still invisible in the thick brush. An ambush? His breathing quickened, the air chill in his nostrils and adrenalin surging through his veins so that he had to clench his teeth to stop them from chattering.

If whatever was up ahead was human and had a gun he'd be an easy target, but there was a wide clump of overgrown topiary that might provide an opportunity to turn the tables. He quickened his pace, reassured by the butt of the automatic warm in his palm, and then ducked and ran crouching toward the bushes, expecting bullets to whip through the branches around him at any moment.

Reaching cover, he knelt down on one knee and listened, his gun out of his pocket and the safety catch off. The stale smell of the inside of his coat came up to him and he stayed absolutely still, listening to the sound of someone moving carefully through the scrub, and he lifted the barrel of his gun a little higher with each approaching step.

He waited. And then the sounds stopped abruptly. They were just the other side of the dense bush, no more than ten yards away, close enough for him to be able to hear a strange snuffling noise. And then he worked it out — whoever was stalking him was laughing.

"You can come out now, I can see you," Korolev said, his voice sounding a lot more confident than he felt, and the reaction was a giggle, and then the blond boy from the day before came out into the clearing, a toy rifle in his hands and a wide grin on his face. For a moment he didn't see Korolev and that brief interval gave the shaken detective time to slip his gun back into his pocket and rearrange his features into something approaching normality. The Lord save him, he was jumping at shadows now, a wreck.

"I thought I had you," the boy said, pointing his wooden gun at Korolev, "but you were too smart for me." His smile turned downward and the rifle dipped in disappointment. The similarity to Korolev's own son, Yuri, was as apparent as the first time he'd seen him and for a moment he wanted to take the child in his arms to comfort him, or himself, he wasn't quite sure. He smiled at the boy and stood up.

"You did well, Pavel, but why on earth are you sneaking around in the woods, trying to ambush innocent passers-by?"

"Even children have to be prepared to defend the Motherland — I was practicing for when the enemy comes."

His eyes were grave under his black flat cap, dislodged snow on the peak. A button nose, the kind of clear blue eyes that only the very young have, a healthy complexion, cheeks pink with the cold. He'd make a good soldier with those eyes, thought Korolev — those eyes didn't worry about right and wrong. Not yet, anyway.

"Practicing for the enemy, you say," Korolev said, putting his hands in his pockets.

"I'll be a sniper when I'm older and I'll parachute behind enemy lines. When did you first spot me?"

"About a minute ago."

"Not bad, not bad. I had you under observation from when you entered the wood. If I'd had a real rifle I'd have got you easily."

"Under observation? Where do you learn this kind of thing?"

"In the Pioneers, of course. I'm a deputy team leader. Pavel Riakov, at your service."

"Korolev," he said, shaking the boy's hand. "Alexei Dmitriyevich."

"The famous detective?"

"The ordinary detective."

"But you've been sent from Moscow to investigate poor Masha's killing and you've arrested Andreychuk the caretaker."

"Not for her murder, for something else," Korolev replied, wondering what Rodinov would make of the fact that even children knew why he was here. Well, at least the youngster didn't seem to know about Ezhov.

"I hope it isn't for something serious."

"It's up to Major Mushkin."

"Good. Andreychuk is a fine fellow and Major Mushkin will see that. He's a famous

Chekist himself."

"So I've heard," Korolev said. He remembered who the boy was now from Rodinov's file. He was playing the lead role in the film, the young Pioneer who betrays his family to the Militia for withholding grain. The boy seemed to be able to read his mind, a proud smile forming.

"How come you aren't filming today?" Korolev asked.

"I am, but I'm not wanted for an hour. Is that where you're going? To the filming? Are you going to make another arrest?" His voice rose in excitement and his wide eyes shone.

"No," Korolev said, shaking his head. "I'm just going over there to talk to a few people."

"I'll show you where they are, and you should question me on the way. I knew Masha as well as anyone."

The boy pointed him back toward the path and Korolev fell into step beside him.

"All right, then. How about you tell me when you first met Citizen Lenskaya?"

"That's easy. Three months back, when I was selected. She was assisting the maestro."

"Comrade Savchenko?"

"Who else? They must have called in every kid in Moscow, but I was the one chosen." The boy paused for a moment, his face

268

becoming solemn again. "A great honor. She was nice to everybody, you know. All the kids liked her; she was a real world-class comrade."

"And how about here? How was she here?"

"She was sad — she said that was just because she was busy. But she wasn't sad in a way that made me think she might have killed herself. She was tough, a real commander. Why do you think she was killed?"

"That's what I'm trying to find out. Any ideas?"

"Counterrevolutionaries is my guess." The youngster offered his professional opinion. "We have to remain ever vigilant for those rats."

Korolev laughed, but without much humor. "I don't think so. Why would they murder her and not, say, Comrade Savchenko?"

The boy lowered his voice. "Perhaps she was working on a secret mission."

Korolev looked at him, wondering whether it was just childish enthusiasm for all things heroic and dangerous, or whether the youngster knew something after all.

"Why do you think that, young Pavel?"

"Because she went to somewhere near Krasnogorka with Comrade Andreychuk —

and that's near the border with Romania. And she knew Comrade Ezhov as well, you know. Personally. Perhaps he asked her to help him out?"

Korolev allowed himself a bitter smirk — the boy *did* know about Ezhov. But leaving that aside, what the hell had the girl been doing in Krasnogorka?

"When was this?" he asked, keeping his voice even.

"A week ago, I heard them talking about it."

"Where?"

"On this very path, Comrade Captain. I was stalking them and I was just about to jump out at them when I heard what they were talking about, and I thought I'd better leave them to it. They sounded very serious."

"And you heard them say that they'd been to Krasnogorka? Together?" And wasn't it a coincidence that Lomatkin had not more than an hour ago been telling him how he wanted to make a visit to Krasnogorka to write some article about the Stalin Line? He'd be having another word with that journalist before the evening was out.

"No, they were planning the trip — Andreychuk was going to drive the College's truck and Masha was telling him they had to be very, very careful that no one found out. That it must be absolutely secret. And Andreychuk said he knew how to get there so that no one would see them. And even if they were seen, he had a pass."

"I see — anything else make you think they were on a secret mission?"

"Well, another time I heard Comrade Babel ask her how Commissar Ezhov was and she said that the commissar was overworked but that she did her best to help him. So you see? She was helping him in his work in Krasnogorka. I've told no one except for you about this, of course. But they say Ezhov sent you down to look into the matter, so I'm guessing you know all this already."

"See that you carry on keeping it to yourself all the same," Korolev said, wincing at the thought that everyone suspected, rightly, that Ezhov was ultimately responsible for his arrival on the film set.

"There they are," the boy said, pointing at a blur of yellow light that illuminated a scattering of motor vehicles, equipment and people gathered around a group of white-bloused peasants brandishing scythes and forks. One of the men who was standing near a camera mounted on the back of a truck beckoned to the boy.

"I'm sorry, Comrade Captain. I think they want me."

He held up his hand in farewell, but the boy was already fifteen feet away. Korolev followed at a slower pace, spying Babel sitting on a box, his hands hanging loose over his knees and his bald patch reflecting the camera lights' glare. He was listening to a man whom Korolev recognized from the papers as Savchenko, a soft peaked cap worn backward over his unruly hair.

"Here he is, fresh from detection no doubt," Babel said, raising a hand in greeting.

Savchenko got to his feet, brushing his trousers and looking accusingly at the drum he'd been sitting on before turning to Korolev with an appraising glance.

"Greetings, Comrade Korolev. Babel and I have just been discussing your investigation. Give me two minutes so I can wrap up this scene and I'll be with you."

"Willingly, Comrade Savchenko."

The film director squeezed Korolev's hand, patted his shoulder and then walked toward the camera and a waiting Shymko. The production coordinator offered him a board with a page clipped to it which the director took absent mindedly, his attention focused on the huddle of peasants.

"So Andreychuk's in the slammer?" Babel said, pointing Korolev to the vacated drum.

"Not for the killing. It's Mushkin's affair now, what to do with the fellow. My responsibility doesn't extend that far."

"You've ruled him out?"

"Not exactly," Korolev began, quickly filling Babel in on the developments, but leaving out the conversation he'd had with Kolya. It wasn't that he didn't trust his friend, but information like that could be a death sentence.

"Krasnogorka?" Babel asked when he'd finished.

"Yes, I don't know the place. It's on the Romanian border, I believe."

"I know it. A border town, as you say. It had a reputation for smuggling a few years back — I don't know if it's still the case."

"The Stalin Line's there now. Not much smuggling where there are machine guns and artillery."

"Don't be so sure; even Red Army men have eyes that can turn the other way."

"Perhaps. I'd like to know what the two of them were up to there, certainly. What do you think about the morphine?"

"I don't think you need to worry too much about the way it was done — everybody knows it will knock you out if you take enough of it. It could have been put in her food, she might have drunk it or she might have taken it thinking it was something else. The question is how it was obtained. It doesn't seem like something you would just come across, not out here. And the other question is who'd have had access to it. An addict perhaps?"

"We're looking into it. And you — any luck with the filming from that night?"

"I don't think it's going to help you much, brother. There isn't a familiar face there, apart from Andreychuk's. The crew were all behind the camera, and only one or two of the cast are in the shots we've looked at so far. I've left one of Shymko's girls going through it. Don't worry," he said, anticipating Korolev's objection, "I'll check through it myself as well, but it's the note-taking slows you down. And I asked her to find someone from the village who might know the extras — I don't know many of them myself."

Korolev shrugged; perhaps it had been too much to hope for that the film would show anything useful.

"Attention, everyone," Shymko's voice boomed loudly. The production coordinator was holding a megaphone in his hand and standing on top of a stepladder. Korolev

274

stood to watch.

"Crowd to your places. Everyone ready?"

Savchenko was helped onto the back of the truck, where he fixed an eye to a small silver box on a tripod that Korolev presumed was a camera. After a long pause, he stood up and looked to the crowd, raising his arms. The crowd responded by shaking scythes, pitchforks and axes in a warlike manner. Then Savchenko, while still gesticulating, made an angry face, all the while not uttering a sound, and the crowd obliged him again. Satisfied, Savchenko turned to the camera operator and the rest of the crew.

"Motor," Savchenko called out and Shymko repeated the word into his megaphone.

"Start," Savchenko said and as Shymko's megaphone echoed the instruction, a young lad snapped a clapperboard shut in front of the camera and the crowd began to advance, indignant and hostile. Then from the side young Pavel appeared, and began to dance, lifting his knees, waving his elbows and prodding at the path in front of the advancing peasants with outstretched toes. The crowd, apparently as bewildered as Korolev, came to a halt. One began to point at the boy and laugh, and suddenly the whole crowd had to lean against each other to

275

avoid collapsing into a helpless heap. And still Pavel danced. Even Korolev couldn't help but smile.

"And stop," Savchenko said.

"That's it," announced Shymko and the crowd's laughter died instantly, and Pavel went from a high kick to a slouching walk that took him back toward the camera. Savchenko pointed out Korolev to the production coordinator and raised the thumb and fingers of his left hand.

"A short break now, don't go far," Shymko announced, and the extras began rolling cigarettes and bending their heads in conversation.

"And they pay you for writing this?" Korolev said.

"Not enough," said Babel, putting his hands in his pockets.

"Korolev, thank you for your patience. Babel here has been telling me all about you and, given you probably know all about me as well, I take it there's no need for cumbersome introductions. Let's take a walk over this way, where we can talk properly." The director led him away from the film crew, and for a moment Korolev thought Babel was going to try and join them, but the writer caught his warning glance and stayed where he was.

"So, let's get straight to the point, Comrade Korolev. I knew Maria Lenskaya well. I'm sure you know that by now. She was my lover, or I was hers — I can't remember which way around it was. Anyway, I'm sure someone among that crowd of gossips has told you by now." The director pointed a thumb back toward the cast and crew.

"Yes, I've been informed, but I'm also aware that you were filming throughout the crucial period, and every one of them is a witness to that as well."

"They have their uses, I suppose."

"So do you have any idea who could have killed her?"

"I don't. And that concerns me because the likelihood is that it was one of us." Although the director didn't seem so much concerned by the thought as intrigued.

"I have to ask about your relationship with her, of course."

"Certainly. It ended some time ago, although when she came to America with Belakovsky I'll admit there was a little flirtation. Nothing serious, but it was so nice to hear beautiful Russian spoken by a beautiful woman. I couldn't resist her."

"Did you meet a man called Danyluk at that time?"

"The defector? Yes, I met him once or

twice. He was in the technological group, not the creative part of the delegation."

"Did Lenskaya have much to do with him?"

"Nothing, as far as I'm aware. He was an insignificant man. I suspect his defection was opportunistic. But I only met him a couple of times, as I said."

"I hope you don't mind me saying this, Comrade Savchenko, but you don't seem overly saddened by her death."

Savchenko, rather than being offended, as Korolev had half expected, considered the suggestion seriously for a moment.

"Don't be misled, Captain, I'm deeply upset," he said. "I valued Masha highly, as a worker and colleague, and as a person. It's the way my mind works, though, to look at such a sadness and speculate around it. A story like this is fascinating for me. I look at it from every angle, consider it, remember it. This is work for me, just as much as if I were digging a ditch. But more importantly, this film has to be finished — why do you think Belakovsky is down from Moscow? To apply pressure, that's why. I have a responsibility to the people who are working with me on this project not to be distracted. We all do. I'll grieve for poor Masha later."

Korolev understood the point. Work that

was behind schedule on a construction project or in a factory could lead to arrests for sabotage and wrecking — so why not a film? Film makers had quotas to achieve, same as everyone else, and if they didn't achieve them fingers started pointing and cell doors started opening, and worse. It was the way things were.

"I apologize, Comrade. I have to ask these things."

"I understand."

And so Korolev asked the questions he had to ask — who had liked her and who had disliked her? Who had been her close associates in Moscow? Who else had she had romantic entanglements with? He asked about Andreychuk, and morphine and her background and every other question he could think of. Savchenko was as helpful as he could be, but he didn't provide any new information. He was, however, intrigued by the idea that she had been drugged before being strangled.

"Keep it to yourself please, Comrade Savchenko."

"Of course, of course, but it's positively romantic, don't you think? It's almost as though she had to die and the killer decided to make it as painless as possible. Perhaps he loved her but she rejected him. Or loved someone else."

Korolev looked at the director to see if he was joking, but he wasn't. It was just as he'd said — he'd taken the bare facts and used them to build a story, but it was an interesting theory and one that Korolev thought might just have something to it. They heard a cough and saw that Shymko had approached, his clipboard at the ready. Savchenko shrugged his shoulders, as if he were being torn away from a fascinating conversation rather than a murder interrogation.

"One final question before you go, Comrade. Do you have any idea why she would have visited Krasnogorka in the company of the caretaker Andreychuk last week?"

"Krasnogorka? Shymko, she went to see a church last week — was it near Krasnogorka?"

"Not far away," the production coordinator confirmed. "A few miles only, I think."

"What church was this?" Korolev asked.

"Some church she'd heard was to be destroyed, and we thought we could use it for the final scene in the film — when the church is burned down by the peasants. I have the details in the office."

"It might be useful. And why did Andreychuk accompany her?"

"She couldn't drive. Nothing more complicated — Andreychuk was helping us out. Is it true you've arrested him?"

Korolev half-expected that if he looked behind him he'd see Indian smoke signals coming from the village, so widely had the information spread.

"Ask Major Mushkin. Anyway, Comrade Savchenko, thank you for your assistance — if I have any further questions?"

"You know where to find me."

Korolev walked with them back toward the camera crew and saw that the peasants had re-formed in the same positions, but before he got any closer a car's lights came bumping though the forest and from it stepped the young Militiaman from the village, Sharapov. He nodded to Savchenko and Shymko, and then indicated to Korolev with a small nod of his head that they needed to talk, and away from the others. Korolev felt his stomach sink — whatever the uniform had to tell him, it looked like it wasn't going to be something he wanted to hear to judge from the youngster's face.

"Sergeant Slivka sent me to fetch you. It's about Andreychuk, Comrade Captain. It's not good news."

For a moment, Korolev thought that Sergeant Gradov had beaten the caretaker to a pulp and that Sharapov had been sent to tell him that the old man wouldn't be helping with the inquiry for the foreseeable future.

"Is he all right?"

"As far as I know, Comrade, he's fine. But the wretch has made a run for it."

CHAPTER SIXTEEN

By the time they arrived at the Militia station, Slivka had already established that the Agricultural College's truck was missing and, efficient girl that she was, she'd called Marchuk and been assured that roadblocks would be set up along likely escape routes and that all stations would be on the lookout for the fugitive. However, by now it was dark and it had to be expected that Andreychuk, with his head start and the cover of night, had a reasonable chance of making good his escape. Korolev listened to her report and then stood for a moment considering the problem that faced them. Sergeant Gradov stood in the corner, a sullen look on his face.

"Well?" Korolev said, turning toward him.

"I went to the house to pick up Sharapov. I left the cell door locked and locked the door to the station as well. But when I came back the door was open and so was his cell and he'd gone."

"When did you last see him?"

"About fifty minutes ago. I wasn't gone for much more than a quarter of an hour. I called Sergeant Slivka up at the house immediately."

"Did anyone see him leave in the truck?"

"I heard an engine starting at about six o'clock," Slivka said. "About forty minutes ago. The sergeant called me about ten minutes later. I remembered the noise of the truck, verified it was unaccounted for and immediately called Odessa. The roadblocks should be in place by now."

"Forty minutes. Slivka, what does that mean?"

Slivka considered the question.

"If he had to make his way to the truck, that would have taken about fifteen minutes from here if he was moving quickly. It's difficult."

"Are you sure of your timings, Sergeant Gradov?"

"It could have been an hour."

"It could have been an hour," Korolev said, not bothering to hide his disdain, before turning back to Slivka. "Let's presume it was him and he's driving hell for leather. Ask Marchuk to act accordingly."

He turned back to the sergeant while

Slivka made a call.

"So let me get this straight — you left a prisoner in the station without a guard, is that correct?"

The sergeant seemed to resent being asked such a question, and Korolev felt anger scour his stomach. It might well be the sergeant's dereliction of duty had caused this mess, but he had a sneaking suspicion that a certain NKVD major named Mushkin would be delivering the blame to Korolev's doorstep. If time wasn't of the essence he'd take some pleasure in telling this idiot exactly what he thought of his negligence — the man had put not only Korolev at risk but all those whom Korolev held dear. He turned to Slivka, suddenly putting two and two together.

"He's from a village near Krasnogorka called Angelinivka, isn't he?" Korolev said, thinking aloud. "What's more he went on a trip with Lenskaya in that direction last week, according to Shymko. The actor boy also overheard Andreychuk say he could get there without being detected. If it's near Krasnogorka, it must be close to the border so my guess is, if he's running, he's running for Romania."

"I'll call the border guard."

Slivka picked up the phone once again,

tapping the cradle for the operator. Korolev turned back to Gradov, his words quick and urgent.

"What have you got to say for yourself?"

"I'm sorry, Comrade Captain, I don't know how he got out."

"Perhaps he was let out. Did that ever occur to you?" Korolev felt a cold anger possessing him that wanted to wrap itself around the neck of this incompetent and squeeze the life out of him.

"Tell me, who else has keys to the station?"

"I do. No one else."

"You didn't have the keys with you, did you?" Korolev heard his voice rising in disbelief.

"I leave them under a brick around the side when I'm out, in case one of the others comes back while I'm away."

Korolev was struck dumb for a moment, turning to Slivka for confirmation that his ears hadn't been deceiving him. Her grim look of contempt confirmed they hadn't.

"Show me this brick," Korolev said, his voice revealing some of his rage. "Slivka? If Firtov's still up at the house taking people's prints, get him to come down. Make sure no one touches anything in the meantime."

Slivka nodded and Korolev turned to see

the sergeant reaching for the door handle.

"What did I just say?" he barked.

"About the fingerprinting?"

"And what the hell are you doing now? Understand this, Sergeant, you do not touch one damned thing in this station until Firtov has been through this place and given it the all clear. And even then you ask permission — do you hear me?"

The sergeant nodded, and Korolev pointed him back to the wall and picked up a cloth from the desk that looked relatively clean, relieved to hear that Slivka seemed to have got through to someone in the border guards.

"It's near Krasnogorka, Comrade," she said, "but you'd better make it a general alert. Now here's his description. Ready?"

Korolev carefully opened the door, touching only the thin sides of the handle that would yield no fingerprints. Then he picked up a rock and placed it against the door to wedge it open so that no one else would contaminate the handle until Firtov and the Greek had done their work.

"The brick?" he said, looking around outside.

"Here it is, Comrade Captain," the sergeant said, walking to the corner of the building and pointing down the narrow alley between it and the Party offices. A yellow clay brick lay on its side, illuminated by the light from the Militia station window. Korolev looked from the brick back to the road — anyone passing could have seen the sergeant hide the keys, but not even that would have been necessary, given it was his long-term habit to conceal them this way.

"I doubt there's a man, woman or child in this whole village doesn't know you leave the keys there," he said. "Did you see anyone on your way up to the house?"

"No one, Comrade Captain. All the village is at a meeting in the tractor barn. Those that aren't are over with the film people."

"On the way back?"

"I saw Comrade Lomatkin near the house, and Comrade Mushkina was out for a walk. I saw no one else."

"I see. And this brick — you left it flat, correct? And it's now on its side?"

"Yes, Comrade Captain."

"Right, Sergeant. You stand here beside this damned brick and this damned door and you protect them with your worthless life until the forensics men get here. And I mean with your life. No one is to touch anything except for Comrade Firtov. And if it rains you will cover the brick and the door

288

handle with your body rather than let one drop of water fall on them."

Which would be difficult, given they were some distance apart, but a point had to be made.

The worst thing was he now had to call Rodinov and inform him of this mess and it wasn't a conversation he was looking forward to. Telling Slivka he needed to go to the investigation room, he got into the car, turned the key, and pounded the driving wheel with frustration when the starter motor wouldn't turn. The sergeant looked over at him nervously and Korolev pointed at the bonnet.

"Don't just stand there, man — crank it."

The sergeant was soon cranking the starting handle for all his worth and the engine growled into life. Perhaps wisely, Gradov retreated quickly from in front of the vehicle, and placed the starting handle on the back seat as if it were burning him. Korolev leaned out of the window.

"Who was he friendly with? In the village? Someone must have helped him."

"No one, really. He kept to himself up at the College. Maybe some of the people who worked up there knew him better."

"Find out who. And find out if anyone saw him leaving. I don't need to tell you where you're heading if we don't track this man down, and fast."

Korolev pushed the gearstick into place and, with the angry scream of an overrevved engine, the car bounded forward.

Korolev felt utter fury, but he understood himself well enough to know that his anger came from fear and guilt as much as it did from exasperation. After all, if he was the man running this investigation then it was his responsibility to ensure it ran properly — he knew the likely consequences of failure, not only for himself but for others as well, and he should have taken appropriate precautions. He should have realized the village Militia station wasn't secure — he'd interviewed Andreychuk there, after all, and seen how it was run. And it was no excuse to say he was tired. All right, the old man probably wasn't involved in the murder itself, but he almost certainly had vital information — if nothing else, then about that trip to Krasnogorka. Damn it.

He pulled the car up outside the stable block where the investigation office was and caught a glimpse of his face in the mirror — he looked like a man about to kill someone. Or be killed, he thought to himself as he opened the car door.

The phone was ringing as he entered the investigation room and he wondered grimly if it might be Rodinov, already calling to blast him for his incompetence. But it wasn't.

"Comrade Korolev?" The operator's voice.

"Yes, that's me."

"I have a phone call for you. I'm putting him through now." There was a change in the crackling noise from the receiver.

"Korolev," he said warily.

"Good evening, Comrade Captain, it's good to hear your voice." That deep actor's intonation with its undercurrent of menace. Count Kolya. The Thief.

"It's good to hear yours as well, Citizen," Korolev said, wondering how the hell the gangster had managed to get hold of the telephone number.

"All going well with your investigation?" Kolya asked.

"Not too bad, not too bad. Berry by berry, and the basket will be full."

"I hear one berry has rolled away." Kolya laughed and Korolev felt his hand tighten on the receiver. This was ridiculous. Kolya must have someone in the Militia headquarters feeding him information. Damn the man.

"I think we know where it's rolling to,"

Korolev said, trying to keep his voice matter-of-fact.

"Good for you," the Thief said, with the implication that he couldn't care less. "Anyway, you asked a question, about morphine. I looked into it. Go to your journalist, he might have an answer for you."

Lomatkin? But he'd been in Moscow. How could he have been responsible? Korolev coughed, clearing a throat which felt a little constricted, like his brain.

"He was some distance from here at the time in question," he managed to say. "Are you sure?"

"I'm sure of nothing — all I know is the fellow has a past, and the past involves the substance in question."

"I see," Korolev said, wondering where it left him.

"And another thing. The delivery I mentioned. They've found another way. It's happening tomorrow night."

The guns. The German guns.

"Are you sure?"

"Certain," Kolya said, his voice laconic.

"Where?"

"That we've yet to find out. But we will."

"You'll let me know?"

"It's our business."

"Then why are you telling me?"

Kolya laughed again, a tinny sound on the crackling line.

"It's a good point — I'll let you know when I know. But remember our conversation. There's a way of handling this and it isn't your way. Tell Slivka to call her mother."

"Her mother?" Korolev was confused. Then it occurred to him that Slivka's mother would be the channel through which Kolya would pass on news of the gunrunning. He was about to confirm his understanding when Kolya hung up, and the line became a steady hum.

It was probably just as well, as through the window he could see Mushkin approaching across the courtyard, the heels of his brown leather boots battering the cobblestones into submission. The major looked in through the window at him as he approached and it wasn't a look that promised a long life to its recipient.

"A pretty mess you've made of this, Korolev," Mushkin said without further ado as he entered the room.

"The escape of Citizen Andreychuk isn't ideal, that much I'll give you," Korolev said, after a pause. "But we weren't holding him on suspicion of murder, you should know that. In fact I wasn't holding him at all. It was up to you to decide what to do with him. Effectively, he was in your custody."

"My custody?" Mushkin said, an amazed smile cracking his stony face. It wasn't a pleasant smile — it was a smile children ran from screaming.

"You as in the local Organs of State Security — I make no personal reference, Comrade Major, but I don't see how a Moscow detective who arrived yesterday can be held responsible for the way things are done here. That responsibility must lie elsewhere. And particularly given that it took that Moscow detective less than twenty-four hours to uncover an Enemy of the State who'd gone unobserved by these same Organs for nearly ten years. It seems to me the least the local Organs could have done in the circumstances is ensure such a person's secure captivity when he was, finally, uncovered. He worked with your mother, didn't he? You knew him as well, I believe."

Korolev felt his toes curling in anticipation of a furious response. But this was, he was pretty sure, the way he had to play it and hope he could rely on Rodinov to back him up. Perhaps Mushkin had also thought through his personal associations with the escapee because he didn't react with fury.

Instead he contemplated Korolev at his leisure.

"Interesting, Korolev. Very interesting. Unfortunately for you I've just spoken to Colonel Rodinov and he's most upset at *your* failure to secure the prisoner — what do you make of that?"

Korolev shrugged his shoulders, hoping he appeared indifferent to the implicit threat. He suspected that Mushkin's comment was a shot across the bows — a reminder that Korolev was a Militiaman, whereas Rodinov and Mushkin were brother Chekists. It didn't change anything, once you thought about it. Whether Mushkin had spoken to Rodinov or not, Korolev's fate had been in Rodinov's hands since that young Chekist had knocked on the apartment door.

"I'm just about to call Colonel Rodinov myself," Korolev said. "As you know, I have to report all matters concerning this investigation to him directly. Shall I let him know that you're taking all steps to apprehend the criminal Andreychuk?"

Mushkin exhaled a thin wisp of smoke that curled up out of his mouth, along the side of his face and then seemed to get trapped for a moment underneath the brim of his cap. "Make sure you keep good notes,

Korolev," he said. "When I take this matter over I don't want to have to repeat every single interview."

The Chekist tapped the drooping ash from his cigarette onto the floor and left the room, closing the door carefully behind him.

Korolev wished he'd slammed it; the carefulness was unsettling. He sighed, lit one of his own cigarettes and made the call to Moscow.

Colonel Rodinov listened with surprising patience to his account of the escape and then got straight to the point.

"Mushkin thinks you're an incompetent fool."

The words were a little bald, but the colonel's voice was neutral in tone.

"He has shared with me his thoughts on my abilities, Comrade Colonel."

"But you're satisfied that this man was not responsible for the murder?"

"Comrade Colonel, I consider it unlikely that Andreychuk would have killed his own daughter without a good reason, and we've been unable to establish any such reason. There are also other elements of the crime that would appear to be beyond him."

"Such as?" the colonel asked, and Korolev told him about the morphine, the cleaning up of forensic evidence and the fact that the caretaker was unlikely to have had the strength to lift the body on his own.

"But he could have worked with someone else. The man was an enemy, hiding among us for many years while wearing the mask of a loyal Soviet citizen. He could have been waiting for an opportunity like this to attack. The girl's murder is potentially embarrassing to higher levels of the Party, as you well know — particularly now that it turns out her father fought with Petlyura. To a rat like that the murder of his own daughter might well be justified if he believed it would damage the Revolution."

"Comrade Colonel, I don't deny that he fought with Petlyura, and that he concealed his identity to avoid retribution, but my impression of him was of an old man who regretted his earlier mistakes. I accept I may be naive in these matters, but if he had been waiting all these years to sabotage the Revolution, why kill his own daughter, and then disguise it as a suicide? Why not, for example, kill Comrade Savchenko or Comrade Sorokina? Surely the death of such a famous film director or actress would damage the Revolution more."

There was silence as Rodinov considered the point and Korolev waited. After some moments, the colonel sighed.

"There might be a good reason, Korolev — the one which caused you to be sent down there in the first place." It was true, the girl's connection with Ezhov could well be behind her murder, but he still had trouble seeing Andreychuk as the killer. And then, of course, there was Mushkina's information about the typewriters, which placed Andreychuk at the film shoot while either the killer or the victim switched them. He explained this to Rodinov.

"And there's another lead I'm following up on, Comrade Colonel," Korolev continued, deciding it was time to fill the colonel in on the trip close to the border that Andreychuk and the dead girl had made. "It's possible that they were visiting a church that might be used in the film. I'm waiting for confirmation."

The colonel didn't respond immediately, and all Korolev could hear from the receiver was the crackle of a bad line.

"It may be nothing, of course," Korolev said, as much to hear the sound of his own voice as anything.

"It might be something though, something serious." The colonel's voice sounded as though some part of him was being squeezed uncomfortably. "What if he *was* a spy? There might be an entire conspiracy down there — don't you read the newspapers, Korolev? The State is besieged on every side — Lenskaya may even have been involved in the damned thing. And where the hell would that leave us?"

The line wasn't that good so it was difficult to say exactly, but the colonel sounded more than a little shaken. It seemed that Korolev wasn't the only one coming to conclusions that he wasn't entirely happy about.

"There's also the matter of the traitor Danyluk, Colonel, the Ukrainian who absconded from the delegation to America."

"Yes, I remember him."

"I'm only a Militia detective at the end of the day," Korolev said. "This may be beyond me."

Korolev waited for the colonel's next words with some trepidation. If he could walk away from the case he'd thank the Lord with all his heart because it would be as great a miracle as any written up in the Bible.

"No." The colonel's voice was thoughtful now. "You're making progress there, whatever else. It's not good to lose potential witnesses, but it seems to me that you can't be held responsible for local Militia officers who aren't under your direct command. I'll call this fellow Marchuk in Odessa and make that clear to him, and Mushkin as well. If you can unmask this fellow in less than a day then they should be asking themselves one or two questions rather than trying to blame their failures on you."

"Thank you, Comrade Colonel." Korolev spoke with a heavy heart. He was stuck with it, then, although at least Mushkin was going to get it in the neck. That was something.

"Find out what they were doing in Krasnogorka, Korolev. If Andreychuk did kill Lenskaya and you think he might have had help — find out who helped him. And if he didn't kill her, find out who did."

Korolev felt his hackles rise — what the hell did Rodinov think he was doing down here? Taking the waters? Sunbathing?

"I'll do my best, Comrade Colonel." He managed to keep his irritation hidden. "But may I ask one thing of you?"

"What?"

"In the course of my interview with the journalist Lomatkin he told me that he was also planning a visit to Krasnogorka — to view the Stalin Line for some article he's writing. Perhaps your men in Moscow could make some inquiries? I'm confident he's a loyal Party member and so on, but it's an unusual coincidence."

"Lomatkin?" The colonel's voice sounded skeptical, but then perhaps he remembered Stalin's directive to remain vigilant at all times, that even the unlikeliest citizen could turn out to be a traitor. "All right, we'll look into Comrade Lomatkin. Anything else?"

"Morphine. It's not so easy to obtain, even in the hospitals sometimes. It may have come from Moscow, or it could have been obtained locally. If State Security can provide any information that connects it to a suspect, it would certainly help. Again, if your men are looking into Comrade Lomatkin, it might be something to bear in mind."

"I'll ask."

"Thank you, Comrade Colonel."

"Korolev, keep me informed of any progress. And be vigilant for signs of counter-revolutionary activity. I don't like the smell of this one bit."

The colonel hung up and Korolev put his own receiver down.

"Calm yourself," he muttered after a moment or two. "It's a mess and you're in the middle of it, but you need to get your head straight and think it through."

He opened his notebook — a lot had happened in the last few hours, he needed to write it down and look for the way forward.

First things first. The colonel had ordered him to go to Krasnogorka to find out what the girl and Andreychuk had been up to. He'd go, sure enough, first thing in the morning, but he didn't know the country-side around there. It would help if Shymko had a location for this church of his, so he made a note to himself to make sure Slivka checked with the production coordinator. Another thought occurred to him — it was a border area. Did that mean it had con-trolled access? Would they have had to pass through checkpoints that close to the bor-der? There must be a record of their journey somewhere. Andreychuk had said something about having a pass, according to the boy, hadn't he? If he had, it should give details of the limits of his authorization. Slivka would know who to ask, or Mushkin per-haps — as a last resort.

Then there was Andreychuk's escape. Somebody had helped him. And if anyone would know who might go out on a limb like that for the fleet-footed caretaker, it would be Mushkina. Another conversation with the major's mother should be a prior-ity. The sergeant had seen her out and about around the time the cell had been emptied of its occupant, and she'd approached him only an hour or so before about getting An-

302

dreychuk out of prison, hadn't she? It was a ridiculous thought, but what if she'd been the one who'd helped the caretaker out of his cell?

Chapter Seventeen

It had been a long day and Korolev went in search of nourishment, but as he passed the dead girl's office he found himself opening the door. His stomach could hold out for another five minutes.

The desk, the shelves bent under ranks of books, the papers and typewriters, the panoramic view over the lake and the snow-decked woodland — all were unchanged since the last time he'd stood there. He thought of the girl and wondered if the last thing she'd seen had been that same moon, now a luminous orb hanging low over the lake, and he hoped the morphine had done its work and that her end had been quick.

He started on the top bookshelf — Lenin, Marx, Stalin, Engels. He opened each book and flicked through the pages, just in case something might have been left there. Savchenko's *Theory of Film*, a well-thumbed volume, seemed to have been more diligently read than those of Lenin, Marx and the others; then a slew of books in English — beyond his powers of translation except for the words *Cinema* and *Film,* which reassured him he was looking at technical manuals. One of the thicker volumes, filled with diagrams and pictures of cameras and other equipment, also contained a brightly colored postcard with the word "Hollywood" in inch-high red letters on top of which was draped a reclining blonde beauty wearing not very much at all.

"A crucial piece of evidence?"

The suggestion came from behind him and for a moment he felt the urge to put the postcard back in the book as though he'd never seen it, but he recognized the voice, and the amusement in it, and so he held it up for Les Pins to see better.

"They have a different climate there," the Frenchman said.

"It gets hot here in the summer," Korolev replied, which it did. In three months' time the sun would be a constant pressure on the landscape, the windows here would be wide open and the room full of the scent of flowers and the buzz of insects. He turned the card over, but there was no message.

"I take it you're not searching Lenskaya's

room for souvenirs of Los Angeles, Korolev?"

Korolev put the postcard back where he'd found it and replaced the book on the shelf.

"Can I help you?" he said, making an attempt at politeness.

"I was thinking I might help you. I heard you trying to pronounce the titles of those English books."

"Trying to pronounce?" He thought he'd been doing a pretty good job himself.

"Anyway," Les Pins continued, "if I can be of any assistance, it would be my pleasure."

Korolev considered the man: an irritating smile on his face that the fellow must think made him irresistible, gray eyes that appeared benevolent but were more likely to be concealing some self-serving motivation. Unless he was wrong, he'd a good idea what the fellow was after. Information, damn him. This fellow would publish his own living mother's obituary while she was still walking around if he thought it would earn him a few more rubles or whatever it was that they paid the Frenchman in.

"It's all right, Comrade Les Pins," Korolev said. "I'm sure you have other things to keep you occupied."

"Not really. I'm here to recuperate as

much as anything, you see. A fascist put a small hole in my shoulder in Spain, and the comrades there thought I needed a break. Now that I'm here, I'm bored. I'd be happy to help. I'll put it more strongly," he said, smiling that priest's smile of his again, "I'd be grateful."

Korolev had picked a collection of Stalin's speeches from the bookshelves and had opened it idly while they were engaged in conversation. Inside it was a piece of paper, folded in four and typed with Latin lettering.

"What's that you have there?" Les Pins asked.

Korolev's English wasn't up to an instantaneous translation, but it seemed to be some sort of poem.

"The twenty-third psalm," Les Pins said quietly, reading it over his shoulder, "from the King James Bible. 'Yea, though I walk through the valley of the shadow of death, I shall fear no evil. For thou art with me.' "

A smart girl — she knew her geography if nothing else. She'd been in that valley all right, even if everywhere nearby was flat. The paper felt crisp enough to have been newly folded — was this what she'd been typing when Mushkina had passed by, before the typewriters had been switched?

Was it a message and, if so, who for?

"Curious," the Frenchman said. "It's as though she had a presentiment of death."

"You'll excuse me, Comrade. I thank you for the translation, but I must ask you to leave."

"Yes, yes. I'm sorry, Captain. I was only trying to offer my assistance."

"It isn't required, but thank you."

"A shame," Les Pins said, not moving away, instead gracing him with a look of sympathetic concern. "But it must be difficult for you. I can understand why you don't want a foreign journalist involved in a murder like this."

There was something loaded in his tone. Enough to make Korolev give the Frenchman his full attention.

"What do you mean, Comrade? Are you suggesting something?"

"Suggesting something? Me? Not at all. I hear the caretaker has run away. Did you arrest him for the murder?"

"No. For something else," Korolev replied.

The Frenchman smiled — a confident smile, the smile of a gambler with a card up his sleeve.

"Just as well, I should think," he said, mischief in his eyes, "what with her being such a good friend of Comrade Ezhov's."

Korolev felt a chill at the back of his neck. "The Militia investigates every crime with the same diligence," he said eventually, as carefully as a man walking through a mine-field, and holding Les Pins' gaze.

Now the Frenchman laughed before looking away.

"But seeing as you're here, Comrade," Korolev said, trying to steer the conversation onto a different track, "perhaps you could tell me where you were on the night of the murder. And whether you saw anything suspicious."

"Suspicious?" The Frenchman shrugged his shoulders. "No. I went down to watch the night shoot. Everyone was there, I think."

"Would you be prepared to give us a list of who you saw, and when? What you remember of the evening — even the most trivial details — might provide invaluable assistance." Korolev kept his gaze steady on Les Pins, and his voice quiet, but he spoke as forcefully as he dared. And the Frenchman seemed no longer to find the situation quite so amusing.

"With pleasure, Comrade Captain. I'll let you have it tonight."

"And were you outside this afternoon? At around six o'clock perhaps?"

"Me? No, I was in my room reading — was that when Andreychuk bolted?"

Korolev said nothing, just looked at the Frenchman unblinkingly until Les Pins glanced away once again, and Korolev saw the fellow's throat move as he swallowed.

"Your recollections from the evening in question would be most useful, Comrade Les Pins," Korolev said and turned back to the books, waiting until Les Pins left the room before he allowed himself to breathe deeply.

Korolev thought about the significance of the typed psalm as he walked back toward the stable block carrying a small enamel pot by its handle. He'd liked to have eaten his dinner in the dining room, but the reaction when he'd walked in — twenty-five pairs of gawking eyes, several pairs belonging to actors familiar throughout the Soviet Union, and complete silence — well, it had been enough to persuade him to ask the girl serving the food if he could take it back to the investigation room, and the enamel pot, lid and handle included, had been quickly forthcoming.

At least the case was making some progress — they now had an ever-lengthening list of people who were accounted for during the crucial time period. And their questioning was revealing more and more about the dead girl, some of which was perhaps a little worrying, but definitely progress. Of course, this Andreychuk business was a disaster and he prayed the border guards or one of the Militia roadblocks would pick him up, and alive, as it seemed likely that the caretaker would have something to tell him about the murder, and maybe about this conspiracy Kolya had told him of as well — and he was desperate to talk to him. It was frustrating, but he felt the investigation was now in the hands of others. He was waiting for a phone call, either to hear from Kolya where this "delivery" was taking place, or to be told someone had picked up Andreychuk. He saw Slivka coming out of the investigation room and raised a hand in greeting.

"Any news on our runaway?" he asked her.

"Shymko dug out the name of the church they were supposed to have been visiting — you were right. It's in Angelinivka. Right on the border, quite close to Krasnogorka. The border guards are searching the area as we speak."

"Any sign of the truck?"

"Not yet, although it's possible Andreychuk could have abandoned it somewhere

311

and be making his way on foot. But the steppe will be no place to hide come the morning."

"No," Korolev agreed. Apart from the lines of trees that split up the fields there wasn't much vegetation in this part of the world, and even the trees wouldn't provide much in the way of cover at this time of year. "If we could find out who helped him out of his cell, they might tell us which way he was headed."

"Firtov and the Greek think they have some good fingerprints. Whether they can match them to anyone is the question. Anyone other than the uniforms from the station, that is."

"We'll see what comes of it," Korolev muttered, conscious that his stew was getting cold. "And we'll take a drive out to this place Angelinivka in the morning and see what we see."

Korolev remembered he hadn't told Slivka about his conversation with Kolya, and wondered how to approach it.

"Your uncle called," he said, after a moment or two, having decided there was no way to broach the issue other than directly — particularly not with a hot dinner in his hand that was making his stomach hollow with hunger. Slivka's eyes seemed to widen slightly, but it was difficult to tell in the darkness. He took a look around, just in case they could be overheard.

"That thing we spoke of? With the guns?" he said, lowering his voice. "He thinks it will happen tomorrow."

Slivka spat on the ground. It was difficult to tell what the action signified. He wished he could see her face more clearly. He wasn't much used to women spitting, if the truth were told, and it left him feeling nonplussed, but he supposed that these days it was her right to behave in just as uncultured a way as her male comrades, just as it was to do the same job.

"What do we do about it, Chief?" she said after a long pause.

"That's the question, Slivka. We don't know where or when it will happen yet, or even if it will happen. But you're to call your mother."

"Call my mother?"

"I don't think it's to inquire about her health. I think Kolya will let us know what's happening through her. Anyway, get yourself some food, let's send Larisa off to bed and we'll have a think about it. A collective decision is always better."

Larisa looked up as he entered the investigation room. The girl's fingers must be worn to nothing from rattling that machine for most of the day and a lot of the evening. She looked exhausted. He pointed a thumb over his shoulder toward the Orlov House.

"Larisa, there comes a time when even you must rest. Now's the time. We'll see you tomorrow morning. Thank you for all your efforts."

The girl didn't argue, just nodded, quickly put the papers she'd been working on in order, and then left, her arms crossed and her head hanging forward.

"Thank you again, Comrade," Korolev said as she passed, touching her shoulder with his hand. Then he shut the door behind her, made his way to the desk, opened the enamel pot and inhaled — it was good, very good. These film people lived well. He picked up the fork they'd given him with one hand and the receiver with the other, and, his mouth already half-occupied with a succulent piece of meat, asked the operator to put him through to Yasimov's communal apartment in Moscow.

Unsurprisingly it took a while for the operator to call him back. Moscow was six hundred miles away and, as a man who'd walked a few miles in his time, he knew that was some distance. But eventually he was

314

connected. A child's voice answered. Korolev checked his watch — it was late for a youngster to be up and about.

"Dmitry Alexandrovich, please."

"Captain Yasimov?"

"The very same."

"I'll get him."

There was the sound of revelry in the background and then a glass breaking to the sound of a cheer. Someone picked up the receiver in the *kommunalka*.

"Yasimov," a voice said, Mitya's voice.

"A party going on there, I can hear."

"Lyoshka," Yasimov said. "Khabarov's son got married. I'm turning a blind eye to the *samogon*."

If Korolev could judge from Yasimov's voice, he wasn't just turning a blind eye to the moonshine, he was testing it to make sure it was what it purported to be. He'd be lucky if he didn't end up turning two blind eyes to it, given the quality of some of the stuff that was going around these days.

"My congratulations to the groom."

"I'll pass them on. Listen, Lyoshka, I was going to call you first thing. I asked around about your girl."

"Any luck?"

"Let me step into my office."

Korolev had visited Yasimov's *kommunalka*

315

— a former merchant's residence that had been divided, sub divided, and then divided once again so that there were now seventeen rooms in which bakers, factory workers, teachers, accountants, and one Militia detective and his family sweated and froze hip to hip. For privacy Yasimov would take the receiver into the toilet beside the phone, if by some miracle the convenience was free.

"There we go," Yasimov said as the background noise diminished considerably. "In here I'm a king as well, you know. Sitting on my throne."

Korolev laughed at the wordplay on his name, as much for the pleasure of hearing a joke he'd heard a hundred times before as anything else.

"What have you got for me?" he asked.

"You sound dreadful — got a cold or something?"

Korolev felt his shoulders relax and a smile tug at the straight line of his mouth. "Mitya, it's good to hear your voice, I can tell you."

"Now, don't get all emotional on me. Everything all right down there?"

"Could be better — the local uniforms have just managed to let our main suspect escape. And the likelihood is he's doing his best to slip across the border as we speak."

There was a pause, and he could almost hear Yasimov doing the computations. Korolev knew what conclusion his fellow detective would come to — a mishap like this wasn't good news for Korolev, of course, but it probably wouldn't be much better for people he knew and worked with. In other words, Yasimov.

"But you're on it, right? You'll catch up with him." Yasimov's voice had an edge to it now.

"I hope so. I don't think the fugitive killed the girl, which is something at least, and we've a good chance of picking him up before he gets too far. We'll see. Anyway, what did you find out about her?"

"Some things, I'm not sure how useful, though. The orphanage people spoke highly of her — proud, they were. I didn't find out much about her background for you, except for the name of her mother. Elizaveta Andreyevna Lenskaya. From down that way."

"Her mother?"

"Yes, when she died the girl was sent to the orphanage."

"I think that's her aunt — one moment." Korolev flicked back through his notebook. Andreychuk's wife was dead all right, she'd died back in 'thirty-three. What had her name been? Here it was. Anna. Anna Andreyevna Andreychuk. The patronymic was the same — Elizaveta must have been the sister who'd lived in Moscow. The one whose death had resulted in Lenskaya ending up in the orphanage.

"Yes — her aunt, most probably — but I thought they didn't have any information on her family."

"I'm guessing someone tidied the official file up a bit — it had that feel to it. But when we looked back at the admissions book the details were all there. The older Lenskaya was from some place called Angelinivka down near you — age at time of death thirty-three, occupation wages clerk. They lived in a communal apartment in Presnaya, but no one remembered them there. I dropped in and had a look around all the same. According to the housing office records, they shared a room with a family of five, so the orphanage was probably a change for the better."

"Angelinivka, you say?"

"That's what it says in the register."

"A place I'm visiting tomorrow, as it happens. Anything else?"

"Well, I asked around about her out at Mosfilm — a nice enough girl, I was told. Ambitious. By that they meant —"

"That she was friendly with Belakovsky?"

"That's the fellow. No one could think of a reason why she'd be murdered, though. I have the names of some other men she'd been friendly with. One will be familiar to you."

"Who's that?"

"Babel the writer."

"Babel?"

"A surprise?"

"Anything firm?" Korolev asked, ignoring Yasimov's question for the moment as his mind scrambled to fit the new piece of information together with what he knew already. Why had the writer not told him he was romantically connected with the victim? Unless, of course, he'd a damned good reason not to.

"Rumors. Want me to see if I can flesh it out a bit?"

"If you can find out *anything* useful to do with this damned case I'll be forever grateful, Mitya — it's turning out to be a pig. And the more about the girl's personal life the better."

"I'll see what I can do. One more thing, before you hang up."

"Go on."

"You asked about Lomatkin."

"Yes?"

"I had a sniff around. Interesting fellow

319

— a man about town, although not so much in recent months. He used to have a bit of a reputation — a few people have mentioned him spending time with undesirable elements and gambling at billiards. By undesirable elements, I mean elements with blue fingers." Thieves. In Moscow. Kolya's people, then. So there might be something in what the Thief had said about Lomatkin. "And there's some suggestion he might have dabbled in cocaine," Yasimov continued. "Although apparently he's a reformed character since he began seeing the dead girl. Make of that what you will."

Cocaine. Was that what Kolya had been getting at in his phone call?

"Anyone mention morphine?"

"No. Want me to go back and ask again?"

"It might be worth it. And see if you can find out more about these undesirable elements, will you, Mitya? And whether any of his acquaintances might be down here on the shoot. I'm interested in the cocaine — the autopsy shows the dead girl was drugged with morphine, that's why I'm asking."

"Got you," Yasimov said.

"Did you visit where she lived?"

"Yes — a small room in a *kommunalka* near the Mosfilm studios. Plain, simple, clean. A couple of shelves of books, quite a few of them foreign. A gramophone. Three records. Nothing much else. I sealed it in case you wanted a forensics team to look over it."

"Any letters, diaries, that sort of thing?"

"Nothing, but one of her neighbors told me she did keep a diary."

"I haven't found it if she did, but you can be sure I'll be searching hard for it now."

The door opened and Slivka looked in at him inquiringly, a pot of her own held in her hand. He waved her toward the chair in front of him.

"Mitya, brother, I owe you a favor."

"Lyoshka, you owe me a number of favors, and I owe you as many in return. Be careful there and come back to Moscow soon — the Thieves miss you."

Korolev hung up and filled his mouth with the last of the now cold stew.

"An interesting conversation, that," he said, still chewing, and relayed Yasimov's information about the dead girl, her possible relationship with Babel and about Lomatkin's blue-fingered friends.

"Angelinivka?" she said. "There's a coincidence."

"Yes — another coincidence, and I don't believe in coincidences. Not much, anyway."

"What are you thinking, Chief?"

"Thinking?" Korolev said, thinking, and therefore a little distracted. "Nothing much. But if Lenskaya's family are from this place, Angelinivka, then maybe that's why Andreychuk took her there. A family reason. His wife died in 'thirty-three. A tough year, but why wouldn't he bury her there if he could? It's not that far away. And when their daughter shows up out of the blue, what would she want to see? Her mother's grave, perhaps? It's a guess, but I've a feeling about it. She'd have been twelve when they parted ways, old enough to remember her mother well."

"So you still don't see him in the picture for the murderer?"

"When we catch him we'll see what we can get out of him — I've a feeling he'll have a story or two to tell us. But for now I want to find out about this trip they took. Seeing as it's so close to the border, it could fit Kolya's information as well."

"We'll see what tomorrow brings," Slivka said, taking a mouthful of food, and Korolev had to wait while she ate. "As for this Babel rumor, I've been going through the interviews earlier, the ones that the uniforms did. Babel is one of the people we haven't been able to confirm as being at the night shoot."

Korolev thought he knew the writer well enough to be pretty certain his friend was no killer. That was inconceivable. He'd a suspicion Babel would happily sit down with a murderer in a bar and drink with him while listening to his story, but that was another thing — a different thing. His curiosity was undeniable, but that didn't mean he'd ever actually pull the trigger on someone, or garrotte them for that matter.

"Anyone else we're missing?" he asked.

"All the crew are accounted for, although one or two of the actors aren't. At least so far — the actress Sorokina, for example."

Which reminded Korolev about what Babel had said to Sorokina about not giving away all her secrets. Perhaps it *had* been a warning.

"What are you thinking, Alexei Dmitriyevich?"

"I'm thinking you need to talk to Sorokina and I need to talk to Babel."

The writer looked disgruntled in the candlelight — the electricity was off for some reason, a power cut or some pressing industrial need, perhaps. On top of which the empty classroom was as cold as a prison cell. Korolev had bundled him out of bed and marched him across to the stable block, but Babel at least had had the good sense to put on his trousers, his boots and a heavy overcoat.

"I think now is as good a time as any to tell me about your relationship with Masha Lenskaya. Don't you?"

"What relationship?" Babel's irritation at his treatment was clear. There would be none of his usual jocularity this evening.

"That's what I want you to tell me. I've been informed, by a reliable source, that you were more than a friend to her. More like a lover — or so they're saying."

"That's ridiculous, who could think such a thing? Me, a middle-aged man, seducing a girl half my age? Do they really think such a thing is possible?" But the idea that he was still thought capable of seducing young women had apparently improved his mood.

"How old are you?" Korolev asked.

"How old do you think I am?" Babel lifted his head, interested.

"Isaac, tell me about the girl," Korolev asked with a patience he didn't feel.

"Forty-two, as it happens."

"So not twice her age, then. She was twenty-six. I don't know why you think it's strange — I don't think Tonya is much older."

Babel raised an eyebrow at the mention of

his wife.

"I wasn't sleeping with Masha Lenskaya, Alexei. Yes, I knew her, that's true — a lot of people knew her, after all. I may have provided fatherly advice from time to time but no more than that."

"Fatherly?"

"Yes. Fatherly. Or perhaps more like the advice an uncle might give. Or possibly an aunt familiar with the world."

"Aunt-like?"

"Something approximating to aunt-like, yes. Really, Korolev, you're a prude under that dynamite-proof cynicism of yours. We would speak from time to time, she and I. Not so strange. The girl had no living relatives, or so she thought, and she enjoyed having someone like me to talk to. Anyway, I've told you all this — that I knew her and what my assessment was of her character. I didn't think I needed to spell out every single detail. If you don't believe me, I'm beginning to think our friendship is built on sand."

Well, Yasimov had only said the girl was "friendly" with Babel. Perhaps on this occasion the rumors had been incorrect. Korolev took out his cigarettes and offered one to Babel — a peace offering.

"Isaac, I warn you. Now's the time to tell

325

me the truth about Lenskaya. If there's anything I should know — spit it out."

"When have I ever lied to you, Alexei? I had a relationship with her but it was a pure one."

"Aunt-like."

"Exactly."

Korolev decided to give the writer the benefit of the doubt, but he wasn't finished with him just yet.

"Isaac. Last night, just before I was going to interview Sorokina, you told her not to go giving away her intimate secrets. What did you mean by that?"

For the briefest of moments Babel looked like a small boy caught with his hand in a jar of sweets.

"You see, we've been doing our best to account for everyone's whereabouts at the time of the murder, Isaac," Korolev continued. "You seem to be missing. And so does Comrade Sorokina."

"All right, all right. I was with Barikada. An innocent walk in the moonlight, nothing to get het up about."

Korolev sighed. It was the sigh of a weary man being made even more weary by the antics of others.

"You should have told us straight away — now it looks bad. Did you spend the entire time with Sorokina? And I mean every moment."

"Yes."

"Now tell me about this walk."

"It was a walk. I wasn't needed on the set and neither was Sorokina. We slipped off. We're old friends, you see. We left just after the filming started and were back for the last take — nine-thirty."

"I see, and you're sure she didn't leave your sight — while I can't see any reason for you to kill the girl, she's a different story."

"Barikada? A killer?"

"She was Ezhov's mistress."

"I'm aware of that," Babel said, stubbing out the cigarette on the sole of his boot, "but she had nothing to do with the girl's death — I'll swear to that. I didn't lie to you, Alexei, I just didn't tell you everything. I thought it was for the best. Not so much for my sake, as for hers. She's with Savchenko now, you see, and if her walk with me had come to light it might have complicated matters. Not just for her, but for me as well."

"This is a murder investigation, Isaac. It's not up to you to decide what you should tell me."

"I understand that —" Babel began.

327

Korolev held up a hand to stop him. "Don't bother. Is there anything you need to tell me about this moonlight walk of yours?"

"Only that I think you can rule out Andreychuk as the killer." Babel put a hand in his pocket and produced what seemed to be a list of names. "I looked for you earlier to give you this, but I couldn't find you. These are the names of the people we have identified in each scene and the times of filming. Andreychuk first appears at eighteen minutes past eight and is in every scene until the end."

Babel handed him the piece of paper.

"I see," Korolev said, looking over it. "But there is still a small window of opportunity."

"No, there's a scene that was filmed just before eight which he isn't in. It had to be reshot because a soundman dropped his microphone boom in front of the camera. Barikada and I were there for that scene, whatever your witnesses may say."

Korolev looked through the list of scenes, each with a precise time and a list of names. Andreychuk's appeared in each one, sure enough.

"Well?" Korolev said, not sure why this was as significant as Babel seemed to think.

"We saw Lenskaya after that. At about ten

minutes past eight, I would say. She was sitting at her typewriter in her office and alive."

"But why didn't you tell us this before?" Korolev said, mystified.

"It wasn't until I started doing the timings that I realized. I thought we saw her before Andreychuk locked up the house, but that isn't possible. The film shoot is a minimum ten minutes' walk from the house. We must have passed Andreychuk on the way, although we didn't see him. When we saw her, Andreychuk would have already been down in the village."

Korolev looked at the timings once again. If the caretaker hadn't committed the crime, who had? And who'd helped him escape, and why?

CHAPTER EIGHTEEN

The bedroom window squeaked as Korolev rubbed at it, clearing the mist. The sky outside was a dark, dark blue. Dawn was imminent and it looked promising — it wasn't raining, and it wasn't snowing, even if at some stage during the night a thin carpet of white had been spread across the landscape. To his surprise, he found himself optimistic about the day ahead — it was a day that promised to be one of revelations and developments, and in his experience that was the sort of day you wanted to get a head start on. He turned to look at Les Pins, snuggled under what appeared to be an unfair allocation of blankets, and then made his way to the bathroom.

Ten minutes later he was making his way across the courtyard when he saw a familiar figure come out of the corner cottage.

"Comrade Mushkina," Korolev called out.

She turned toward him, her eyes squinting as if struggling to identify him.

"Korolev?"

"Yes, Korolev. I was wondering if I could have a few moments of your time."

"I'm just going for a walk," Mushkina replied, indicating the path that led around the side of the house with a flick of her stick.

"I'm sure it won't take more than a moment. We could go back inside if you'd like."

Although, now that he thought of it, her cottage contained the angry Chekist major who was also her son. Why hadn't he offered to talk to her in the investigation room? It was almost as close.

"Come in and welcome," she said, opening the door to a small hallway and leading the way. Korolev took off his hat and dipped underneath the lintel even though it wasn't that close to his head. He followed Mushkina through to a large sitting room.

"I'm sorry to disturb you," he said.

"That's quite all right, Korolev."

A copy of Furmanov's *Chapayev* lay on the table, the faded lettering of the title barely legible on its upturned spine. It looked as though it had been read more than a few times. She'd been a political commissar herself, hadn't she? Perhaps the book had some resonance for her.

"What can I do for you?" she asked, following his eyeline to the book, then examining him in turn as though searching for the answers to some questions of her own. Korolev had to remind himself that he was the one meant to be interrogating her, not the other way round.

"I've heard about the events down at the Militia station, if that's what you've come to tell me about," she said, before he had a chance to ask her anything. "A great surprise. Andreychuk always gave the impression of being a good worker but it seems we must be careful of even those we feel we know quite well these days."

Korolev took his notebook from his overcoat pocket, opening it at the first clean page.

"It's about Citizen Andreychuk I've come."

"I guessed as much."

"It's possible he took a journey over toward Krasnogorka last week. With Citizen Lenskaya. Do you know anything about that?"

"I think he said something about having been asked to drive one of the film people somewhere, but he didn't mention where to, or who had asked him."

"Do you remember the day?"

"Thursday, perhaps. I'm not sure. He said it wouldn't affect his other duties, so I agreed and gave it no more thought."

"He went to a village called Angelinivka; it's on the border."

"Yes, the Dnester runs past it. Although it's wide at that point."

"Did he have a pass to visit the area?"

"He would have had, yes. We have connections with kolkhozes in the border areas, and have students over there at this very moment."

"So he could have been over that way quite often recently?"

"Several times since the new year."

It occurred to Korolev that if Andreychuk *was* involved in some kind of terrorist conspiracy, this would be a perfect cover. He considered the point for a moment before changing tack.

"Did you see anything unusual yesterday — at the time of Andreychuk's escape? I believe you were walking near the village at around six o'clock."

"Yes, with Comrade Les Pins. We didn't go into the village itself, but we were close enough. If I'd seen anything suspicious you can be assured I would have informed you directly."

"I'm sure you would," Korolev replied,

flicking back through the pages of his notebook to check his memory of his conversation with Les Pins the night before. "Did you say you were with Comrade Les Pins?"

"Yes. He speaks a Russian you don't hear much these days. I like to listen to him."

"I was curious about that," Korolev said. "Where he acquired such Russian, I mean."

"His father was a diplomat in Petersburg for a few years at the end of the last century; he went home with a Russian wife," Mushkina said, before correcting herself. "In Leningrad, I meant. But Les Pins is still a good comrade, despite his class background. He has some interesting insights into the situation in Spain."

"And where did your walk take you?"

"Around the house and the College mainly."

"I wonder if I could have your exact route, Comrade Mushkina. At what time you started walking, at what time you finished, and who you met. If anyone."

Mushkina looked at him sharply, but her voice, when she responded, was calm.

"Timing is difficult, Comrade Captain. I don't wear a watch. But if you say it was at six o'clock then I won't disagree with you. It could well have been, it was certainly get-

334

ting dark. I would think we left not long before five-thirty, we took a walk around the lake, and then he accompanied me around the College. We saw a few of the film people and Gradov, the sergeant from the village. But we didn't speak to anyone. I would imagine we finished here no later than six-thirty."

"And you went nowhere near the village?"

"No."

"And you didn't see Lomatkin, the journalist?"

"Should we have seen him?"

"Not necessarily. And if you didn't see him, you didn't see him. Now, if you don't mind, let's go over it once again — and if you can give me the descriptions of the film people you saw, I'd be grateful. It may be they saw something that you didn't."

The shadows cast by the courtyard buildings were long in the watery dawn sun when Korolev left Mushkina's cottage. As he walked back toward the house he wondered why Les Pins had said he was reading in his room at the time of the escape, when in fact he'd been with Mushkina. And then there was Andreychuk driving around the border area at will — what was he to make of that?

He looked up to find himself face to face

with Slivka. She looked surprisingly chirpy for first thing in the morning.

"You look like you slept well," he said.

"Spectacularly, Chief. Really — a world-class sleep. A sleep the like of which an American millionaire would give his last dollar for."

"I'm pleased for you."

"We've had a bit of luck," Slivka said, smiling. "Lomatkin's print showed up in the station. Firtov just called to tell me."

"Lomatkin's?" Korolev said, thinking hard. "Where in the station?"

"On the bars of the cell."

"Interesting. Anywhere else?"

"Not so far."

"Any other unidentified prints?"

"They're still going through them. But don't you see? This means he was there."

"You're right, it's good news. Did you call your mother, by the way?"

"I did, she was pleased to hear from me. She thinks it will snow again later on."

So no word from Kolya yet, then.

"Well, let's have a word with the famous journalist, shall we?"

They fell into step and walked toward the house as he told her Mushkina's news.

"What do you think?" he asked as they climbed the stairs to the veranda, in front of the windows Lenskaya had sat behind the night she'd died.

"Did we ever fingerprint Les Pins, Chief?"

"I believe so, but check with Firtov," Korolev said as they entered the dining room. There was laughter at the far end, but it fizzled out as Korolev's cold gaze searched for Lomatkin among the faces that turned toward the door in curiosity. Shymko was sitting with Belakovsky at the nearest table and Korolev approached them, leaning down to ask quietly for the whereabouts of the journalist.

"He left about ten minutes ago," Shymko said.

"For the western defenses." Belakovsky confirmed. "Comrade Babel went with him. But he left you a note, didn't he?"

"Lomatkin?"

"No, Babel."

"Babel left me a note?" Korolev said, wondering what the writer was up to. "Where is this note?"

It turned out the note was with Larisa in the investigation room and it was short and to the point:

Dear Korolev,
Lomatkin is visiting Krasnogorka and I've decided to go along with him. I

hope we'll be able to meet tomorrow instead.

Babel

Korolev was confused. He wasn't supposed to be meeting Babel. He turned to Slivka, showing her the piece of paper.

"I think we need to call your friends in the border guards again."

Slivka drove, her peaked cap turned backward on her head as if this would in some way improve the car's aerodynamics, and her shoulders hunched over the wheel as if her pushing it forward would propel the vehicle faster. After yet another two-wheeled corner Korolev decided it was time to rein her in.

"Listen, Slivka, it won't do much good if we arrive in a pair of coffins."

Slivka looked at him in frustration.

"But what if he escapes?"

"Lomatkin? We've alerted the whole countryside — if the border guards haven't set up roadblocks on every cart track from here to Kiev I'd be surprised. Don't worry, we'll catch up with them soon enough."

Indeed, they were approaching a checkpoint even as he spoke — a khaki-colored car had pulled into the side of the road and a truck with brown canvas sides was barring the way ahead. The spot had been chosen well; on both sides of the road there were deep drainage ditches that would soon put a stop to anyone who tried to break through, but the heavy machine gun aiming at them would probably halt most vehicles short of a tank long before that.

Slivka stopped the car and Korolev showed his identification to the officer who approached them, hand on the butt of his holstered revolver.

"What's a Moscow detective doing in this part of the world?" the border guard asked, having examined the Militia card for long enough to have spelled it out letter by letter.

"I'm assisting Odessa CID with a murder inquiry. I take it you fellows are looking for someone called Andreychuk. Well, so are we. You're doing it at our request."

The fellow looked down at the Militia card once again, and then back at Korolev, his face relaxing from warily vigilant to something more quizzical, possibly even amused. He pointed to the identification photograph.

"Korolev. Alexei Dmitriyevich? Didn't you used to play football for Presnaya? A few years back — central defender?"

Korolev examined the border guard afresh — he didn't look that old. Twenty-five maybe? It was strange to have your past brought up in the middle of the steppe by a fresh-faced youngster.

"A long time ago, perhaps. But even I've half-forgotten that."

"My father played goalkeeper. Ivanov?"

"Ivanov?" Korolev looked at the boy's face and caught the echo of another one. Nikolai Ivanov. "I remember him. Spared our blushes many's the time. You must be young Alexander. Sandro, isn't it?"

"Yes, that's me." The boy's face creased into a pleased smile.

"How did you end up here?"

"I was posted," Ivanov replied, looking around at the boundless horizon, flat in every direction except for the occasional line of trees marking the edges of the fields and calming the wind that whistled across them. The proud lift of the chin didn't quite convince Korolev that Sandro wouldn't rather be serving somewhere else.

"If you see my father, tell him I'm well," the boy said, handing him back his Militia card.

"I will. But, tell me, we're also looking for two men who might have come this way not so long ago — Lomatkin and Babel. We asked that they be detained."

"We heard nothing of it," Ivanov said, looking concerned. "They came through about fifteen minutes ago — heading for Krasnogorka. Not every day we get famous people traveling on these roads."

"I see," Korolev said, disappointed but not surprised that the alert hadn't reached him. "Do you have a radio?"

"We do."

"Can you call ahead and request that the next checkpoint hold them?"

"The next checkpoint is in Krasnogorka."

"That'll do. There should be an alert out for them already — but just in case."

"You're looking for this fellow Andrey-chuk, you said? Are you going to look over his truck?"

"His truck?" Korolev asked, confused as to what Ivanov was talking about. His face must have given him away because the boy pointed over his shoulder.

"You don't know? We found the truck — in Angelinivka. About an hour ago."

Korolev turned to Slivka, who was waiting for his decision. Follow the truck or Lomatkin and Babel?

"How do we get there from here?" Korolev asked, making his decision. The border

341

guards would hold Babel and Lomatkin for them.

"Go straight ahead, you'll see a signpost in a few miles."

"Thank you. One last thing?" Korolev asked, extracting one of the photographs of Lenskaya he'd brought with him from the dashboard. "Have you seen this woman recently?"

Ivanov looked at the photograph for a few moments, then shook his head.

"No, and to be honest I'd remember a girl like that if she came through a checkpoint around here."

Korolev took the picture back from Ivanov. Was that the thing he'd missed? How different she was? Now that she'd been in Moscow for twelve years, and America as well — that here, in the land where she'd been born, she was as exotic as Barikada Sorokina?

"Good to see you, Alexei Dmitriyevich," Ivanov said as Korolev pointed Slivka toward the road ahead.

"I'll remember you to your father."

The signpost for Angelinivka seemed to have been used for target practice, on top of which what was left of the letters had been sanded by the wind to the point where they

342

were barely legible. Slivka slowed down and then halted, looking to Korolev for a final decision. He looked around them. There wasn't a clump of brush big enough to call a bush for a mile in any direction and the few winter-stripped trees that were visible looked like black skeletons praying to heaven for forgiveness. It was a grim enough place. The Lord knew he'd be glad to get away from here and back to Moscow. And the thought of Moscow, six hundred miles away, reminded him of Valentina Niko-laevna and the way she'd put her hand on his chest when the NKVD man had knocked on the door. He wondered what it had meant, that small moment of intimacy. It was something he'd avoided considering in the time since, but now, for some reason, the way she'd looked at him and the feel of her hand pressing against him seemed like something to hold on to. He nodded to Slivka, who turned left toward Angelinivka.

The village itself, when they got there, barely deserved the name — two dusty lines of dilapidated buildings that met at a rutted crossroads. There was no sign of the border guard or the truck Andreychuk had stolen. In fact there was no sign of anyone at all. Slivka drove slowly past the long low peas-ant houses, with wooden walls more gray than brown emerging from mud foundations and straining under snow-topped damp thatch. A dog with legs as thin as whips tottered to its feet in front of them, baring its teeth but unable or unwilling to muster the energy to bark. Korolev had seen more depressing places, but he couldn't for the life of him remember when.

"Where are the people?" Slivka asked.

"I don't know, Slivka, but there's the church — and that's what Andreychuk and Lenskaya came to see."

The church stood about a hundred yards past the last house in the village and around it stood the wooden crosses of a graveyard. As they drove toward it, Andreychuk's truck came into view, along with two cold-looking sentries, who unslung their rifles when they saw them.

"Militia," Korolev said, holding out his identity card for inspection. A tall youth with an acned face looked down at the card, his brows contracting as he read it. His comrade, another one barely out of his teens but half the other's size, stood to the side, his rifle held at waist height aiming at a spot just behind Korolev's ear.

"Point that damned gun somewhere else," Korolev said, and the short boy's eyes came to life. He turned to his comrade, who handed Korolev's Militia card back to him as though it was red hot.

"You're happy with my identification, are you?" Korolev growled.

"Absolutely, Comrade Captain," he said.

"Good," Korolev said, opening the door, pleased to see he had at least three inches on the two sentries, and a good deal of weight to boot.

"When did you find it?"

"An hour back, Comrade Captain."

"I thought your people searched the village last night," Korolev said to the taller guard.

"Yes, Comrade Captain. At eight o'clock and at eleven, but it wasn't here then."

Korolev walked over to the truck, noticing the thin even layer of snow on top of the hood. It had been there for a while.

"Are you searching the area?"

"Two sweeps have gone north and south on a two-mile width, Comrade Captain. Men every twenty yards." The guard pointed across the fields to where some men with rifles could be seen walking in line some distance away. "And we've been through the village as well, and the church of course."

Korolev looked up at the dome of the church. Close up it was clear the facade had suffered since the arrival of Soviet Power, and not just the paint either — bullet holes marked the stone walls in a steady line, on top of which the crucifix was gone from the dome and, to judge from the chipping around the stump, it too had been the target of the machine gunner's attention.

"Why is the village empty?"

"They were moved to the kolkhoz farm up the road last week, Comrade Captain. Soviet Success. It's about two and a half miles away." Again he pointed, this time along the road that led away from the village and to a new future. "They're knocking this place down. It will be fields by the summer."

Clearly no one had told the emaciated dog about the move.

"We should look inside," Korolev said.

The church's interior was even colder than outdoors — the solid, still cold of a meat locker. Predictably it had been desecrated. Who knew who'd done it? Party activists who'd come from the cities to lead the peasants to collectivization by example, and had ended up forcing them to it at gunpoint? Soldiers? Border guards? It didn't matter now — the damage had been done. They picked their way through the debris gingerly — to judge from the stench the place had been used as a latrine — but there was nothing to indicate the caretaker had been there, or his daughter.

Stepping outside again, Korolev looked at the two sentries, huddled in the lee of the truck, inhaling warmth from cigarettes they protected with both hands. Korolev nodded toward the worn-looking wooden Orthodox crosses in the cemetery — crosses that were from a different time, when such a symbol wasn't considered to be a political statement. After not more than a minute's searching, they came across the recently tended grave of Anna Andreychuk.

"His wife?" Slivka asked.

"Possibly," Korolev said, running a finger along the wooden plank that spelled out her demise. No cross for Andreychuk's wife under Soviet Power. So was this the reason for the visit Andreychuk had made with his daughter to this place? A final act of remembrance before the village was bulldozed and forgotten? At least Andreychuk's wife would still be here when the Lord came looking for her on the day of judgment. Nothing else would. Not the house she'd been born in, nor the church where she'd worshipped. Even the marker on her grave would be removed when they turned the cemetery into tillage.

They were just getting back into the car

when a soldier came running from the fields.

"We've found him," he shouted breathlessly to the sentries, "down by the river. Dead."

CHAPTER NINETEEN

From a distance the body looked like nothing more than a pile of crumpled clothing, the worn boots only a foot away from the wide river's bank. The only thing that marked Andreychuk out as anything other than rags was the puddle of frozen blood that surrounded him.

"Has anyone touched the body?" Korolev asked the captain commanding the detachment.

"If anyone has, it was before I got here," he replied. "I was a Militiaman myself for two years, in Omsk."

Korolev watched the wind turn the white hair on the dead man's head. Then he looked across the river.

"You did well," he said after a long pause. "Can you get a message to Dr. Peskov at the School of Anatomy in Odessa? I'd like him to see the body as it was found." He studied the sky — it was clear for the moment. Hopefully they wouldn't have to cover the corpse. "We'll need a forensics team to come out as well; Peskov can pass the message on."

As the captain left, Korolev turned his attention back to the river bank, approaching a little closer to examine the dead man. Andreychuk's face — robbed of life — seemed thinner, the beard more disheveled. His eyes were open and Korolev resisted the temptation to lean down and close them.

"Only the crayfish becomes more beautiful with death," he muttered to himself.

"What was that?" Slivka asked.

"Nothing. Just a stupid saying." He didn't feel comfortable repeating it and fortunately she didn't press him. The entry wound was in the nape of the neck, and while there was a revolver in Andreychuk's hand, it seemed unlikely that he would have shot himself in such a way. This looked like murder to Korolev. He leaned forward to look more closely at the gun. A Nagant. Could it be a souvenir of Andreychuk's fighting days? Korolev had carried a Nagant himself when he'd fought for the tsar, and another when he'd fought for the Red Army in the Civil War. They were still standard issue for the Militia and the army, and Korolev was an exception in that he carried a smaller

Walther he'd acquired from a Polish officer back in 'twenty-two — but then there were different rules for detectives. Andreychuk's weapon looked as though it wasn't long from the factory, but he didn't like the barrel one bit. It looked shorter than the army version and, as far as he knew, these short-barreled Nagants were only issued to the Militia or State Security. He pointed it out to Slivka.

"It looks like it could be one of ours," she said, peering down at it. "Easily checked, though. It will have a serial number and there'll be a record."

"Well, let's see what we can find out about it."

It looked as if the dead man had been kneeling when he'd died, and the body had fallen forward and onto its side. Korolev mimicked holding a pistol behind his head to see if suicide was even remotely possible.

"Don't do it, Alexei Dmitriyevich. The case isn't over yet," Slivka said in a dry tone. He almost smiled, putting his hands back in his pockets and looking again at the corpse. Snow covered parts of the body, and more had gathered along the dead man's side where the wind had pushed it.

"Time of death, Slivka, that's what we're looking for," Korolev said as the border

351

guard captain returned. "Comrade Captain, when did it stop snowing? He obviously died before then. And there's snow on the truck as well."

"I'm not sure. Before six anyway; it hasn't snowed since I started on duty. I'll check with the sentries at the nearest control point."

"I'd be grateful." Korolev glanced across the field toward the church. There were tracks in the snow here and there.

"There were no tracks around the truck when we found it," the captain said, as if anticipating his thoughts. "They were the first thing I looked for."

Korolev nodded and turned to Slivka.

"Stay here with the body until Dr. Peskov and the forensics boys arrive. Don't let Firtov and the Greek start till Dr. Peskov has had a good look and, likewise, don't let Peskov take the body away until they've done their work. We'll need a proper autopsy done in Odessa, but ask him for his preliminary impressions."

"Of course, Chief."

"And show Lenskaya's photograph around — see if any of these border guards recognize her. Or Andreychuk for that matter. Someone must have seen them when they visited last week."

Slivka nodded and he put a hand on her arm for a moment by way of thanks.

"Comrade Captain." Korolev turned to address the border guard officer. "Have you got tracking dogs nearby?"

"I can have some here within thirty minutes," he said, curiosity narrowing his eyes.

"I'd like to see if they could trace the dead man's steps from the church. Just to make certain. And to see if he was alone when he arrived, or if he brought his killer with him."

"We'll see what we can do."

"Thank you, Comrade."

Korolev took the keys to the car from Slivka and walked back across the field toward the church, wondering what Lomatkin would have to say about Andreychuk's escape from the station and his death beside the Dnester with a bullet in the back of his neck.

It didn't take Korolev long to drive to Krasnogorka, and any concerns he'd had about tracking his quarries down were soon allayed — Lomatkin and Babel's car was parked beside a border guard checkpoint just before the road entered the town. They looked around as he approached and Korolev was not surprised to detect anger in Lomatkin's animated reaction. Damned

Korolev this, damned Korolev that, he didn't doubt. They were probably half-frozen by now — come to think of it, he wasn't that warm himself after walking around graveyards and fields.

"Captain Korolev, Militia CID." He held up his identification card for the border guard sergeant to inspect. "You're detaining those two for me."

"We are. That Lomatkin fellow has been threatening all sorts, Comrade Captain."

"We'll see about that. Have you somewhere I can talk to them?"

"There's the barracks in town."

Korolev considered the offer and then decided to interrogate Lomatkin in the car. It would be quicker.

"I'll speak to them here," he replied. "Could you bring Citizen Lomatkin over first? Let me see if I can't calm him down."

When summoned, the journalist approached the car with his bottom lip pouting like a stubborn child's. Korolev produced his notebook and wet the graphite tip of his pencil with his tongue as Lomatkin settled himself into the passenger seat.

"What the hell is all this about, Korolev? You're sabotaging vital work — I have to file a piece for *Izvestia* by this evening and that's not looking likely now, is it?"

Korolev wrote the time and date at the top of the open page, allowing his pencil to linger over each letter.

"Well, come on — out with it. Why have you detained us?"

Korolev did his best to look surprised.

"Why do you think I had you detained? We all have vital work to do, Citizen Lomatkin. And orders to follow."

"Are you making fun of me? We're held here with no explanation and then you just happen to drive past? Of course you're responsible for this."

"You think I can boss border guards around? A simple Militia captain from Moscow giving that lot orders? It doesn't work that way, Lomatkin. You should know that. I could ask them, certainly — but would they comply? Difficult to say."

The journalist's petulant look began to be tempered with unease.

"Comrade Ezhov could order them, I expect," Korolev added, taking a cigarette from his pocket. "They report to him, of course. All of them. This particular platoon, I suppose, would have to go through a few layers of command, but eventually they most certainly do report to Comrade Ezhov. Yes, I expect Comrade Ezhov could order them to do just about anything he wanted them to do, and then it would happen as day follows night. And as we both know, he was very fond of Masha Lenskaya."

Korolev struck a match for his cigarette and the flare splashed Lomatkin's pale face with yellow light. The journalist had the look of a man concentrating very hard.

"What do you want, Korolev?"

"Well, for a start, you might explain why you saw fit to ignore my instructions not to leave the film set."

"You never gave me such instructions. You told me not to leave tomorrow for Sebastopol, but this is a short trip. I'd have been back at the house by now if you — if someone — hadn't delayed things."

"My instructions were clear, Lomatkin. You're a suspect and you stay where I tell you to until I say otherwise."

It wasn't the first time Korolev had found his temper bubbling up since he'd got off the plane from Moscow, but this time he felt it boiling over.

"I'm a suspect? But I was in Moscow, Korolev. It simply isn't possible that I could be responsible for her death."

"I don't care if you were on the moon, Lomatkin. You were her lover, you've told me you wanted to marry her, you have, let us say, a dubious background and she was sleeping with other men. So maybe you didn't kill Lenskaya yourself, fair enough — but you could have conspired with someone else to do it, or paid them. I don't know which, but I don't want you skipping over the border before I've found out."

"What do you mean?" Lomatkin protested. "What dubious background? I'm a Party member, Korolev. And you'd do well to remember it."

"A Party member, is it? I doubt you bring up your cocaine addiction in any Party meetings, do you? And I'm guessing the bosses at *Izvestia* don't know about it either."

"Cocaine?" Lomatkin's voice rose to a shrill pitch. "I'm not addicted to cocaine. Are you mad?"

"So you just took it from time to time, is that right?"

"I don't know what you mean . . ." The journalist dragged out each word, but it wasn't Korolev's job to be giving Lomatkin time to think.

"What? You've forgotten all those games of billiards with those Thief friends of yours? They've slipped your memory as well, have they?" Korolev was filling in a bit of detail but, to judge from Lomatkin's shocked expression, he wasn't too far off the mark.

"Those are gross exaggerations — as a journalist sometimes I have to —" But Korolev held up a hand to stop him.

"Don't waste your breath, Citizen Lomatkin. For a start, I don't have time to be writing down your worthless excuses and, second, I'm investigating a murder — no — two murders now. Believe me, if you irritate me by not cooperating fully, I'll make sure what I know is passed on to people who take an interest in these things."

"Two murders?"

"Your friend, Andreychuk. He's lying on his face with a bullet in the back of his neck six miles from here."

"Andreychuk's dead?"

"You sound surprised."

"I . . ." began Lomatkin, "I heard he'd escaped — but for him to be dead . . ."

"You know nothing about his death either, of course."

"No, of course not. What are you suggesting?"

"I'm suggesting I'll see about that. And I'll take my time seeing. You're under arrest."

Lomatkin's face paled. "For what?"

"For letting Andreychuk out of his cell, that's what. And then conspiring with someone to have a bullet placed in his skull."

Lomatkin fell silent. He looked at Korolev, speechless, and Korolev wondered whether he was in shock at the uncovering of his crime, or just bewildered at the predicament he found himself in.

"Letting him out of his cell?" the journalist eventually repeated.

"That's what I said."

"What makes you think —" Lomatkin began, and Korolev took his hand and turned it palm upward. He tapped each fingertip one by one.

"Little. Fingers. Leave. Little. Prints. And these little fingers left prints all over Andreychuk's cell door. Now, seeing as I've just left Andreychuk's body not so very far from here with a bullet hole in his head, and seeing as I'm now sitting here with you and the same little fingers that smudged up that cell door, I'm wondering is that just a coincidence or something else? To put it bluntly, I'd like you to do some explaining."

"About the fingerprints?" Lomatkin asked, his eyes now round with terror.

"Yes, about the damned fingerprints, about the way you decided to drive over here to a place where Andreychuk ended up dead. While we're at it, we'll have a little talk about the morphine we found in Lenskaya's stomach and whether that might have some connection with the cocaine you enjoy so much."

Lomatkin took a deep breath, as if he were trying to gather his courage, to calm himself.

"I can explain," he said.

Korolev folded his arms and settled himself into the seat.

"Explain, then."

Lomatkin took another deep breath.

"The truth is I went to the station yesterday. I went to visit Andreychuk. I wanted an explanation from him, to understand something about Masha's death."

He paused, sighing.

"Anyway, when I arrived the door to the station was open so I just walked in. There was no one there, Korolev. No Andreychuk, no Militia, nobody. The cell is right there, and it was open as well. I also called upstairs just in case, but the whole place was empty. I looked inside the cell, I must have touched the bars or the wood when I did, but Korolev — he was already gone. And when I got back to the house and I heard he'd escaped, I kept my mouth shut. That was stupid, I see that now, but I swear I had nothing to do with his escape."

"What kind of a fool do you take me for?"

360

"It's what happened, Korolev. God help me, it's what happened. I wanted to ask him about Masha, what he knew, why it had happened. That's all."

Korolev considered the journalist's story and took his time doing it. Lomatkin looked back at him unblinkingly — if he was lying, he wasn't bad at it. And he must be lying.

"And what time did this all happen?"

"About six o'clock."

"About? You need to be more specific than that, Lomatkin."

"Just before six, then. I'm not sure exactly, I didn't look at my watch. It could have been a quarter of an hour before. Now that I think of it, I'm sure of it. About a quarter to six, that's when I arrived."

Korolev considered the timing, almost allowing himself to entertain the possibility that Lomatkin might be the victim of extraordinary bad luck, but then he remembered he wasn't there to witness miracles, but to uncover the truth. And the fellow would know the timings just as well if he'd let the caretaker out as if he'd stumbled upon the escape after it had taken place.

"You say you saw no one, not even in the village?"

"The village was deserted. I saw one of the Militia near the house, but apart from him, no one."

That would be Gradov, who'd seen Lomatkin as well.

"You didn't see anyone driving past? The truck Andreychuk drove, or Sergeant Gradov in the Militia car, perhaps?"

"I didn't walk back along the road. There's a path through the trees."

It occurred to Korolev that if he looked at the situation from a different point of view, an interesting question presented itself. How had Lomatkin known the station would be open, or rather that the key would be hidden under a brick around the corner and the uniforms away? Helping Andreychuk to escape would have required some local knowledge which the journalist probably didn't have and a large dose of luck — or assistance. And then there was also the fact that Lomatkin couldn't have put the bullet in the back of Andreychuk's head because he'd been back at the College when the caretaker had died, at least if the snow was anything to go by. But why shouldn't there have been two of them involved? Clearly someone else had killed the caretaker and perhaps that person had been the one with the local knowledge. And that person had probably also killed Lenskaya.

"Who are you working with, Lomatkin?

And why did you need to free Andreychuk in the first place? That's what I'd like to find out. Did he know enough to point the finger at you for Lenskaya?"

"I'd nothing to do with Masha's death, Korolev, and nothing to do with Andreychuk's escape. And I know nothing about the murders either — I swear on my mother's grave, I know nothing about anything."

Korolev looked at the journalist and wondered whether his mother was even dead. He wound down the window and beckoned the border guards over.

"Comrades, can you hold this man for me for a little while? He's under arrest."

He heard Lomatkin let out a low moan which he ignored, instead leaning across him to open the passenger door as the border guards came round.

"You'll be seeing the inside of a cell again before the day is out, Citizen Lomatkin," Korolev said, irritation as much as anger adding a gravelly growl to his voice. "Only there won't be anyone coming along to let you out."

"But this is a mistake, Korolev," Lomatkin said, his eyes black in his white face.

"I doubt it."

The border guards stood beside the car, either side of Lomatkin's door, waiting. The journalist glanced out at them, then back to Korolev, looking like a man who'd been handed a death sentence, and stepped out of the car. As the guards led him away, Korolev lit up a cigarette, thinking that there was something about smoking that kept a man sane in this job of his, then got out and walked over to the other car, where Babel waited.

"Alexei," the writer said as Korolev opened the driver's door. "You got my message? I thought it best to hitch a ride in case he was making a bolt for it. Did I do the right thing?"

Korolev shrugged. "You did the right thing. We found his fingerprint on Andreychuk's cell door, so it looks like he had something to do with his escape. But what made you suspect him?"

"The morphine. I remembered what you said about the morphine and then I recalled Lomatkin had a past with such things. When he said he was going off toward Krasnogorka I thought I'd better go too."

Korolev examined the glowing end of his cigarette, trying to work out whether there was enough tobacco left for another go at it. He decided there was and felt the heat on his lips and his fingers as he inhaled.

"Have you arrested him?"

Korolev looked at Lomatkin, a lonely figure as he walked toward the town between the two border guards, and sighed.

"Yes."

CHAPTER TWENTY

A quick call from the local Militia station to Colonel Marchuk in Odessa and a secure cell in the Bebel Street headquarters was set aside for Lomatkin. It wouldn't be ideal having him locked up so far away from the College, but at least he would be there when Korolev went looking for him. The arrangements made, Korolev called Colonel Rodinov and brought him up to date on Andreychuk's death and Lomatkin's arrest.

"I see," Rodinov said finally, when Korolev had finished speaking. There was a long pause and Korolev began to wonder if the strange whirring of machinery coming down the line wasn't the sound of the Chekist's brain turning over.

"I'm concerned by these developments, Korolev," the colonel said eventually. "It seems to me it would be better if I were nearby. I'll fly down tomorrow. We need a resolution to this business, Korolev.

And soon."

Korolev felt his stomach plummet to the toes of his boots, where it stayed for the rest of the conversation, stayed while he watched Lomatkin placed in the back of a police van bound for Odessa and stayed there throughout the journey back to Angelinivka. The village was still deserted, the only difference being that the skeletal dog had now passed on to a heavenly hunting ground and his body was being picked over by two quarreling crows. Korolev pulled the car over just past the church and got out.

Slivka was waiting for him beside the border guard truck — he'd been gone for nearly three hours, but she'd waited for him. She looked up from her notebook as he approached and nodded. The body had gone and he supposed that meant they had a date with Dr. Peskov in the School of Anatomy.

"Any news?" Korolev said, offering her one of his three remaining cigarettes.

"A couple of things, Chief," Slivka said, cupping her hands around the match he lit for her. "Firtov has more fingerprints from the station. They don't belong to the Militiamen, Andreychuk, or Lomatkin. Or us, for that matter. They're working on identifying them. At this stage they think it's one individual."

"They could belong to anyone, of course."

"They've fingerprinted most of the villagers for the Lenskaya matter and Firtov says the Greek will crack it, if anyone can. He seemed confident. And that's not all — Firtov said the Greek was making progress on the partial fingerprint, the one on the bracket from which the girl was found hanging."

"What does he mean by 'progress?' "

"As of this morning, the Greek had limited the possible matches to six people, and Firtov reckons he'll have narrowed it down still further by now."

Korolev felt a stab of irritation.

"Narrowed? What's this narrowing good for? Why can't he just tell us who's on this list of his now? We're detectives, not judges. If they give us the names we can do some narrowing of our own. What's the point of keeping quiet about it?"

"He wants to be sure — there isn't much of a print, he says, and the Greek takes his time. But the important news is they're sure the fingerprint doesn't belong to Andreychuk and it doesn't belong to Shymko either."

Korolev hesitated, more curious than ever about this damned fingerprint. Andreychuk and Shymko had been the ones who'd cut the girl down and if the fingerprint wasn't theirs, who did it belong to? He'd have some names out of the Greek before the day was out — even if the fellow couldn't speak and didn't want to tell him.

"What did Firtov make of Andreychuk?" he asked, swallowing his frustration along with a lungful of smoke.

"Same as us — murder. He took the gun back to Odessa, as well as Andreychuk's truck."

"I see. And Peskov?"

"The same. Gunshot wound to the back of the head. Death instantaneous."

Slivka pointed at where the snow had been cleared away to reveal a spray of frozen gore.

"He was pretty confident that Andreychuk was kneeling when he was killed, but he said he'd have a better idea once he'd examined him at the School of Anatomy."

Korolev grunted, not relishing the thought of another autopsy — if he never had to attend one again he'd die a happy man.

"Anything else?"

"The captain had his dogs running around here for a while, but they came up with nothing. But he checked with the nearest roadblock — the snow stopped falling at around two in the morning."

Korolev considered the new information.

"Did you get a chance to call your mother?" he asked eventually.

Slivka looked pointedly around her at the desolate landscape.

"All right," he said, his tone resigned. "Let's go and see what Peskov has to tell us about Andreychuk."

As they walked across the field toward the car, Korolev was tempted to light up his last cigarette but, after a moment of consideration, he decided to save it for after the autopsy. The thing about morgues, autopsies and the like was that the smell got inside you: inside your nostrils, inside your mouth, into the very fabric of your clothing. That cigarette would go some way to burning away some of that heavy scent of chemicals and death, and remind him he was alive after all.

That was the thing about working outside Moscow, Korolev decided as he stood on the pavement, feeling as though his body had been beaten with an axe handle. After a couple of days of being battered by bad suspensions and rotten roads, you were pretty much finished. He stretched gently, ignoring Slivka's smirk, deciding the woman must have the constitution of a bear. Here he was, half-dead from the bruising he'd got from all their hithering and thithering and bumping and battering, and there she was, looking as fresh as an early summer rose.

Damn the young, he thought to himself as he nodded to her to lead the way around the side of the university to where the School of Anatomy was situated.

As it happened, Peskov already had Andreychuk's body naked on the stainless-steel autopsy table and, if Korolev wasn't wrong, the external examination completed. Peskov, in apron, white gown, surgical cap and gloves, turned his attention away from a tray of medical instruments to greet them, frowning with some concern as he examined Korolev.

"Ah, Captain Korolev, you look quite pale. Are you in good health?"

"I was fine until I walked in here," Korolev said, the words slipping out before he could catch hold of them.

He smiled an apology and took a step forward to look at the gray body on the table, struck by the pelt of white hair that covered much of Andreychuk's chest. The dead often looked surprisingly calm and Andreychuk was no exception — his skin smooth now that gravity was pulling it tight.

"You've been quick — getting him prepared, that is," Korolev said after a moment, hoping to make amends for his earlier remark.

"I understood it was a matter of urgency." Peskov smiled at him. "You look anxious, Comrade Korolev."

He *was* anxious — he had a Chekist colonel flying down in less than twenty-four hours; he wanted to get across the city to Bebel Street and find out who was on the Greek's list of possibilities for the partial fingerprint; and then he had to give Lomatkin a thorough grilling. And if that wasn't enough, he had Kolya's gunrunners on his mind. Yet here he was, about to see a human being cut open from head to toe, all so that he could be told that the fellow had been shot in the head.

"I'll be straight with you, Doctor," Korolev said. "The investigation has produced a number of leads which need to be followed up as soon as possible. So, while I know it's not the way you probably like to do things, I have to ask you — what do you think? Are you going to be able to tell me anything I don't already know?"

Peskov considered the question, running a finger along the dead man's arm. Korolev wondered whether he was checking the muscles for rigor mortis or whether it was an inadvertent action — the type of thing a man who works with dead bodies would think perfectly normal — even though it set Korolev's teeth on edge.

"At this stage," Peskov said, nodding, "I can tell you that the bullet entered from extremely close range — about an inch away judging from the burn marks."

He looked up at Korolev, who nodded his agreement.

"Time of death," Peskov said. "Last night, late, or very early this morning. It's a guess, based on a number of factors. You see these marks that look like bruising?" Peskov pointed to a patch of discoloration on the skin. Korolev had been in enough autopsies to know what he was talking about.

"Hypostasis?"

"Very good," Peskov said. Then, seeing Slivka's puzzled expression as she looked up from her note-taking, he explained. "The blood follows the natural laws of gravity, Sergeant. What you're seeing isn't bruising but the dead man's blood accumulating in the part of his body which was closest to the ground when we found it. It doesn't generally manifest itself for at least eight hours. It was present when I examined him by the river, so that tells us he'd been dead for at least that long. On top of that, look at his eyes."

Peskov placed a gloved finger against an eyeball. It gave under the pressure like the softest of jelly and Korolev felt his stomach twist, but he managed to nod his interest, not trusting himself to speak.

"If I were to put my finger in Captain Korolev's eye, there would be elasticity," Peskov said, and Korolev thought there might also be an uppercut that would lift the doctor a foot or so into the air.

"But here we have flaccidity, and that normally occurs only after approximately twelve hours. Sometimes as long as eighteen. On top of which rigor mortis has not quite set in, although the first signs are visible at the back of the neck and lower jaw. It might seem delayed, based on the other indicators, but the dead man is old, is quite muscular and the temperature was below freezing point last night. All of these factors would have impeded the process."

"He was last seen at about six in the evening out at the College," said Slivka looking up from her notebook. "And it seems clear he was shot in Angelinivka from the blood spatters."

"What are you asking?" Peskov said.

"We're looking for the time of death. The village was searched last night at about eleven and the truck wasn't there. The snow on his body indicates he was shot before two a.m. Can you narrow it down any further?" She looked to Korolev for approval, which he gave with a slow inclination of his head.

"Not at this stage," Peskov answered. "And, in any event, it's difficult to be specific about these things. Every corpse is different — I'll take the temperature of his organs, of course, but that won't tell me anything that you don't already know — my examination would agree with a time of death between eleven p.m. and two in the morning. I think I have one good piece of news, though."

Peskov leaned forward and turned the dead man's left forearm so that it was more easily visible for Slivka, pointing to a small round hole in the skin. Korolev had noticed the wound earlier and been confused by it.

"There's no sign of an exit wound, so if I'm not mistaken we may be able to retrieve the bullet. It might give Firtov something to work with."

Peskov glanced up for a reaction and whatever look was on Korolev's face, it seemed to be enough for the doctor to set to work, opening the wound wide with a swift stroke of his scalpel. Korolev forced himself to look as Peskov began digging and twisting into the dead man's flesh and moments later held up a small metallic nugget that had once been the business end of a bullet.

"I'll be able to tell you more about internal trajectory later on, but at a guess there was some deflection within the skull and when the bullet came out it lodged in his arm, luckily enough up against the radius. Take it to Firtov, see what he makes of it."

The bullet chinked in a glass jar in Korolev's pocket as he and Slivka walked up the steps that led to Pasteur Street.

"Well, Chief," Slivka asked, looking over at him, "what did you make of that?"

Korolev grimaced.

"It's a strange one. Someone helps him get out of his cell and then, likely as not, helps him to make it all the way to the Romanian border as well. And having done all that, this same person, or one of their allies, shoots him and leaves him for us to find. And even though he had a gun in his hand, his killer managed to shoot him in the back of the head. He must have had a reason for it being in his hand — some sort of threat, but he was facing the other way. And where did his gun come from?"

"The barrel on it worries me," Slivka said. "I'd swear it was a Militia weapon. Or . . ." She stopped mid-sentence and Korolev had an idea he knew why. If it was an NKVD weapon, the only Chekist involved in the case and close to hand was Mushkin.

The drive to Bebel Street took less than five minutes, and all the way the questions they both had about the gun were a tangible presence in the car. Asking the questions seemed to risk turning suspicion into a fact, so they kept quiet and, in Korolev's case, tried to think about more pleasant matters, which yet again turned out to be the memory of Valentina's hand on his chest.

When they arrived, Firtov seemed to share their unease. He nodded toward the Nagant, sitting on a wooden desk in front of him. Firtov was wearing a dirty apron to protect his clothes and white fingerprinting dust covered the gun from end to end.

"I traced the serial number," he said, a dour expression making his cavalryman's mustache seem less ebullient than usual.

"Well?" Korolev said, bracing himself.

"It was issued to Sergeant Gradov in October 1935."

"Gradov?" Korolev felt a flood of relief. "That fool not only left a prisoner un-

377

guarded, but provided him with a gun as well?"

"Perhaps," Firtov said cautiously. "He was disciplined for its loss last year — in June. It was stolen from the station, or so he claimed, but the investigation at the time led nowhere. He was lucky to keep his stripes and if Major Mushkin hadn't interceded on his behalf he'd certainly have lost them. Or worse."

"Mushkin?"

"I spoke to the man who led the investigation — he wanted to throw the book at Gradov, but Mushkin went right to the top and Gradov got away with it. For losing his weapon, no less."

"So it's possible Andreychuk could have been the one who stole it?" Slivka interjected, perhaps a fraction too forcefully.

"He must have got hold of it somehow," Firtov said.

It would be helpful, Korolev thought, if they could find another stage in the Nagant's journey from Gradov's possession to Andreychuk's cold hand — but that Andreychuk had taken the gun was the most logical explanation. In fact, he was almost grateful to Sergeant Gradov; at least the gun didn't come cursed with a State Security background — apart from, of course, Mushkin's intervention on the sergeant's behalf.

"How about fingerprints?" he asked, after a brief pause to offer a prayer to the Virgin for that small mercy.

"On the gun? Yes, and they belong to the dead man. That's what the Greek thinks anyway, but he's checking them once more. Speaking of fingerprints, we have a shortlist for that partial on the wall bracket."

"So I heard," Korolev said, doing his best to keep his anticipation under some kind of control.

"Three names. Antonova, she's a cook in the canteen; one of the cameramen, Belinsky; and a more interesting one — that Frenchman, Les Pins."

"Antonova was in the crowd scenes that evening," Slivka said. "And Belinsky was filming them. It's possible Belinsky helped take the girl down, but I don't remember anything about that from the interview notes."

"And Monsieur Les Pins?" Korolev said, knowing the answer. They'd never properly questioned him and now his fingerprint had shown up on the bracket from which the dead woman was hung. "He told us he was down at the night shoot, but it's never been confirmed, has it?"

"No," Slivka agreed. "Of course, up until

now it's been hands off for the Frenchman."

"It was. It may not be anymore. On top of this, there are some inconsistencies as to his whereabouts at the time of Andreychuk's escape. He said he was in his room, but Comrade Mushkina says he was with her, walking near the village. I think we need to have a chat with the fellow, don't you, Sergeant?"

"I'll call the Militia station. See if we can locate him. Do you want me to drive out there?"

"No, I've a feeling we should stay in Odessa today," Korolev said, thinking about gunrunners and Slivka's mother. "Ask them to bring him into Odessa, if it's convenient for our honored French guest. If it isn't, well, we'll deal with that eventuality when it comes to pass. And order Gradov to report here directly — he seems a careless sort of a fellow with regard to poor Andreychuk, doesn't he? Leaving his key for him to escape and losing his gun for him to shoot himself with."

"I'll see to it, Chief."

"And call your mother, Slivka."

She nodded her agreement, giving Firtov a put-upon shrug of her shoulders. The forensics man turned toward Korolev with a look of puzzled respect.

"You've tamed that one," he said as the door slammed shut behind Slivka. "If anyone had asked her to call her mother a week ago, they'd have been walking bow-legged till September."

"I believe in encouraging youngsters to have respect for their elders." Korolev spoke with a grave expression. "You'll call me if you come up with anything else?"

"Count on it," the cavalryman said.

Korolev turned to leave, but then he stopped, hearing the chink of the bullet in his pocket. He pulled out the glass container and showed it to Firtov.

"I almost forgot," he said. "It's the slug that made the hole in Andreychuk's head. The doctor pulled it out of the dead man's arm."

Firtov took the jar from Korolev, examined it for a moment, his face impassive, then placed it on his desk. The dented bullet seemed to have a dark presence, despite the glare of the electric light. He pulled across a set of weighing scales and decanted the bullet into one of the brass baskets, before adding and subtracting various tiny weights.

"Not from a Nagant. Most likely a nine-millimeter. We'll have a look at it, anyway, me and the Greek, and see what we make of it under a microscope."

"I'd be grateful. Tell Slivka I've gone down to check in on our journalist friend — maybe a little time in a cold cell has warmed up his memory."

CHAPTER TWENTY-ONE

Lomatkin was sitting in his shirtsleeves, beltless and bootless, his open collar revealing the top of a gray vest. Korolev felt a pang of sympathy for the bewildered-looking man — after all, he himself had sat in a not dissimilar cell not too many months past, an experience he wouldn't wish to have again.

Korolev sat down, and they looked at each other for a long moment, hands tucked into their armpits, each a mirror image of the other.

"This isn't so bad, is it?" Korolev said, glancing around him. "A cell to yourself? Clean, more or less, and a bench to sleep on? You're lucky if you ask me. You should see the cage I've just passed. Some real types in there I can tell you — they'd have fun with a cultured man like you."

"I saw the cage," Lomatkin said, his voice measured. "Is that how it works? If I don't tell you whatever it is you want to hear you put me in there with them?"

"No," Korolev said, pretending to consider it. "I always think information gained in such a way is unreliable."

"You're a paragon of virtue," the journalist replied.

Korolev laughed and took a packet of cigarettes from his pocket.

"These all right for you? They didn't have a wide selection at the kiosk. Mind you, they could have had old boots and I'd have bought them. I'd smoked my last one after Andreychuk's autopsy and this case needs tobacco. As well as a few answers from you, of course."

Lomatkin took one, running its length underneath his nose as though it were the finest cigar. Korolev offered him the packet again.

"Take a few, for later."

"Later?" Lomatkin asked.

"Well," Korolev said, shrugging his shoulders, "you must see how things stand. You won't be buying cigarettes for yourself for a while."

"I'd nothing to do with Andreychuk's escape, or his death. I've told you that already. I shouldn't be here. Now or later."

"The evidence doesn't back you up,

Citizen, and that's the truth of it. In fact the evidence points to you having let the fellow loose and then conspiring with a person or persons to plant a bullet in his skull. But let's leave that aside for the moment. Let's talk about something else. Let's talk about crimes against the State. Let's talk about espionage."

Now Lomatkin's eyes were like a pair of car headlights — as if someone had seized him by the nether parts and treated them unkindly. Korolev forced himself to be patient, allow the fellow to sweat. He deliberately settled back onto his chair, moving from side to side to extract every possible fraction of comfort from its hard frame, uncrossed his arms and slipped his hands into the pockets of his overcoat.

"Yes," he continued, when he'd finished. "I know all about it. Forget Andreychuk is my advice, you have bigger problems. What's the local equivalent of the Butyrka in these parts? I hope the cells are as nice as this."

"You know . . ." Lomatkin began eventually, before his voice tailed off. Maintaining an impassive expression, Korolev considered what he knew and what he was guessing. Putting facts together and producing possibilities from them was what being a detective was all about, of course, but in this case

he didn't have many facts to back his sup-
position up — all he had was Kolya's suggestion that Lenskaya had been bringing
valuable secret information to the Ukraine
that was being traded for guns. The girl had
been killed, so it seemed likely to Korolev
that she'd been killed because of her espionage activities, although he wasn't certain
of that by any means. But if her death *had*
had to do with spying, it seemed probable
she'd died because she'd been a threat to
the traitors in some way. And Lomatkin's
relationship with her, his arrival the day
after her death, his assistance in Andreychuk's escape, his visit to Krasnogorka —
whether or not with the intention of escap-
ing across the border — all pointed to him
being involved. And, with him being a
defense journalist for *Izvestia,* why shouldn't
he be the source of this mysterious secret
information? The Germans wouldn't hand
out guns for statistics about road-building
in Kazakhstan — no, they'd want military
information, and Lomatkin could have been
the man to provide it.

"I don't know everything," Korolev continued, "but I know enough. It occurs to
me that you could avoid the worst of what's
in store for you if you're frank with me —
the guns are what I'm after at this stage. If

you help me prevent them from falling into the traitors' hands, then I'll help you, you've my word on it. You made a mistake, your record will stand you in good stead if you're open and straightforward with me. And if you aren't — well — there are others who will ask the same questions in a different way."

"Guns, Korolev? Guns? I don't understand a word of what you're saying. And I don't know what this espionage talk is about either."

Imagine if they'd managed to find the dead girl's diary that Yasimov had mentioned, Korolev thought to himself. Imagine if it had made life easy for them by explaining exactly what was going on here. The journalist had certainly reacted to the suggestion of espionage — he was sure of that. But the mention of guns seemed to have given the fellow confidence again. Perhaps he didn't know about the guns.

Korolev decided to take a risk.

"We found her diary, Lomatkin."

"Her diary?"

"Her diary. You knew she kept one, surely? So we know she was bringing information down from Moscow — and your role in it. What you might not know is that your information was being passed on for guns,

387

German guns. That's what she was killed for. We know about your role. It's the others we're after now. Tell me everything, Lomatkin, and you might get out of this in one piece. Did they have something on you? Was it the drugs, or something else?"

Korolev hoped his face didn't betray his own fear. If he'd got this wrong, if Lomatkin turned out to have nothing to do with anything, then Korolev had revealed Kolya's information and the journalist might blather about it to Mushkin or someone similar and Korolev was pretty confident that the Chekists would be interviewing this fellow sooner or later. Korolev scanned Lomatkin's face for reassurance, a small sign of guilt, but it was as if the journalist's expression was frozen solid — only his eyes seemed alive, staring at Korolev with unnatural intensity, and he had a sudden temptation to lean across and twist the man's nose. What a strange impulse, he thought to himself, holding Lomatkin's gaze and doing his level best not to blink. And it was an impulse that was still there, making his fingers twist in his pocket, when they rubbed against a piece of paper, which suddenly seemed a most useful thing to produce.

"We also found this, Lomatkin. Lenskaya typed it just before she died." And Korolev handed him the typed page he'd found the night before in the book of Stalin's speeches.

Lomatkin looked at the piece of paper for a long time, his mouth moving slowly as he read it. Perhaps his English wasn't that good — but Korolev was confident the journalist understood it all right.

"She wasn't religious, you know," Lomatkin said.

"It doesn't matter to me if she was or she wasn't."

"But this psalm meant something to her — I suppose it means something to all of us these days."

Korolev waited as a frown darkened the journalist's face. It was as though Lomatkin was asking himself a difficult question — and after a time, it seemed he'd found an answer to it.

"What did she write about me in the diary?" he asked. The journalist spoke quietly and Korolev had the feeling that Lomatkin was bracing himself for a dead lover's recriminations. But it occurred to Korolev that if he were in the journalist's shoes he'd like to hear he'd been forgiven, if there was anything to be forgiven for.

"She cared about you, Lomatkin," Korolev said, a somber tone deepening his voice. "She loved you, it seems. She didn't hold you responsible for the mess she found herself in."

Lomatkin smiled sadly, turning his eyes up to meet Korolev's. "You never found a diary, did you?"

Korolev started to speak, but before he could think of anything to say Lomatkin shook his head to stop him.

"Don't bother, Korolev, it doesn't matter. I'll be open with you. I knew it would end up like this. But I'd nothing to do with her death and nothing to do with Andreychuk's escape, I promise you that much."

"I'm listening," Korolev said, hope stirring.

"You know about my indiscretions — my dubious past as you called it. Perhaps that's what first made them think they could blackmail me. After all, these days an anonymous denunciation based on lies can result in a ten stretch. And they had more than lies, Korolev. But they were clever, they dug a little and must have found out about Masha's past along the way. I might have risked the consequences of what they knew about me — it was mostly gossip and I have friends who could have helped me — but Masha's father having been a Petlyurist officer and her living under a false identity, well, those things alone would have resulted

390

in her death. I know enough about Ezhov to know that much. It would have been done quietly, but he couldn't have allowed her to live."

It was true, Korolev thought: to be discovered having a dalliance with the daughter of a counterrevolutionary would have been a political disaster for the Central Committee member responsible for State Security, no matter what Comrade Stalin said about the sins of the parents not being visited on their children. No, someone with a class background like Lenskaya's, particularly someone who'd obscured it so effectively, would be an Enemy of the Revolution in the eyes of the Party, and a traitor to the State.

"To start with they didn't seem to want much from me," Lomatkin continued. "Nothing more than what they could have read in *Izvestia* two days later anyway. They just wanted to know the stories I was working on — the launch of a new submarine, the range of a fighter bomber. Really, it was the kind of thing I'd have told anyone over a glass or two of beer."

"They were leading you on."

"Of course. I closed my eyes to the risks at first. I knew the man who approached me. A Ukrainian, like me. Living in Moscow, like me. A Party member, like me. When he started talking about a separate Ukrainian state with support from European powers I realized the mess I was in, but by then they'd enough on me to have me shot four times over, and in my own handwriting no less. Then they squeezed me, and they squeezed me till there was nothing left."

"So what was the information you provided after that?"

"More confidential, much more confidential. Detailed plans for a new tank, inch-accurate maps of the western defenses, locations of armaments factories, our preparations against chemical warfare. In my position I had access to such information on a regular basis, and when I did I passed it on. I was afraid of ending up in a place like this, and of Masha ending up here as well, but now that I'm here, and Masha's dead, well, there's nothing to be afraid of, is there?"

Korolev wasn't sure about that, but he let it go.

"How did they find out about her, do you think?"

"It must have been when she came down here scouting for the film location. I suppose she was curious to see where she came from and it was she who suggested to Savchenko that they shoot down here. That her father turned out to be the caretaker at the College was a complete coincidence, I think. They kept it a secret between them, I'm sure of that — I didn't even know about it. But someone must have known."

"Who?"

"I've no idea. It must have been someone who knew her father well. Perhaps someone who knew her mother too. That would be my guess. Masha'd kept her mother's maiden name — someone must have been able to put the names together, do the research, find the evidence."

"What evidence?"

"They had a baptism record. I showed her a copy."

"She knew about the blackmail?"

"I told her it was just for money and that I'd dealt with it. I never put Andreychuk and the baptism certificate together, though. He'd changed his name, of course."

"Of course," Korolev agreed. "Why do you think they killed her?"

"It was my fault," Lomatkin said. "I kept her out of it as much as I could, but when Masha started coming down here so often, their man in Moscow, the Ukrainian, wanted me to slip the documents into her belongings. Sometimes microfilm was hidden in the binding of a book and when she arrived here the book would be swapped for a duplicate, and the film retrieved. It was their idea, not mine. But I should have resisted because, you see, she must have found it this time. That's why I had to come down so suddenly. They'd put something in the binding of a report she was working on, but when they went to find it, it was gone."

Belakovsky's report on his plans for a Soviet Hollywood. Korolev whistled. This wasn't something a Moscow flatfoot should be involved in. This was something for Rodinov when he arrived. No matter what the risk. He'd have to tell the colonel everything now and the sooner the better.

Lomatkin went on. "They must have thought she was going to expose them. Whoever it was, I don't think Andreychuk had any part in it — but if he was a Petly-urist during the Civil War . . . well, who knows?"

"I don't think Andreychuk was responsible — I'm not sure who was, though," Korolev said. "This report — it was for Belakovsky? Some idea he has for a film town — Kino-grad, I think."

"Yes, I believe so."

"It was missing when he went to look for it," Korolev told him, wondering what its absence might mean. "Tell me, we found a fingerprint that puts your friend Les Pins at the spot where Lenskaya was found hanging. What do you make of that?"

"Les Pins? He can't have been involved in this, can he? What would a Frenchman have to do with this?"

It occurred to Korolev that, all things considered, Lomatkin was remarkably calm — especially given that his life expectancy had radically shortened in the last couple of minutes. But that was sometimes the way it went with criminals who'd been living with guilt for a long period of time — when they were finally uncovered it was almost a relief. He extracted his cigarette packet and offered the journalist one.

"I'm guessing it's to do with these guns," Korolev said as he lit up.

"I know nothing about guns," Lomatkin said, and Korolev noticed how his face had grown a little paler. It could be the effects of the cigarette but more likely it was the mention of that terrible word, plural. Guns would mean the NKVD wouldn't go easy on him when he fell into their clutches, and into their clutches the journalist was inevitably going to fall.

"The information you were passing on through Lenskaya has been exchanged for a shipload of Mausers, or so I've been told."

"Mausers? Do you know how many?"

"I don't. But if there are guns coming from abroad to counterrevolutionary terrorists then things aren't good. And it occurs to me that the only foreigner we have in the locality is a certain Monsieur from France — if that's where he really is from. What do you know about him?"

"Les Pins? A journalist — a friend of the Socialist movement. His articles on Spain were published all over the world — in *Pravda* as well. I'm sure he must be a Party member. Wasn't he wounded in the fighting for Madrid? I know he met Savchenko in America back in 'thirty-four, and that's why he's visiting here before going on to Moscow. He's giving speeches in support of the Spanish comrades — I believe he's to meet Comrade Stalin himself. I can't see him being mixed up with German guns."

"But you say he was in America? Did Lenskaya know him from there? Wasn't there a traitor involved in that delegation to America?"

"There was — Danyluk. He wasn't someone she had much to do with, thankfully, but I don't know if he knew Les Pins. All I know is that Masha didn't come across Les Pins on the delegation, or if she did, she never told me."

This was a new angle, and one whose ramifications Korolev could only begin to consider. If Les Pins was yet another who'd been in America, why had no one mentioned it before? And who else had been there? Danyluk, the traitor — of course. The dead girl — yes. Savchenko and Belakovsky — indeed; although neither could have had anything to do directly with the girl's death.

"Was there anyone else in America at the time? Anyone who might have had contact with Les Pins or this fellow Danyluk? Anyone involved in the film's production, perhaps."

Lomatkin shook his head, looking utterly exhausted now. "I wasn't there. I wouldn't be the person to ask. And I know nothing about the guns, Korolev, or I'd have spoken up before — the man I had contact with in Moscow is called Topolski. Babel knows him, he's a member of the Writer's Union and easy enough to track down. Give him my regards when you do."

"I will," Korolev said, and was about to go on when he was distracted by the sound of footsteps approaching quickly along the corridor outside. Generally, in the cells, things moved slowly — there was no rush, the prisoners and their guards had all day long to do whatever they had to do — but here were people moving with intent and urgency, and coming toward their cell.

"In here," a voice said, then a key turned in the lock.

"Chief," Slivka said when the guard had opened the door, her face almost as pale as Lomatkin's. "I got through to my mother."

CHAPTER TWENTY-TWO

Korolev's mind felt assaulted by suggestions, identities, locations, timings, possibilities and a hundred other scraps and facts — and this great swirl of information was twisting and turning and colliding and fragmenting as it rattled around the inside of his skull so that he couldn't even begin to put it into any semblance of order. Instead he found himself concentrating, with a certain amount of self-pity, on the small ache in his forehead that all this *thinking* was making appreciably worse. What this case needed was someone with a bit more brainpower and that was the truth.

"They're both missing?" he managed to ask, speaking quietly in case they could be overheard. "Both of them?"

"I'm not sure missing is the correct word to use, Chief. But they can't be found, that's true enough."

Korolev looked at Slivka quickly to see if

she was making fun of him.

"But Gradov is a Militiaman — a sergeant no less." Korolev could hear the plaintive note in his voice, and so he allowed himself a brief pause to pull himself together before proceeding in a more appropriate growling whisper. "He's in charge of the damned station, the dog — he can't just go wandering off whenever he wants to."

Slivka began to look uncomfortable so Korolev, with some difficulty, stopped himself once again, and then continued in what he hoped was a more measured tone.

"He left no message? Perhaps he was feeling unwell — a visit to the doctor?"

"Sharapov says the last he saw of him, he said he was going up to the house, got into the car and hasn't been seen since. Larisa has a good view over the courtyard from that office of hers and says she's certain he never arrived."

"I see. And Les Pins?"

"Apparently went for a walk after lunch and hasn't been seen since either."

"A coincidence?"

"There's more."

"Tell me."

"I told Sharapov about the morphine in Lenskaya's stomach. When he was looking for Les Pins, he went up to his bedroom and took a quick look through his belongings. He found a packet of morphine tablets."

"Morphine tablets?"

"Do you think —" Slivka began.

"He had a bandaged shoulder — it's possible there was still some pain. But yes, perhaps that's where the morphine in her stomach came from."

"But if he had a shoulder injury, how could his print have ended up on the bracket?"

"He would have had help, that much is certain," Korolev said and then a thought occurred to him. "Did we ever ask where the uniforms were at the time of her murder?"

Slivka's face was enough of an answer.

"Why would we have?" Korolev said. "It's not your fault, Slivka. It's mine if it's anyone's."

"Gradov," Slivka said bitterly.

"It could well be."

"We have to put out an alert. Another one."

Korolev considered the suggestion and what it would mean — more roadblocks, more reasons, more explanations. It didn't take him long to shake his head. This investigation was meant to be a quiet one, and he'd already had the entire region alerted twice. If he did it again, and for a foreigner, that really would make a stink.

"Not for Les Pins," Korolev said, thinking aloud. "No, I'll need to get instructions from Moscow to do anything about him. But seeing as Sergeant Gradov is in the habit of losing guns and prisoners, I think we can ask your boss to put a quiet word out on him, don't you?"

"I'll ask."

"Do that," Korolev said. "How long will it take us to get to Moldovanka and this bar?"

"We're driving?"

"I think it would be a good idea to have a car — in case we have to move quickly."

"It might be. But I have to tell you, there's a good chance it won't all be there when we've finished."

"I trust your family to look after it."

Slivka laughed at that. "More fool you then, Chief. I'd only trust them to make off with anything saleable. Particularly if they know it's a Militia car — it would be a point of honor with them."

"How long to walk?"

"Twenty minutes."

Korolev looked at his watch — it was five o'clock. According to Slivka's mother, they were to meet Kolya and his men inside the

Moldovanka bar at seven. In the meantime it was essential he called Rodinov for instructions about this damned Frenchman, and tell him exactly what was going on.

Another thought occurred to him. "What about Antonova and Belinsky? Did you double-check whether they were in the room when the body was discovered?"

"Antonova is accounted for. She went back to the village with two other women after the night shoot. Likewise Belinsky, who was still packing up camera equipment when the girl was found."

"I see," Korolev said, his head hurting even more now. He wished the investigation would slow down for a few hours, to allow him to bring some sense to it, but the meeting with Kolya was close at hand and between now and then every minute would be precious. The more he thought about the Moldovanka meeting, the more he was convinced that if things came to a tussle with armed terrorists it would be good to have a fast car close to hand. On top of which, he didn't like the idea of doing this without his back being covered.

"Is there someone we could trust to keep a car nearby, someone quiet? What about Firtov? Or the Greek?"

"I could ask them."

"Do it, Nadezhda Andreyevna, and find me somewhere private to call Moscow. There are matters we need direction on, and from the highest level."

It was strange the silence that came when Korolev asked the operator, a police operator no less, to give him a line to Moscow, the Lubianka, Colonel Rodinov. It lasted a few long seconds and when the operator finally spoke it sounded more like a thirsty man's croak than speech, but it was refreshing how quickly you could sometimes be connected when the recipient had such an impressive address.

"Rodinov," came the voice down the line, the colonel pronouncing his name as though he were chewing a piece of raw meat. And Korolev told him everything.

"Les Pins, Lomatkin, Danyluk, this rat To-polski in Moscow, the girl's father and this damned Militiaman. It's a conspiracy, Korolev — the Devil alone knows where it might end. We've got to intercept those guns, do you hear me? I'll call our people in Odessa — they'll have that place surrounded in ten minutes' time and then we'll have the lot of them, and we'll see what holes the rats crawled out of, and what holes we can find to put them in when we've finished with them."

"Colonel, as I understand it, Moldovanka is a tight neighborhood, inward looking, the kind of place where strangers are viewed with suspicion. And if I know Kolya and his cohorts, they'll be on the lookout — if not for Chekists, then for the terrorists. If you send the wrong type of people in the wrong numbers, well — it might be counterproductive. We don't know where the guns are yet, after all."

There was a pause at the other end of the line, and Korolev shook his head in self-admonition. What kind of idiot was he? Offering advice to a Chekist colonel on how to do his job? He ought to be locked up in a place where he couldn't harm himself or others. How he'd managed to survive this long in a hard world was a mystery to him.

"Now's not the time for explanations, Korolev." The colonel seemed calmer now and his voice was an interesting mixture of curiosity and menace. "But you'll be telling me before tomorrow is out, face to face, why the Thieves think you're a man to be trusted. And I can't wait to hear your explanation."

If I survive that long, thought Korolev, I might even give you one.

"Of course, Comrade Colonel," he said,

deciding that if the colonel was happy enough to wait for twenty-four hours then there was no point in jumping the gun.

"You may be right," Rodinov continued. "All the same we'll quietly monitor any movements out of the city. It's crucial those guns don't get away. If you fail, we'll try a different approach."

Korolev didn't want to think about that and, anyway, there was another sensitive subject he needed to raise.

"Comrade Colonel. About Major Mushkin."

"Go on."

And so Korolev did, reminding Rodinov that the major had interceded for the missing Sergeant Gradov when his gun had gone missing.

"Mushkin's father was a Petlyurist, of course," Rodinov said when Korolev had finished.

"I wasn't aware of that."

"Oh yes, Mushkin's mother shot him herself — a famous story and an example to all Bolsheviks." There was a lengthy pause. Eventually the colonel came to a decision.

"Mushkin will be informed and be part of the operation, but he won't be heading it and he won't be given all the information until the last moment. Leave that to me. As for what you say about the Moldovanka — I'll talk to our people and see what can be done, quietly as I've said. And, if necessary, we'll be ready to shut the city down tight as a clam. Is this girl Slivka trustworthy?"

"I'd stake my life on her."

"And how much does she know?"

"Only as much as I considered necessary. I've been careful with information, as you said," Korolev said, which wasn't entirely a lie.

"Keep it that way. And these men you're asking to drive the car?"

"Solid fellows."

"Good. Call if you have any news — there will be someone here to take a message, no matter what the time. Tell Slivka and these solid fellows of yours the same. Just in case. Leave a trail, Korolev, and we'll follow it."

In case you don't make it back, Korolev thought to himself. The door to the office Slivka shared with two other detectives was locked when Korolev arrived and he rapped quietly on it with his knuckles.

Slivka opened up and ushered him in, looking past him into the corridor to make sure there was no one around. "I got us some artillery," she said as she locked the door behind him and, sure enough, on her desk were two solid, snub-barrelled machine guns, about two and a half feet in length.

"PPD 34s," Slivka said proudly. "Don't ask me where I got them."

Korolev put a hand on the closer of the guns and ran his fingers along the dull gray metal.

"Where did you get them?"

"Ah, Chief, I told you not to ask," Slivka said with a grin. "Well — the border guard uses our armory and I've borrowed them. We have to get them back by first thing in the morning."

"You *borrowed* submachine guns?" Korolev said, not bothering to hide his amazement. "From the *border guard?*"

"Well, I thought that if we needed guns then we might as well have good guns."

"But what if we lose them?" Korolev asked, picking one up and beginning to warm to the evil weight in his hands.

"There's only one way we're losing them, Chief, and if that happens — well, they can't shoot us twice, can they?"

"No," Korolev agreed, clicking out the magazine — easily done — and slipping it back into place. "No, you're right there, Slivka. You're sure no one will notice?"

"Someone owed me a favor, now I owe him one. He turned a blind eye, and he'll turn another tomorrow."

Korolev found his finger on the trigger guard. The guns were small enough to go underneath an overcoat on a long strap and they could chop a man in half in less time than it took to say hello. If it came to shooting, they'd be glad to have them.

"Eight hundred bullets per minute," Slivka whispered, as if inviting him to bed, "and I've four magazines for each of them."

"That's a lot of bullets."

"A great deal of bullets," Slivka agreed, her teeth white in the low light.

"And I even managed to get you a spare clip for your Walther, Chief. And there's a Nagant for you, if you want it."

Korolev shrugged his shoulders.

"Better to be safe than sorry. What about Firtov and the Greek?"

"It's agreed. Firtov will drive the car and stay close if he can. I've worked out some meeting spots with him in case he loses us. Don't worry, Chief, I know Moldovanka like the back of my hand and so does Firtov. He'll keep close to us and he'll have the Greek to follow on foot if it comes to walking."

Korolev couldn't help but think that Sergeant Slivka was a little too excited at the prospect of the evening ahead. But that

was youth, he decided, and it was probably
no bad thing.

CHAPTER TWENTY-THREE

"What time is it?" Slivka asked.

"Time to go," Korolev answered, and checked his machine gun for the third time before repeating the exercise with the Nagant and then with the Walther.

"The Greek will stay as close as he can," Firtov said. They'd parked, at his suggestion, a few streets away from the bar in a quiet lane behind a warehouse. They hadn't told the two forensics men everything, but they'd told them enough and, as far as they knew, the Greek was close by, although they'd dropped him off some distance away.

"Use your discretion, Comrade," Korolev said. "Stay back and report to the colonel in Moscow if things get rough — there's a bigger picture here than our skins."

Slivka nodded her agreement, a firm movement, and Korolev was reassured by her determination.

"All right, Slivka, let's see if we can make

it to this bar of yours without clanking too much."

At least the evening air was fresh compared to the stale atmosphere inside Firtov's car and Korolev breathed in a lungful with something approaching pleasure as he adjusted his clothing to cover his weaponry.

Moldovanka wasn't a plush area, by any means, and even if its buildings were low, the streets themselves were wide and straight. The district still had more than an echo of the grandeur of the center of Odessa, even if much of the paintwork was peeling and some of the plasterwork was well nibbled. When they turned out of the alleyway into a larger street they found it busy with workers returning home, and despite the temperature and the limited light from the street lamps there was a buzz of conversation as friends greeted each other and discussed the day's happenings. Korolev kept his eyes moving as they walked, scanning the crowd for danger, so it was all the more of a surprise that he was almost on top of Mishka before he spotted the rotten-toothed rascal.

"Nadezhda, darling," Mishka said with an insolent smile, "you must keep better company than this. Come on, this summer —

you and I — we'll go to Yalta and drink real champagne in the finest hotels. Caviar, you name it, we'll have it. Hanging around with persons like this will give you a bad reputation."

"But Mishka, you're a sewer rat," Slivka said to the Thief in mock bewilderment.

The Thief laughed, not in the least offended. "At least a rat like me would look after you, not take you out on dates to dumps like this."

What was this about a date? Slivka and he were Militia detectives on an important assignment.

"Hey, Mishka. Enough from the monkey. Take us to the organ grinder," Korolev growled, and his irritation turned to cold fury when the Thief's response was to laugh again. At him. In front of witnesses, no less.

"Did you hear that, Fox? These Moscow Terriers have dirty mouths on them."

Mishka addressed his remark to a tall wiry individual with thick red hair who was dressed, like Mishka and, indeed, Korolev and Slivka, in a long overcoat that probably hid a similar amount of armaments. As he looked around him, Korolev saw that Fox was one of several men who'd appeared in their locality, all with an equally antisocial look about them. It seemed as if half the toughs in Odessa were out for an evening's promenade.

"Greetings, Fox," Slivka said with a small nod in the red-headed man's direction.

"Evening, Nadezhda. Kolya said to bring you and the flatfoot into Petya's when you showed." Fox pointed in the direction of a bar on the corner of a wide crossroads. More men were posted around it; they looked hard and vigilant, men made in Fox's image.

"What have you got under your coat, Korolev?" Mishka asked with that irritating smile of his.

"Something that's as good as a shovel if you want to dig yourself a grave, little Mishka."

Mishka seemed ready to take up the challenge, a vein in his forehead visibly beating as his clear blue eyes, completely devoid of anything resembling emotion, contemplated Korolev, narrowing to slits as he did so.

"Mishka, take a couple of the boys around the block — make sure we're clear there."

Kolya's voice was like gravel pouring into an empty hole, remorseless and undeniable. The young Thief blinked, looked at Korolev as though he'd forgotten who he was, then nodded his agreement.

"Fox? Benya? Let's go."

"You brought something for us, Alexei Dmitriyevich?" Kolya said, nodding at the shape in Korolev's coat in turn.

"Something useful."

"I hear you brought some friends along as well."

"Friends?" Korolev asked, wondering if Rodinov had sent some dim-witted Chekists blundering into Moldovanka to keep an eye on things.

"You've a car and a driver parked three streets away, in behind the box factory. Not a friend of yours? It's a Militia vehicle and known as such."

"That's Firtov," Slivka said, moving a little closer to intercede. "Firtov's all right, Kolya. We need a car for later, but he'll stay back. He's trustworthy."

"I know who's in the car, Nadezhda," Kolya said slowly, not looking at her, keeping instead his steady gaze on Korolev. An interesting gaze it was as well — inquisitive and yet menacing. As if Korolev were a curious question that needed to be examined from more than one perspective and then dealt with.

"Well, Kolya?" Korolev asked.

"You should have told us about Firtov. If he hadn't been recognized it might have gone badly for him. And now we wonder if

415

we can trust you."

"We needed the car," Korolev replied firmly, "and I'd no way of telling you about him."

Kolya nodded, then gestured to the hard-looking men who stood out by virtue of their stillness and intensity among the neighborhood's evening crowd.

"Let's go inside. Your car will be there when you need it. And Firtov too."

They followed the Thief into the half-empty bar, and at a nod from Kolya a bottle of vodka and some dark rye bread arrived at the small table he led them to, followed swiftly by glasses. Korolev, after a moment's consideration, unbuckled the strap of his machine gun and placed it on the floor, Slivka following suit with her own weapon.

The presence of two machine guns in the bar aroused little comment from the other drinkers, which wasn't surprising given that everything from a bayonet to a cut-down shotgun was sitting on the tables around them.

Korolev was pretty certain that the half-dozen men in the room, including the bartender, had almost, but not quite, smiled with approval.

"Nice artillery," Kolya said, placing a Luger on the table, followed by a saw-toothed knife.

"We came prepared. So what's the situation? It looks like there's enough weaponry in here for a small war."

"A small war is what we might have on our hands." Kolya squinted at his watch, then smiled. "But in an hour or two we'll bring the war to an end, I think."

"You know where the guns are?"

"Yes. They have a place in the catacombs they think no one knows about, but they're wrong."

"Catacombs?" Korolev asked.

"This city is built from limestone. Where do you think it all came from? Underneath the city is where — they've been cutting it out for a hundred years now, and once you start making holes like that beside the sea, pretty soon gentlemen like me link them up and make tunnels, and then you have a nice way of getting something from the port up to the town if you want to do it quietly. You can travel from one end of Odessa to the other without seeing daylight, they say. And even if they're prone to exaggeration around here, it's possible they're talking the truth on this."

"So how do you know about this place of theirs?"

"We have one of their men out the back,

and he has a wife and children. He'll show us where his friends have their stash."

"What's in this stash of his?" Korolev asked.

"At least forty crates, he says — I don't know more than that and there's still more coming in, but we should catch most of it." Kolya looked at him keenly for a very brief moment, then resumed his impassive expression.

"It's understood that any weapons are for us, Kolya," Korolev said.

"You can have anything that shoots or blows, that's agreed. For guns and suchlike, we'll only take away what we bring. We want a quiet life — and these guns are noisy. They're of no use to businessmen like us. Shall we drink on it?"

They emptied the small vodka glasses, drank in unison, and Korolev felt the alcohol warming his throat and stomach.

"So how many guards?"

"A few."

"Well?"

"More than one, fewer than twenty. All we know is that they want to take the guns out of the city tonight and if there are forty crates — well, they'll need some bodies to shift them."

Once again Korolev had the feeling there

was something he wasn't being told.

"Come, Kolya, all I have to do is call Marchuk or Mushkin and this city can be shut down so that not even a bicycle can move three feet."

Kolya rubbed his chin, as if doing this would help him come to whatever kind of decision he was attempting to make.

"I'll be honest with you, Korolev, we want to deal with these people ourselves — we owe them a thing or two for the last week. On top of which, we don't need the Chekists and your boys tightening the screws on the city at the moment — it would be bad for business. And we don't want them poking around the catacombs either. We've things of our own hidden there, not that there'd be much chance of them finding our belongings, or their guns for that matter, but still . . . Nadezhda, explain to him."

"Chief, the tunnels are everywhere under the city. Every building you see above the ground came from within it, so you can imagine how many there are. Some of the catacombs are linked, but many are independent of each other, or the connections are well hidden. People get lost down there and are never seen again. If the guns are properly concealed, we might never find them."

"You see, Korolev? But with you and these little guns of yours, we should do it easily enough. Anyway, we know where they are right now. By tomorrow they could be somewhere else. There's no time to waste."

"The guns stay with us?"

"On my word. We want what we want, nothing more."

"You're telling me you're going to risk life and limb to foil a terrorist plot for nothing?"

"Not for nothing, Korolev. We're calling in a debt — a blood debt."

Korolev grunted his disbelief — there was something else to this, he was sure of it. He considered standing up and walking away. If he slipped a clip into the machine gun there wasn't much anyone could do about it, but his duty was to see that the traitors were stopped. An armed uprising, at this time and moment, might lead to a civil war for all he knew, and he'd seen enough of the last one not to want to see another.

"All right, Kolya, we'll play it your way," he said, and felt for a moment as though he'd signed away his soul to the Devil.

Chapter Twenty-Four

It was dark and damp and the tunnel they were making their way along had been cut for smaller men than Korolev, and he cursed as a drop of water went down his collar. After twenty minutes of walking bent over and regretting every spare round he was carrying, Korolev was not in the best of moods.

He was also becoming increasingly worried — after all, he'd no idea how to get out of this damned place if the matter in hand didn't go according to Kolya's sketchy plan. If he could see something, Korolev thought to himself, then perhaps he could get his bearings. He'd felt the drafts from passages they'd passed to the right and left, and once had even been surprised to look up and see the yellow glow of what might have been a street lamp, far above him in what must have been an air vent. But otherwise the only illumination was from a flashlight carried by the guide at the front of the column, and even that had been covered with a piece of gray cotton. All in all, it was the kind of situation that could eat into a man's confidence.

But still they pressed on, inch by inch, step by careful step. And the farther they went, the more Korolev was beginning to wonder if he'd ever be able to stretch himself up to his full height again.

He was almost at the point of despair when the man ahead of him stopped and turned to place a hand on his shoulder.

"The Count wants you up in front." He spoke in a low mumble that Korolev presumed was meant to be a whisper. Korolev squeezed past him and three others before the shaded flashlight showed him a man lying crumpled on the floor and the faintest outline of Kolya's face as he leaned over a piece of paper that a gray-bearded old man was marking up with lines and crosses.

"Greetings, Korolev. The place is up ahead. Not far, but we split here."

"What happened to him?" Korolev asked, nodding down at the guide.

"He served his purpose. Mole here knows where we are and how to go about the thing. This fellow wasn't telling us the entire truth, so we sent him up to God to ask forgiveness for his sin."

In the faint light Korolev saw that what he'd taken for a shadow was a puddle of blood spreading out from the dead man. Korolev nodded again, keeping his lips firmly pressed together — now wasn't the time to be splitting hairs about how and why the man had died. Anyway, if the Chekists had got their hands on him his fate would have been the same.

"We're here," Kolya whispered, pointing at a cross on the page. "And they're there." He pointed at another cross in the center of a square box.

"That's a chamber about fifteen yards by ten. Two side rooms. Here and here. Not where this fellow told us, though. But Mole knows these tunnels as well as any man knows the streets above. I suppose the fellow thought he could lead us into a trap — more fool him."

He drew two small boxes to the side and below the larger box to signify the side rooms. Three lines ran from the chamber on the rough map, and Korolev decided these must be the tunnels that led into and out of it. One of the lines led directly to the cross that Kolya had pointed out as their current location and the Thief now ran his pencil along it.

"This is the passage ahead. If you stay here, Mole will take the rest of us through the side passages and we'll have them trussed up nicely. Give us ten minutes to get into position and then come along the passage shooting and shouting while we hit them from behind . . . or pick them off as they run," he added, after a moment of contemplation.

"So we do all the work," Korolev asked, incredulous, "while you pick off the survivors?"

Kolya smiled and put a hand on the barrel of Korolev's machine gun.

"Would you hang around in a tunnel if two pepper grinders were coming along it spitting lead?"

"No, but I might leave them a farewell present of a grenade without its pin."

"You've a better plan?"

"We all hit at once — hard and fast. Get in as close as we can before we start shooting and then cut down anything that moves. Excepting each other, of course."

Kolya nodded his agreement, and handed him a small flashlight from his pocket.

"Make sure you know who you're shooting at. I'll leave Mishka with you. I know you two don't love each other, but if anyone comes along the tunnel Mishka's the fellow you want waiting with a knife in his hand."

Korolev grunted, thinking that was just as good a reason not to have Mishka with you. Still, now that he thought of it, they could always send the rat in first when it came to the shooting.

"You have a watch?" Kolya asked, tapping the strap of his own.

"Yes," Korolev answered, feeling slightly offended. He was a detective, after all. Where would he be without a watch?

"Mole?" Kolya went on.

The older man nodded.

"Let's set our watches now for half-past eight. In fifteen minutes we go in. Unless something happens sooner, of course. In which case we don't wait for an invitation, right?"

"Agreed," Korolev said, doing his best to make it clear that he wasn't being ordered about here.

Whispered instructions proceeded down the line of men and then, with surprising stealth, a procession of burly gangsters squeezed past him — only the faintest of sounds coming from men not inches away. He counted them as they passed. Ten. Twelve including himself and Slivka.

"Nervous, copper?"

Thirteen, Korolev remembered, regretting

that there wouldn't be more of Mishka to hide behind when they sent him down the tunnel first.

In a whisper not much louder than a breath, Korolev told them the plan. He looked at his watch.

"In five minutes, we start to move. Very slowly. Mishka, you go first — if we meet someone on the way, you give him the directions to heaven."

"With pleasure, *jefe*."

There wasn't anything more to be said and so they sat there, on their haunches, in the pitch black, listening to the sound of the water dripping from the roof not far away, and Korolev found himself rubbing gently at the trigger guard of the machine gun as he counted off the seconds until it was time for them to make their move. At one stage there came a noise that sounded like the scuttle of small pebbles, but where he couldn't tell, and he felt his hand clench around the gun before reassuring himself that it had probably been just a rock fall. He listened with a concentration that made his ears hurt, but there was nothing else. Then, shielding the flashlight's bulb in his hand so that his bones were outlined in the ghostly red light that shone through his fingers, he checked his watch.

"Time to move," he whispered and the click of the flashlight's switch as he slid it off was joined by the noise of safety catches being moved to the appropriate position and rounds being chambered. Despite their painstaking care, the sounds seemed unnaturally loud and he felt the familiar electric surge through his body that always came with the approach of danger. Swallowing to relieve his dry mouth, he followed Mishka down the tunnel, each step as careful as a tightrope walker's.

Step after careful step and breath after controlled breath they advanced. Then from up ahead came the sound of a companionable laugh — the kind a man might give in response to a familiar joke. Korolev's entire body froze in mid-step before he allowed it, very slowly, to move forward and come to a more comfortable rest.

Without a word, Mishka moved forward and Korolev followed, sensing rather than hearing Slivka coming behind him. The laugh sounded once again. Deeper this time and more drawn out. Was it a different man? Older perhaps? Korolev kept moving, wondering how far away the men were. Now there was a glimmer of light up ahead, at first only a vague coloring of the darkness but growing stronger as he advanced, and it revealed the Thief's silhouette, twenty paces ahead of them, moving with the smooth stealth of a cat approaching an unwary bird, a knife in one hand while his other slipped the heavy revolver he was carrying into the back of his belt. Korolev upped his pace — he wanted to be close at hand when the gangster did whatever he was going to do.

They were near enough now to hear the murmur of conversation and other incidental sounds as well — the scrape of a heavy wooden object along stone, the squeal of a nail being levered out of its tight wooden resting place. Now that Korolev was able to make out, even if only faintly, the walls and roof of the passage they were following, he increased his pace — just as Mishka disappeared around a corner up ahead. Korolev, arriving at the same point not more than a handful of heartbeats later, found the Thief holding a black-haired youngster in his arms, Mishka's free hand guiding the gushing blood from a slit throat onto the dead man's clothing at the same time as he lowered the body gently to the floor.

They were now in a small chamber lit by a sputtering candle, on two sides of which benches had been carved out of the stone itself. A rifle, shining with newness, leaned against the bench on which the sentry had been sitting, or more likely sleeping, until Mishka had brought his life to a close.

"Help me with this, can you?" a voice said from beyond the far entrance.

"Let me finish this first," another answered, and Korolev was half-convinced that he could hear the invisible men breathing hard as they set about whatever work was occupying them. Mishka grinned at him, his teeth golden in the candlelight, as he wiped his bloody hand clean on the dead sentry's arm. Was it Korolev's imagination or did the wide eyes of the corpse show surprise that he was lying prone on a cold stone floor, his throat a bloody gash?

Korolev looked at his watch. They were early by two minutes and close enough, it seemed to him, to hear the men next door wheezing away like steam engines. He glanced over at Slivka's grave expression — a contrast to Mishka's, who was looking at the two of them with a smile on his face, as if he were sitting in the front row at the cinema. If the situation were different, Korolev would have had the greatest of pleasure in throttling him, but instead he held up two fingers to indicate how long was left. He pointed his weapon at the doorway, and was pleased to see Slivka follow suit. Mishka, winking at Korolev as he did so, pulled his long-barrelled hand cannon from his belt.

And all would no doubt have proceeded in an orderly fashion if there hadn't come the sound of approaching feet from the tunnel along which Korolev and the others had so painstakingly advanced. Even Mishka lost his jaunty grin when the noise became unmistakable — at least half a dozen men cutting off their retreat. Korolev looked at Mishka, wondering if the approaching footsteps might be friends. Mishka shrugged his shoulders. Could they be Chekists? No, NKVD men would have approached slowly and stealthily. These fellows were bowling along as if they were out for an evening walk and Korolev wouldn't be surprised if they were carrying weapons not dissimilar to the nice shiny rifle the dead sentry had been cuddling.

Korolev gestured Mishka and Slivka to cover the chamber ahead, extinguishing the guttering candle with a quick pinch of his fingers before turning back to the tunnel and lifting his machine gun so that the butt sat snugly inside his elbow.

"Militia. Drop your weapons and lift your hands to the ceiling." Korolev spoke quietly. There was a moment of silence, a conversation stopped mid-sentence and seven or eight men came to a halt about five yards away. The lead man, carrying a lantern to illuminate the tunnel, smiled as Korolev turned the corner, but the smile slid away now that he found himself looking down the barrel of a machine gun. As the silence extended, Korolev thought there might just be a chance the rats would indeed drop their guns, but then one of them began to point what looked like the sawn-off stump of a hunting gun while two of the others unslung their rifles, and Korolev fired the entire magazine in three short bursts — the muzzle's yellow flash splattering the walls as the recoil bucked the gun in his hands. The lead man's lantern was still falling as Korolev stepped back around the corner, already dropping the magazine to the floor, and in its light he was able to register the carnage caused by a couple of dozen forty-four caliber bullets fired at close range in an enclosed space.

He ducked back just as the first bullet slammed into the wall beside him, slipping in a new magazine as he did so. The bullet was followed by a blast of shotgun pellets, and ricochets spattered his face and coat like hailstones. He was half-deaf but could still hear Slivka's gun sounding like an eight-hundred-rounds-per-minute death

431

sentence behind him, and he glanced over to see Mishka's revolver jerking up like a French can-can dancer's leg. All good — they were doing some damage to the rats, and that was what mattered.

This time when he went around the corner, he thought it prudent to do so at a low level, and so bent down on one knee. The lantern he'd seen before was now half-covered by a body and not giving out much light, but the muzzle flash from the quick bursts of three or four bullets that he sent in its direction was enough to tell him that at least five of the bandits were down and out of the battle. Bullets were still cracking back toward him, however, showering him with loose chunks of rock. He fired off the last of the magazine and ducked back into relative safety, pursued by another shotgun blast and the screams of a severely wounded man.

A quick glance told him Mishka and Slivka were gone, hopefully to finish off the last of the devils next door. He slid another of the magazines into the machine gun and, in the moments of relative silence between fusillades from either side, listened as well as he could with his ringing ears to what was happening in the passage he was defending. To his surprise he felt warm liquid on his face and a sudden consciousness of pain told him he'd been nicked. He decided it was time to beat a retreat, turning the corner to fire off a farewell gift, but the machine gun only managed to loose off two slugs before it jammed. Korolev was about to swear when he was hit in the shoulder by something very damned solid. It fell to the ground with the unmistakable metallic roll of a grenade and Korolev didn't hesitate, turning and running toward the next chamber, almost tripping on the body of the sentry that Mishka had done in, but somehow managing to keep his balance as his feet and legs tangled and tumbled him across the room. He dived through the entrance pursued by a blast that sent rock shards and shrapnel to help him on his way.

It took him a moment to gather his senses — he'd landed awkwardly on the useless machine gun, but apart from a few bruises he seemed to be intact. He reached for the Walther under his armpit and looked around him as a blast of machine-gun fire from some way off reassured him that Slivka was still alive and kicking. Good for her. The chamber was much bigger than the one he'd just been blown out of and three crumpled bodies, one of which had been flung backward over an open wooden chest, were testament to Mishka's and Slivka's shooting abilities.

He surveyed the situation. He was battered and bruised, and had suffered a scratch or two along the way, but he was alive for the moment. His firepower was reduced, but at least the Walther was reliable, unlike the jammed coffee-grinder, and he still had that Nagant as backup. He could hold the doorway here so long as they didn't throw anymore of their damned grenades at him. After all, the others should be back soon, or so he hoped.

Wherever Kolya and Slivka were, the bandits were closer still — there was movement in the smaller chamber. He couldn't see the men who were approaching clearly, but he could hear them well enough.

"We got him," a nervous voice declared in a whisper.

"Be careful," came the response. "He wasn't on his own."

At least three of them, and maybe more from the sounds of quiet movement. Korolev stood with his back to the chamber itself, ready to turn and fire into the next room. There was more gunfire from Slivka's direction.

"That must be our boys giving them hell," the first voice said.

"But where are they, then?"

"That's not one of them. That's poor Borya." A different voice now.

"Damn it, it is. Will I throw in a grenade?"

"Are you mad? There's a couple of tons of ammunition in there."

Korolev glanced around at the crates full of munitions of one sort or another and didn't like the look of them one bit. There was another footstep — too close now — and he moved to fire two quick shots at a dark shadow, which dropped to the ground shooting as he stepped back. The others joined in and ricochets whined around the chamber behind him as all hell broke loose.

It was time to give up this spot, he decided, pulling out the Nagant and, sticking his hand around the corner, firing three random shots into the gloom to a predictable response. Keeping low as bullets cracked and whined around him, he retreated as quietly and carefully as he could, stepping over a body and taking cover behind the crates. He kept his guns aimed at the entrance to the smaller room and kept moving until he reached the comforting dark of the far entrance. At least from here, he'd be the one able to see — and not be seen.

The enemy must have come to the same

conclusion, as a bullet clanged into one of the lanterns that hung from the ceiling and it exploded in a ball of flame as it soared across the room, fortunately landing in an empty corner where it did no damage except to light the room even more brightly. Korolev felt sweat break out along his spine, and it wasn't from the sudden rush of heat as much as the thought of what might have happened if the oil lantern had landed on an ammunition crate. The same thought must have occurred to the bandits, as there was silence for an appalled moment which ended with a shouted warning and the sound of three shots. Two of the bandits came backward into the light, firing through the doorway they'd just come from. Korolev shot twice, missing both times, and before he could fire a third time one of the men was clutching a wounded arm, his pistol lying on the floor, and the other one had also dropped his weapon and raised his hands in surrender.

Strange, thought Korolev, as he moved toward them, one gun covering them, and the other trained on the entrance they'd piled through. Very strange.

CHAPTER TWENTY-FIVE

The Greek wasn't in a position, not having acquired the power of speech in the short time since Korolev had last seen him, to explain how he'd ended up in the passageway behind the bandits. But however he'd done it, it was his arrival that had resulted in a happier ending to the underground gunfight than Korolev had necessarily been expecting. The Greek clearly knew it as well, to judge from his pleased smile.

"Good work, Greek."

Not taking his eyes from the prisoners, the Greek nodded his proud agreement. He'd appeared out of the dark entrance shepherding a wounded man, who'd joined the two earlier arrivals. The prisoners now stood against the wall with expressions indicating they'd already thought their futures through and they didn't like the look of them.

"Anyone alive back there?" Korolev asked, pointing along the corridor.

The Greek held up two fingers, before shrugging and reducing his estimate to a single finger. A tough man, the Greek — not that Korolev was complaining.

Korolev collected the guns the bandits had dropped, an ancient imperial army Smith & Wesson revolver and a more recent Nagant, emptied the remaining cartridges onto the floor and threw the guns into an open rifle chest. He picked up his machine gun and worked the side bolt to dislodge the jam and loaded the last magazine. Then he held his flashlight alongside the barrel of the gun, before walking into the smaller chamber the Greek had appeared from. There were sounds from the passageway beyond, but they were the sounds of the half-dead rather than the living.

Korolev was cautious, taking his time, playing the flashlight beam back and forth. Five dead, that was certain — a machine-gun bullet at close range was an unforgiving visitor and not many of the fifty-odd he'd sent down into the mass of men seemed to have missed. But one man was still alive — Sergeant Gradov. One of the bullets had pulled an ear from his head, and others had torn at his thighs and an arm — but it looked as if he would live, and also as though he might be able to talk.

Korolev took no chances, advancing slowly, picking up any weapons he came upon, emptying the ammunition they contained and throwing them behind him — all the time keeping his gun pointing at the sergeant. Korolev felt his jaw tighten as he stepped over dead men, a feeling of nausea rising in him at the smell of warm blood and cordite mixed with the chill damp of the tunnel. He'd killed these men. All right, they'd have killed him as soon as blink, and no doubt about it — but still. He'd sent their souls to the Lord whichever way you looked at it, and who was to say the Lord wouldn't look on them kindly for resisting the Soviet Power that had destroyed his Church? Korolev felt despair dragging at him, and reminded himself not to think about such matters — maybe things weren't perfect in this Soviet State of his, but at least he'd done his duty. And that was all there was to it — thinking about right and wrong was a dangerous game these days.

While Korolev was making his slow approach, Gradov had managed to push himself up so that he was now leaning against the tunnel wall, his weight balanced on one buttock, face haggard with pain and effort.

"Go on, then — finish me off." His voice was hoarse as he summoned the energy to speak.

"So, Gradov — a traitor."

Gradov adjusted his gaze to look behind the flashlight's beam.

"Captain Korolev?" he asked.

"Yes."

"I told them you were trouble, but they wouldn't listen to me. 'If he came all the way from Moscow, it must be for a reason,' I said. But they knew better."

Korolev took a step closer. He could hear voices from the room in which he'd left the Greek, Slivka's among them. The battle was clearly over.

"How did a fellow like you get involved in this? You don't look the type."

Which was true — he looked like a brute and a bully, sure enough, but not the kind who would take a risk if it didn't involve lining his pockets.

"We all have a past, Korolev."

"They had something on you as well, did they?" Korolev said, thinking of Lomatkin and how he'd been led astray.

"They had me where they wanted me. If I didn't do as I was told, there was a letter

440

addressed to the Chekists with my name inside it. And proof I'd fought with Makhno and shot a commissar or two one April morning back in 'twenty. Not just any commissars either. I picked some high-up ones, friends of today's high-up ones, to make matters worse."

Korolev nodded. A past like that didn't leave much of a future.

"Well, they did for you anyway. Tell me who it was. That you owe them nothing is certain."

"They did for me? No, Korolev, you and that damned gun of yours did for me."

"I didn't put you in this hole, Gradov, believe me. Others were responsible for that and you'll give me their names if you have any sense."

"Don't waste your time, Korolev."

"It was Mushkin, wasn't it? He's the link. He knew about you and he knew about Andreychuk — he even made sure you weren't disciplined when you lost your gun."

The sergeant didn't say anything, but Korolev caught the ghost of a smile before the wounded man looked away and spat. Then there was the sound of someone approaching from the passageway behind him, picking his way among the bodies, and he turned to see Kolya, the Thief's face taking on a sudden look of anger in the half-light given off by the flashlight. Korolev didn't even have time to open his mouth before the pistol in Kolya's hand fired twice, each blast like a punch that pushed him backward.

"What the . . ." Korolev began to say before his feet slipped on someone or something, and he tumbled backward onto the sprawl of bodies, all the time waiting for the pain of the bullets.

"Did he hit you?" Kolya asked, before answering his own question. "No, he couldn't have. What happened to you, then?"

"What do you mean, 'What happened to you?'" Korolev began indignantly, before he realized he hadn't in fact been shot. He was still holding the flashlight and, pointing it at Gradov, he saw that a neat round hole had appeared in the center of the sergeant's forehead. He lowered the beam of the light and saw a small automatic in the dead sergeant's good hand, before turning it back to the newly minted bullet wound.

"Nice shot," he said reluctantly.

"He pulled on you when you turned your back."

Korolev got to his feet, using the stock of his machine gun to lever himself upward.

The embarrassment and anger he felt at having made such a stupid mistake was one thing, but to have been helped out of the consequences by Count Kolya — well, that was another thing altogether. He thanked the Lord that the darkness gave him the opportunity to marshal what little dignity might be left to him.

"You took your time — we had them coming at us from all sides while you dawdled along."

"So I can see. That gun of yours dealt with them, though. Was the grenade yours or theirs?"

"Theirs. Did you get them all?"

"We missed one or two — things were confused in the dark. Slivka and Mishka sent them running, but Fox's men weren't ready for them. We lost a couple of ours in the tunnel, and a couple of them got past — but you have your guns all the same and the battle's won."

Korolev looked at Gradov. Six dead here, then. One in the next room, three in the chamber with the guns. Two of Kolya's men and on top of that however many of the gunrunners who had been killed in the tunnels trying to escape. As quick and bloody an evening's work as he'd ever heard of.

"I hope it was all worth it."

"I'd say it was worth it, Korolev. They wouldn't have been able to keep their fingers from the triggers of that weaponry, and they wouldn't have been shooting at crows with them either."

But Korolev was just a bit too old for all this killing and that was the truth. He'd never been much good at it, if he was honest, but he'd done what was asked of him.

"Are you all right, Chief?" Slivka asked as he emerged into the relative light of the big chamber. She looked at his forehead with a frown, and Korolev remembered the graze he'd picked up during the shooting and lifted a hand to wipe away the blood.

"I'm fine," he said, surprised by how much blood there was — his fingers were red with the stuff and he dragged them down the wall to clean some of it off. "We need to think what to do with these guns, Slivka. And these bandits for that matter. Greek," he said, turning to the doughty forensics man, "can you find your way out of here?"

The Greek nodded.

"And back as well?"

The Greek nodded again.

"I need you to get above with the prisoners. Slivka, you'll go with him. Get our men down here as soon as possible. If a couple of them managed to get free, they might chance it and come back — so time is important. If you're not sure of the way, Kolya will lend you his guide."

But Kolya shook his head when Korolev looked to him for confirmation.

"That can't be, Korolev. We worked together on this job because we had good reasons to — to go after these rats who were killing ours. But if I sent Mole with you, that would be something else again."

The other Thieves nodded their agreement, and Korolev understood. The Thieves' code forbade them helping the Militia or any other representative of the State. Not for the first time Kolya had bent those rules when it came to Korolev, but the justification for it this time no longer existed.

"Don't worry, Korolev," Kolya said, as if reading his thoughts. "We'll keep to our part of the deal."

"Come back as soon as you can," Korolev instructed the Greek, who nodded, looking deliberately at each of the Thieves as if to remember their faces. Korolev shared his concern, but he wasn't about to admit it.

"You'd best be off before our people arrive," Korolev said, as his colleagues and the prisoners left. All the Thieves' eyes were on him now, and they seemed to be waiting for something. Mishka had that slanting smile of his that boded no good and Korolev found that his hand had slid under the belly of his machine gun of its own accord and that he was pleased to feel the cold metal of the trigger against his forefinger.

"Yes, we'll be off soon enough," Kolya agreed, leaving something unsaid — as if he were considering how to broach an awkward subject.

"Off you go, then," Korolev said, moving backward to lean against the nearest wall. He tried to do it nonchalantly, but it seemed he'd convinced few of his audience, and certainly not Mishka, whose smile broadened as he opened that hand cannon of his and discarded the empty brass bullet casings, dropping each one theatrically to the ground, where they bounced and rolled, and then filling the chambers left vacant with live bullets extracted from the pocket of his jacket.

"We have something we need to take with us, Korolev," Kolya said eventually. Polite, but firm. Well, Korolev thought, bracing himself — at least the others were clear of this now, with luck.

"I thought we had a deal, Kolya. Those guns are going nowhere."

"Not the guns, Korolev. The leather suitcases over there in the corner, I think. The guns you can keep."

Korolev saw the two bags he was talking about. Battered brown leather. No distinguishing marks. He looked around at Kolya's men and saw that there wasn't one of them didn't have a gun in his hand. And the truth of it was if he tried to stop them, it wouldn't make a difference. He'd done well to make it this far into the night, and there was a long way to go till morning.

"What's in them?"

"Money. You can't start a revolution with bullets alone."

Korolev nodded, looked around him at the determined faces and nodded once again.

"What bags?" he asked, when his mind was made up.

"That's very reasonable of you, Alexei Dmitriyevich," Kolya said.

"I'm a reasonable man, and I have more important things to do this evening than worry about a couple of bags I never saw."

"Mishka, Fox?" Kolya said, turning his head slightly to speak over his shoulder. "Take a hold of those things and let's be on our way."

When Mishka and Fox had the bags in

their hands, the Chief Authority of the Thieves of Moscow raised a finger to his forehead and saluted Korolev, then followed his men down the far tunnel.

CHAPTER TWENTY-SIX

Korolev looked at his watch — ten minutes past nine — and sat down on one of the wooden crates, wondering how the hell he'd got into such a situation. It was unheard of, really. Maybe in Chicago the gangsters had shoot-outs like this, but you didn't expect such a thing in the Soviet Union. Of course, there were criminals here just as there were in the Capitalist countries, but this was extraordinary. To have so many dead in one place outside of a war was unbelievable. He took a cigarette from his pocket and lit it, looking down into the empty eyes of one of the gunrunners. It made you wonder. It certainly made you wonder.

The trembling that he'd managed to suppress until that point started up again in his left foot. He tried to stop it by wedging the toe of his boot into the gap between a crate and the wall, but that did nothing. The trembling spread up to his knees. He was cold, so very, very cold. What the hell was wrong with him? He pulled an arm across his face, feeling his coat sleeve pushing a layer of sweat across the skin as he did. He was worn out, that was all. Tired. And then this damned bloodbath. And how close death had been this evening. He looked down at the dead terrorist and thought how easily it could have been him lying there, an empty husk of cold skin and bone.

When he was calm again, he gathered the dead men's guns from the surrounding tunnels — for something to do as much as anything else. There were sixteen corpses altogether, and that wasn't even counting the unwilling guide whose throat Kolya had slit before the main shooting had started. And all he wanted was to get out of this tunnel and out of this city and away from this place as soon as could possibly be managed. Back to Moscow, where he knew what was what, more or less.

He'd put the last of the weapons with the ones he'd gathered earlier into an empty crate when he heard the sound. Nothing at all, probably, but he hid behind a pile of crates, putting a round into the chamber of his machine gun. Another more distinct noise, like the sound a hob nailed boot makes when it is trying to move quietly.

He didn't recognize the youngster who came into the room, but he had the look of a Chekist about him — a well-built fellow in a short black woolen overcoat, gray cavalry trousers twisted into high brown boots that glinted in the light from the two remaining lanterns. He also had a punchy-looking revolver in his hand and an expression of extreme apprehension. Korolev watched the Chekist's gun barrel draw wide arcs in the air as it led his gaze around the destruction until eventually he saw Korolev and the machine gun. The Chekist gave an explosive gasp of fear and his hands, gun included, flew upward in a declaration of surrender. Korolev doubted he'd come all this way on his own, so he decided to keep quiet and wait and see what happened next.

"We have you surrounded," a familiar voice called in from the next chamber along. "Put down your weapons and you'll be treated fairly."

"Come on in, Comrade Major," Korolev called out, deciding to play the situation straight. "The room is secured."

"Korolev?"

"The same, Comrade Major. And pleased you've shown up, I can tell you." Korolev hadn't intended his words to sound ironic, but there it was. Mushkin came around the corner, his gun pointing at the floor and a look of bemusement on his face as he looked at the dead men and crates full of guns. He even smiled as he slipped his pistol into the holster of the Sam Browne belt he had strapped across his chest.

"Well, Korolev, you've been busy I see," he said, turning to the young Chekist. "Put your hands down, Petrov. This is Korolev, the Militia expert from Moscow."

"No, he can keep them up for the moment, Comrade Major. You too, for that matter."

"What's this, Korolev?" Mushkin asked.

"How did you find your way here, Comrade Major, if you don't mind me asking?"

"How did I find my way here? What kind of question is that?" Mushkin's anger was beginning to show.

"Did you have a look at any of the dead out there, Comrade Major? One of them is your protégé, Sergeant Gradov from the village station. You'll remember him — the fellow on whose behalf you interceded when he lost his weapon last year."

"Gradov?"

Irritated, yes, but no sudden fear or concern.

"Yes, Gradov. He was one of the terrorists — that's what he was doing here. Helping

452

run guns for a rebellion against the State is how your Sergeant Gradov was passing his time."

"Gradov? A terrorist? I don't believe it."

"So my question to you is how did you end up down here, Comrade Major? I ask this because it's not a place you just stumble upon."

"I didn't just stumble upon it, Korolev. Petrov here is friendly with a woman whose husband disappeared yesterday. A stone-cutter. She thought he'd got involved in some smuggling operation and came to Petrov for help, and he came to me."

"How convenient. And you managed to make your way to this exact spot."

"I'm not sure what you're suggesting, Korolev, but I haven't been inside these tunnels since the Civil War. And wouldn't be down here now if Petrov hadn't brought me down here."

"Olga Ivanova gave me a map." Petrov's voice was a barely audible whisper.

"And why would she tell you to come down here?"

"Because her husband didn't come home last night. She had a bad feeling about him. And she was right. We found him with his throat cut back along the passageway. But she knew where this place was."

453

"Petrov came to me, as I said," Mushkin interjected, "and since Rodinov told us this business had something to do with the catacombs, we followed it up." Mushkin's voice sounded angry now. "So put the damned gun down, Korolev. You've done your duty — you've asked the questions — but enough is enough."

Suddenly the sound of more people approaching came from the direction the Greek and Slivka had left in. Petrov looked concerned, as well he might, but it was Colonel Marchuk's voice that called into the chamber.

"Korolev?"

"In here, Comrade Colonel."

The room was soon flooded with uniforms, all armed to the teeth. The colonel looked around at the weapons and the men lying dead, and nodded his grim approval to Korolev. Then he set to work.

In a whirlwind of activity the colonel sent for more men, congratulated Korolev, praised Slivka and the Greek, calculated how long it might take to move the weapons, identified some of those lying dead and cursed the traitor Gradov for a black-hearted villain. And at some point, amidst all the bustle and confusion, Mushkin disappeared.

■ ■ ■

"Comrade Petrov," Korolev asked. "Where's your boss gone to?"

"Major Mushkin? He's gone to report to headquarters. He wants our people to take over down here."

Korolev looked around for Slivka. She was at his elbow, bless her.

"When did he go and which direction?"

Petrov indicated the far tunnel, confused as he realized that the Major had chosen a different way out from the way he'd come in. Odd, given he'd said he hadn't visited the catacombs in fifteen years.

"When?"

"Not more than two minutes past, Comrade."

Korolev turned to Slivka. "Run after him. If you find him, follow him. See where he ends up."

"Petrov," Korolev said, after Slivka had gone, "tell me why there weren't more of you down here? Why just the two of you?"

"The major said we had to keep it strictly confidential, Comrade Korolev. Between ourselves."

"So no one else apart from you and the major knew you were down here, or about

Olga Ivanova's map."

"No one."

"I see," Korolev said.

CHAPTER TWENTY-SEVEN

Things were moving quickly now, and Korolev had to admit he was impressed with Marchuk. In less than an hour the captured weapons had been moved out of the catacombs and into the security of the Bebel Street station. On top of this, Marchuk had put every Militiaman in Odessa out on the streets, had closed down the railway station, blocked the roads out of the city, and now even ships were to be prevented from leaving the harbor. Even Rodinov was pleased.

"Marchuk has done well," he said when Korolev telephoned to inform him of the latest developments.

"I agree, Comrade Colonel."

"And you've done well also, Korolev."

As for Mushkin, Rodinov had seemed strangely unconcerned when told that he'd disappeared and that Slivka had been unable to track him. Almost as if he'd expected just such an outcome.

"Don't worry about Mushkin, Korolev. He doesn't like you and you don't like him, but that doesn't mean he's a traitor. No, we must look elsewhere for the source of this conspiracy. Tell Marchuk I approve his every action, but that from now on the Odessa NKVD will be taking over this affair directly. Petrenko is in charge now, tell Marchuk that — they'll know each other, I'm sure of it — and all prisoners are to be transferred to his custody. As for you, Korolev, you keep on as you've been doing."

"Shall I ask this Comrade Petrenko for instructions?"

"You report only to me, Korolev. No, you started off looking for the girl's killer and you should carry on doing so. Petrenko will handle the rest. I suggest you go out to the Orlov House immediately. If Les Pins is there, take him into custody. If not, I want you to search his belongings and seize any potential evidence. And remember this. Discretion is required. Absolutely required. That's why I'm sending you and not Chekists. And why you're not to talk to anyone else about this case, except me."

There was nothing friendly about the instruction and Korolev took the point. He might well have uncovered this conspiracy, but he wasn't to be allowed to give either

Marchuk or this new fellow Petrenko any information that might link the matter back to the People's Commissar's mistress or to the People's Commissar himself. And now it was his job to secure any incriminating evidence.

Korolev's grimace drew Slivka's attention away from the road ahead and he shook his head to tell her it was nothing. In accordance with the colonel's instructions they were driving toward the Agricultural College, the car splashing the uneven road ahead with the only light in a world as dark as the inside of a grave.

"The uniforms should have secured the place by now," Slivka said, glancing at her watch. The Militiamen from the village station had been told to prevent anyone from leaving until they arrived, and also to hold anyone who attempted to enter the premises in the meantime.

Two minutes later the car's headlights illuminated the Odessa Regional Agricultural College's name, the foot-high concrete letters golden in their beam as they turned into the entrance, but there was something oppressive about the way the night closed in behind them as they drove along the tree-lined avenue. The faint outline of the Orlov

House showed ahead, ghostly pale against the black sky with not a glimmer of welcoming light to be seen. There was no sign of the Militiamen.

"Let's leave the car here, Slivka," Korolev said. "I have a feeling about this."

Slivka killed the engine and the headlights, and the car coasted to a halt. They sat there for a moment, listening to the silence of past midnight on the steppe. Not even a mouse was turning in its sleep. The only sound was their own shallow breathing and the creak of the car's warm hood as it adjusted to the subzero temperature.

They stepped out of the car, closing the doors very quietly, and waited for their eyes to become adjusted to the darkness. The air had the moist, frigid density that preceded snow, and Korolev felt a speculative flake land on his cheek. They began to walk slowly toward the Orlov House, moving into the darker shadows on either side of the avenue, where the trees overhung it, and were grateful they had when lights suddenly glowed up ahead — the long windows on the ground floor of the Orlov House and the white outside lamps of the college buildings dusting their immediate surroundings with a silvery sheen. Korolev looked away from them to preserve his night vision, thinking there must have been a power cut that had just been repaired.

It wasn't so much the silence that disturbed him or the absence of the Militiamen who should have been challenging them. It was something else again, something much more intangible. And he was grateful for the snug feel of the Walther in his hand when the light spilling from the windows and open front door of Mushkina's cottage showed a crumpled body lying on the cobblestones in front of it.

With Slivka covering him, Korolev carefully approached, recognizing the young uniform from the village, Sharapov. Wet blood oozed down the boy's pale face. Korolev leaned down to feel for a pulse and was surprised by the wave of relief when he felt it. But the relief was tempered with caution — Korolev looked around the courtyard, concerned that the boy's attacker might still be close by. The lights flickered, then went out once again and they were left in darkness. Slivka had already positioned herself beside Mushkina's open doorway and he made his way to her, crouching as he did so.

"Who's that?" she whispered.

"Sharapov — someone's knocked him out cold."

In the dark, he couldn't see Slivka's reaction.

"What do we do about this someone, Chief?" she asked, her voice calm.

"We see if we can find him and we deal with him." Korolev took a deep breath and stepped inside Mushkina's cottage.

Inside it was as dark as the bottom of a coal mine and Korolev pushed himself against the wall, lifted his Walther and turned on his flashlight, running it quickly around the room. It looked just as he might have expected except for the slumped figure lying across Mushkina's writing desk.

"It's clear, but we've another body," he whispered to Slivka, who entered behind him and covered him as he approached the desk.

"The Frenchman," he muttered as he turned Jean Les Pins' head, the dead man's hair surprisingly soft and his skin, even more surprisingly, with a trace of the heat of a living person. But a thin strip of rope was still dug deep into his neck. And then the smell struck him. The perfume of hot wax. He put a finger to the wick of the candle beside Les Pins' head — still warm and the wax underneath still liquid. The killer must have left only moments before they arrived.

"Who is it?" Slivka asked, moving slowly across the room, gun held out in front of her with her left hand supporting her right.

"Les Pins. Strangled. Whoever did it is still close, Slivka. Be careful."

There was no sign of a struggle, and yet here Les Pins was, garrotted, and Sharapov lying unconscious outside with a lump on his head the size of a lemon. There was a door leading further into the house and Korolev, followed closely by Slivka, crept toward it and, gun first, made his way into the kitchen. A quick scan of the room with his flashlight showed the back door was ajar.

"Do you think we disturbed them?"

"I don't know, but I'm going to check upstairs."

Leaving Slivka to cover his back, Korolev climbed the stairs to the upper story, his feet seeming to find every possible creak in the steps as he went. A shirt lay discarded on the small landing and it was clear that someone had ransacked the two bedrooms — Mushkina's clothes were strewn everywhere, a mattress had been thrown from the bed and cut open with a knife and books littered the floor, their spines and boards filleted. A very thorough job, but hastily done, Korolev decided, wondering what the ransacker had been looking for, and why similar havoc hadn't been visited on the rooms downstairs. Perhaps they *had* disturbed the intruder. Or perhaps Les Pins had.

"Well, Chief?" Slivka called up to him in a loud whisper.

"That someone's been up here, Slivka — and searching for something by the looks of it. No sign of Comrade Mushkina."

He turned off his flashlight and went back downstairs — whatever they'd been looking for must be worth having.

"Where's Mushkina's telephone?"

"I'll find it."

"Get it winding, Slivka, and get people out here, soon as you can. I'll bring Sharapov into the kitchen before he freezes."

By the time Korolev had dragged the young Militiaman inside the front door, fat snowflakes were beginning to fall in earnest and already a thin coating of white covered the cobblestones. He could hear Slivka frantically turning the handle on the telephone she'd found on the kitchen wall.

"No line, not even a crackle. It must be the electricity."

"Or perhaps that 'someone' fellow cut it, just to make things easy for us. Come on, help me get Sharapov into the kitchen."

"Chief," Slivka said a few moments later, speaking quietly as she placed a cushion under the unconscious Militiaman's head, "do you hear something?"

He heard it all right — the sound of an approaching motor, its engine barely turning over, but audible enough despite the snow. They crossed the room to the small window that overlooked the courtyard and saw a small truck coming up the lane where they'd left the car at a pace that a man on crutches could have kept up with, its lights off.

"There's a phone in the investigation room and one up at the house," Slivka whispered. "Shall we try for them?"

"You go, Slivka. I'll stay here. We can't leave Sharapov on his own."

Korolev sensed that she was about to disagree, but he took hold of her shoulder and pushed her firmly toward the back entrance.

Slivka turned as if she might resist, but then she kept on moving and closed the door behind her. Good girl, he thought, then retrieved Sharapov's Nagant from its side holster. He cracked it open and ran a thumb around the chambers before snapping it shut. Good, it was fully loaded — he'd keep the Walther for later. He slipped off the safety catch and returned to the window just as the truck disgorged three people at the very spot where Sharapov's body had lain just minutes before.

CHAPTER TWENTY-EIGHT

The first man into Mushkina's sitting room looked around nervously, apparently not knowing what to expect, before retreating. When the tall man returned, he was accompanied by another shadowy figure who aimed what looked like a revolver into the darkness. Korolev wasn't sure where the third member of the crew was, but he hoped he'd stayed in the truck. He waited until the two men reached the middle of the room before aiming the flashlight at their eyes to dazzle them.

"Militia. I've a gun pointed right at you so put your hands up and drop your weapons to the floor. One wrong move and I shoot."

Korolev flicked the beam back and forward between the two men — he didn't recognize the taller man, but the second man was familiar, even if it weren't for the Militia overcoat. Blumkin from the village station. There was a clatter as Blumkin's

467

pistol hit the floor.

"Who are you?" Korolev asked the stranger, his voice sounding far more measured and calm than he felt.

The man opened his mouth to speak and then thought better of it. Blumkin seemed to be trying to slowly back away toward the door until Korolev fixed him to the spot with a warning flash of the light.

"Blumkin, try anything and you'll be breathing through a hole in your chest. Kick your gun over here."

The Militiaman moved back toward his gun in order to comply, while Korolev, his eyes never leaving Blumkin, addressed the tall man.

"You. Surname, name, patronymic."

But the stranger was looking at a point behind Korolev's shoulder and even Blumkin had stopped moving, waiting for something. It wasn't much of a surprise when a voice came from the kitchen doorway.

"Don't move, Korolev. It would be a mistake if you did."

It was the voice of a person who had a gun pointed at a fellow's back and a bullet ready to plant a hole the size of a baby's fist between his shoulder blades if he should so much as shiver. But Korolev started to turn anyway. After all, he recognized the voice well enough.

"That's enough, Korolev. Put your gun and the flashlight on the table beside you."

"As you wish," Korolev said, placing Sharapov's Nagant down as instructed and noting without surprise that Blumkin had recovered his pistol and was pointing it straight at his throat.

"Damienko, pick up that gun and take the light."

"What's going on, Comrade Mushkina?" the tall man asked.

"Trouble is what's going on, Damienko. And your only way out of it is to do as I say."

Mushkina's voice had enough iron in it to armor a tank and the stranger did as he was told, checking the magazine of Sharapov's Nagant and making sure there was a bullet in the firing chamber. Whoever he was, he'd handled a gun before. Korolev was conscious of the weight of the Walther in his pocket, but with three guns now trained on him it seemed to him the best place for his hands was pointing upward, which was where he put them.

"What happened to Les Pins?"

"We found him searching for certain information. A guest who overstayed his

469

welcome — in more ways than one — and a loose end that needed tying up."

Korolev sighed: it didn't take much detective work to realize he was another loose end that needed tying up — permanently. Still, he had a gun in his pocket and Slivka was out there somewhere. The game wasn't over yet — not for as long as he was allowed to keep playing it, anyway.

"So it was you, all along, Comrade Mushkina. Pulling the strings, finding enemies and counterrevolutionaries and bringing them together. Killing anyone who stood in your way."

"Finding them, Korolev?" she repeated bitterly. "That wasn't hard — there isn't a man, woman or child in this part of the world who doesn't know that the Revolution has failed them. I don't have to search for people who are against the Revolution — around here *everyone* is against the Revolution. Ask people in the village about hunger and they'll tell you stories that will turn your blood to ice. They were left with nothing for a long winter — but I know where it all went. Do you know where, Korolev? Abroad. To the Capitalist countries. To the imperialists and bankers. To prop up fascists and oppressors while our own people starved. And there's nothing that wasn't eaten here at that time. Leather, grass, the bark of trees and worse, much worse than that. This is what the Revolution gave these people — the same people it was meant to be freeing from tyranny and want. Let me tell you, Korolev, the tsars were better to the people around here than Stalin, and that's the truth of it."

Korolev turned to look at the elderly woman. The light from the flashlight held on him by Damienko showed the silver in her hair, the dark hollows of her eyes and cheeks. There was no doubting her sincerity.

"I don't involve myself in political matters, I'm a detective."

"You were sent by the Lubianka, Korolev. You're no ordinary detective."

"I was sent here, as you say, by the Lubianka — but I'm no Chekist. And, believe me, if I had my way I'd be in my bed in Moscow right now rather than having guns pointed at me. But you know who the murdered girl was connected to, and it was my misfortune to come to his attention on another case. Political matters aren't for the likes of me, Comrade, but I go where I'm sent. That's what an ordinary detective has to do — his duty."

"Ordinary, you say? Do you know how

much trouble you've caused us?"

"My job is to investigate crimes, Comrade. I don't apologize if I make it inconvenient for the criminals."

As soon as he'd said it, Korolev regretted the comment. It wasn't the time to be pointing a finger at people who were pointing guns at him.

"We're no criminals, Korolev," Mushkina eventually said, her voice seeming a little quieter than before. "The criminals are Stalin and the Party, who've murdered the People. I know the truth."

Korolev wanted a cigarette and he wanted to see his son Yuri one more time. To ruffle his fingers through the boy's soft hair and hear him laugh. It looked as if the odds on seeing Yuri were long, but he might have a chance with a cigarette.

"Mind if I smoke? I've some in my pocket. I even have a few spare." Well, why not offer them around? The likelihood was he wouldn't be finishing them himself.

"I have some questions that need answering," Mushkina said by way of agreement.

"I've a few of my own," Korolev responded, his fingers reaching slowly for the breast pocket of his overcoat. "But I'll answer yours better if I have some smoke in my lungs."

"Slowly, then."

When he struck the match, the spark's light briefly showed the faces of his captors: Blumkin looked determined, Damienko as if he wanted very much to be somewhere else and Mushkina could just as easily have been discussing the weather as aiming a loaded gun at a Militiaman's head. The Frenchman, on the other hand, looked as dead as ever.

Korolev's cigarette tip glowed orange as he blew out the match.

"How did you find out about the guns?" Mushkina asked, her voice gentle.

"A fellow I know told me about them. It seems you tried to force the wrong people to shift them for you."

"Not my work. Some men must always take the hardest way. I choose the way that gets me to the destination safely. I knew it was an error to cross the Odessa Thieves."

"You know what happened, then?"

"In the catacombs? Yes. Some of our people escaped."

"Not for long. When I left Odessa the place was crawling with Militia and Chekists. A mouse in a bread box had better have his papers in order tonight."

"Not so many that I couldn't make my way out, Korolev — age and standing in the

Party count for something, even these days. Tell me, how did you find out about Les Pins and Gradov? We know you were looking for them. Blumkin here was ordered to hold them on sight."

"Gradov? Well, it was his habit of losing guns that turn up in dead men's hands, and given Andreychuk had escaped on his watch — well, even I began to wonder whether he might be worth talking to. As for Les Pins, we found his fingerprint on the bracket the girl was hung from. And Sharapov spotted the morphine tablets he used to drug her in his bedroom."

"The girl was another mistake. She could have been dealt with a different way."

"I wanted to ask you why she was killed. You must have known she was Ezhov's lover — everyone else did. Surely killing her could only cause you trouble."

"I knew it, but this fool didn't. And didn't bother asking either." She flicked the barrel of her gun in the dead Frenchman's direction. Korolev didn't need to see her face to be certain it reflected the contempt in her voice. "And then it turned out she was Andreychuk's daughter. If I could have talked to her, I would have reminded her that our exposure was her own death sentence, but he was an adventurer, an amateur. How he pulled the wool over the eyes of the Comrades in Spain, I've no idea."

"Who was he?"

"A Russian mother, a French father, a German spy. He was with the French in Odessa when they intervened in 'nineteen, and stayed on as an observer with the Whites. When he became involved with the Germans I don't know, but fascists have their own loyalties. To him, we were a means to an end. To us, he was a source of guns, so much the same. We gave him something he wanted and he gave us what we wanted. But then he decided he should be the one making the decisions, and some of our people agreed with him. And I was overruled."

"And they paid the price?"

"They listened to him when he said they could force the Thieves to ship in the guns. And look where that got them."

"Why did he kill the girl?"

"She found out what she was bringing in from Moscow."

"And what? Threatened to reveal everything to the authorities?"

"Not quite — she realized Lomatkin was compromised and wanted an end to the arrangement. Les Pins overreacted, and before the information had been recovered as well."

"It was him who drugged her?"

"Yes, although Gradov was the one who killed her."

"And then he killed Andreychuk as well?"

"I don't know — I'd arranged to get him across the border, but when the boat came for him, they found him dead. Perhaps it was Gradov, or perhaps someone else. Andreychuk was a good man — he fought with my husband in the war — but maybe Les Pins only had one way of dealing with problems like that."

"So that's how you knew Andreychuk."

"My husband was a Party member before the Revolution, but when he was asked to betray the Petlyurists he was dealing with to the Whites, he refused and went over to them. Now, of course, I see he was right — but then . . ."

"And your son, he came to the same conclusion?"

"Him? He's still as loyal to the Party as a dog."

Korolev could hear something close to hatred in her voice.

"But he was involved in your conspiracy, wasn't he? Isn't that why he was here?"

"Him? Never — the strain of being a butcher for twenty years is the reason he's here, nothing else. If he'd known one tiny fraction of this — well, you must know what would have happened."

At that moment, two quick bursts of electricity energized the filaments of the light bulbs in the room to dramatic effect. It was like seeing two photographs, almost identical, each for a fraction of a second. The first flash of light left them all dazzled, but Korolev was sure he could see a figure standing in the doorway behind Blumkin and the peasant, wearing a greatcoat. Slivka? If it was her, Mushkina saw her as well because she called out a warning and there was a gunshot. Then the lights came on once again, illuminating a scene that was more confused than the first. Blumkin's eyes were wide open and his body seemed to be lifting off the ground, blood spurting from a bullet wound in his shoulder. Damienko had disappeared, probably hiding under the table. But the figure in the doorway and Mushkina were standing still, each with a pistol aimed in the other's direction, both guns blazing.

Korolev dropped to the floor, pulling out his Walther as shot after shot blasted across the room, and the shooting didn't slacken for an instant when the lights went out again. It was like a wall of noise, so quickly were they firing, and the muzzle flashes showed Mushkina standing there shooting toward the doorway and Blumkin firing at random, the wall slick with his blood as he slipped lower and lower. It was impossible to work out what was happening and a bullet hitting the table beside his head convinced Korolev it was safer not to try. Finally there was a pause, then one last shot and then nothing more.

What followed the explosion of light and gunfire was silence, broken only by a long whistling sigh from somewhere near the doorway and then a single word.

"Mother." It was more like a long exhalation than anything and it sounded like Mushkin's voice. Still, Korolev stayed where he was.

At first he could hear nothing except for the truck's engine outside, still turning over, then he heard running feet from the direction of the Orlov House and the distinctive sound of empty brass cartridges falling nearby onto a wooden surface — someone in the room was alive and reloading.

"Chief?" called a voice from outside, and Korolev felt his spirits rise. It was Slivka — he might get out of this yet — and now a flashlight's beam was angling in through the window, cutting into the darkness.

"Come out with your hands up," Slivka

demanded, and then Korolev heard another familiar voice in the background.

"That's Militiaman Blumkin by the wall, over there," a boy's voice called out. It was young Riakov.

But there was no response from the room and no sound other than Korolev's pulse thudding in his ears and his unnaturally rapid breathing. More people were coming at a run now and Slivka was telling them to keep back. Somewhere outside he could hear Belakovsky's voice asking what was happening. Sorokina was proclaiming that it was a terrorist attack on the film while Shymko was telling everyone to stay where they were.

"Be careful, Slivka," Korolev said quietly, "take your time. I'm beside the table but I can't see anything."

There was a gunshot and a bullet cracked over his head and both he and Slivka fired in response; then there was more silence. Slivka's light shone into the room once again.

"Are you all right?" she asked.

"I'll live."

"I think one of us just shot Comrade Mushkina," Slivka said, unsure, by the sound of it, that this was a positive development.

"Good," he said. "Who was it in the door-way?"

"Major Mushkin," Slivka said. "He's not looking good. Finished, I'd say."

"And Blumkin?" he asked.

"In a bad way, but still conscious."

"There's a fellow called Damienko in here as well."

"I surrender," Damienko said. "Don't you worry about that." And there came the sound of a gun skittering across the floor.

Then Korolev rose to his feet just as the light came back on and he looked around him at the dead and the wounded and thanked the Lord for preserving his poor sinner's life once again.

CHAPTER TWENTY-NINE

Korolev stood beside Slivka's car on the village's solitary street thinking back to the night before. When the lights had come on again, it had been chaos. There'd been actors and technicians, production girls and all sorts swarming into Mushkina's cottage as soon as it was clear it was safe, and more histrionic dramatics than on a bad night at the Bolshoi. In the end, he'd had to fire a shot into the ceiling, and even then it had required a firm talking to and a reminder of his duty as a loyal Pioneer to persuade young Riakov to leave.

After that, it had been a question of waiting until reinforcements arrived and adding up the butcher's bill. Mushkin had caught a bullet in the chest and was dead, his face a mask of pain — and Korolev couldn't help thinking it was the knowledge that his mother had probably fired the bullet more than the injury. Blumkin and Mushkina were both clinging to life and had been ambulanced to the care of Dr. Peskov's colleagues at the university hospital in Odessa, along with the concussed Sharapov. Damienko had emerged from his hiding place uninjured but terrified and was now sitting in a cell in the Militia station, not twenty yards away from where Slivka and Korolev were standing, having a mysterious conversation with the newly arrived Colonel Rodinov.

Snow had fallen throughout the night and most of the morning and it had pushed up against the walls of the village in deep drifts. Korolev, after all the excitement of the previous days, was utterly exhausted. He rubbed his hands together and stamped his feet to try and revive the circulation.

"He's taking his time," he said, turning to Slivka.

"I wonder why he wanted to talk to him."

"Best not to ask, and even better not to know," Korolev answered. He'd spoken to Rodinov the night before, immediately after the gunfight in Mushkina's cottage, and a lengthy silence had followed his report of the events that had taken place.

"This Damienko fellow — you said he looked as though he'd handled a gun before."

"Yes," Korolev had answered. "A soldier at some stage, I'd imagine. I haven't asked him yet — I thought I'd speak to you first."

"Good. Hold him at the village station. Have that pathologist fellow of yours take Les Pins and Mushkin into his morgue — but not under their own names. I'll talk to Colonel Marchuk to make arrangements. This fellow Blumkin — what is his condition?"

"Conscious. More than that I can't say."

"And Mushkina?"

"She took a few bullets." Omitting to mention that they'd come from Slivka and himself. "She's not talking much, but she's tough."

"And you really think she shot Mushkin?"

"It looks that way. It wasn't me and Damienko's gun wasn't fired. It could have been Blumkin, but my money would be on Mushkina."

"A husband and a son," Rodinov said, and there was a note of admiration in his voice. Korolev made no comment. It wasn't the kind of statement that required one.

"He was loyal all along — Mushkin, that is. You know that now, don't you? He even had suspicions about his mother, but I didn't believe him. I thought his exhaustion was playing tricks on him."

"I see it now. I had my doubts."

"He had his doubts about you as well, Korolev."

"Yes, Comrade Colonel."

"But you got the job done between you."

"I hope so, Comrade Colonel."

"The guns are safe, and most of the conspirators in custody — I'd say you completed the task assigned to you. But what happens to them now you don't need to bother about."

"As you say, Comrade Colonel."

There was a pause that reminded Korolev, yet again, of the precariousness of his situation. He opened his mouth to say something, but what could he say? After a few moments, Rodinov spoke again. The voice was slow and deliberate, each word weighted with menace.

"You said the film people thought it was a terrorist attack."

"That was their initial reaction."

"Don't disagree with that explanation, Korolev. Tell them the matter is still under investigation. Where possible, encourage them in their belief but without confirming it. Understood?"

"Of course, Comrade Colonel," Korolev replied.

There was another pause.

"No one, including you, is to speak to this Damienko until I arrive. The same applies to Mushkina and Blumkin. I will talk to Petrenko and Marchuk to ensure this happens, but this instruction applies to you more than anyone. Just in case you were to become confused about the extent of your responsibilities in the meantime, this matter is now in my hands — no one else's. Is that clear?"

It was clear enough, and Korolev had followed the colonel's instructions to the letter — to the extent that now he and Slivka stood in the snow, stamping their feet to keep warm and uncomfortable under the close inspection of the four goons who'd come with the colonel from Moscow. Hard men, young, hungry — looking like hunting dogs waiting for an order from their master.

"I hope that's it," Slivka said, breaking the silence. Korolev turned to find her looking up at the sky.

"What?" he asked, curious.

"The winter. I hope that's it finished now. That we can leave it behind us at last."

"Yes," Korolev said, a little distracted. "The spring is always welcome."

Their attention was diverted by the sound of the door to the Militia station closing.

Rodinov stood in front, pulling on his gloves.

"Korolev?" he said, looking around the village for a moment, as if to remember it forever. Korolev raised his hand to his hat in salute.

"Come with me."

Korolev followed the colonel to his car, its engine still running. At Rodinov's invitation he joined him in the back seat.

"Well, Korolev. You did a good job."

"Thank you, Comrade Colonel."

"Don't thank me, thank Comrade Ezhov. He's pleased with how things have turned out and wants you to know it."

"I'm grateful for that."

"You should be. Of course there are a few matters that still need to be resolved, and that's what I'm here to do."

"I see," Korolev said quietly, wondering if he was one of them.

"Yes." The colonel took off one of his gloves and examined his fingernails. "A little tidying up is called for. So I will now tell you what exactly happened here over the last few days, in case you become confused when you read about it in the newspapers. Are you listening carefully?"

"Yes, Comrade Colonel." Korolev tried to make sure his face was devoid of any indications that could be construed as confusion, although his mind was racing.

"What happened is this," Rodinov continued, not looking at Korolev and speaking as though to an invisible audience. "A young comrade, the late Maria Lenskaya, beautiful, dedicated and utterly loyal to the Soviet State, came across her estranged father — the traitor Andreychuk — whom she knew to be a former Petlyurist officer and suspected of being an active counterrevolutionary. The rat didn't recognize her and so she was able to observe him behaving suspiciously — we'll fill in the exact details later on. It helps, of course, that he was involved in such activities."

He glanced at Korolev, as if looking for approval, and so Korolev nodded, beginning to understand.

"Alerted to his evil intentions, she informed Comrades Mushkina and Les Pins about her fears and, under Mushkina's direction, Lenskaya and Les Pins, together with Comrade Lomatkin, I think, infiltrated a conspiracy to create an independent Petlyurist state in the Ukraine — with German backing. With me so far?"

Korolev nodded again.

"Very good. The conspiracy was led by that fellow Damienko, a Ukrainian exile

who had returned to the country from —"
the colonel paused to think — "Budapest.
Fortunately the efforts of Comrade Lenskaya and her fellow loyal Party members to
bring the conspirators to justice were ultimately successful and resulted in the seizure
of a large quantity of weapons and the death
and arrest of all the conspirators, but at a
terrible price. Comrades Mushkina, Les
Pins and Lenskaya laid down their lives so
that the Revolution might be preserved.
They have joined the pantheon of Bolshevik
heroes, along with Militiamen Gradov and
Blumkin, of course. And we should never
forget Major Mushkin. Especially not Major
Mushkin. A Chekist hero of the highest
valor. I shouldn't be surprised if his mother
and he weren't buried in the Kremlin wall
itself. Oh, and that journalist Lomatkin. He
was a hero as well."

"All of their lives?" Korolev couldn't stop
himself from asking the question; as far as
he knew Blumkin, Mushkina and Lomatkin
were still alive.

"Yes," Rodinov said, drawing a finger
languidly down the fogged-up window
beside him. "All of them. Their selfless
sacrifices for the Socialist Motherland will
be an example to us all. They will be
awarded the highest honors, of course. Post-

humously."

Rodinov seemed lost in thought for a moment and Korolev sensed his own fate was hanging by the narrowest of threads.

"Which brings us to you and Sergeant Slivka."

"We're happy to do our duty, as you direct."

"I don't doubt it. Slivka is a Party member?"

"Komsomol, I believe."

"I see, but you aren't — isn't that right?" The colonel's eyes were boring into him now, but Korolev sensed no hostility as such — not yet, at any event. He hesitated, considering how best to respond.

"I've never thought myself worthy of being considered for an active political role in the Revolution, Comrade Colonel." Korolev spoke carefully.

"Yes, I think you should focus on what you are good at, Korolev — digging out answers for people like me."

There was a hint of irony in the colonel's voice, but there was no trace of it in his expression.

"You, Korolev," he said after another pause, "you will go back to Moscow and resume your duties."

Korolev felt relief well up in him, but the

colonel wasn't finished.

"I understand there are vacancies in Moscow CID that haven't been filled. Semionov was a junior lieutenant, wasn't he?"

"That was his Militia rank."

"Then we shall promote Sergeant Slivka. You work well together. I'll explain it to your chief. You may give her the good news. The People's Commissar believes you may be of use to him again, sometime in the future."

"Thank you, Comrade Colonel."

The colonel waved a hand in acknowledgment.

"Now these forensics men you worked with — are they reliable?"

"I put my life in their hands, Comrade Colonel. And they came through."

"Well, we shall look after them as well."

Korolev's face must have revealed his fears because Rodinov raised a reassuring hand.

"Don't worry, Korolev, they served the State loyally — they have nothing to fear." Rodinov's expression was still cold, but Korolev sensed that the danger had passed. "What did I tell you again and again during this investigation, Korolev?"

"That discretion was vital, Comrade Colonel."

"Be sure your new colleague knows it as

well as you do. The Party is grateful for your contributions to the successful outcome of this matter, but you must never speak of it again."

"I understand."

Rodinov studied him. "You have a son, Korolev, haven't you?" he said in a detached voice.

"Yes. He's eleven now."

"He lives in Zagorsk, doesn't he?"

Korolev said nothing, fear paralyzing his vocal cords, wondering how Rodinov knew about Yuri, and whether the threat in the question was intended, and then certain beyond doubt that it had been. He found himself trying to swallow, but there was no saliva in his mouth, wondering should he say something, assert his complete reliability, his devoted loyalty to the Party, his dedication to the revolutionary cause, but instead he just looked into the colonel's cold eyes and kept his face as expressionless as he could.

"You still have ten days before you need to be back at work, Korolev. Go and visit the young lad. The permits will be arranged for you. You deserve it."

A few moments later Korolev found himself outside in the sun, in something of a daze, the freezing air sharp on his face and unexpected tears icy on his cheek. He turned away from Rodinov's car and walked toward the Orlov House, his feet moving of their own accord and his mind not concentrating on anything much except the fact that he'd made it through this mess after all and that he'd be seeing his son. His glance fell on the ruined church and for an insane moment he found himself walking toward it, fully intent on going inside to thank the Lord for his good fortune.

But instead he pulled a hand across his eyes to dry them and then over his unshaven chin, and felt the tiredness of the last few days like a weight on his back, and with the last of his energy he turned, smiling at Slivka as he walked back toward her.

AUTHOR'S NOTE

The Darkening Field is a work of fiction, but I've tried to ensure it has a sound basis in fact. There have, however, been some compromises, particularly with regard to place names — the Orlov House, for example, is loosely based on the Kuris Manor near the village of Petrivka, not too far away from Odessa. Sadly it burned down in 1990, but I've posted some photographs of it in its current condition on my Web site, www.william-ryan.com, for those who might be interested. Likewise the village of Angelinivka and the town of Krasnogorka can also be found near Odessa, but they bear no resemblance geographically or otherwise to the way I've described them in the book.

The film *The Darkening Field,* from which the novel's title derives, bears some resemblance to Eisenstein's lost masterpiece *Bezhin Meadow* — from which it can reasonably be assumed that the character

Savchenko has a very slight connection to the great Russian film director. As it happens, the writer Isaac Babel was involved with the screenplay for *Bezhin Meadow* and, as he appeared in *The Holy Thief,* it seemed a good idea to set the novel on a fictional version of the film set. Unfortunately for Babel and Eisenstein, the concerns about the political soundness of *Bezhin Meadow* meant that it was never shown publicly. It's believed the only copy of it was destroyed by a German bomb in 1941.

For more detail on the historical background to the novel, I'd encourage readers to visit www.william-ryan.com, where I have given a more detailed description of the research I undertook for the novel, including a bibliography of sources, photographs, and other material.

I'm in debt to a large number of people for their support and assistance during the writing of *The Darkening Field.*

Elena Andreeva and Anna Andrievskaya showed me around Odessa and the surrounding region — Elena, in particular, managed to spirit me into places I really wasn't supposed to go, which was both stressful and invaluable.

Larisa Ivash was a source of very useful suggestions and was a careful and helpful reader of an early draft, as were Ed Murray, Barney Spender, Kelley Ragland at Minotaur, Nina Salter at Éditions des Deux Terres, and my wife, Joanne.

My agent Andrew Gordon and his colleagues at David Higham Associates, particularly Tine Nielsen, Ania Corless, and Stella Giatrakou, have been brilliant, as has George Lucas at Inkwell in New York.

Finally, I'm grateful to everyone at Macmillan — Sophie Orme, Katie James, Liz Cowen, and Eli Dryden in particular, but most of all Maria Rejt for her consistently to the point and accurate editing. The novel wouldn't be whatever it is without her.

ABOUT THE AUTHOR

William Ryan is the author of *The Holy Thief,* which was a Barry Award Nominee for Best First Novel and shortlisted for the Theakston's Old Peculier Crime Novel of the Year. Born in London, Ryan attended Trinity College, Dublin, and completed his master's in creative writing at St. Andrews University. This is his second novel.

VISIT HIM ONLINE AT
WWW.WILLIAM-RYAN.COM.

The employees of Thorndike Press hope you have enjoyed this Large Print book. All our Thorndike, Wheeler, and Kennebec Large Print titles are designed for easy reading, and all our books are made to last. Other Thorndike Press Large Print books are available at your library, through selected bookstores, or directly from us.

For information about titles, please call:
(800) 223-1244

or visit our Web site at:
http://gale.cengage.com/thorndike

To share your comments, please write:
Publisher
Thorndike Press
10 Water St., Suite 310
Waterville, ME 04901

Young Scientist and the Dentist

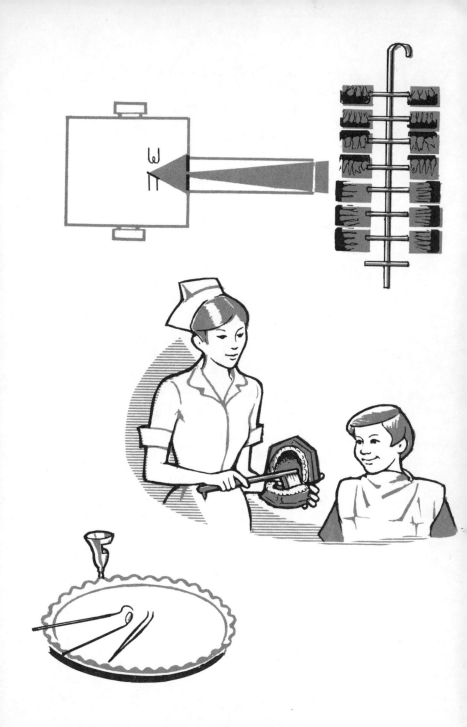

YOUNG SCIENTIST
AND THE DENTIST

by George *Barr*

Consultant in Elementary Science,
Board of Education, New York City

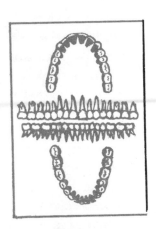

Illustrated by Mildred Waltrip

McGRAW-HILL BOOK COMPANY

71-393

New York   Toronto   London   Sydney
St. Louis   San Francisco   Mexico   Panama

Also by George Barr:

Preface

I am especially grateful to my own affable dentist, Robert C. Tesch, D.D.S., and also to Herbert N. Gross, D.D.S., both of New York City. They granted me time in their very busy schedules for clarifying facts. They also went over my finished manuscript with a fine-toothed comb and offered excellent suggestions. Another keen reader of the manuscript was one of my former science students, Gilbert J. Kringstein, D.D.S., Chief of Oral Surgery, Jewish Hospital and Medical Center in Brooklyn, New York.

The American Dental Association sent me large packages of popular leaflets and also reviewed the manuscript for accuracy. I am particularly thankful to Dolores E. Henning, Assistant Director of the Bureau of Dental Health Education; also to Joanna A. Carey, Assistant Director of the Bureau of Public Information. My thanks also go to Donna B. Finkler and to the dentist consultants for their excellent suggestions.

I also appreciate help received from the National Institute of Dental Research, the International Association for Dental Research, the National Bureau of Standards, and the Research Laboratories of the Dental Colleges of New York University and Columbia University. Considerable help also arrived from the Office of the Assistant Surgeon-General for Dental Services, Department of the Air Force.

Dentistry is a fast-moving field utilizing every pertinent discovery and invention in our modern technological age. This information was supplied to me by over 100 dental-equipment supply companies.

I am especially indebted to James Ryan, Jr., Vice-President of the Densco Company, for assisting Mildred Waltrip, my illustrator. I also carried on a correspondence with Weber Dental Manufacturing Company, Ritter Equipment Company, Pelton and Crane, Mid-West American, Cavitron-Ultrasonics, Star Dental Manufacturing Company, Cheyes Dental Instrument Corporation, J. F. Jelenko and Company, Inc., Hanan Engineering, Torit Corporation, Eastman Kodak, and others too numerous to mention. Big companies with big hearts!

I must hasten to include my gratitude to my wife, Hylda, for patiently wading through my rough copies to produce one original and four carbons of a beautifully typed manuscript.

George Barr

Contents

Introduction

If you accidentally had a tooth knocked out, would it be possible to implant it into its original socket?

Why did George Washington's teeth chatter when he spoke?

Are there people who never get a single tooth during their lifetime?

How does a dentist's grinding instrument rotate at speeds of almost half a million turns a minute?

Why are baby teeth rootless and hollow when they fall out?

How effective and safe is fluoridation of drinking water?

Is hypnotism ever used in dentistry?

Why are research dentists studying barnacles?

How good are mouthwashes for bad breath?

Did barbers ever do the work of dentists?

In the old days, for various reasons, people lost their teeth one at a time, and by the time they were middle-aged they had very few teeth left. But today, with knowledge and care, one can go through life with all one's own teeth.

This book explains the *why* about teeth. It describes in nontechnical terms the art and science of dentistry. You will learn how your precious teeth started to develop many months *before* you were born, and also how teeth are engineered by nature for great strength and varied utility. Your attention is also alerted to the many scientific principles at work in a dentist's office. This book will point out and help you understand the up-to-the-minute technical devices used for dental treatment. Your dentist will appreciate your knowledge because he knows that an educated patient is a better patient.

This, then, is a guide to exciting discoveries which can be made during visits to the dentist. For science-minded boys and girls who are alert and curious, these trips can be absorbing adventures. Some home experiments are also included. *Young Scientist and the Dentist* should give you many ideas for science-fair projects.

To Elsa:
  How sweet and delightful—
  your first pearly tooth!

Count Your Teeth

As you know, there are different kinds of teeth. Our 32 permanent teeth fall into the following classifications: incisors, canines, premolars, and molars.

As a first step in learning about your teeth you should obtain a hand mirror and find each tooth as it is being discussed and illustrated in the following pages. Then you will better understand what the tooth looks like, what it does, and where it is situated in your jaws.

At your age you may be surprised to discover that your total tooth count will be less than 32. You may have only 28 teeth. The mystery of your 4 missing teeth will be cleared up when you find out about your tardy wisdom teeth.

Incisors

As you can see in the chart of the upper and lower jaws on page 19, the incisors are the sharp cutting teeth in the front of the mouth. Four are in the middle of the upper jaw; two on the right and two on the left. These are opposed by four similar but smaller incisors in the lower jaw. The tooth near the middle of the jaw is the

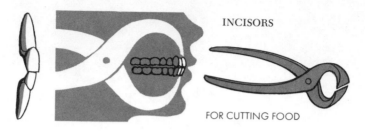

INCISORS

FOR CUTTING FOOD

CENTRAL INCISOR. The one more toward the side is known as the LATERAL INCISOR.

The Latin word *incise* means "to cut into." Incisors have broad sloping surfaces which come to a knife-sharp edge. They serve as shears when they come in contact with the incisors on the opposite jaw. These teeth cut off particles of food, which are then forced by the tongue and mouth muscles backward to the rear teeth. Here the particles are ground into smaller pieces by the larger and flatter teeth.

Canines

These are often called "dog teeth" because they are long and sharp like certain teeth of a dog. Dogs are in the family of animals called canines. There is one canine tooth on each side of the incisors in each jaw, making a total of four.

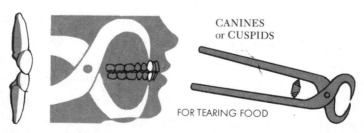

CANINES
or CUSPIDS

FOR TEARING FOOD

A canine tooth is also called a CUSPID. *Cusp* is the Latin word for "point," and the crown of a canine tooth is spear-shaped. This tooth has about the same cutting action as an incisor, but in addition it can efficiently pierce and hold food materials during tearing. Canines are especially adapted for their work by being located in the corners of the mouth. These teeth also have extra strength because their roots are long.

A canine tooth is often wrongly called an "eye tooth." Galen, the famous Greek medical authority of the 2nd century, believed that the canine teeth received branches from the eye nerves. This is not true, but the popular name "eye teeth" has persisted through the years. In the same way, the canine teeth in the lower jaw are erroneously called "stomach teeth."

Premolars

As the word implies these 8 teeth are located in front of the molars. There are 2 in each side of the upper and lower jaws between the canines and the molars. They are also called BICUSPIDS since they are most often double-pointed teeth. The one next to the canine is the FIRST BICUSPID or first premolar. The next tooth toward the rear is the SECOND BICUSPID or second premolar.

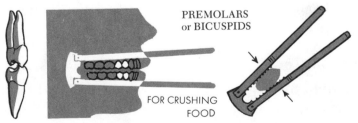

PREMOLARS
or BICUSPIDS

FOR CRUSHING
FOOD

Premolars have surfaces which can be considered somewhere between canines and molars.

Molars

In Latin *molar* means "millstone." Molars have broad surfaces and are the flattest of all teeth. They are the largest and strongest because of their large crown size and also because their root development furnishes firm anchorage.

The molars in the *upper* jaw usually have 3 roots each, but the molars in the *lower* jaw generally have only 2 roots each. The loss of a molar is serious because it furnishes the most important support in the stabilization of tooth and jaw relationships.

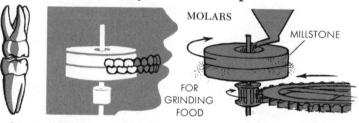

MOLARS

MILLSTONE

FOR GRINDING FOOD

There are 12 permanent molars, 3 in the rear of each side of the upper and lower jaws. They are called first, second, or third molars, counting from the front toward the rear. However, the molars which are located farthest to the rear usually do not appear until long after the other molars have arrived.

Wisdom Teeth

The third molars mentioned above are popularly called WISDOM TEETH because they come in between the ages of eighteen to twenty-five, when a person is supposed to have reached the age of wisdom and can make his own decisions.

Wisdom teeth are sometimes very troublesome for an interesting reason. People today have the same number of teeth as the cavemen had. However, as the result of evolutionary changes through the ages, there has been a shortening of the jaws in all civilized races. This has crowded together the teeth so that there is little room for the last (third) molar or wisdom tooth.

Sometimes the wisdom tooth does not appear at all, because it does not develop properly in the jaw. What is worse, it may be IMPACTED. This means that it is wedged against another tooth and perhaps lying on its side under the gums.

Wisdom teeth usually decay prematurely, perhaps because they are so far back and are thus more difficult to reach with a toothbrush. In general, it is not easy to cleanse teeth in the rear of the mouth, because there is little muscular action of the lips and cheeks to help remove particles mechanically. Many scientists believe that in future evolution man will lose his wisdom teeth. This is a trend in evolution we can readily see because of our own experience with these troublesome teeth.

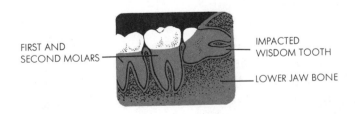

FIRST AND SECOND MOLARS

IMPACTED WISDOM TOOTH

LOWER JAW BONE

Naming Your Teeth

Look at the labeled chart and in no time at all you can easily learn the name of each tooth. Next time you go to the dentist, surprise him by referring to your teeth like an expert; for example, "my lower left first premolar," or "my upper right central incisor." Practice looking into the mirror and identifying each tooth in your mouth without referring to the chart.

Your upper jaw which, by the way, *does not move*, is called the MAXILLA. The lower jaw, which is movable and hinged, is the MANDIBLE. Sometimes the dentist will refer to the upper teeth as maxillary teeth and those in the lower jaw as mandibular (man-DIB-yah-lar). In addition, he may sometimes use the word ANTERIOR to indicate that a tooth is toward the front of the mouth. POSTERIOR means toward the rear.

Numbering Your Teeth

The dentist also has a simple numbering system for easy record-keeping on a patient's chart. There are several systems used in the profession. In one, each tooth is numbered from 1 to 32. Or a dentist may simply number the teeth from 1 to 8, starting at the central incisor as No. 1 and going back to No. 8, which is the wisdom tooth. He then indicates by special symbols shown in the illustration whether the tooth is left or right, and in the upper or lower jaw.

For example, if he writes $\overline{6}$, he is referring to the sixth lower left tooth, which is a first molar. If he writes $\underline{1|}$, then the tooth is the first upper right one—a central incisor.

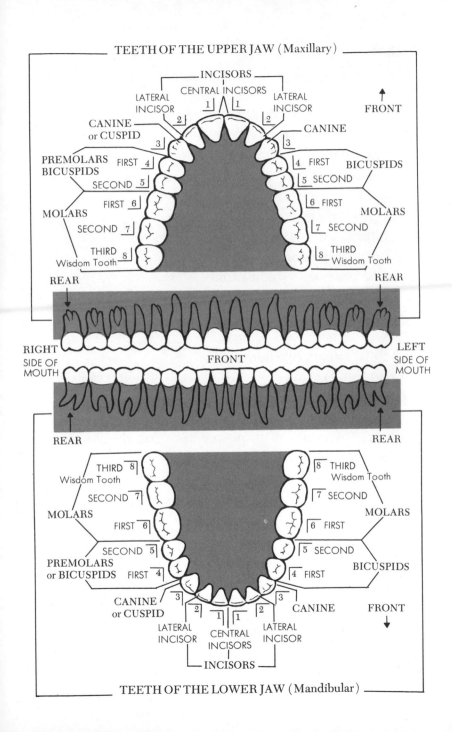

TEETH OF THE UPPER JAW (Maxillary)

INCISORS
CENTRAL INCISORS
LATERAL INCISOR — 1 | 1 — LATERAL INCISOR
FRONT

CANINE or CUSPID — 3 — CANINE

PREMOLARS BICUSPIDS — FIRST 4 — 4 FIRST — BICUSPIDS
SECOND 5 — 5 SECOND

FIRST 6 — 6 FIRST — MOLARS
MOLARS — SECOND 7 — 7 SECOND

THIRD 8 — 8 THIRD
Wisdom Tooth — Wisdom Tooth

REAR   REAR

RIGHT SIDE OF MOUTH   FRONT   LEFT SIDE OF MOUTH

REAR   REAR

THIRD 8 — 8 THIRD
Wisdom Tooth — Wisdom Tooth

SECOND 7 — 7 SECOND

MOLARS — FIRST 6 — 6 FIRST — MOLARS

SECOND 5 — 5 SECOND

PREMOLARS or BICUSPIDS — FIRST 4 — 4 FIRST — BICUSPIDS

CANINE or CUSPID — 3 — 3 — CANINE

LATERAL INCISOR — 2 — 1 | 1 — 2 — LATERAL INCISOR
CENTRAL INCISORS
FRONT

INCISORS

TEETH OF THE LOWER JAW (Mandibular)

What Was Your Count?

The mirror has shown you the number of teeth you possess. If you have all your permanent teeth and have never lost any, you should have a total of 32. However, if no wisdom teeth have come in yet, you should have only 28 teeth.

Here is a tally for a complete set of permanent teeth:
16 maxillary (upper) teeth (8 right, 8 left), consisting of:

    2 central incisors

    2 lateral incisors

    2 cuspids (canine)

    2 first premolars (bicuspids)

    2 second premolars (bicuspids)

    2 first molars

    2 second molars

    2 third molars (wisdom teeth)

16 mandibular (lower) teeth (8 right, 8 left), same as in upper teeth.

Now that you have counted your blessings, are you all there? Good! With proper care you should be able to stay this way for a lifetime. Be true to your teeth or they will be false to you!

The Marvelous Architecture of Teeth

Do you know that your teeth started to develop about 7½ to 8 months *before* you were born? You were still in your mother's body and less than 1 inch tall! The cells which formed your teeth originated from the same cells which later became your skin, hair, and nails.

The growing tooth cells are called BUDS, and scientists have studied them under the microscope. At birth, each bud is in its correct location in the jawbone so that the baby teeth can be completely formed months later. Each bud is like a seed in the ground. In this case, of course, the "ground" is your jawbone. At birth, only the crown or hard enamel top of a tooth is developed in the jaw. It is not yet visible, but x-rays can show that the teeth are there, ready to appear at the right time when they are fully grown.

A tooth is a marvel of nature's handiwork. Each one is designed to fulfill a certain task. Some sharp ones are used for seizing, tearing, and cutting foods, while flat teeth crush and grind foods.

A tooth has two general regions on the outside: a CROWN and a ROOT. The crown sticks up above the sur-

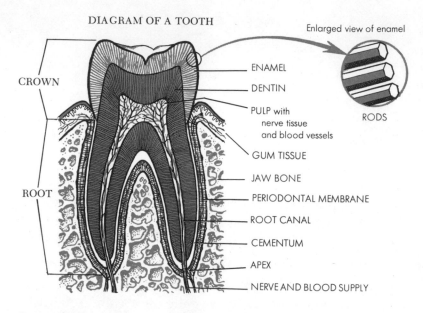

DIAGRAM OF A TOOTH

Enlarged view of enamel

CROWN

ROOT

ENAMEL

DENTIN

PULP with
nerve tissue
and blood vessels

RODS

GUM TISSUE

JAW BONE

PERIODONTAL MEMBRANE

ROOT CANAL

CEMENTUM

APEX

NERVE AND BLOOD SUPPLY

face of the gum. It is the part which is visible when you smile, and the part of a tooth which you brush. Sometimes the dentist will also mention the NECK of a tooth. This is the part between the crown and the root, just at the gum line.

Look at the cut-away diagram of a tooth. Refer to it often as you read the following description of each part.

Enamel

This is the material that covers the crown of the tooth and extends to just below the gum line. It is the hardest substance in the body—as tough as the topaz, a precious gem of great hardness and durability.

ENAMEL owes its firmness to the great number of tiny mineral crystals of calcium compounds. Throughout the enamel there are millions of 6-sided rods extending at right angles to the base of the enamel. The position of these columns of hard minerals supplies additional strength where it is needed. Notice that the enamel is thicker at the biting surface than near the gum line.

While enamel is very hard, it is also quite brittle, and a tooth can break like glass when struck by a hard object. It also does not have good strength at the edges, and can be worn away by acids. One of the unfortunate facts of dentistry is that once enamel is damaged or destroyed it cannot repair itself and grow back.

Dentin or Dentine

This is the yellowish substance that makes up the bulk of a tooth. As you can see, it extends from under the enamel in the crown to the root tip. It is a form of bone which looks like ivory. However, DENTIN is harder than bone and softer than enamel. As long as a tooth is alive a little bit of additional dentin can be formed. Dentin is capable of transmitting pain, although a definite nerve supply has not been found in it.

Pulp

This is the soft, jellylike living material in a tooth, and is in a PULP CHAMBER completely surrounded by dentin. It is the most important substance responsible for the health of a tooth. Pulp has tiny arteries which supply it with fresh blood containing nourishment and oxygen. In addition, it contains veins which remove impure blood and carbon dioxide.

23

There is also nerve tissue in pulp which is sensitive to irritation, such as heat, cold, and pressure. When you have a toothache this is usually the part which aches. Pain is a signal that decayed areas are becoming extensive. Pulp is able to repair itself, and in fact can return to normal—*if the damage has not gone too far.*

As a person gets older, the pulp chamber becomes shorter and narrower. This fact can sometimes be used by the Police Medical Examiner as a basis for determining the age of a badly decomposed corpse.

The pulp is often wrongly called the "nerve" of the tooth. In reality, pulp contains the nerves. When the pulp is removed from a tooth, the nerves are of course also removed. And when the pulp dies, so does the "nerve."

Cementum

This is a thin layer of bonelike tissue covering the root of a tooth. It is continuously forming. Each time the tooth changes its position, new layers of CEMENTUM are made. Cementum supplies a firm anchorage in the jawbone, as explained below.

Periodontal Membrane

This tough membrane occupies the space between the root of a tooth and its socket in the jawbone tissue. Strong bands of fibers coming from the membrane are firmly attached to the cementum surrounding the tooth. Other fibers are also firmly anchored into the jawbone.

24

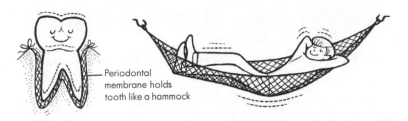

Periodontal membrane holds tooth like a hammock

In this way the tooth is held in a kind of sling or hammock in its socket. The fibers act like a group of rubber bands stretched between the tooth and its socket. Like a shock absorber, this serves to lessen the impact caused when the teeth come together in biting or chewing. In an x-ray the PERIODONTAL MEMBRANE appears as a dark line around the root.

Root Canal

Notice how the pulp chamber narrows down and becomes a tube to the tip of the root. Blood vessels and nerves enter and leave the pulp through this passageway, which is often very small.

Apex

This is the bottom of the root, through which blood vessels and nerves enter the root canal containing the pulp.

Why Different Types of Teeth?

Biologists agree that living things will best survive in this competitive world if they are better suited to deal with conditions around them. As scientists examine plants and animals they discover special life-saving characteristics in each species which have helped them adapt to their environment.

Those species which were not able to defend and feed themselves, or to find shelter or undergo other necessary life processes, have slowly, but relentlessly, disappeared from the face of the earth.

A study of animal teeth shows that they are particularly designed to help animals obtain and chew the special food they need to survive. A CARNIVOROUS animal, such as a tiger, eats only the flesh of other animals. The tiger has special sharp teeth for seizing, tearing, and cutting its meat. On the other hand, a cow, which is an HERBIVOROUS animal, eats only vegetable matter. Accordingly, it has teeth suited to cutting vegetable fiber and grain, and also flat teeth for grinding.

Man is OMNIVOROUS, which means that he eats all foods, both meat and vegetable. He has been endowed by nature with types of teeth which are found in carnivorous and herbivorous animals.

CARNIVOROUS TEETH

HERBIVOROUS TEETH

Your Pearly Baby Teeth

As you know, every person receives two sets of teeth in a lifetime. A favorite joke of the dentist is that if you do not take care of your first two sets you will have to buy a third set!

The first or primary set consists of only 20 teeth, 12 less than an adult has. The back 3 molars of the permanent set on each side of the upper and lower jaws will not appear until years later. Actually there is no room for 32 teeth, since a baby's mouth and jaws are quite small. Also, a young baby's jaw muscles are not well-developed, so that there is not too much need for the back molars to do heavy chewing and grinding. That is one of the reasons why a baby is at first fed strained rather than coarse food.

The primary teeth are called BABY or MILK TEETH. The dentist may also refer to them as DECIDUOUS (dih-SIJ-uh-was) teeth. This comes from a Latin word meaning "to fall down," which is what the baby teeth will do between the sixth and twelfth year. Perhaps you already know that certain trees, such as maples and sycamores, lose their leaves in the Fall and are called deciduous trees.

Development of Teeth

When a baby is born there are no teeth visible in its tiny mouth. However, an x-ray will show that the teeth are there, hidden away under the gum and ready to come out at the proper time. They started to grow about seven and a half months before birth. Each growth started from a thickened area of tiny cells called a BUD. Each of the 10 compact masses in each jaw corresponds to the exact location of a baby tooth.

The fascinating fact discovered by researchers is that the microscopic buds for the SECONDARY or adult set are also developing in the unborn child! In fact, the first permanent molars, *which will not appear until the age of six,* have already developed their hard crowns at the time of birth. These show up in a most interesting manner on x-rays of a newborn baby's jaws. From the buds, the hard, enamel crown part of a tooth develops first. When the crown is fully developed, the root begins to grow. After birth, when the baby's first tooth appears at about six to nine months, the crown is very hard and the root is about two-thirds formed.

Every once in a while you will hear tales about babies being born with one or several teeth already visible. These stories are true. There are many cases where nature's timetable has not been accurate. Stranger things have been known to happen. There are medical histories of people who *never* developed teeth throughout their lives—neither primary nor adult teeth! Such things can happen when tooth buds fail to develop

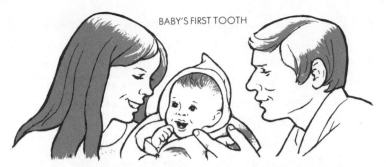

properly. Dentists will also tell you of seven-year-old children who have already lost all their teeth because of faulty development, decay, and disease. In such cases, complete sets of artificial teeth are made for the unfortunate children.

Appearance of First Teeth

The time when the first pearly baby tooth breaks through the baby's gum and makes its welcome appearance is a moment of great joy in a family. This happy event usually occurs between six to eight months. But there is such a wide variation in time that physicians and dentists tell mothers not to worry about late arrivals.

When a tooth is coming through the gum it is said to be ERUPTING. Can you see any similarity between an erupting volcano and a baby tooth forcing its way through the gum? Many babies become uncomfortable and cranky at this time because the gums often become deep red and swollen. The teething baby may lose its appetite and have trouble sleeping, and may frequently run a slight fever. But these are normal signs of teething. Doctors tell mothers not to be too concerned. It is one of the natural nuisances we all endure.

The irritated and painful area in the baby's mouth stimulates the nerve endings and increases the amount of saliva. This accounts for the excessive drooling we see at this time. The baby likes to chew anything which can maintain pressure on the gums, and it is a good idea to supply a hard crust of bread for this purpose. Special teething rings (not nipples or pacifiers) are also recommended for the teething baby.

To this day, scientific researchers have not found a logical explanation of why a tooth erupts, when it does, or exactly how the process occurs. Much research is going on at the present time and several theories have been advanced. It will be a great triumph in the science of dentistry when this question is finally completely answered.

The first teeth to appear are usually the 2 lower front ones—the central incisors. Then the 2 upper central incisors appear. Baby teeth are smaller than adult teeth, but because the baby's mouth is so small they seem to be quite prominent. The first teeth are also whiter than permanent ones. That may be one of the reasons why children's teeth have been compared to pearls by adoring parents. Everyone loves the bright smile of a happy child.

In general, after the central incisors, the teeth appear in the following order: lateral incisors, first molars, canines, and second molars. The lower teeth of each kind usually appear before the upper ones. Often the teeth

THE PRIMARY TEETH

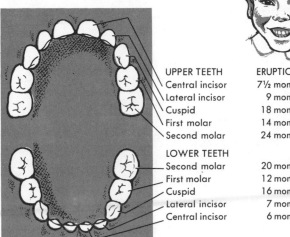

UPPER TEETH	ERUPTION	SHEDDING
Central incisor	7½ months	7½ years
Lateral incisor	9 months	8 years
Cuspid	18 months	11½ years
First molar	14 months	10½ years
Second molar	24 months	10½ years
LOWER TEETH		
Second molar	20 months	11 years
First molar	12 months	10 years
Cuspid	16 months	9½ years
Lateral incisor	7 months	7 years
Central incisor	6 months	6 years

erupt 2 at a time or come at very close intervals. As you can see in the chart, all the primary teeth have erupted by the time the child is twenty-four to thirty months old.

Importance of Primary Teeth

Experience has shown that it is necessary to preserve the first set of teeth until the second set comes. Many people disregard the proper hygiene for keeping the baby teeth clean and free from decay. Their reasoning is that these are temporary, and that a brand-new good set will eventually come along. But their logic is faulty, as you will see.

When a primary tooth is lost prematurely, and a space is left in the jaws for a length of time, there is a

31

shifting of the neighboring teeth in the gums. The teeth in the opposite jaw may also drift out of their normal positions.

The child's upper and lower teeth may not come together properly and the child may not be able to chew thoroughly. The teeth may also start to grow crooked. Then, when the adult teeth come in, they are not properly guided by these crooked teeth and they too assume poorly aligned positions. This can damage the appearance of the face and jaws, and badly affect the child's personality development, as well as his speech and physical health. Expensive teeth-straightening procedures may be necessary to remedy conditions brought on by ignorance and neglect.

The careful parent sees to it that the child starts very early to practice the essentials of dental health described in detail on page 144. These consist of the proper brushing or rinsing of teeth after meals, restriction of sweets, eating proper nutritional foods, and making regular visits to the dentist. Every family dentist works on children's teeth, but one who specializes in dentistry for children is called a PEDODONTIST.

Each dentist advises the parent on how to instill good dental habits in the young child. He also has informative pamphlets on the subject. Today there are painless, psychological, and often enjoyable methods of treatment for the very young patient.

If the dentist feels that there is an undesirable space left by the loss of a primary tooth, he can often insert a simple and harmless device called a SPACE MAINTAINER.

32

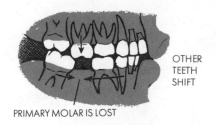

OTHER
TEETH
SHIFT

PRIMARY MOLAR IS LOST

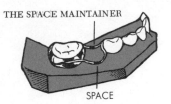

THE SPACE MAINTAINER

SPACE

This will prevent excess movement of surrounding teeth until the secondary teeth erupt.

How Primary Teeth Are Lost

When a child is about five years old, the spaces between front teeth will increase slightly because the jaws have grown larger. Open spaces are usually seen between the teeth. This is especially obvious during a smile. If these spaces are not too excessive, they are not the result of neglect, but rather nature's way of providing room for the larger front permanent teeth which will replace them.

The natural loss of primary teeth is called SHEDDING. At the age of about six to seven years the first teeth start to be shed. These are usually the lower central incisors. You will remember that these front teeth were also the first to erupt. Among the last baby teeth to be shed are the 2 upper canines, sometimes at as late as twelve years. As you can see from the chart on page 31, in general the lower teeth are shed first and then the uppers follow.

When a primary tooth is ready to fall out, it gets very loose in the gums. In most cases a child can pull it out painlessly when it becomes uncomfortably loose and

wobbly. Frequently, *at the very end,* when the tooth is about to come out by itself, the final removal is hastened by parents who resort to methods handed down through the ages. However, dentists caution parents not to be impatient. The loose tooth will fall out almost bloodlessly in a short while.

Much superstition and folklore have been developed around the loss of a child's tooth. The favorite one is to put the tooth under the pillow at night, in the belief that the "Good Fairy" will replace the tooth with a silver coin. This is not very scientific, of course, but for countless ages it has given children a very successful method of obtaining spending money from loving parents and relatives. So who would want to change such a beautiful custom?

It has often been said in jest that to even the score the child should give the parents some money or another gift for each tooth coming in. How does that strike you?

Not too long ago, ignorant people believed that the secondary teeth would arrive sooner if the child were in possession of a tooth belonging to another person. Teeth were sold for this purpose—even teeth acquired from corpses or from poor people.

It had long been believed that the primary teeth are shed by being pushed out of their sockets by the growing secondary teeth. However, research has shown that a certain group of cells called ODONTOCLASTS forms around the root tips of the primary tooth. These special cells dissolve the root part of the primary tooth.

Finally, when enough of the root is gone, the tooth loses most of its anchorage and is held in place by only a few strands of tissue. The final separation may occur by itself, or, at most, may need only a slight coaxing.

Look at the shed primary tooth in the illustration. See how most of the hard calcium section of the root has been lost and is almost hollow. The tooth now consists mainly of the crown. The nerves and blood vessels have also dissolved. Now you can understand why the loss of a baby tooth occurs with hardly any pain or loss of blood. Isn't nature wonderful and quite considerate of little children in this instance?

 A SHED PRIMARY UPPER MOLAR—NO ROOTS

Eruption of Permanent Teeth

At about six years of age the child's first adult tooth arrives. It is called the permanent first molar or six-year molar. Parents often think that this is just another tem-

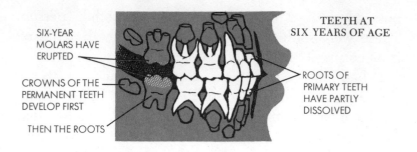

SIX-YEAR
MOLARS HAVE
ERUPTED

CROWNS OF THE
PERMANENT TEETH
DEVELOP FIRST

THEN THE ROOTS

TEETH AT
SIX YEARS OF AGE

ROOTS OF
PRIMARY TEETH
HAVE PARTLY
DISSOLVED

porary tooth which is arriving late, especially since usually none of the temporary teeth have started to fall out.

Do not confuse this tooth with the temporary first molar. As you can see in the chart on page 37, the permanent first molar does not replace any primary tooth. It is located in the rear of the last primary molar. The jaw has increased in size and there is ample room for it.

In other words, the permanent first molar will erupt into a spot which had *no* tooth before, so will the 2 permanent molars in the rear. The former temporary first and second molars in each side of the upper and lower jaws will be replaced by permanent first and second bicuspids, also called premolars. Notice that the addition of the bicuspids gives the permanent set 4 types of teeth while the temporary set only had 3 types.

The 4 permanent first molars are of great importance. They are considered by dentists to be the "keystones" or "cornerstones" of the dental arches. Since they arrive years before many of the other teeth, their correct position will determine the stability of the teeth around them.

These six-year molars are in the mouth for a longer period than the other permanent teeth. It is also more difficult to clean them because of their position and type of surface. They are therefore subject to more decay, especially during the most vulnerable childhood years. Because of their critical role, dentists make strong efforts to keep these teeth in good health.

A child's jaw reaches maximum growth between the ages of approximately sixteen to eighteen. By this time most children have already received their complete set of adult teeth, with the exception of the wisdom teeth.

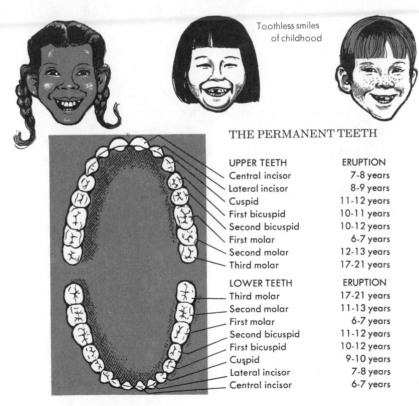

Toothless smiles of childhood

THE PERMANENT TEETH

UPPER TEETH	ERUPTION
Central incisor	7-8 years
Lateral incisor	8-9 years
Cuspid	11-12 years
First bicuspid	10-11 years
Second bicuspid	10-12 years
First molar	6-7 years
Second molar	12-13 years
Third molar	17-21 years

LOWER TEETH	ERUPTION
Third molar	17-21 years
Second molar	11-13 years
First molar	6-7 years
Second bicuspid	11-12 years
First bicuspid	10-12 years
Cuspid	9-10 years
Lateral incisor	7-8 years
Central incisor	6-7 years

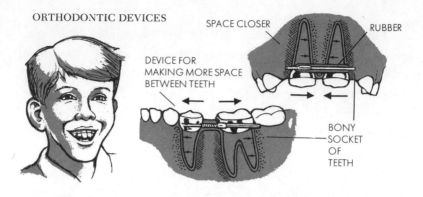

ORTHODONTIC DEVICES

SPACE CLOSER

RUBBER

DEVICE FOR
MAKING MORE SPACE
BETWEEN TEETH

BONY
SOCKET
OF
TEETH

Orthodontics

Sooner or later you, or someone you know, will be wearing a brace or some other teeth-straightening device. This is applied by a dentist who specializes in ORTHODONTICS (or-thah-DON-ticks: *ortho*-straight, *dontics*-pertaining to teeth).

Teeth and jaws are constantly in a state of change. This is especially true in childhood and adolescence because of the growth of the facial bone structure. Because of this movement, many children develop poorly aligned biting and chewing positions of the upper and lower jaws. This is called MALOCCLUSION. For many other reasons some teeth may grow crooked. It becomes necessary to correct these conditions in order to achieve good oral health, as well as a pleasant appearance, so necessary in the development of one's personality.

Orthodontics works on the principle that teeth can be moved or turned in the mouth, without loss of their bony support, when small forces are constantly applied. The side of the bony tooth socket in the jaw which is

38

facing away from the pressure is subjected to compression. This squeezing force makes the bone become resorbed and slightly smaller.

The bone on the side of the tooth which is *facing toward* the pressure of the orthodontic tightening device is undergoing tension. This pulling force stimulates bone to be deposited.

The orthodontist uses a variety of appliances including metal bands, wire bars, jackets covering teeth, springs, strings, rubber bands, and hooks. Constant tightening of the devices exerts a pressure and causes a movement in the desired direction. Special exercises of the jaws are often part of the therapy. Photographs taken before, during, and after treatment show the progress.

Results are generally slow, frequently requiring many months. But the patient is rewarded if he cooperates and follows the instructions of the dentist. Orthodontics is an investment in one's future.

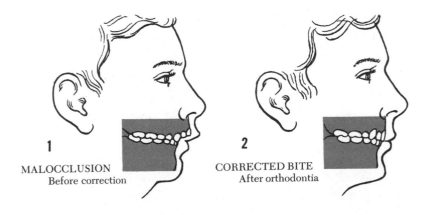

1
MALOCCLUSION
Before correction

2
CORRECTED BITE
After orthodontia

Civilization's Affliction—Tooth Decay

One of the annoying diseases of mankind, as prevalent as the common cold, is DENTAL CARIES (KAR-eez), ordinarily known as tooth decay. *Caries* is the Latin word for "rotten." In the United States fewer than 5 persons in 100 go through life without experiencing the distress and expense caused by this breakdown of the tooth structure. Dentists say that dental caries seems to be increasing over the years, so that today they hardly ever see a patient who never gets a cavity.

Theories of Dental Decay

Most researchers will agree that the illness of dental decay seems to have increased through the centuries as people became more civilized. Man is no longer only a hunter, dependent upon raw meat, wild fruits, berries, and roots. As he developed socially and industrially he also began eating more luxuriously prepared foods, especially more refined sugars and starches.

Historians and medical men have long suspected that diet may in some way be responsible for dental troubles. They point to less dental decay found in certain tribes

40

studied in various parts of the world. These under-developed cultures usually do not have too many highly refined foods, but eat those which are usually in the rough natural state.

During the recent world wars certain countries were not able to import much sugar. It was then found that there was a definite decrease in dental decay, whereas before the war this disease was epidemic. After the war, when sugar again became available, the amount of dental caries rapidly increased once more. Two such countries studied were Norway and Italy.

Much research is going on to find the cause of dental decay, but it is still not completely understood. There are many theories, and these are matters of dispute among scientific investigators. However, there is agreement that the disease begins with acids eating away the hard enamel of the outer tooth. These acids are produced by certain types of bacteria in the mouth which act on fermentable carbohydrates.

After a small part of the hard covering of the tooth is softened and dissolved by the acid, various kinds of bacteria enter the weakened tooth and digest away the softer inside material.

Bacteria in the Mouth

When a baby is born its mouth is practically free of bacteria. Almost immediately, this moist, dark, warm, and nourishing area becomes the haven for a great many kinds of bacteria. This condition will continue throughout life.

Various strains of microscopic organisms, many of which are harmless, will always be present in the saliva. But bacteria also accumulate on the tooth enamel in a soft, usually invisible film called DENTAL PLAQUE (PLAK). This thin layer sticks to the teeth because of a gluelike material extracted from the saliva and also from sugars and starches. Plaque contains tiny particles of food and cast-off cells from the tissue which lines the mouth. All this becomes the food and ideal breeding grounds for the bacteria which thrive in the plaque.

Even the cleanest mouth will contain teeth having some plaque. Areas which are constantly swished by mouth fluids, or scraped by the chewing process, will have less of this chemical-bacterial film. Frequent and proper brushing helps remove most of it. Plaque tends to develop most strongly in areas where food particles can be trapped and which cannot easily be rinsed or brushed away: for example, between the teeth and in the rear teeth. Research has shown over and over again that in teeth where many cavities develop there will adhere more than the normal amounts of plaque.

Making Plaque Visible

Because plaque and certain types of stains on teeth are often difficult to see, the dentist will use a DISCLOSING SOLUTION. This is a harmless vegetable dye which will color the plaque or stain. It is usually red, and may be brushed on the teeth or swished between the teeth.

You can purchase disclosing wafers at any drugstore, or ask your dentist for a sample. Make a dramatic test

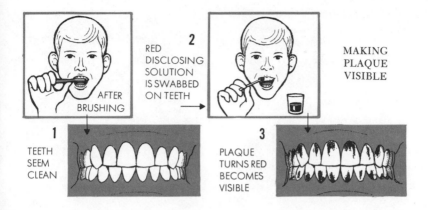

1 TEETH SEEM CLEAN

2 RED DISCLOSING SOLUTION IS SWABBED ON TEETH

3 PLAQUE TURNS RED BECOMES VISIBLE

AFTER BRUSHING

MAKING PLAQUE VISIBLE

to show the presence of plaque, even after you brush your teeth as well as you can. It may shock you to see all the reddish areas on the teeth. This will teach you to try to brush those places more carefully. However, in most cases only the dentist will be able to clean them completely.

You can make your own disclosing solution by applying on your teeth some tincture of iodine or Mercurochrome which you may have in your medicine chest. Use a toothpick applicator with a cotton tip. Only dip into the bottle *once* so that you do not contaminate your family's antiseptic solution. Try various vegetable colorings also. The disclosing stains will soon disappear.

Tartar

If dental plaque is not removed, but is allowed to accumulate, it may lead to the formation of TARTAR, also known as CALCULUS. This is a hard mineral-like substance which forms on the surface of the teeth, slightly

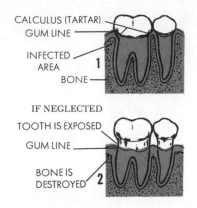

CALCULUS (TARTAR)
GUM LINE
INFECTED AREA — 1
BONE

IF NEGLECTED
TOOTH IS EXPOSED
GUM LINE
BONE IS DESTROYED — 2

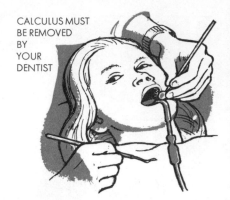

CALCULUS MUST BE REMOVED BY YOUR DENTIST

above and below the gum margins. This is a favorite protected area for bacteria to collect and grow.

Once formed, tartar is extremely difficult to remove. It cannot be cleaned by brushing or by chemicals. Only a dentist or his assistant (who is a dental hygienist) can remove it by careful use of special scaling and filing instruments. This treatment is included in the cleaning and polishing service a dentist calls ORAL PROPHYLAXIS. It should be done at regular intervals. If tartar is allowed to build up, it can irritate the gums and eventually push this tissue away from the teeth and contribute to their loss. Tartar is a frequent cause of bleeding gums.

Acid-Forming Bacteria

Scientists are aware that some of the bacteria normally found in all people's mouths are harmless. But for many valid reasons, they have become very suspicious of certain other strains. Studies have shown that

44

usually there are more cavities when there are present more bacteria called LACTOBACILLI ACIDOPHILUS.

These rod-shaped bacteria feed on CARBOHYDRATES, which is a class of foods including sugars and starches. Bacteria are one-celled plants and have no mouths. They "eat" by giving off certain digestive chemicals called ENZYMES. The enzymes make the surrounding food soluble, and only in this condition can the food be absorbed into the cell body of the bacterium.

In this fermentation process which keeps the bacteria alive and nourished, lactic acid and other acid waste products are produced. It is believed that these acids are the guilty ones which dissolve the enamel on a tooth and make openings for other infectious bacteria to enter. Where there are cavities, the affected areas on the teeth have been repeatedly shown to be more acid than similar areas on healthy teeth.

The production of acids from sugar and starches begins to take place *within minutes* after a person eats. Some of the acid is neutralized by the saliva, but, of course, not enough. That is why it is strongly recommended that rinsing or brushing be done *immediately* after eating.

In fact, there is a certain CARIES-SUSCEPTIBILITY TEST in which the number of *Lactobacilli acidophilus* is counted in a person's saliva. If the number is above-normal, the patient is supposed to be more "cavity-prone." The test however is not 100 percent accurate and is the subject of some controversy among dentists.

Other bacteria, especially streptococci, have also

been accused of causing tooth infection and decay. Almost all researchers now believe that dental caries is caused by not one, but several strains of microorganisms.

Experiments are constantly being made on rats and hamsters which are raised in germ-free containers and fed sterile foods. It has been shown that they will *not* develop cavities—even though they are fed large quantities of sugars and starches. Only when bacteria found in mouths of animals having cavities are introduced will the dental-decay process begin in the infected rats. *In other words, bacteria responsible for dental caries can be transferred from one mouth to another.*

Investigators now believe that since dental caries has been shown to be infectious, (caused by germs), it may be possible to develop protective vaccines some day in the near future, just as it is now for many other bacterial diseases.

Dental researchers are also working on new harmless chemicals and enzymes which dissolve or wash away plaque by destroying its sticky properties. One such remarkable substance is DEXTRANASE.

Solving the problem of dental decay is not simple. Many other factors must be considered, such as diet, heredity, general health, and oral hygiene. Even emotional condition is being studied. It is definitely known that people living through a prolonged emotional period develop more cavities. Adolescence is a period of such stress—and this is also a time when many cavities occur.

The three overlapping circles in the illustration sum-

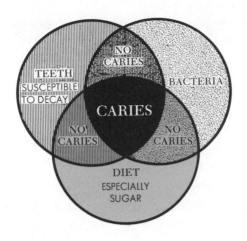

marize visually the three conditions which must be present to produce dental decay or caries. The first is to have teeth which are not resistant to decay. This includes almost the entire American population. Very very few of us are not susceptible.

The second condition is the presence of bacteria which can cause decay. The last circle indicates diet, especially sugars and starches which are eaten frequently and allowed to remain in the mouth.

As shown in the overlapping circles, one condition does not induce caries, neither do two of the conditions. Only in the very dark section, where the three circles overlap, can caries be produced.

How a Cavity Develops

As you have learned, the acid-producing bacteria and other microorganisms live in the dental plaque which forms on the teeth, and are sheltered in certain spots in the mouth. Cavities usually begin under these areas.

The flat crown surface of a molar is also a very vulnerable location. As shown in the illustration, it consists of pits and fissures (cracks) in the enamel. These tiny holes and deep lines are quite weak and easily become deeper as the acids erode them.

Another favorite spot for decay bacteria to do their dirty work is between teeth. It is here that food particles can become wedged. Cavities also form more readily at the gum line, where tartar deposits have been allowed to accumulate.

On page 22 you saw that the enamel is made up of a great many closely packed, tiny, 6-sided rods pointing toward the surface of the tooth. It is now known that the cavity-producing acids work their way into the spaces between these rods.

In due time the penetrated enamel dissolves. Now the tooth's outer defenses have been invaded. The bacteria enter, find shelter, and grow colonies. If not stopped here by the dentist, the acids will continue to eat deeper into the tooth.

The bacteria still cannot get too much nourishment from the enamel itself, since it is composed mainly of rocklike nonliving matter. The bacteria feed mainly upon the particles of food remaining in the crevices.

However, once the dentin is reached, the acid-forming bacteria, and also the bacteria of infection, are able to grow at a faster rate. They are now surrounded by the richer food of which dentin is composed, especially

HOW A CAVITY IS FORMED

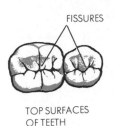

FISSURES

TOP SURFACES
OF TEETH

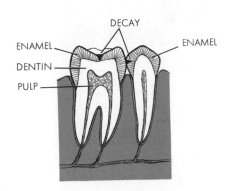

DECAY

ENAMEL

ENAMEL

DENTIN

PULP

1 DECAY STARTS IN ENAMEL

protein, fat, and carbohydrates. Decay is therefore intensified.

Notice in the illustration that the decay area is large where the bacteria penetrate the enamel. This area becomes smaller and shaped like a cone as it advances toward the dentin. Once it touches the dentin, the decay area enlarges very rapidly, and then again becomes cone-shaped as it approaches the pulp.

When the decay is only in the enamel, a person may not have a toothache at all, or have only a very low-intensity toothache. However, the enamel-dentin junction is a sensitive area and when decay reaches this area the toothache may become more annoying. Some people, as you know, react to pain more strongly than others.

If the tooth is treated now by a dentist it can save later pain, damage, inconvenience, and expense. But if this condition is neglected, the decay finally reaches the pulp cavity and the real trouble starts.

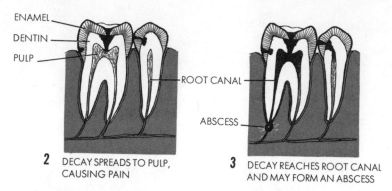

ENAMEL
DENTIN
PULP
ROOT CANAL
ABSCESS

2 DECAY SPREADS TO PULP, CAUSING PAIN

3 DECAY REACHES ROOT CANAL AND MAY FORM AN ABSCESS

When the infection reaches the pulp, the bacteria feed on the living tissue, and decay then proceeds very rapidly. The nerves in the pulp chamber soon are in direct contact with the mouth fluids and the atmosphere. This causes sharp burning pains. Hot or cold fluids irritate the exposed nerves. In time the pulp will be killed, and extensive decay may undermine the enamel and dentin. The weakened portions of the tooth may cave in.

The infection may also spread down the root canal and come out of the tooth and enter the jaw; a dangerous and swollen pus pocket called an ABSCESS may form at the base of the root. Pus is a creamy liquid composed of dead and live white blood cells which help destroy bacteria. It also contains bacteria and particles of destroyed body cells.

Unless treatment is given, the infection may keep destroying living tissue in the jaw. Even the jawbone can be eaten away. In upper teeth, infection may even enter the sinus cavities. Frequently glands alongside the neck will swell painfully because of infected teeth.

50

If infection enters the bloodstream it may affect one's entire system.

It must be pointed out that dental decay is a *progressive disease*. Once it starts, it will continue, unless it is properly treated. It is true that the body has certain defenses against invading bacteria, but these are not able to stop most dental caries. It is also a fact that some dentin can be formed at the pulp-dentin junction, but not fast enough to stop a destructive infection. Sometimes the nerve tissue itself is destroyed, and no pain is felt—but the destruction still continues.

What Is a Toothache?

The pulp contains tiny blood vessels as well as sensitive nerve branches interwoven into the tissue. When the pulp is injured by the invading and destructive bacteria, it reacts by becoming inflamed. More blood is brought to the area. The tissue grows very warm and swollen.

Since the pulp chamber is a confined area, the expanded tissue and blood vessels have no place to go. When the pressure continues to increase, the nerves become squeezed and irritated. This triggers messages of pain to the brain.

Another source of pain is an abscess formed in the jaw at the base of the root. The enlarging pocket of pus then presses on nerves which register pain. In a badly infected tooth the nerve tissue in the pulp is destroyed, but the pain persists because it is registered by nerve endings which are mainly in the periodontal membrane around the tooth.

You may find it difficult to accept, but pain is actually of great help to our bodies. Pain notifies us that something is wrong. When we have a toothache we quickly seek the aid of a dentist. He ascertains where the pain originated, and does what is necessary to eliminate the cause. Pain is an alarm system, which keeps most diseases from developing too far to be treated satisfactorily.

Can you explain why you can feel a throbbing in a bad tooth during a toothache? Pain and excitement will usually speed up your heartbeat and raise your blood pressure. This makes the confined blood vessels in the pulp expand and press harder against the injured tissue with its irritated nerves. The oversensitive nerves pick up the pulsations every time the heart beats, and you feel a throbbing pain.

Strangely enough, a toothache often feels worse when you lie down on a pillow in an effort to get some relief. This is because lowering the head brings more blood to it because of gravity. Once again, the increased blood pressure expands the blood vessels, which squeeze the nerves, and the pain increases.

When you drink cold or hot liquids during a toothache, the pain can be quite intense. The reason is that certain nerve endings are especially sensitive to cold, as well as to hot stimulation.

Tapping a bad tooth will usually cause pain. It also hurts to bite down on an infected tooth. The tooth may frequently seem higher than the neighboring ones. The reason for the above sensitivities is that the inflamed

52

nerve endings in the dental pulp, and also around the tooth, are being compressed in each instance.

What to Do for a Toothache

At first sign of pain phone your dentist. No matter how busy he is he will always treat an emergency. He knows how miserable one can be because of a toothache. Call him early. If you wait too long his office hours may be over, and you may have to suffer through an unbearably long night, or even a weekend. If you cannot visit him he can give you advice on how to get relief.

Your parents may give you aspirin to swallow for temporary relief. Oil-of-cloves is another age-old remedy. Place a small amount of it on a wisp of absorbent cotton and apply it over the decayed or painful tooth. Do not use too much for too long because this medicine can cause a chemical burn. Actually, oil-of-cloves is mainly effective when it is placed within the cavity so that the liquid contacts the exposed nerve. There are also other preparations sold by pharmacists for obtaining relief for a toothache.

Dentists always point out that a bad toothache can be avoided with regular dental care. Periodic visits to a dentist can spot trouble before a bad situation develops.

What Is Fluoridation? (floor-uh-DAY-shun)

In certain communities in the United States people's teeth developed blotchy brown stains on incompletely developed enamel. This is known as "mottled enamel," and scientists traced the cause to a greater than normal amount of fluorine in the drinking water.

However, a surprising fact soon became obvious. In spite of the disagreeable stains on the teeth, the children and adults who grew up in these sections *had fewer dental cavities* than the rest of the population in the United States.

After considerable research, public health authorities also discovered that one part of fluorine per million parts of water did not produce mottling. Yet it was sufficient to reduce dental decay, especially in the developing teeth of children. Scientists suggested adding fluorine to public reservoirs all over the country where sufficient fluorine does not occur naturally. In some areas the drinking water contains a natural concentration of fluorine which is in excess of the correct amount. Fluorine is then extracted until the adjusted concentration is satisfactory.

This has now been done in many cities with good results. In cities where tests were made there were dramatic decreases in dental cavities—up to 65 percent —especially in children who had been drinking fluoridized water since birth. These conclusions have been accepted by the foremost scientific, medical, dental, and public health organizations in our country.

However, as in all matters, it is impossible to get total agreement. Some very angry groups of people, for religious, political, and even scientific reasons vigorously object to having fluorine added to public drinking water.

Nevertheless, fluoridation is being carried out in more of our cities, and also in foreign countries. Fluorine is even added to drinking water at our military bases. Scientists agree that fluorine is safe and effective in concentrations of one part per million. This is equivalent to one drop of fluorine in a full bathtub of water. In fact, millions of people in the United States have lived for years in areas where the drinking water exceeded one part per million. No harmful effects were ever found besides the mottling mentioned above.

Expert studies using powerful electron microscopes show that fluorine solutions penetrate the surface of the enamel. It is believed that this changes the chemical nature and gives the tooth protection against being dissolved by acid.

If the drinking water is not fluoridated, dentists can give children this protection by placing a weak solution of a fluoride on the teeth. This is allowed to remain there for about 3 minutes. The treatment is repeated several days apart. However, there are variations to this procedure. In some cities schoolchildren have received this treatment by biting their teeth on sterile plastic mouthpieces which have been moistened with a special fluoride preparation.

You have already heard of fluoride being added to many toothpastes. Some people believe it should also be added to table salt and foods we eat daily, or perhaps taken in pills.

Fluoridation as a public health measure has joined vaccination against smallpox, immunization against diphtheria, chlorination in reservoirs to obtain germfree water, fortification of milk with Vitamin D, and enrichment of baking flour with minerals and vitamins.

Ancient Man's Dental Troubles

Mankind has been having trouble with teeth ever since people first appeared on earth. Archeologists know this from studying skulls which they have dug up. They find that they can usually make very clear examinations since teeth generally do not crumble into dust, but remain as well preserved as bones for long periods.

It is believed that one of the most serious problems prehistoric man had with his teeth was that the teeth became worn down considerably. No doubt chewing and grinding of the coarse foods which early man ate was responsible for this excessive wear. There is evidence, too, that prehistoric man had a heavy bite because of his larger and stronger jaws.

Dentists say that after the enamel and the underlying dentin of the caveman's tooth were worn away, the living material in the pulp chamber became exposed and grew infected. This must have caused agonizing toothaches, like some we experience today.

There is also evidence that early man must have suffered from poor alignment of the teeth and jaws, diseases of the gums, infections of the jawbones, and also from the buildup of tartar. But, in general, scientists tend to agree that while some clear signs of dental decay are occasionally found in man's fossilized remains, this condition was not as widespread as it is today.

It is believed that the reason for this is that modern man eats more soft foods than the caveman did, especially those containing refined sugars and cooked starches. As you have learned, the present theory of dental decay holds that decay is caused by the erosive acids produced when certain bacteria break down sugars and starches.

No race or tribe of people yet discovered has ever entirely escaped dental troubles. However, one of the persistent findings of research is that the amount of dental decay (cavities) and other diseases of the teeth increases as the level of civilization rises.

There is very little evidence from the fossilized remains that the caveman did anything to remedy his dental troubles. No sign of dental repair work has ever been found. Neither have studies of ancient man's tools shown that he tried to treat himself. One wonders whether any pain-ridden, inventive caveman ever used the method shown in the cartoon to extract a loosened, infected tooth.

Inside the Dentist's Office

When the smiling dental assistant beckons you into the office, you enter a highly specialized, professional workshop, elaborately designed and engineered to fill every need of an efficient, busy dentist. Of course, the familiar chair and equipment-studded dental unit shown in the illustrations dominate the scene. But you can also see an x-ray machine, a special light fixture, instrument cabinets, sterilizers, and other interesting scientific equipment.

Do not believe that because the devices have handsome colors and compact, streamlined appearances they are simple. Many scientific principles are brought into action at the turn of a switch, valve, or dial. Out of sight, and behind the removable service panels, lies an industrial maze of metal pipes for water, air, gas, and electricity. There are also rubber hoses, valves, gauges, wires, fuses, machines, and many special controls.

In dental work there is need for slightly warmed drinking water for the patient who wishes to rinse his mouth. Notice how the water cup fills itself when it is on the special stand in its receptacle near the cuspidor.

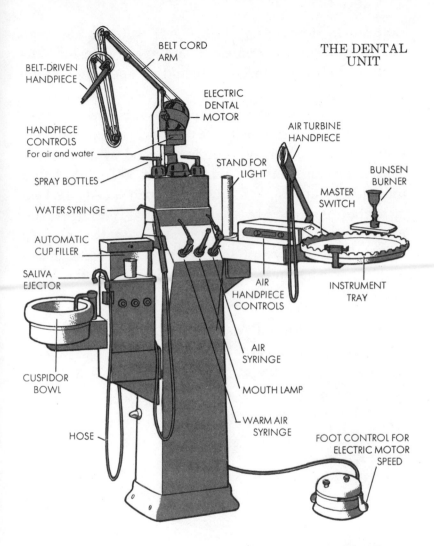

BELT CORD
ARM

BELT-DRIVEN
HANDPIECE

ELECTRIC
DENTAL
MOTOR

AIR TURBINE
HANDPIECE

HANDPIECE
CONTROLS
For air and water

BUNSEN
BURNER

SPRAY BOTTLES

STAND FOR
LIGHT

MASTER
SWITCH

WATER SYRINGE

AUTOMATIC
CUP FILLER

SALIVA
EJECTOR

AIR
HANDPIECE
CONTROLS

INSTRUMENT
TRAY

AIR
SYRINGE

CUSPIDOR
BOWL

MOUTH LAMP

WARM AIR
SYRINGE

HOSE

FOOT CONTROL FOR
ELECTRIC MOTOR
SPEED

The water is shut off automatically when a valve closes
because of the increased weight of the filled cup. In
most units the valve is operated by an electromagnet
called a SOLENOID. A switch is closed when the filled

59

cup moves downward. Lukewarm water is also constantly used by the dentist in syringes for flushing the teeth of debris produced by grinding and other dental work.

Another important use of water is in connection with the high-speed grinding tool called an AIR-TURBINE HANDPIECE. Compressed air is directed against vanes. This force can make the shaft turn at 300,000 to half a million revolutions per minute. At such speeds the heat of friction produced by the cutting or grinding attachment would dangerously overheat the tooth and even kill it. That is why a pressurized stream of water mixed with air is constantly being directed against the tooth and gums as shown in the illustration below.

Uses of Compressed Air

In addition to powering the air-turbine handpieces, compressed air is also used for operating the dentist's air syringe. This directs a strong blast of filtered, dried,

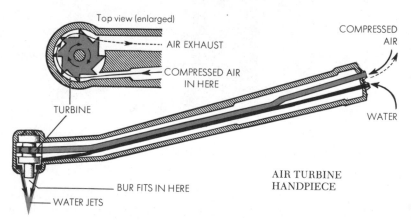

Top view (enlarged)

AIR EXHAUST

COMPRESSED AIR IN HERE

COMPRESSED AIR

TURBINE

WATER

BUR FITS IN HERE

AIR TURBINE HANDPIECE

WATER JETS

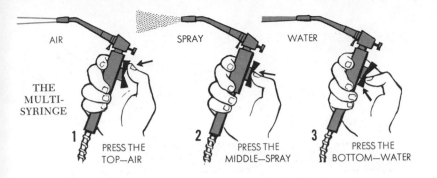

THE
MULTI-
SYRINGE

AIR

SPRAY

WATER

1   PRESS THE
TOP—AIR

2   PRESS THE
MIDDLE—SPRAY

3   PRESS THE
BOTTOM—WATER

and heated air against a tooth in order to clean and dry it. The medicated water spray is similarly activated by the compressed air.

The automatic, electric air compressor and its tank are usually in another location, away from the dental unit, so that the motor is not heard. During compression the invisible water vapor in the air, called humidity, condenses and drops down to the bottom of the tank. This must be drained off at frequent intervals by hand, or automatically, because in dentistry only dry, clean air can be used.

In addition, there is another way of removing any moisture remaining in the compressed air. Before going to the syringe, spray, or air-turbine handpiece, the compressed air passes through a drying chamber. This contains a chemical called SILICA GEL, which absorbs moisture. The material must frequently be heated to reactivate it by driving off the water. This, too, is usually done automatically.

Saliva Ejector

This is a suction device used to draw out saliva and

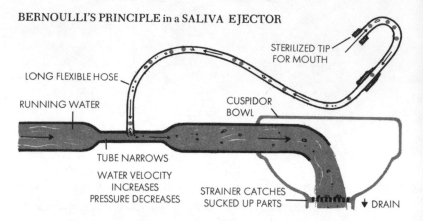

LONG FLEXIBLE HOSE

RUNNING WATER

STERILIZED TIP
FOR MOUTH

CUSPIDOR
BOWL

TUBE NARROWS

WATER VELOCITY
INCREASES
PRESSURE DECREASES

STRAINER CATCHES
SUCKED UP PARTS

DRAIN

other fluids from the mouth. The unit is connected by a long flexible hose to a sterilized curved mouthpiece which the dentist hooks over the lower teeth in the patient's mouth.

The SALIVA EJECTOR is really a water-powered vacuum pump operated on a well-known scientific principle called the BERNOULLI EFFECT, whereby a fast-moving stream of fluid produces an area of reduced pressure around it. The pump is activated by turning on the water, which flushes the small sink called a CUSPIDOR near the dental chair.

Water enters a sealed chamber containing a narrow passageway. As the water leaves this small opening, it speeds up, and a lower pressure is created around this fast flow. The end of the saliva-ejector hose is in this area. The other end of the hose is attached to the mouthpiece. Since the pressure in the mouth is *higher* than the pressure in the unit, the mouth fluids are forced to move into the hose toward the lower pressure.

In some complicated units compressed air is used instead of water. In that case, the moving air is made to speed up by passing it through a narrower tube, just as in the water unit. The rest of the hose attachment is similar to the one using water.

Before the substances drawn from the mouth can escape into the sewage drainpipe, it must pass through an easily accessible fine strainer. This prevents the loss of valuable excess or "scrap" dental materials which may be sucked up and redeemed by the dentist as precious scrap metal.

During certain procedures where it is necessary to quickly remove much liquid and debris from the mouth, the dentist will use a larger hand-held tube connected to an ORAL EVACUATOR. It is really a special electric suction pump, very similar in design to a tank-type household vacuum cleaner.

More About Handpieces

The modern high-speed, air-turbine handpiece has removed the pain from most dental grinding and cutting procedures. Incidentally, dentists do not like to use the term "drilling" when describing the action of this instrument, since tiny steel cutters or little grindstones are mainly used. The dentist does the required work very quickly, and with hardly any vibration or pressure by the handpiece. He practically brushes away the tooth structure. In fact, if he exerts anything but a feather touch, the instrument may stop turning.

One of the problems created by a part which is rotat-

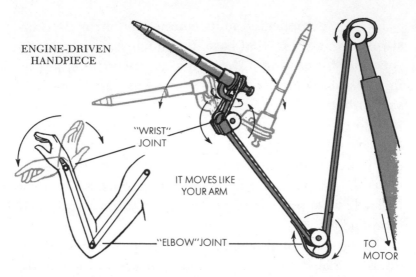

ENGINE-DRIVEN
HANDPIECE

"WRIST"
JOINT

IT MOVES LIKE
YOUR ARM

"ELBOW" JOINT

TO
MOTOR

ing at speeds which sometimes exceed 450,000 revolutions per minute is that the bearings will be quickly worn out. This difficulty has been solved by designing an "air bearing." The end of the metal air-turbine cartridge does not touch a metal bearing. Instead it "floats" evenly inside a frictionless cushion of air.

For certain types of work dentists still prefer to use the older engine-driven (electrical) handpieces which operate at much slower speeds. Slower handpieces also have more turning force, called TORQUE (tork), than the air-driven turbines. Greater torque means that they are not stopped as easily. Since each type of handpiece has its special use, most dentists have both kinds.

The electrical handpiece is driven by a long, round belt intricately wound around several pulleys from the motor to the handpiece. The extension arms coming from the motor on the dental unit are like a person's upper and lower arm. This arrangement allows the dentist to reach the patient in any position, regardless of the adjustment of the dental chair. The handpiece is attached to the "wrist" of the extension arm. Soon these cumbersome belts and pulleys will become things of the past. Today a dentist can obtain a handpiece which contains a small, lightweight electric motor, powerful enough to do what the dentist demands.

On the floor, close to the base of the chair, is a foot control for adjusting the speeds of the handpieces. Some have pedals which must be pressed. Others have rings which are turned. Different controls are used by various manufacturers. Some also have foot valves for water control.

Modern handpieces have come a long way since the slow, awkward rotary tool used in George Washington's day. The first models were made from spinning-wheels.

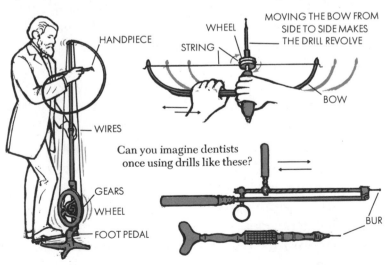

HANDPIECE

WIRES

GEARS

WHEEL

FOOT PEDAL

WHEEL

STRING

MOVING THE BOW FROM SIDE TO SIDE MAKES THE DRILL REVOLVE

BOW

Can you imagine dentists once using drills like these?

BUR

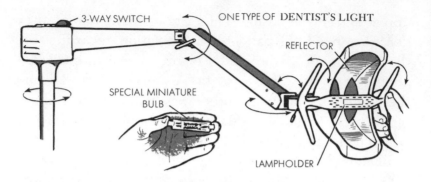

ONE TYPE OF DENTIST'S LIGHT

3-WAY SWITCH

REFLECTOR

SPECIAL MINIATURE
BULB

LAMPHOLDER

Various inventions were later designed using foot trea-
dles and gears. These increased the rotational speed of
the shaft leading through the handpiece. Of course, the
use of electric motors was a big step forward. They
were used for many years until the air-driven turbine
handpiece revolutionized the dental field.

Lighting

Lights used by dentists were greatly improved when the
electric bulb was invented by Thomas Edison. Before
this the dentist used a gas flame whose light was magni-
fied by a lens and focused on the teeth.

The modern dentist's light is extremely important in
his work. Engineers have taken care to produce a light
which is very intense, yet not glaring or too hot. When
switched to its brightest light it is about 15 times as intense as a 100-watt bulb. The source of the light is
usually quite small and may come from a special
quartz-iodine lamp. Brighter and cooler lamps are constantly being developed by the dental-supply industry.

Special mirrors or other means help to eliminate

shadows, so that the instrument in the dentist's hand does not block the light. The light can also be adjusted in a great many positions. Good dental lights are color-corrected. This means that anything held under it will have practically the same color that it would have in sunlight. This is extremely important in matching colors of cements and artificial teeth. There are fluorescent lights which are specially designed for color-matching.

The light can be mounted on the wall, chair, or unit. Some units also have a special small mouth lamp which can be pulled out and shone into the mouth. This is used when it is necessary to get more illumination in certain areas in the mouth than the overhead light can give.

Dental Chair

The chair in the dentist's office looks somewhat like a barber's chair. Perhaps it is because the oldtime barbers actually extracted teeth. Then when dentistry became a profession, a very similar chair became part of a dentist's equipment because it was very practical and adjustable. A similar condition existed when the first automobiles very closely resembled horseless carriages.

A modern dental chair has a soft, restful, sponge-rubber seat and backrest for the patient's comfort. It is covered with topgrain cowhide. The armrests can move up and down, and there is a platform for the feet. The padded headrest can be moved to cradle the head snugly.

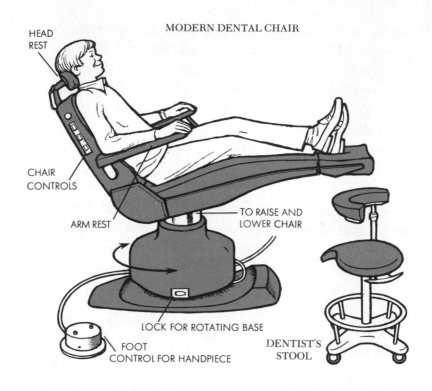

HEAD
REST

CHAIR
CONTROLS

ARM REST

TO RAISE AND
LOWER CHAIR

LOCK FOR ROTATING BASE

FOOT
CONTROL FOR HANDPIECE

DENTIST'S
STOOL

There are controls for lowering and tilting the back and raising the legs, so that the patient can be placed in an almost horizontal position. It has been found that fainting or dizziness rarely occurs in this position, since it is not easy for the blood to leave the brain, which causes fainting. There are also special lounge-type chairs which conform to the curves in one's back. Research has found that astronauts can withstand tension much better in this contour position. The dentists simply borrowed this idea for their own use.

The entire chair can be raised or lowered by oil pressure. It can be rotated on a pedestal through an arc of 60 degrees and locked into any position. Most new chairs are worked by electricity and have switches in various locations, as you can see in the illustration. A dental chair is a marvelously engineered device. No wonder most of them cost over $2,000. Many dentists can tell of patients who found their positions so restful and cozy that they actually fell asleep.

Sit-Down Dentistry

Most dental chairs have places where the dentist and his assistant can hook on their own comfortable, adaptable chairs. Dentistry is very difficult. A dentist used to stand on his feet all through a long day, frequently in a strained position, and in time could develop a painful back condition. That is why dentists have sought work-simplification devices while seated.

Lights, instrument panels, service trays, chair positions, handpiece extension arms, and all other equipment are designed to make it possible for a dentist to work sitting down. To make his work even easier he tries not to hold his elbows high.

Many operators have even dispensed with the cuspidor so that a patient need not sit up to rinse his mouth. The dentist uses a high-speed ASPIRATOR which is really a fast-working, heavy-duty saliva ejector. During treatment, a tray with the instruments rests constantly near the patient's face and within easy reach of the dentist and his assistant.

Instruments and Other Office Equipment

Dental Mirror

The small round, dental mirror is one of the handiest devices in dentistry. It is used for observing surfaces of the teeth that are not in the direct line of vision. By reflection it can throw light on dark areas. It is also used to move aside the lips, cheeks, or tongue, and can even protect tissue from injury when an instrument slips.

Many procedures need to be done on teeth where the dentist's only view is the reflected image from a mirror. It is not easy for a student dentist to learn to use a mirror, because the image is reversed and movements must

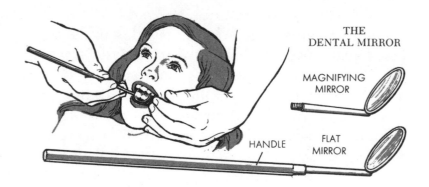

THE
DENTAL MIRROR

MAGNIFYING
MIRROR

FLAT
MIRROR

HANDLE

HOLD
MIRROR
TO
REFLECT
MESSAGE
ON CARD

TRACE MESSAGE BY LOOKING
ONLY AT THE REFLECTION

be made in directions opposite to those which appear to be correct.

You can see for yourself how confusing it can be to follow a reflected image. Write a message or your name on a card. Lay the card down on the table with the writing facing away from you. Hold a mirror so that you see the reflected writing. Now try to trace the words on the card as you see them by looking only into the mirror.

In addition to the flat mirror, there is a concave mirror which gives an enlarged but distorted view of the teeth. Some mirrors have lights attached to them. Others are combined with air tubes for blowing away chips or fluids. All these instruments can be sterilized.

A common problem with mirrors is fogging. Fogging is caused by the condensation of the warm water vapor exhaled from the lungs on the cooler mirror surface. The dentist has several methods of preventing or removing the moisture. He can warm the mirror slightly by

71

passing it through the Bunsen burner flame, or dipping it in warm water. Of course, a blast from the air syringe will clear it very quickly.

He may also dip the mirror into special commercial liquids containing detergents which prevent drops from forming on the mirror as the vapor condenses. Glycerine is also used to produce this effect.

These solutions lower the surface tension of the water. Surface tension is the attraction which water molecules have for each other, and is responsible for the formation of spherical droplets on the mirror. When these droplets cannot develop, only a very thin transparent film of water appears on the mirror. The dentist can see through this.

Sometimes it is necessary to have close-up magnification with both hands free. The dentist then wears a pair of binocular magnifiers held in place over his eyes by means of a headband.

Pulp-Vitality Tester

The dentist can usually find out whether the nerves in the pulp have been completely destroyed or whether they still have some life. He may do this by tapping, called a percussion test, but this is not a conclusive test since a pain reaction may be given by nerves *outside* the teeth.

More effective methods are the application to a tooth of a heated pellet of wax, a very cold tool, a piece of ice, or a dash of cold water. If the tooth is dead, no pain will be felt. This is called a thermal test.

These tests may be very painful to a patient whose aching tooth is extremely sensitive. That is why dentists also use an electronic PULP-VITALITY TESTER. This instrument often rests in a niche on the dental unit. When the dentist touches the probe to the tooth to be tested, he introduces a harmless, adjustable, minute electric current into the tooth.

At first the current used is very feeble. A numbered regulating dial or a meter on the instrument indicates the intensity of the current as the dentist slowly turns the dial. The patient is instructed to raise his hand at the first awareness of a "pins and needles" sensation.

At this point the dentist notes the dial setting. He then tests the same tooth on the opposite side of the mouth as a control and compares the readings. A good tooth, with its healthy nerves, will bring forth a response from the patient to the electric current sooner than one whose pulp and nerves are diseased or dead.

For example, suppose a sound tooth caused a response to the electricity at a dial setting of 7, and the suspected tooth at 15, which represents a higher current setting. The dentist would have good reason to believe

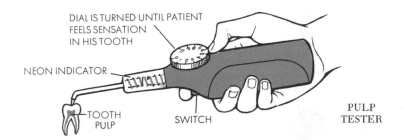

DIAL IS TURNED UNTIL PATIENT
FEELS SENSATION
IN HIS TOOTH

NEON INDICATOR

TOOTH
PULP

SWITCH

PULP
TESTER

that the pulp or nerve and blood supply in the suspected tooth was practically destroyed.

Many dentists do not consider this test completely reliable and use it only as an extra clue in their diagnosis. For example, during a bad toothache a false conclusion can easily be drawn from the fact that an inflamed pulp, with its oversensitive nerves, might register pain *sooner* than the pulp of a normal tooth.

Electronic pulp testers do not work where large metal fillings or crowns are present. Also, a tooth which has several roots might have one vital pulp and one destroyed one. The tester might not indicate this.

Instruments

Dentists take great pride in the useful steel instruments which fill their shallow cabinet drawers. These are specially designed for all dental procedures. They are kept sharp, clean, and shiny.

Hand-held instruments have three main parts. The SHAFT or HANDLE, which is long and hexagonal to prevent slipping. The BLADE is the sharp end, if the instrument is used for cutting. If not used for cutting, the working end is called the NIB. For example, the blunt end of a CONDENSER or PLUGGER which is used for packing down cement is called a nib. A cutting tool has a slanted edge on the blade called a BEVEL.

The SHANK is the part which connects the shaft and the blade or nib. Many handy instruments have blades or nibs on both ends. Dental instruments usually have angles or bends at the ends in order to reach every surface of different teeth.

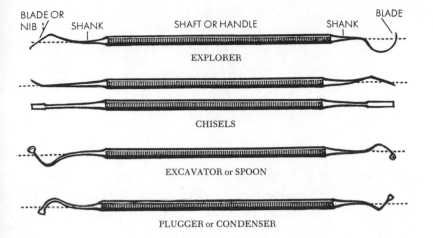

BLADE OR NIB   SHANK   SHAFT OR HANDLE   SHANK   BLADE

EXPLORER

CHISELS

EXCAVATOR or SPOON

PLUGGER or CONDENSER

Notice in the illustration that the tips of the angled blades or nibs always end very close to the imaginary continued line of the long axis of the shaft. This type of instrument has been found to have less tendency to turn in the dentist's hand. There is less strain on him, and he can use leverage with more effective force.

Cutting instruments get their names from the type of work they perform and also from their shape. For example, an EXCAVATOR is used to remove decayed material from cavities. There are three kinds: hatchet, hoe, and spoon excavators. Other cutting instruments are SCALERS, FILES, KNIVES, CHISELS, and LANCETS.

One of the first instruments employed by the dentist in his examination is the familiar EXPLORER. This has a large, curved hook which is quite thin and sharp. By probing the surfaces of the teeth, including those below the gum line, the dentist can discover tiny cavities and other conditions, such as tartar. He can actually do this

by sense of touch alone, because the long blade amplifies each tiny vibration produced at the tip.

Watch the hand grips and finger locations of both the dentist's hands when he uses any instrument. He rests his fingers in definite positions so that his working hand will be steady and supported. The fingers also act as guards, so that if the tool slips it will not cut into the lips, cheek, or gums.

Cutters for Handpieces

There are several types of cutting, drilling, and grinding devices which are gripped and rotated by the dentist's handpiece.

BURS are small steel cutters used for rapid removal of tooth structure, to open and prepare a cavity for filling. As you can see in the illustration, burs come with heads in many shapes: round, cylindrical, pointed inverted cone, and others. The various heads enable the dentist to make any kind of cavity wall he desires. Burs are made of extremely hard tungsten carbide steel for high-speed work.

STONES are small grinding wheels on steel shafts.

76

MANDREL

They contain some abrasive such as diamond dust, carborundum, or aluminum oxide held together by some strong binding material such as plastic, hard rubber, or baked clay.

Stones are also supplied to dentists in a multitude of shapes. Some unmounted stones are not on shafts. They look like little wheels and must be attached to a MANDREL. This is a shaft that fits into a handpiece; the front end has a removable screw to hold the stone.

This same mandrel can also hold various types of rubber wheels, cups, and brushes for polishing natural and artificial teeth. Some common polishing materials are pumice, very fine chalk, and jeweler's rouge, which is mainly reddish iron oxide. DISKS are also mounted on a mandrel. They are similar to small round circles of sandpaper with a mounting hole in the center. They are made of cloth and may have abrasive on one side or both sides. The powdered abrasives bonded to the cloth or waterproofed paper can be carborundum, sand, aluminum oxide, diamond, cuttlefish bone, pumice, chalk, and many other materials. The disks are widely used for polishing teeth, gold, and plastics to an extremely fine finish.

77

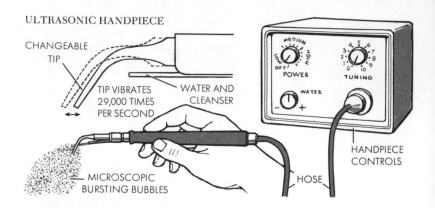

ULTRASONIC HANDPIECE

CHANGEABLE TIP

TIP VIBRATES 29,000 TIMES PER SECOND

WATER AND CLEANSER

MICROSCOPIC BURSTING BUBBLES

HANDPIECE CONTROLS

HOSE

POWER

TUNING

WATER

Ultrasonics

This is a new electronic principle used instead of a rotary or a hand instrument for certain procedures. A specially designed instrument tip is made to vibrate about 29,000 times a second. The human ear can only detect up to 20,000 vibrations per second—the word ULTRASONICS means beyond the limit of sound.

In operation, water and an abrasive are introduced on a tooth surface as a thin mixture. When this mixture is caused to vibrate at ultrasonic speed, there are created countless microscopic bubbles having high vacuums. These bubbles grow and suddenly collapse inwardly with great force. The impact actually blasts loose the nearby solid particles such as cement, tartar, and stains.

At present most dentists use ultrasonics mainly for removing tartar. There are also special cleaning baths for instruments. The principle is still being developed so that it can be used for other dental work. Perhaps some day it will be used to accurately cut and prepare teeth for fillings and crowns.

Laser (LAY-zer) Beam

Much experimentation has been done to utilize LASERS in dentisty. This modern word stands for "Light Amplification by Stimulated Emission of Radiation." Specially grown chemical crystals are electronically stimulated so that the excited atoms are forced into very high energy levels.

The tremendous energy is soaked up by the laser material like a sponge. When triggered by a complicated circuit, this energy is released in a huge burst of light (radiation).

The beam is highly destructive to tooth structure as well as other tissue. Lasers are presently too difficult to control for the delicate work needed in dentistry. Nevertheless, much research is continuing in this field.

Sterilization of Instruments

A sterile instrument is one which is free from germs. Merely scrubbing with soap and water may make it *clean,* but not necessarily *sterile.* Most bacteria are killed by boiling water, but steam under pressure is more effective in killing *all* bacteria. Germs are also destroyed by an open flame and by various chemical solutions.

Every dental office contains an electric steam sterilizer called an AUTOCLAVE. This is the steel container with a temperature gauge whose securely bolted door makes you think of a bank vault. It operates on the same principle as the pressure-cooker used in many homes.

Water, as you know, changes to steam at 212 degrees Fahrenheit at sea level. At this altitude the atmospheric pressure is 15 pounds per square inch. In an open container at sea level it is impossible to raise the temperature of the water above 212 degrees. The water simply does not stay around in liquid form to be overheated, and it steams away.

When water changes to water vapor or steam, it expands in volume almost two thousand times. When water in a container is securely covered and boiled, the steam cannot escape, and therefore the pressure on the water surface increases. The water now will boil and change to steam only at a higher temperature.

The sides of an autoclave are made of strong steel, and the door is very securely and ingeniously locked to prevent a bomblike explosion. There is also a safety valve which opens to allow steam to escape if a dangerous pressure accidentally builds up. Another safety measure makes it almost impossible to open the door until all the steam is released.

The temperature at which the autoclave is operated is usually about 270 degrees Fahrenheit. Some high-pressure units are designed to reach 400 degrees!

Distilled water must be used in autoclaves. If ordinary tap water were used, minerals would remain after the water boiled off and form a crust in the water chamber.

After sterilization, the instruments are removed with sterile tongs or gloves and then wrapped in sterile cloth. Some instruments are wrapped in special paper before sterilization. They are removed from the sterilizer this way and remain covered until used.

Dentists also use sterilizers which do not use steam under pressure. In these the instruments are merely boiled. This tends to corrode certain steel instruments, so "cold" sterilization is frequently employed. In this method the dental tools are placed into a solution of germicidal (germ-killing) chemicals. Alcohol, formaldehyde, and carbolic acid were formerly used extensively, but dentists and their assistants complained about the irritating effects on their hands. Today most dentists use a sterilizing solution containing zepherin chloride, which is not so harsh.

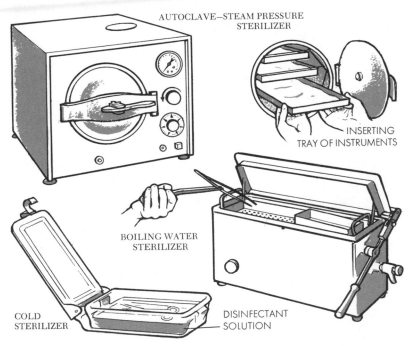

AUTOCLAVE—STEAM PRESSURE STERILIZER

INSERTING TRAY OF INSTRUMENTS

BOILING WATER STERILIZER

COLD STERILIZER

DISINFECTANT SOLUTION

Seeing the Invisible with X-Rays

Next to pain-killers, or anesthetics x-rays have revolutionized the practice of dentistry more than anything else. These penetrating rays were discovered in 1895 by Wilhelm Konrad von Roentgen, a German scientist. But it was not until 1913, when a practical x-ray tube made its appearance, that dental x-ray machines came into general use.

The first models were large, crude, and frightening. Many dentists sent their patients to commercial x-ray laboratories which were operated by trained technicians. In 1923 the first shockproof and simplified x-ray machines were placed on the market. Soon every dentist was stimulated to buy his own machine, and today this invaluable device is standard equipment.

Dentists depend heavily upon x-rays for making a diagnosis. Sometimes when the location of a toothache is difficult and uncertain, x-ray pictures may provide excellent clues as to its origin. An x-ray check-up can also uncover tiny or hidden cavities which are just beginning, and which are not visible through ordinary examination. These are usually found between two

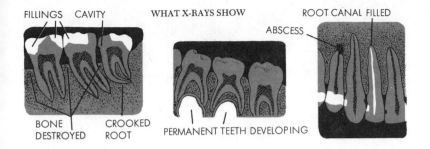

FILLINGS CAVITY

WHAT X-RAYS SHOW

ROOT CANAL FILLED

ABSCESS

BONE DESTROYED CROOKED ROOT

PERMANENT TEETH DEVELOPING

contacting teeth or below the gum line. Frequently, new decay can be observed beneath old fillings through the use of x-rays.

A dentist also uses x-rays to reveal an abscessed tooth, or one which is impacted and not able to erupt because of its abnormal position. X-rays also disclose the absence of the development of a permanent tooth in the jaws. Before extracting a tooth, the dentist can tell whether the root is crooked and then take proper precautions. Without x-rays he would have to guess about this.

Verification is also made of hidden infections and growths in the jawbone, destruction of bone, various diseases of the gums, tartar, and faulty fillings. X-rays are of vital importance in root-canal work.

How X-Rays Work

X-rays are another form of radiant energy like radio, television, heat, and light. However, x-rays have very short wavelengths—about 10,000 times shorter than those of light. (A wavelength is the distance between a point on one wave to a similar point on the next wave.)

83

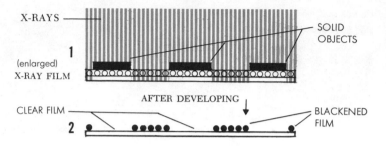

X-RAYS

1

(enlarged)
X-RAY FILM

SOLID OBJECTS

AFTER DEVELOPING

CLEAR FILM

2

BLACKENED FILM

X-rays have the ability to stream through many solid objects. They go through flesh, gums, and soft tissue much more easily than through bone, teeth, or metal.

The rays blacken photographic films just as visible light does. The dentist places a small, covered x-ray film into your mouth behind the teeth he wishes to investigate. It is held with a special hold, which is secured between the upper and lower teeth. He carefully positions the x-ray cone against your face. Then, after he moves away for a short distance, he makes a very brief exposure.

The film is processed in the darkroom just as for any

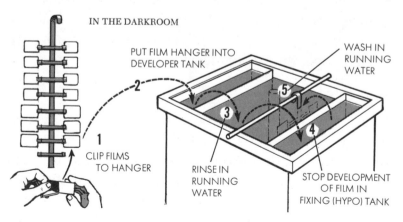

IN THE DARKROOM

PUT FILM HANGER INTO DEVELOPER TANK

WASH IN RUNNING WATER

CLIP FILMS TO HANGER

RINSE IN RUNNING WATER

STOP DEVELOPMENT OF FILM IN FIXING (HYPO) TANK

black and white photograph. The finished product is a dried x-ray negative showing varying densities from black to clear.

The hard enamel, dentin, and former fillings or other opaque dental work will appear clear on the negative. They did not allow the x-rays to pass through to the film. The darker sections on the negative represent the less solid or open areas where the x-rays were able to go through without being stopped.

As you can see by studying the illustrations on page 83, a cavity shows up as a darker area, since a bit of the solid part of the tooth has been eaten away. An abscess appears as a blacker area because tissue has been destroyed and more x-rays can strike the film. The same is true for bone destruction. Training and experience have taught the dentist how to expertly interpret many other x-ray pictures.

Did you know that the black part on a processed negative consists of microscopic particles of pure silver?

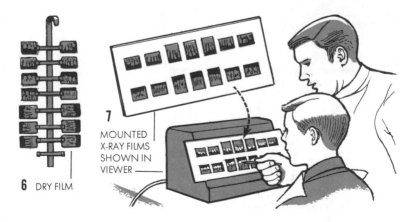

7

MOUNTED
X-RAY FILMS
SHOWN IN
VIEWER

6 DRY FILM

Before exposure, the sensitive part of the film consists of silver bromide. This chemical is held embedded in hardened gelatin on a plastic sheet of cellulose acetate. Wherever the x-rays strike the film, pure grains of silver will be deposited and trapped in the gelatin during the development in the darkroom.

How X-Rays Are Produced

These rays are generated in an x-ray tube as shown in the illustration. Most of the air in this tube has been removed. A low-voltage electric current heats up a coil of wire, called a FILAMENT, until it is white-hot. The coil is also known as a CATHODE or NEGATIVE ELECTRODE. If the air were not evacuated from the tube, the glowing metal filament would combine with the oxygen in the air and immediately burn up.

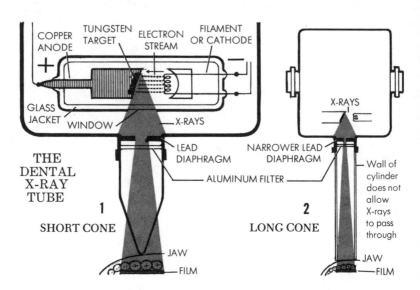

While the filament is very hot, it gives off ELECTRONS. These are negatively charged particles and so they are attracted to the positively charged ANODE. This is a copper bar on whose surface, facing the filament, is a small block of heavy tungsten metal called the TARGET. From 40,000 to 100,000 volts, supplied by a step-up transformer, are changed to direct current and then applied across the cathode and anode.

The high voltage and the vacuum help the streaming electrons acquire very high velocities. When they strike the anode target, the electrons plunge deep into the tungsten atoms and are stopped. Most of the energy of these speeding negative particles is then transformed into heat, but a small fraction becomes x-rays. These rays are deflected downward toward the patient by the slanting target.

Since about 99 percent of the expended energy produces wasteful heat, most dental x-ray tubes are completely immersed in oil. This allows the heat from the anode to be drawn off before the metal melts and the tube is destroyed. Transformers are usually also bathed in oil to prevent excessive build-up of heat.

Safety with X-Rays

You may have heard that although x-rays are useful, they also have the ability to destroy living tissue. Because of this harmful effect, dentists and manufacturers have taken many safety precautions.

The tubes are designed and shielded so that the x-rays can only go out through the desired port, without scattering in many directions. The size of the x-ray beam is limited so that only a small area of the face is irradiated. This is accomplished primarily by a lead diaphragm placed near the tube; the diaphragm has a certain size opening in its center. This is an effective shield which allows only a portion of the center of the beam to reach the patient.

There is also a sheet of aluminum through which the beam must pass. This filters out certain rays in the beam which have been found to be harmful. The cone itself is shielded so that the rays do not scatter in all directions.

In addition, many dentists place special cut-out metal shields between the beam and the patient. This removes all possibility of unwanted x-rays reaching any part of the face but the desired area. Many dentists also use protective aprons containing lead which can be placed over a patient's chest and lap.

By far the biggest improvement in reducing excessive radiation has been the use of high-speed x-ray films. Exposures can now be made of very short duration, sometimes as low as $1/60$ second. To control the accuracy of such short exposures, the dentist has an extremely reliable timer. Most timing switches work from a distance by remote control using wires. Some electronic timers operate by radio and have no connecting wires.

Radiation Records

X-ray damage to tissue has been found to be cumulative. That means that radiation received today must be added to radiation received yesterday or in the future. Experts say that each person in his lifetime can only take a certain amount of harmful radiation from all sources. Besides teeth, chest, and other medical x-ray examinations, one must also include exposure to radiation from radium and other radioactive atoms.

After one's life limit is reached, the body tissue is supposed to lose its resistance to radiation injury. It has been suggested that each person keep a cumulative record listing each exposure to radiation. To be meaningful and accurate, this must include the strength of the radiation and the duration of each exposure.

X-Ray Monitoring

People who work near x-rays or radioactive materials wear special warning badges called MONITORS. Some badges contain sensitive chemicals which darken visibly after dangerous exposure. Others must be developed in photographic solutions. Still others are sent to laboratories where the extent of the radiation is calculated. There are also various pencil-type pocket instruments called DOSIMETERS which are clipped to a smock. Some are designed to give instant checks of the amount of radiation.

The dentist and his helpers who do much x-ray work may wear a small unexposed, covered x-ray film on their uniforms. There is a paper clip or other opaque object attached to it. After a week or longer, they develop the film. If they see the outline of the clip on the negative, it means that they are receiving some of the stray x-rays. A dentist may leave such test films in various locations near the x-ray unit. In many cities regular checks are made of dentists' x-ray apparatus by the Health Department.

Dentists and their assistants protect themselves by using the remote control timer at a safe distance from the patient having an x-ray picture taken. If possible, they stand facing the rear of the x-ray tube. The film is *never* held in the patient's mouth during an exposure. Instead, an x-ray holder is used.

X-Ray Units

The new x-ray machines used by dentists today are streamlined, handsomely designed, and colorful. They are safer than ever before and easily operated. There are dozens of models to suit each dentist. Some are stationary models, while others can be moved to the next room if necessary. Wall models fit closely against the wall in order to be out of the way. When needed, the tubehead can be extended on its bracket far out into the room.

The controls are simple. You can easily read them next time you visit the dentist. All models are different, of course, but they usually have the following dials, meters, lights, and switches.

There are selector dials so that the dentist can choose the required voltage and amperage (current). The abbreviation "kv" stands for kilovolts (kilo=1,000). Any voltage from about 40,000–100,000 (40–100 kv) may be

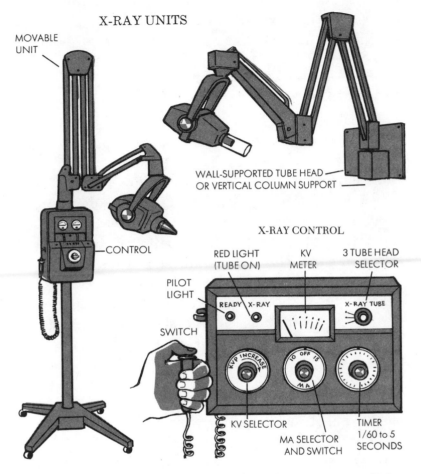

X-RAY UNITS

MOVABLE UNIT

WALL-SUPPORTED TUBE HEAD
OR VERTICAL COLUMN SUPPORT

CONTROL

X-RAY CONTROL

RED LIGHT (TUBE ON)

KV METER

3 TUBE HEAD SELECTOR

PILOT LIGHT

READY   X-RAY

X-RAY TUBE

SWITCH

KVP INCREASE

TO OFF 5
MA

KV SELECTOR

MA SELECTOR
AND SWITCH

TIMER
1/60 to 5
SECONDS

chosen. An electric meter verifies the accuracy of the selected kilovoltage.

The current or amperage selector is labeled "ma," which means milliamperes. A milliampere is $\frac{1}{1,000}$ ampere. Some control panels may also have a meter to check this. There may also be a timer ranging from $\frac{1}{60}$ second to 5 seconds. A red light will go on during an exposure. Of course, there is an on-off switch, and on the side of the unit the coiled remote-control switch may be hung.

Types of Cones

The conventional x-ray tubehead which the dentist places close to your face ends in a *short, pointed cone*. This type spreads out the beam like a fan. This allows radiation to go beyond the film in all directions.

Dentists also use a *long cone,* which is designed to produce a narrower beam. This type has a long, open tube over it to further shield the radiation coming out of the open end. This restricts the size of the x-ray beam to the part of the body to be examined. It confines the beam to the size of the film being used.

Another disadvantage of the short cone is that the picture may be distorted. This is because the x-ray tube is so close that it produces a broad, spreading beam, and may cause the shadow of one tooth to over-lap its neighbor on the film. The long cone produces more parallel rays and allows a clearer, unobstructed shadow of the tooth being x-rayed to fall on the film.

Regardless of which type is used, the dentist must position and center the cone for each exposure. This must be carefully done to prevent interference from the other teeth which may be in very close contact. He works so fast and efficiently that most patients do not re-alize that for each tooth to be properly x-rayed the angle of the cone must be adjusted. Otherwise the pic-ture may not be of much value.

There are new tubeheads which contain a light which casts a shadow of crosshairs over the patient's face. This shows where the most effective part of the beam's rays are going to act. It saves much time for the dentist and is more accurate.

An unusual x-ray device has been invented for taking exposures of all the teeth in a jaw *at one time* in a few seconds! It is called a PANORAMIC x-ray machine and was developed by the National Bureau of Standards for the United States Air Force. In this case the film is *not*

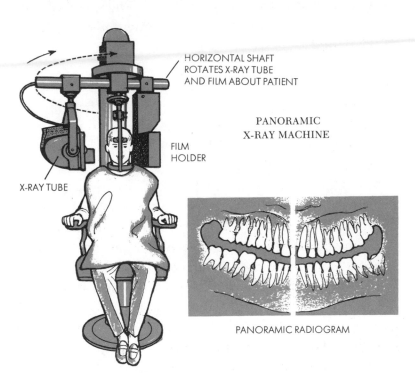

HORIZONTAL SHAFT
ROTATES X-RAY TUBE
AND FILM ABOUT PATIENT

PANORAMIC
X-RAY MACHINE

FILM
HOLDER

X-RAY TUBE

PANORAMIC RADIOGRAM

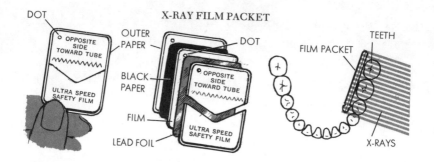

X-RAY FILM PACKET

in the mouth. The x-ray source and the film are rotated around the patient while he is seated. The speed of rotation is not constant because of the noncircular curvature of the dental arches.

X-Ray Film

The film most frequently used by your dentist comes in a small packet and is probably obtained from a wall dispenser like one which holds paper cups. This film dispenser however is lightproof.

The film is 1¼ by 1⅝ inches. It usually can show three teeth at a time. It has an outer wrapper which is lightproof and waterproof. Inside this wrapper the film is sandwiched between protective paper on the front side and a thin lead sheet backing.

The paper allows x-rays to pass through it, but the lead foil prevents the x-rays from going into the mouth past the film. The packet is pliable and can be bent slightly so that it can be held close to the jaw.

The printing on the packet tells which side to face toward the tube. If the packet is placed backward, zig-

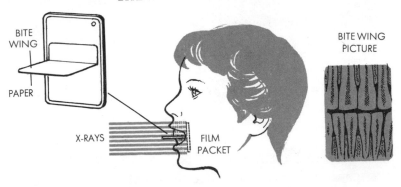

BITE WING

BITE WING

PAPER

X-RAYS

FILM PACKET

BITE WING PICTURE

zag lines will appear on the film because the lead foil has these lines. There is also a raised dot on each film to orient the dentist when examining the developed film.

Another commonly used *small-sized* film is the BITE-WING film. It will record about two thirds of the length of several upper and lower teeth while they are in a biting position. As shown in the illustration, this packet has a flap or wing on which the teeth of the patient bite to hold the film in position.

Anesthesia—Blessed Gift to Dentistry

Having a tooth extracted or prepared for filling is such a painless matter today that one sometimes takes this for granted. Mankind was not always so fortunate and sustained great suffering in the past. It must have been torture to have a tooth torn out of one's jaw without any effective way of deadening pain.

History tells us about the many attempts made in every civilization to conquer pain. People in ancient times knew of only a few narcotic drugs. Some were made from opium, hemlock, or cocoa leaves. A favorite way of putting someone into a deep sleep was to place the seeds of Indian hemp on a bed of hot coals. The vapors which were formed were inhaled deeply by the patient. Usually, a blanket held over the patient's head, and also over the coals, helped direct the vapors more efficiently.

Another method of falling into a stupor was to soak the root of the mandrake plant in wine. A person then drank this wine until he became unconscious. Actually, the stupefying effect of alcohol was known since biblical days. It was used up to the time of the discovery of the anesthetics in use today.

However, all attempts to find a good pain-killer failed. All methods used had undesirable side-effects. They did not completely kill all pain, and they harmed and sometimes killed the patient. Most of the time they made the person ill.

One of the schemes used to produce insensibility was hypnotism. About 1778 in Paris, Franz Mesmer, a German-Swiss doctor, was able to place a patient into a deep sleep using this method. While in this condition the person felt no pain regardless of what was done to him.

Many doctors and other people learned this technique, but it finally fell out of favor. It is still practiced to this day. There are dentists who use hypnotism routinely.

Discovery of Nitrous Oxide

About 1800, Sir Humphrey Davy, a famous English physician and scientist, discovered that a gas, nitrous oxide (N_2O), could put people into a deep pain-free sleep. But nobody followed up this observation.

However, professional entertainers learned that this gas could make people behave as though they were drunk. Persons from the audience would be called up on stage to inhale the gas. After a while they would run around like insane people. They would sing, dance, and make noises like animals, to the amusement of everyone. Since those who were under the influence of the gas laughed a great deal, the gas became known as laughing gas.

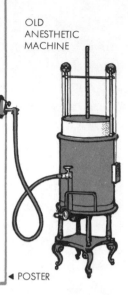

OLD ANESTHETIC MACHINE

A GRAND

EXHIBITION

OF THE EFFECTS PRODUCED BY INHALING

NITROUS OXIDE, EXHILERATING, OR

LAUGHING GAS!

WILL BE GIVEN AT

Memorial Hall

Saturday EVENING, *May 15th* 1845.

70 GALLONS OF GAS will be prepared and administered to all in the audience who desire to inhale it.

MEN will be invited from the audience, to protect those under the influence of the Gas from injuring themselves or others. This course is adopted that no apprehension of danger may be entertained. Probably no one will attempt to fight.

THE EFFECT OF THE GAS is to make those who inhale it, either

LAUGH, SING, DANCE, SPEAK OR FIGHT, &c. &c.

according to the leading trait of their character. They seem to retain consciousness enough not to say or do that which they would have occasion to regret.

N. B. The Gas will be administered only to gentlemen of the first respectability. The object is to make the entertainment in every respect, a genteel affair.

The History and properties of the Gas will be explained at the commencement of the entertainment.

ENTERTAINMENT TO COMMENCE AT 7 O'CLOCK.

TICKETS *12 ½* CENTS,

◄ POSTER

One of these amusing exhibitions of laughing gas was witnessed in 1844 by a dentist, Horace Wells, of Hartford, Connecticut. He saw one subject accidentally receive a severe blow on the leg, which then started to bleed. After the show Dr. Wells spoke to this man and learned that he had felt absolutely no pain at the time of the accident, or until the effects of the gas wore off.

The alert dentist saw the possibilities of using nitrous oxide in his practice. First he decided to try it on himself. He inhaled the gas from a bag until he lost consciousness. Then another dentist, a friend, extracted one of Wells' teeth. When Dr. Wells awoke he was delighted to find that he had felt no pain. A practical anesthetic had at last been found. It was a tremendous gift to mankind.

Wells used the gas successfully in his practice. Then he tried to introduce this anesthetic to medicine. He decided to demonstrate the gas by extracting a patient's tooth before a group of prominent physicians. However, during the extraction, the patient cried out in pain. Something had gone wrong. Probably not enough gas was used. Wells was publicly humiliated and pronounced a humbug.

The sad part of this story is that this great benefactor became very frustrated and despondent. In fact, he committed suicide the next year. However, he is recognized by historians as the discoverer of anesthesia.

Despite many new discoveries of anesthetics, nitrous oxide is still in use today. It is mixed with a controlled quantity of oxygen (at least 20 percent), to produce release from pain. This condition is called ANESTHESIA, which means "loss of sensation." Different levels of anesthesia can be produced by varying the proportions of the gases.

It has been found that if a mixture is made of about 25 percent nitrous oxide and 75 percent oxygen, the patient does not become unconscious, yet remains free from pain.

This is used when a very temporary pain-killer is required. The patient hears, sees, and understands what is going on and can obey instructions, but cannot feel pain. Dentists call this absence of pain without loss of consciousness, ANALGESIA. The patient is immediately revived by administering pure oxygen. The gases, of

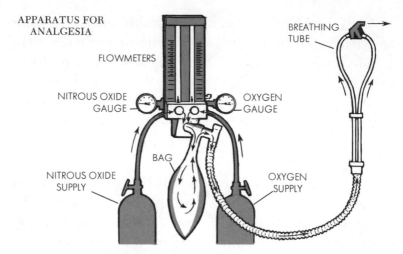

APPARATUS FOR
ANALGESIA

FLOWMETERS

NITROUS OXIDE
GAUGE

OXYGEN
GAUGE

BREATHING
TUBE

BAG

NITROUS OXIDE
SUPPLY

OXYGEN
SUPPLY

course, are inhaled through special masks placed over the nose and mouth.

The account of the development of "laughing gas," was provided because of its importance. Actually, your family dentist mostly uses local anesthetics, such as those in the Novocain family. If you ever need a *general anesthetic* he will probably send you to a specialist. A safe anesthetic commonly used by such specialists is sodium pentothal. It is administered by injection into the vein of a patient's arm.

Dental Syringe

This is the instrument used to inject a local anesthetic into the gums. A dental syringe is not the same as the one used in medicine. You know how a physician draws a certain volume of liquid from a vial up into his glass syringe. Most dentists prefer to buy the anesthetic in sterile, sealed glass or plastic tubes called CARPULES

100

or CARTRIDGES. One of these is slipped into the metal syringe and locked into place as shown in the illustration. One end of the cartridge is sealed with a thin rubber cap. The other end contains a rubber plunger.

The lower end of the syringe holds the special hypodermic needle, which is sharpened at both ends. When a cartridge is in place, the cap end is down. The sharp end of the needle inside the syringe pierces the cap. The fluid can now be ejected out of the hollow needle when the syringe piston moves down the plunger of the cartridge.

There are also in use disposable units which contain the cartridge and the *attached* sterilized needle in one unit. New models are constantly appearing. Each one has a slightly different way of piercing the rubber seal.

There is also a new injection instrument which uses no needle at all. Its blunt tip is placed against the gum

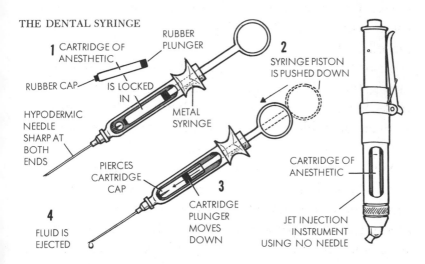

THE DENTAL SYRINGE

1 CARTRIDGE OF ANESTHETIC
RUBBER PLUNGER
RUBBER CAP
IS LOCKED IN
HYPODERMIC NEEDLE SHARP AT BOTH ENDS
METAL SYRINGE
PIERCES CARTRIDGE CAP
4 FLUID IS EJECTED
3 CARTRIDGE PLUNGER MOVES DOWN
2 SYRINGE PISTON IS PUSHED DOWN
CARTRIDGE OF ANESTHETIC
JET INJECTION INSTRUMENT USING NO NEEDLE

and a very high pressure forces the anesthetic painlessly into the tissue.   It is excellent for children, but its present limitations do not allow it to penetrate as deeply or as effectively as the regular needle and syringe.

Other Ways of Reducing Pain

The trend among modern dentists is to attempt to reduce tension, anxiety, and even physical pain by psychologically distracting the patient the instant he walks into the waitingroom.   A "livingroom" atmosphere is achieved by a colorful decorating scheme with comfortable furniture, easy-to-look-at wallpaper, good lights, and air-conditioning.

Soft music of the pleasant kind, including waltzes and ballads, is piped in from the dentist's own hi-fi stereophonic unit record-player or radio.   There are also commercial companies which send in soothing music and entertainment especially selected for a dentist's waitingroom and office.   The telephone company's wires are leased for this purpose.

In order to distract the patient and make time move faster, there may be large, interesting, and bubbly fish tanks to watch.   Magazines and booklets for all ages are stacked on tables. Some dentists have games and toys for the young and educational slides for the others.

While in the dentist's chair there may be a choice of several distractions.   Some dentists have television or movie screens mounted for easy viewing by the patient. There may be earphones to enable the patient to listen to a special tape, renewed regularly, which delivers commentaries on the news of the week. Some dentists are amateur magicians and comedians whose amusing tricks and jokes often make a visit to the dentist a pleasant experience.

There are several methods of directly avoiding any possible physical and mental pain. Before a session, most dentists will tell a patient that they will stop the instrument immediately if the patient raises a hand. This is an effective scheme for reducing apprehension, since most grinding is done painlessly and very quickly. Some dentists even hand the patient the actual electrical switch which shuts off the handpiece instrument.

There is a novel pain-relieving invention which sends music and specially designed sounds into the patient's earphones. The theory behind this system is that the pain signals being sent along the nerves can be blocked by loud or unusual music or noise. Here, too, the patient holds a control box with which he can change the volume and quality of the music and other sounds. Many dentists have not found this method effective and consider it only a passing fad.

You have read of many methods available to dentists for distracting the patient. Of course, no dentist will use all the devices described. Most competent dentists rely mainly on a pleasant atmosphere and an able staff with a sincere interest in the patient's welfare.

There are also many commonly used sedatives given to the patient to safely relieve tension and pain. Among such pills and capsules are mild barbiturates as well as tranquilizers.

Painless Extraction of Teeth

One of the things a dentist regrets most, is to have a patient lose a tooth. He will try his best to save it by means of various treatments. But sometimes, in spite of all his heroic efforts, he finds that the tooth is beyond repair and he gives you the bad news that it must come out.

In general, it is good to keep teeth as long as possible, even if a considerable amount of repair work, such as fillings and crowns or root-canal therapy, has to be done. Once a tooth is removed, the empty space *must be filled.* If it is not, then the other teeth on the sides and above the space will move out of their proper positions and cause much trouble.

Another reason for keeping your own teeth as long as you can is that artificial teeth at best are not quite as good as natural, healthy teeth. No bridgework or denture lasts forever in one's mouth. There are powerful mechanical forces and chemical reactions which can cause breakdowns. These are expensive and usually occur at the most inconvenient times. The dentist is aware of this and always makes a gallant try at preventing an extraction.

Years Ago Teeth Were Really "Pulled"!

Years ago when the dentistry profession was young, and repair techniques were not simple, teeth were taken out more frequently than they are today. In many areas in our country there were no practicing dentists or even physicians who were willing to extract teeth. This task was usually performed by barbers who might have advertised in their windows,

HAIRCUT-10 cents
TOOTH PULLED-20 cents

Blacksmiths and traveling medicine men also "pulled" teeth.

The expression "pulling teeth" has become part of our language, because for many years this is exactly what extraction was. Museums and private collectors have obtained many types of evil-looking forceps used in the past to remove teeth.

These instruments, which were usually made by a blacksmith, gripped the victim's tooth and gave it a twist which loosened the tooth. The person's head was often held between the operator's legs and the tooth was actually pulled or even pried out. No doubt some

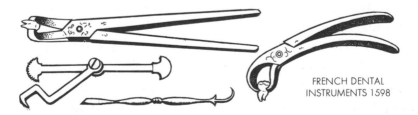

FRENCH DENTAL
INSTRUMENTS 1598

of the tissue around the tooth often went along with the extracted tooth. No anesthetic was given the suffering patient, except perhaps a good dose of whiskey. The effective pain-killers used today were not yet discovered.

Extracting a Tooth Today

It is said that extracting a tooth is a routine procedure. So it is—for the dentist, who does a number of such extractions during the week. As for you, it is not a normal everyday matter, and you have a natural uneasiness about the entire process. You would rather be somewhere else instead of in the dentist's chair.

But even at this age, you are already somewhat of a philosopher and you know that certain inconvenient things have to be done from time to time. The great truth is that having a tooth taken out no longer hurts. Not pleasant, to be sure, but honestly free from pain. Most of your discomfort will be due to your active imagination and incompletely controlled emotions. Almost everybody sails through an extraction in grand style.

The dentist will inject the area around the tooth with an extremely effective anesthetic such as procaine, commonly known as Novocain. You may not even realize that the gum has been pierced, because the dentist often applies some anesthetic on the injection site. It is also possible for him to spray the area with ethyl chloride. This solution evaporates so quickly that it freezes and numbs the tissue. In addition, most dentists today use factory-packed sterile needles only once and then

106

dispose of them. Therefore the needles are absolutely sharp and produce no sting when fluid is injected.

An anesthetic such as Novocain, which is applied only to the place where its pain-killing effect is desired, is called a LOCAL ANESTHETIC. An anesthetic which puts the whole body into a deep sleep is known as a GENERAL ANESTHETIC. Novocain has the remarkable ability to produce a temporary numbness of the nerves that supply sensation to the gums, the deeper tissue, and the tooth itself.

After a short while the dentist tests whether there is any sensation felt around the tooth. When he is convinced that the anesthetic has completely taken effect, he pushes back the gum all around the neck of the tooth. He uses a special instrument for this. The patient usually does not even feel this is being done. The reason it is necessary to push away the soft tissue from the tooth is to avoid loosening excess tissue during extraction. This facilitates removal of the tooth and makes for faster healing.

The dentist is now ready to use the sterilized extraction forceps, which he selects from a large array having different shapes. There are a number of these instruments, since they are specifically shaped for each kind of tooth.

To make his work easier, he must apply force in a vertical direction and not at a slant. This means that he must hold the forceps in a different position when extracting a front, rear, upper, or lower tooth. He therefore has forceps with jaws which are suitably angled for

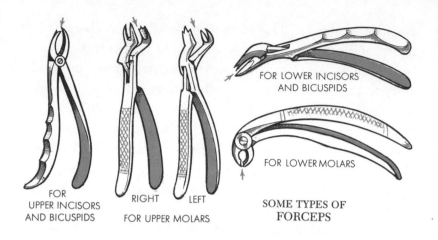

FOR LOWER INCISORS
AND BICUSPIDS

FOR LOWER MOLARS

FOR
UPPER INCISORS
AND BICUSPIDS

RIGHT   LEFT

FOR UPPER MOLARS

SOME TYPES OF
FORCEPS

each tooth. The handles are also designed to fit his grasp in each different position. Because teeth are positioned at different angles, and locations, the dentist uses different positions in front and behind the patient, depending on the tooth.

The jaws of a suitable forceps are then inserted into the pushed-away tissue and tightened around the tooth to be extracted. The tooth is rocked or given a slight twist in its bony socket. This loosens it from the periodontal membrane and the tooth should now be free.

The extracted tooth is carefully examined by the dentist to make sure that no part of the tooth has broken and remains in the jaw. Any small portion of the root, or bone fragment, which remains can delay healing.

The patient has felt no pain, only an awareness that the dentist has used a mechanical force. At any rate, there is now a wonderful sense of relief that the episode is over. If the extracted tooth was one which had been causing bad toothaches, there is reason to be doubly grateful to the dentist. He treated your extraction with gentleness and concern.

Afterward, the dentist will place some sterile gauze into the tooth socket and ask you to bite on it. This hastens the formation of a blood clot which is normal and necessary for quick healing.

Actually, a certain amount of bleeding is desirable in order to form a good clot. Of course, any excess bleeding is controlled before the patient leaves, by applying very effective packings designed for this purpose, or by using other professional means.

Gums bleed easily when injured because they have a great many intermeshed blood vessels. That is why gums are pink.

Most extractions are done by your family dentist. Sometimes x-rays may show that the tooth to be extracted is badly impacted, and will be difficult to remove without disturbing or damaging neighboring teeth. Your dentist may then wish to send you to a specialist who is an ORAL SURGEON.

The dentist also takes special precautions if the patient has a heart condition, is a "bleeder" or diabetic, or has some emotional disturbance.

After an Extraction

It is logical to expect some pain after the anesthetic wears off in several hours. After all, it is like any other injury or wound. Until healing takes place, there is tenderness. Fortunately, a wound caused by an extraction usually heals quite rapidly, because the presence of saliva has a healing effect. If the pain is annoying, tell this to your dentist and he will give you appropriate instructions.

Allow the blood clot in the extracted tooth socket to become firmly anchored. Do not suck on the hole or eat hot foods for about 6 hours. Reduce your activities —no jumping around! It is also advisable not to rinse your mouth with water until the day *after* the extraction. Then for a few days rinse with saltwater, prepared by dissolving ½ teaspoon of table salt in a glass of warm water.

Root-Canal Therapy

Sometimes the dentist can avoid extracting a tooth even though the pulp is badly infected and has extended down to the very thin part of the root canal. There may even be an abscess (pus pocket) at the base of the root. In order to try to save the tooth the dentist must

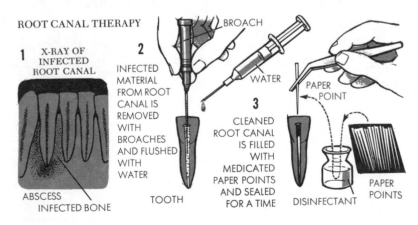

ROOT CANAL THERAPY

1 X-RAY OF INFECTED ROOT CANAL

2 INFECTED MATERIAL FROM ROOT CANAL IS REMOVED WITH BROACHES AND FLUSHED WITH WATER

BROACH

WATER

3 CLEANED ROOT CANAL IS FILLED WITH MEDICATED PAPER POINTS AND SEALED FOR A TIME

PAPER POINT

ABSCESS INFECTED BONE

TOOTH

DISINFECTANT

PAPER POINTS

clean, sterilize, and fill the area. Simple root-canal therapy can be done by any dentist, but severe cases are usually referred to a specialist in this field called an EN-DODONTIST.

Very fine barbed reamers called BROACHES, files, and other highly specialized instruments are used. They are tediously rotated by hand or by slowly rotating handpieces and carefully worked down the root canal. Progress is verified by x-rays. Infected material is carefully lifted out. Sterile paper slivers called POINTS are moistened with medication and inserted into the deep hole and kept there for several days. When the dentist is certain that no more infection exists, he fills the opening.

It is easier to work on a front tooth because there is usually only one canal, while molars may have two or more canals. Many teeth are saved by modern root-canal therapy. Years ago, the only way to fight a badly infected pulp was to extract the tooth.

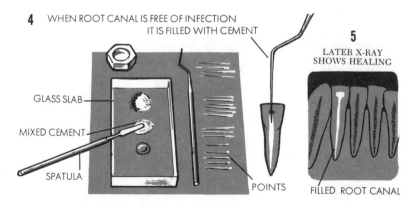

4 WHEN ROOT CANAL IS FREE OF INFECTION
IT IS FILLED WITH CEMENT

5
LATER X-RAY
SHOWS HEALING

GLASS SLAB

MIXED CEMENT

SPATULA

POINTS

FILLED ROOT CANAL

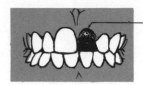 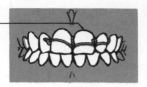

TOOTH KNOCKED
OUT IS WIRED
TO ADJACENT
TEETH

Accidental Loss of a Tooth

Many people do not know that if a tooth is knocked out due to an accident, it can often be successfully replaced. This is especially true for children.

The American Dental Association suggests that the tooth should not be cleaned, but should be wrapped in a wet cloth. If this is brought immediately to the dentist he will replace the tooth into the child's jaw.

The tooth will be securely wired to its adjacent teeth. Under favorable conditions the tooth may become reattached to the jaw. New tissues will be formed, including a blood and nerve supply. This process may take many months. Frequently it is completely unsuccessful. Much research is being done in this field.

Transplanting of Teeth

This idea is very old. Records show that when a Roman soldier in Julius Caesar's army lost a tooth in battle, he would knock out a similar tooth from a prisoner's mouth. Then the tooth would be securely held in the socket of the lost tooth by wires or other means. Modern dentists believe that these transplants were in the main doomed to failure.

112

Today scientific transplanting of teeth is being studied more and more. Perhaps some day we will have many tooth banks, in convenient locations all over the country, similar to the eye and other organ banks, constantly ready for transplantation.

Research dentists are also able to IMPLANT natural teeth in jaws in which new tooth sockets have to be cut. In time the implanted teeth often become firmly anchored. Some dentists specialize in implanting artificial teeth in jaws. Stainless-steel screws and other hardware actually bore into the jawbone and tighten down the teeth.

Another branch of research is attempting to grow live tooth buds in glass flasks. These will be implanted into any jaw for further development into full-grown natural teeth. Perhaps some day this will replace artificial dentures. Wonder of wonders!

Fillings and Other Restorations

Once decay starts in a tooth it progresses relentlessly until something is done about it. A decayed tooth does *not* heal itself as do many other parts of the body. If you wish to save the tooth, you must go to the dentist—the sooner the better. The only practical treatment is for the dentist to thoroughly remove all the involved enamel, dentin, and pulp which is decayed. Following this, he fills the cavity or inserts some other RESTORATION.

In dentistry a restoration is the replacement of a part of a tooth or of an entire tooth by artificial means. This includes a filling, inlay, crown, bridge, denture, and various appliances to straighten teeth. Most of a dentist's time is spent on restoration.

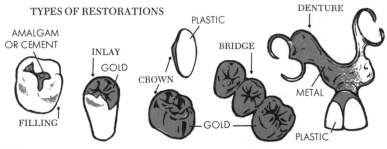

TYPES OF RESTORATIONS

AMALGAM OR CEMENT

FILLING

INLAY

GOLD

PLASTIC

CROWN

GOLD

BRIDGE

DENTURE

METAL

PLASTIC

114

Preparation of Cavity

Many years of training and experience are involved in the dentist's fast and usually painless removal of tooth structure. Each case must be given careful judgment. The cavity must be ground in such a way that it will not weaken the tooth after the filling is made.

The dentist must also keep in mind the various stresses which the finished restoration will have to successfully resist. Some forces which tend to change the shape of the filling are compression or squeezing, shearing or twisting, and tension or pulling. Each shape of cavity, and each type of filling have their own peculiar characteristics studied and known by the dentist.

In using handpieces with high-speed rotating burs and abrasives, much frictional heat is produced when the very hard enamel and dentin are ground away. If this heat were to become excessive, it could be transmitted to the underlying pulp. This living material contains nerves which are very sensitive to heat or pressure.

To avoid pain, the dentist cools the instrument and tooth by means of a stream of water. If the handpiece is not water-cooled, then he works in short intervals and with slight pressure to avoid building up excessive heat. He may also use an air stream for cooling the tooth.

Too much heat can actually destroy the living cells in the pulp. Still another way of destroying pulp tissue is the exposure of the pulp to the open air for a prolonged period. The dentist is constantly mindful of this danger when he uses an EXCAVATOR. This is the hand instrument with the spoon-shaped blade for scooping out decayed matter from a deep cavity.

The dentist has a fairly accurate idea of the size and location of the pulp chamber. It is different in each type of tooth. Also, as age increases, the pulp recedes farther away from the top enamel.

If the cavity is very deep and the pulp is exposed, the pulp must be insulated against heat, cold, and electrical effects. Annoying electrical shocks can occur because of the presence of different metals on the teeth. These form a chemical battery with the acids in the mouth. The pulp must also be protected against the irritating, if not deadly, acids of certain cements used for fillings. For example, a silicate cement is very acid until it sets and frequently even after it hardens.

For the above reasons a lining or sealing layer of a special cement is applied as a base before the regular filling material is inserted into the cavity. One such frequently used insulating sealer contains calcium hydroxide, another is a zinc phosphate cement. A popular cavity lining is ZOE, which stands for zinc oxide and eugenol. The main ingredient of eugenol is OIL-OF-CLOVES which you have probably smelled on a visit to the dentist many times.

If the tooth is painful, or if the pulp is badly infected, the dentist will carefully clean and wash the cavity. He will then dry the area with a blast of air and apply an antiseptic and pain-reducing medication. He will close the cavity with a temporary cement which he can easily remove at your next visit, after giving the medication

116

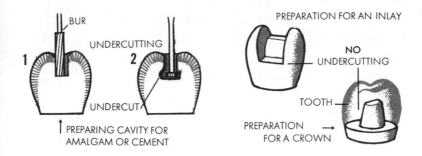

BUR

UNDERCUTTING

1

2

UNDERCUT

↑ PREPARING CAVITY FOR
AMALGAM OR CEMENT

PREPARATION FOR AN INLAY

NO
UNDERCUTTING

TOOTH

PREPARATION →
FOR A CROWN

time to act. Then he will fill the cavity with a permanent cement.

Frequently the cavity is ground so that the hardened filling cannot be pulled out. This is done by making the bottom wider than the top, like a dovetail joint in furniture drawers. Grooves made to lock a filling in place are called UNDERCUTTING.

The dentist sometimes extends the edges of the cavity beyond where the decay is located. He does this to make certain that he has removed all decay. All undermined enamel must be removed, because it can no longer hold up under the forces of chewing. Another reason for extending outlines of cavities is to produce a more logical location for the filling. Some areas are stronger, more easily cleaned, or look better.

More Permanent Fillings

At the end of the last century one of the popular cements for filling cavities was a tarlike, antispetic material called CREOSOTE. Another filling material was GUTTA-PERCHA, which resembled hard rubber. Today there are excellent and infinitely better cements. Yet research has still not produced one which is perfect. Every cement in use today has something wrong with it. Sooner or later a filling will loosen because of the severe chemical and mechanical forces constantly at work in the mouth.

What are some important qualities which an ideal cement should possess? Above all it should not be affected by the constant chemical action of saliva and liquid or solid foods. It should form a very durable, strong, leakproof, adhesive bond with the tooth structure. It must be able to withstand compression and shearing and tension stresses, and also be hard enough not to be worn down by abrasion. An ideal cement should also not be irritating to the gums or pulp tissue.

A dentist does not want a cement which is brittle. Such a cement cracks easily, especially at the thin margins. It should not shrink as it hardens. Shrinking would allow liquids and infection to enter the cavity. A good cement should be easily mixed and not harden too quickly or too slowly. It must not conduct heat or electricity. It should be possible to mix it with other colors to produce desired shades. The odor and taste must be pleasant. It should not spoil in its container while on the dentist's shelf.

Do you think engineers will ever invent such an ideal dental cement? Research in this very important field is going on all over the world. Investigators use the most modern scientific tools—from electron microscopes to radioactivity. Recently scientists have even analyzed the extremely hard cement produced by barnacles which holds them to rocks in the water. Epoxy cements are also being studied. At present they are irritating to the pulp and gums.

Descriptions of some of the cements most frequently used by dentists follow. These are very good when used properly, but as you now know, they will not last "forever and a day."

Amalgam

This is the so-called "silver filling." An AMALGAM is an alloy of mercury and other metals. Mercury is a silvery, liquid metal at room temperature and is also known as quicksilver. To form a SILVER AMALGAM, the mercury must be mixed thoroughly with a powdered silver-tin alloy to form a soft, pasty mass. After a short while this mixture solidifies into a hard mass of interlocked crystals of silver-mercury and tin-mercury compounds.

The amalgamating can be done in a small, deep dish with a glass or ceramic clublike mixing tool. The apparatus is called a MORTAR AND PESTLE, the familiar trademark of a druggist. However, most dentists today use a

PREPARING AMALGAM FOR A FILLING

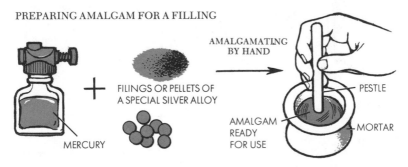

FILINGS OR PELLETS OF A SPECIAL SILVER ALLOY

MERCURY

AMALGAMATING BY HAND

AMALGAM READY FOR USE

PESTLE

MORTAR

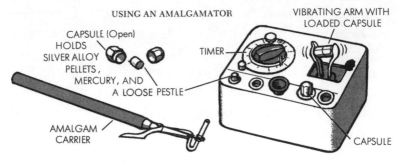

USING AN AMALGAMATOR

CAPSULE (Open)
HOLDS
SILVER ALLOY
PELLETS,
MERCURY, AND
A LOOSE PESTLE

TIMER

VIBRATING ARM WITH
LOADED CAPSULE

AMALGAM
CARRIER

CAPSULE

small machine called an AMALGAMATOR, which mixes the amalgam with speed and precision.

In this apparatus a very exact amount of mercury and alloy are funneled into a small capsule containing a loose pestle. The capsule is then clamped between two arms which extend from the machine and which are automatically vibrated. A timer shuts off the machine after a predetermined number of seconds.

The assistant hands the material to the dentist in an amalgam-carrier. The dentist forces the alloy into the properly undercut and lined cavity, and packs it down against every surface. The tool he uses is called a CONDENSER or PLUGGER. He also has a tiny air condenser the size of a bur which works by air pressure.

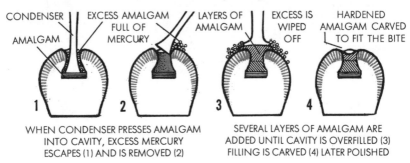

CONDENSER

AMALGAM

EXCESS AMALGAM
FULL OF
MERCURY

LAYERS OF
AMALGAM

EXCESS IS
WIPED
OFF

HARDENED
AMALGAM CARVED
TO FIT THE BITE

1   2   3   4

WHEN CONDENSER PRESSES AMALGAM
INTO CAVITY, EXCESS MERCURY
ESCAPES (1) AND IS REMOVED (2)

SEVERAL LAYERS OF AMALGAM ARE
ADDED UNTIL CAVITY IS OVERFILLED (3)
FILLING IS CARVED (4) LATER POLISHED

MATRIX BAND   TOOTH WITH CAVITY TO BE FILLED   WEDGE   MATRIX BAND

Excess mercury is removed when the mixture is squeezed through a special cloth. The dried mixture obtained this way is always used to finish the filling. After allowing a reasonable time for hardening, the dentist carves the filling to conform to the shape of the tooth. High spots are found by having the patient bite a form of carbon paper called ARTICULATING PAPER which leaves marks on the surfaces which are rubbing against each other.

Sometimes one of the cavity surfaces is an open wall on the side of the tooth. In order to fill such a cavity the opening is closed by means of a very thin strip of steel bent around the tooth. It is called a MATRIX BAND and is locked into place by turning a screw or by some other means. Plastic strips are also used for this purpose. After the filling is made, the matrix is removed, leaving a smooth, contoured, or properly shaped wall.

To prevent saliva from wetting the cavity or filling, the dentist uses a saliva ejector and a roll of cotton under the lip or cheek. If greater dryness is needed, a rubber sheet is often stretched and clamped over all the teeth in a certain area. A punched hole allows only the desired tooth to project. This device is called a RUBBER DAM.

Silver amalgam fillings are cheaper than some other

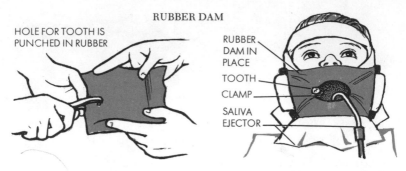

HOLE FOR TOOTH IS PUNCHED IN RUBBER

RUBBER DAM IN PLACE

TOOTH

CLAMP

SALIVA EJECTOR

restorations, mainly because they require less of the dentist's time, but they are quite serviceable. Because of their dark appearance, amalgams are used mainly for inconspicuous areas, such as the rear teeth or the backs of front teeth.

Silicate Cement

This is the type of filling widely used for front teeth, because it can be matched to resemble the shade of one's own teeth. It is often referred to as a porcelain filling, which is not a correct term.

It comes in two containers. In one there is a ground-up mixture of glasslike compounds. The other bottle contains a solution of phosphoric acid and other ingredients. When both are carefully mixed, a soft, thick mass is formed. When this hardens it resembles tooth enamel in appearance. The manufacturer supplies a shade guide with instructions for mixing the different ingredients to obtain the desired color.

SILICATE CEMENT is popular because of its appearance, and it is strong enough for the place where it is used, but it cannot be subjected to much stress such as on a

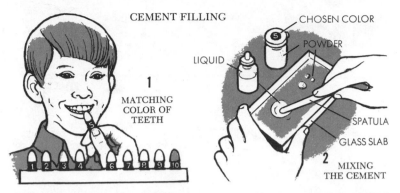

CEMENT FILLING

CHOSEN COLOR

POWDER

LIQUID

1
MATCHING
COLOR OF
TEETH

SPATULA

GLASS SLAB

2
MIXING
THE CEMENT

chewing surface. Neither is it durable. Its biggest disadvantage as a filling is that it is slowly soluble in mouth fluids, and eventually it may loosen and discolor. Often, after a few years it must be replaced.

Acrylic Resin Cement

This is a plastic used for white fillings, its chemical name is methyl methacrylate. It comes in two bottles, one a powder and the other a liquid. On mixing, it first becomes a doughlike mass which gradually turns into a hard substance. The hardness and strength are due to the combining of small molecules to form large chainlike molecules. This is called POLYMERIZATION or CURING.

Crowns

In badly decayed teeth, where several surfaces have been destroyed, it is often impossible to fill the cavities. The dentist will then have to cap the entire tooth with a crown. This is a metal, porcelain, or plastic, form-fitting jacket which is cemented over the tooth.

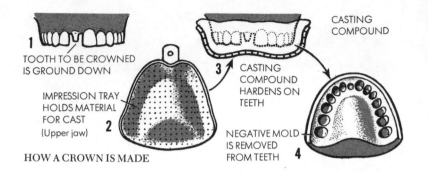

1 TOOTH TO BE CROWNED IS GROUND DOWN

IMPRESSION TRAY HOLDS MATERIAL FOR CAST (Upper jaw) 2

HOW A CROWN IS MADE

3 CASTING COMPOUND HARDENS ON TEETH

CASTING COMPOUND

NEGATIVE MOLD IS REMOVED FROM TEETH 4

Metal crowns are generally made of gold or stainless steel. These metals are used because they are strong, durable, and not affected by oral fluids. In some countries the sight of gold or other bright metal in one's smile is actually thought to be desirable. However, in this country, gold and silvery metals are considered too flashy. These crowns, if used at all, are placed mainly on rear teeth.

Porcelain jackets are more presentable for front teeth. They can be made to almost exactly match the appearance of the neighboring teeth.

The tooth to be covered must first be prepared by being ground down as shown in the illustration. In this way the porcelain jacket will have sufficient thickness and strength when it is finished.

The dentist first takes an impression of the cut-down tooth and its neighboring teeth. There are many impression materials used by dentists. An old standby is plaster of Paris, which hardens into a rigid mold. Many dentists prefer to use substances which never harden like plaster. Instead these substances set into accurate impressions which remain quite flexible. They can be bent out of shape but always return to the form in which they became set. The advantage of this rubber-like material is that there is less danger of breaking or distorting the impression during its removal from the teeth, and it may reproduce undercuts.

Some excellent elastic-type impression materials are made of silicone rubber. Others are made of agar-agar, a gelatinous material obtained from certain seaweeds. Some impression materials must be placed into warm water to soften them before being used. Others are squeezed from tubes and must have an activator added from another tube.

But all impression materials are first soft and almost fluid in order to reach every portion of the teeth and gum lines. They all set quickly for accuracy and to avoid distortion by tongue and mouth movements. Special impression trays are used to hold the material against the teeth.

When the set impression material is removed from the mouth it will contain a shaped hole representing a NEGATIVE of the tooth. After the impression is rein-forced on the outside, a special plaster called stone is poured into the mold and usually vibrated on a shaking machine to remove air bubbles. Sometimes amalgam is used to make the casting.

When the mold is separated, the very hard plaster casting which is obtained is called a DIE, CAST, or MODEL. In every detail, it is an exact duplicate of the prepared tooth. The die will be used as a base for building up and baking a porcelain jacket-crown or forming a metal crown.

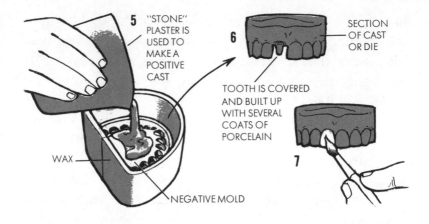

5 "STONE" PLASTER IS USED TO MAKE A POSITIVE CAST

6

SECTION OF CAST OR DIE

TOOTH IS COVERED AND BUILT UP WITH SEVERAL COATS OF PORCELAIN

WAX

7

NEGATIVE MOLD

Porcelain is a ceramic material like the dishes in your kitchen, made by baking certain clays. Crowns require a mixed-up batch of very highly purified porcelain ingredients. By using shade guides, and through experience, dentists know how to obtain a porcelain whose shade matches the patient's other teeth.

The soft porcelain is brushed on the die and fired in a special oven at controlled temperatures, usually between 1,600 and 2,500 degrees Fahrenheit. Several applications of porcelain and a few firings are necessary. The final ones gives the crown the highly glazed, hard finish.

The jacket is carved to conform to the proper shape as determined by the other impressions taken by the dentist. It is then polished and removed from the die. The jacket is now ready for being cemented over the prepared tooth. Any one of the cements previously described will be satisfactory as long as it does not change the shade of the partly translucent jacket.

126

OVEN COVER

8 FINISHED CROWN IS REMOVED FROM OVEN

CROWN IS CEMENTED TO TOOTH AND HELD FIRM UNTIL DRY

COTTON

10

IT LOOKS LIKE A REAL TOOTH

9

If a metal crown is desired, the plaster die can be thinly painted with a material which conducts electricity. Gold and other metals can then be electroplated and built up on the die. There are other, highly technical means of making crowns.

During his years in dental college a dentist learns how to actually perform most of the laboratory work necessary in his profession. He becomes very familiar with the mechanical processes. However, this is a most time-consuming part of dentistry. That is why most dentists feel it is not worth their while to do their own heavy laboratory work. They do however make accurate impressions and pour models or casts in their own small laboratories and also perform several other procedures. But in general they only do the work which must be completed in the mouth. Laboratories do only the mechanical operations away from the mouth and at the prescription or direction of the dentist.

These shops are set up for fast, reliable work. They have expert dental technicians who use the most modern, expensive equipment under standardized and controlled conditions. There is frequent pickup and delivery service by messengers. If this is not available, some dentists use quick mail-order service.

You may be interested and amused to know that stainless-steel crowns are also made for cows' teeth which have been very badly worn down. Veterinary dentists can install these quite inexpensively. Dairy farmers claim that this procedure is a good investment, since they get better milk production from cows that can eat better.

Inlays

When a cavity is too large for a successful filling, and when a gold crown or porcelain jacket is not desired, the dentist may suggest an INLAY. This is a single piece of gold or other metal, or perhaps porcelain, which is cast to fit into the prepared cavity precisely. An impression is made by forcing a softened inlay wax into the prepared cavity which has *not* been made wider at the bottom. The opening in the tooth produces a projection in the impression.

This wax pattern is now completely embedded in a

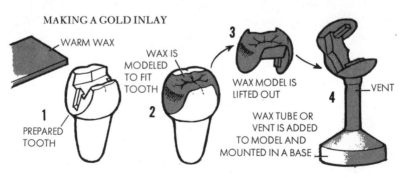

MAKING A GOLD INLAY

WARM WAX

WAX IS MODELED TO FIT TOOTH

WAX MODEL IS LIFTED OUT

VENT

1 PREPARED TOOTH

2

3

4

WAX TUBE OR VENT IS ADDED TO MODEL AND MOUNTED IN A BASE

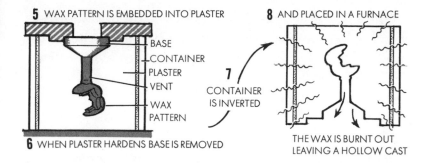

5 WAX PATTERN IS EMBEDDED INTO PLASTER

BASE
CONTAINER
PLASTER
VENT
WAX PATTERN

7 CONTAINER IS INVERTED

8 AND PLACED IN A FURNACE

THE WAX IS BURNT OUT LEAVING A HOLLOW CAST

6 WHEN PLASTER HARDENS BASE IS REMOVED

hard plaster, after a small tube or vent is attached from the wax to a distance outside the embedding plaster. When the plaster hardens, it is heated in an oven and the buried impression wax melts and escapes through this vent.

There is now a hole in the plaster where the wax used to be. This hole is a reproduction of the prepared cavity in the tooth. When molten material is poured through the escape vent, it takes the exact shape of the wax that was originally forced into the cavity prepared for the inlay.

Laboratories have ingenious machines for casting. Partial vacuums and centrifugal effects are used to force the molten material tightly against the mold.

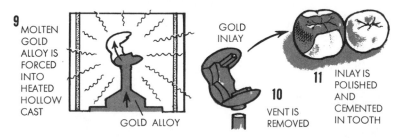

9 MOLTEN GOLD ALLOY IS FORCED INTO HEATED HOLLOW CAST

GOLD ALLOY

GOLD INLAY

10 VENT IS REMOVED

11 INLAY IS POLISHED AND CEMENTED IN TOOTH

The inlay is completed by being made to conform to the "bite" impression taken by the dentist. After a fitting, it is polished and cemented into the cavity. Properly done, inlays are considered better than amalgam restorations under certain conditions.

Bridges

If one or more teeth are missing, and it is necessary to replace them with artificial ones, a BRIDGE may be constructed. In this case the artificial teeth are firmly attached to crowns on neighboring teeth.

If a removable bridge is desired, there are strong metal clasps which are fitted to grasp the adjacent teeth. Very careful impressions and expert dental and laboratory work can produce remarkably accurate and presentable artificial teeth.

An artificial replacement or substitution for a natural part of a person is called a PROSTHESIS (pross-THEE-sus). A bridge is such a device. A *complete* artificial replacement of either the upper or the lower teeth is also called a complete DENTURE

The dental profession has come a long way since the awkward, spring-separated, wooden and animal-bone dentures which were prepared for George Washington. Modern dentures are strong and lightweight, and stay in place because they are perfectly fitted to the gums.

Acrylic plastic, which remarkably resembles living gum tissue, is used for removable partial dentures. It is permanently bonded to a framework made of gold or

130

one of several other alloys.   Beautiful, natural-looking porcelain teeth are securely locked into place.

The dentist can make very presentable temporary crowns, bridges, or dentures for the patient to use while waiting for the laboratory to fabricate the final product. Such "instant teeth" often look good enough to pass as the real thing.

Dental Engineering

In designing a dental bridge the trained dentist takes into consideration the various stresses which will be acting from any angle upon every part of the structure. His analysis can be compared to the extreme care used by engineers who build bridges which span rivers and ravines.

Powerful forces are at work in the mouth.   Our jawbones, muscles, and sharp teeth combine to multiply pressures just as any efficient machine seen in a factory. For example, suppose that the pressure of a person's normal bite is 125 pounds per square inch.   In engineering the word PRESSURE means the force in pounds *per square inch.*

If this pressure had to act perpendicularly only between two very sharp teeth, the actual contacting surface would, of course, be only a small fraction of 1 square inch.   Let us say it is only 1/100th square inch. Therefore the total *pressure* on *1* square inch of the biting surface now becomes 125×100 or *12,500 pounds per square inch!*

Acquiring a Clean Mouth

Nobody yet knows the entire story about dental decay, but it is the considered opinion of many dental experts that the cleaner one's mouth is kept, the greater are the chances of avoiding cavities. Therefore it is recommended that for best results one should brush the teeth with a fluoride toothpaste immediately after every meal, and also after eating any snacks, especially sweets. This will help prevent the formation of harmful acids.

Dentists know that this advice cannot always be followed away from home. They suggest that if brushing is not possible after eating, then one should rinse the mouth with water. And if even this cannot be done, the mouth can be quietly swished with drinking water and swallowed without much ado.

About Toothbrushing

The *chief* purpose of using a toothbrush is to clean the teeth and gums and to remove any bits of food, and not to medicate the mouth, despite many advertisers' claims. Dentists agree that the regularity and the technique of brushing are more important than the type of toothpaste used, with the possible exception of fluoride toothpaste. Brushing should also stimulate the circulation of blood, especially at the gum margins. In a way, brushing should give the gums the stimulation that is missing because of the lack of coarse foods in our diet.

In this country there is a custom of brushing one's teeth on arising, at the same time the face is washed. Then breakfast is eaten, and, sad to say, many of us do not brush again, or even rinse our mouths as we start on our day's work.

Since most people do not feel like brushing twice in the morning, dentists say it is better to omit brushing before breakfast. It is more effective to brush *after* breakfast. If one wishes to remove the bad taste usually present in the mouth on arising, then rinsing with water or a mouthwash should suffice.

An excellent habit to develop is the brushing of teeth before going to bed. During the night the teeth are not subjected to the cleansing action of the saliva, as they are during the day when the tongue and jaws are more active. Therefore it is very important to brush away accumulated food particles. This gives the bacteria less to work on throughout the night hours.

How to Brush Your Teeth

There are various methods of using a toothbrush effectively, but most accepted techniques agree on one point —the sides of the teeth must be brushed *away from the gums*. If the teeth are wrongly scrubbed from side to

133

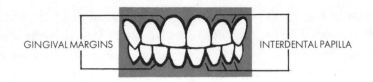

side the stiff brush bristles can injure the delicate edges of the gum which surround and bridge healthy teeth.

You can see in the illustration that the gum outline which hugs the tooth is called the GINGIVAL (JIN-ji-val) MARGIN. Where the margins bridge the gap between two teeth, there is a free area of gum tissue. This is an INTERDENTAL PAPILLA (pah-PILL-ah) and of very great importance.

Brushing from side to side can tear and irritate these tissues and leave loose spaces around the teeth for the accumulation of tartar, food particles, and bacteria. An inflammation of gum tissue is called GINGIVITIS. It may begin as a slight bleeding of the gums, and perhaps end with the loss of one's teeth. Disease of the supporting tissues of the teeth is known as PERIODONTAL (around the tooth) DISEASE and is responsible for a tremendous loss of teeth in people as they get older.

A widely recommended method of toothbrushing is basically as follows. Place the ends of the bristles in contact with the enamel and the gingival margins. The bristles should point at about an angle of 45 degrees toward the biting surfaces of the teeth. Hold the brush handle horizontally.

Press the bristles carefully against the gums and between the teeth. Do this firmly, but not so strongly as

134

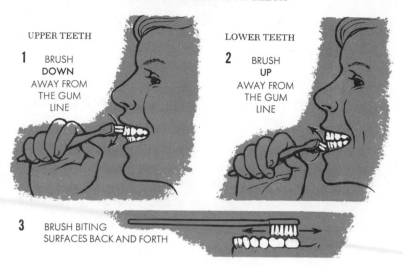

UPPER TEETH

1 BRUSH **DOWN** AWAY FROM THE GUM LINE

LOWER TEETH

2 BRUSH **UP** AWAY FROM THE GUM LINE

3 BRUSH BITING SURFACES BACK AND FORTH

to cause damage. Now give the brush a downward, rolling motion with your wrist as shown in the illustration, so that the bristles sweep *away* from the gums. Repeat about ten times in each area.

Now move the bristles a little less than one brush-length away and do the same for each section of the mouth—upper and lower, inside and outside. You may find it difficult to keep the brush horizontal when cleaning the inside of the front teeth. In this case you may hold the brush handle less horizontally.

The biting surfaces of the teeth, especially of the pre-molars, may now be brushed back and forth. But these are the only places where this motion should be used.

For various reasons your dentist may suggest slight variations in the method shown here. But you will find that in nearly every case you will be asked to brush the upper teeth *down* and the lower teeth *up*.

To be effective, brushing cannot be done with the careless, lightning speed of a little boy washing his face. This only hits the high spots. If you are a 20-second brusher you are really not cleaning your teeth. You are merely exercising your arm!

About Toothbrushes

These have been used since about 1700, yet research is still going on to find the best kind. Dentists say that a toothbrush head should be about 1 inch long. This would make it small enough to reach every section of the upper and lower teeth.

The bristles should be about ½ inch long, bound in tufts which are ⅛ inch apart, pointed and trimmed to the same height. The tufts should be arranged in 2 rows of about 6 tufts each. Medium rather than hard bristles are suggested. However, many dentists have different preferences. They claim that specific brushes should be used for certain toothbrushing methods.

Many bristles, whether natural or synthetic, become soft when wet. That is why it is advisable to own several brushes and alternate their use. One will be drying while the other is in use. Even the best brushes eventually lose their stiffness and then become useless. Many dentists recommend purchasing new brushes every 4 months.

Needless to say, a toothbrush should be washed clean after use and not be allowed to become caked with ac-

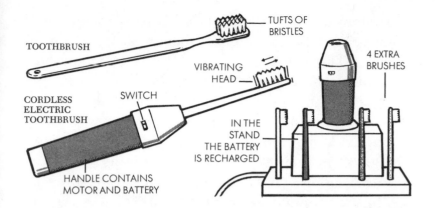

TOOTHBRUSH

TUFTS OF BRISTLES

VIBRATING HEAD

4 EXTRA BRUSHES

CORDLESS ELECTRIC TOOTHBRUSH

SWITCH

IN THE STAND THE BATTERY IS RECHARGED

HANDLE CONTAINS MOTOR AND BATTERY

cumulated toothpaste. A dirty brush harbors bacteria. It should be hung up to dry after washing. Do this in an open area where air is circulating. A wet brush in a drawer encourages the growth of mold and bacteria.

There are many types of electric toothbrushes. Ask your dentist about them. They make it easier to brush teeth faster and perhaps more efficiently, but you must follow the instructions carefully. Some electric toothbrushes can make as many strokes in 3 minutes as a person can in 30 minutes. If not used intelligently this can become a hazard.

Toothpastes

Most dental authorities say that all toothpastes sold by large reliable companies are good. It is difficult to say which is the best. Some may taste better or contain a more highly advertised ingredient. However, the type of brushing one does is probably of greater importance than the medicinal value of the DENTIFRICE itself.

137

Modern toothpastes contain a harmless cleaning and abrasive material, usually a calcium phosphate compound. This gives the teeth a polish. To aid the cleansing, some synthetic detergent is added, but frequently soap is also included to produce some froth. Several well-known brands are sold with a stannous or other fluoride. A gum acts as a binder for all the ingredients and glycerine prevents the paste from drying out.

The decision by a family to continue using a certain toothpaste is probably made because of the pleasant taste. Each brand has its own identifying flavoring agent. Some common ones are oils of birch, cinnamon, clove, rose geranium, orange, spearmint, peppermint, wintergreen, eucalyptol, and menthol. Artificial sweeteners such as saccharin should also be included. Would you believe that many years ago real sugar was used in toothpastes? Many well-meaning parents bought these for their children's dental health. Today we know that this actually hastened the development of cavities!

You can make your own effective toothpowder by mixing one part powdered table salt and two parts baking soda (bicarbonate of soda). If you wish you may use just the soda alone. Place some on a moist toothbrush to brush your teeth.

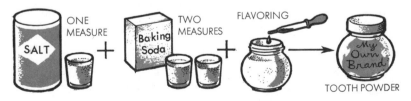

If you want to improve the taste of this, experiment by using various flavoring agents. Make sure they do not contain sugar. Ask your pharmacist to add a drop or two of a flavoring oil mentioned above.

Mouthwashes

Millions of dollars are being spent on advertisements to convince the public that certain mouthwashes will keep one's mouth free of germs. Dentists say that use of the words "antiseptic," "germicide," or "disinfectant" to describe a mouthwash is definitely misleading. According to many dentists, any solution strong enough to kill most germs in the mouth is too dangerous to put into the mouth.

The best that a mouthwash can do is cause a very temporary decrease in the number of bacteria. Some mouthwashes also leave a pleasant taste and feeling in the mouth. Many also have an astringent effect. This causes a pleasant shrinking or tightening of the mouth tissues. But all these are very temporary sensations. The effect of a mouthwash probably lasts no longer than 30 minutes.

Mouthwashes rinse away food particles and other products from the mouth. For this purpose it is just as good and cheaper to use tapwater. A more effective chemical rinse can be made by stirring 1 teaspoon of table salt into one glass of lukewarm water. Instead of the salt, ½ teaspoon of baking soda may be used.

There are certain medicated mouthwashes also sold by druggists. These are used for special sensitive mouth conditions. They are much stronger than the ordinary mouthwashes. Do not use them unless they are ordered by the dentist.

Toothpicks and Dental Floss

Toothpicks were used to remove food particles from the teeth centuries before the appearance of toothbrushes and toothpaste. Wealthy people used to own gold and jewelled toothpicks. Some were even worn on watch-chains. When you use a wooden toothpick, do it carefully. If you use it roughly it can cause damage.

Dental floss can get into places between teeth which toothpicks cannot reach. That is why it is often recommended by the dentist. It must be used with care and not moved harshly back and forth like a saw. It can injure the interdental papillae.

Only Your Best Friends Will Tell You

On all sides Americans are bombarded by advertisements warning them that their recent unpopularity may very well be due to bad breath, known as HALITOSIS. Therefore they are advised to use certain brands of mouthwashes, toothpastes, and lozenges, and once again become the life of the party.

These advertisements are very frank and have made many people aware of the fact that their breath can offend other people. It is not easy for a person to know whether his own breath has a bad odor. The smelling apparatus, situated high up in the nose, tires very

140

quickly. If an odor persists one loses an awareness of it after a while.

There are many different causes of bad breath. An unclean mouth ranks among the foremost reasons. When particles of certain foods are left in the mouth after a meal, they are acted upon by bacteria and enzymes in the saliva. Certain bad-smelling gases are usually produced by these reactions. This is particularly true of protein foods such as fish, meat, eggs, and cheese.

In addition, this condition is made worse if the saliva is allowed to stagnate for a long interval. That is why one's breath is unpleasant upon arising, or going for an extended period without drinking water.

Infections of teeth, gums, mouth, throat, nasal passages, and sinuses are also guilty of causing halitosis. Do you know that odors of certain foods when eaten get into the bloodstream and the odor is exhaled from the lungs? Examples of such offending foods are garlic, onions, peppermint, and certain chemicals.

To attack the problem of halitosis the teeth should be routinely brushed after a meal, and the mouth thoroughly rinsed. An excellent way to clean one's mouth after a meal is to use one of the devices operating on a water-spurting principle. Its trade name is WATER PIC, and it works as follows:

By means of an electric pump, water from a reservoir is changed into a thin stream which makes 20 spurts per second. A nozzle held by the operator directs this

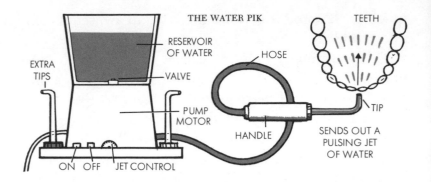

THE WATER PIK

RESERVOIR OF WATER

HOSE

TEETH

EXTRA TIPS

VALVE

TIP

PUMP MOTOR

HANDLE

SENDS OUT A PULSING JET OF WATER

ON   OFF   JET CONTROL

against the teeth and gums. This device does not replace brushing. However, it does clean areas which cannot be reached by a brush. There are other oral irrigating devices which work on different principles.

A visit to the dentist to remove all dental decay and rule out gum and other infections is a must. He will also clean stains and remove tartar. An excess of these has been known to be responsible for bad odors.

If the problem persists one should see a doctor. He will check for sinus and other infections. Sometimes digestive troubles or other sicknesses such as advanced diabetes may be causing unusual odors. Frequently dentists can spot these ailments during a visit.

The use of breath-sweetening lozenges does not eliminate bad breath. These simply mask the odor by substituting a stronger and more pleasant odor. The same is true for mouthwashes. You have learned that halitosis may be caused in many ways. Therefore it is misleading for advertisers to give the impression that their product kills halitosis germs. There are no specific halitosis germs.

142

Preserving Your Teeth

By the time you are thirteen years old you will probably have all the teeth you will ever possess, except all your wisdom teeth. If you are careful and follow the simple rules for dental health you can make your teeth last for life.

There are powerful bacterial, chemical, and mechanical forces constantly at work in your mouth to injure your teeth. If you are careless you are simply turning yourself over to the enemy, and the destructive process is speeded up. Dental records show that between the ages of six and fifteen many students are beginning to have their precious permanent teeth damaged, and some of the teeth are being lost forever.

Importance of Good Teeth

Perhaps the biggest reason for having a strong, well-aligned, healthy set of teeth is for the enjoyment of good health. All types of food are easily and thoroughly chewed, meals are enjoyable, and painful toothaches are minimized or nonexistent.

Healthy, well-spaced teeth give your face a beautiful smile which constantly affects your personality. Good teeth will be a priceless possession in your social, business, and professional life. A full set of teeth also helps shape your face, especially your cheeks, the corners of your mouth, and the lips.

Even your speech is influenced by teeth. It is found that 18 out of 26 letters of the alphabet need the help of your teeth for proper enunciation.

A healthy mouth, free from dental decay and gum disease, is usually also easily kept free from bad breath. And you know what a disadvantage an offensive breath can be in dealing with people.

Rules for Dental Health

1. *Keep your mouth clean.* Brush your teeth after eating. If you cannot brush, then rinse. If you cannot rinse, swish with drinking water and swallow. Be constantly aware that food particles, especially sweets, must not be allowed to cling to teeth.

2. *Cut down on sweets.* If you must eat sweets, do so only at meals. Try not to eat between meals.

3. *Visit the dentist regularly.* Do this every six months, or whenever he suggests. Don't wait until you have a toothache for a check-up, repair work, or ORAL PROPHYLAXIS (cleaning).

4. *Take advantage of fluoridation.* If your drinking water is not fluoridated, ask the dentist for fluoride treatment.

Sweets to Avoid

It cannot be said often enough that particles of sweet foods which are not rinsed out of the mouth are acted upon by bacteria to produce acids *within a few minutes.* Keep this thought in mind and go easy on the following foods when you cannot rinse your mouth for awhile.

Soft drinks sweetened with natural sugar. Most soda pop has a tremendous concentration of sugar.

Candy balls, rolled candy mints, fruit drops. These

144

are very disastrous for your teeth because they dissolve slowly and are kept for long periods between the cheek and the side teeth. The bacteria then really have a ball! In addition, these candies may contain citrus acid which is capable of dissolving tooth enamel.

Sweet doughnuts and muffins. When these are eaten for breakfast *and the mouth is not rinsed,* some sugar will remain on the teeth for many hours.

Gooey pastries, cakes with thick icing, pies

Ice cream, ices, thick syrups.

Chocolate, chewing gum.

Raisins, dates, dried fruits, honey.

And lots more! Many dietetic foods however do not contain natural sugars but use artificial sweeteners.

Eat Fibrous Foods

Certain foods such as apples, pears, raw carrots, celery, cabbage, and other fresh fruits and raw vegetables contain tough fibers and require chewing before being swallowed. They scrape the teeth and gums, and help clean and stimulate them. The jaw muscles are also exercised.

Foods that do this are called DETERGENT foods. It is recommended that you eat more of these since most of our foods are soft. Many soft foods, such as crackers, cakes, and candy, get pressed into the cracks and grooves of the biting surfaces of teeth. Such foods are known as IMPACTING foods. In their wedged and flattened condition, they will remain on the teeth for a long time unless removed with a toothbrush after eating.

Diet and Dental Decay

Many studies have been made to learn whether dental decay can be prevented by including extra amounts of certain vitamins, minerals, or other foods in one's diet. Despite the claims of food faddists, there is at present no scientific evidence that this can be done successfully.

Only fluorine has ever been found to offer some degree of immunity to cavities when it is swallowed. Nevertheless, much research is still going on. In science, the last word is never written about any subject. Dental and medical researchers still have open minds regarding cavities and diet.

It is well known by medical experts that for maintaining good physical health one must eat a balanced diet. This means eating the proper foods in the correct proportions. It has also been found that for good dental health one must eat the same diet which promotes good health for the rest of the body. Good dental health means properly formed and anchored teeth, strong jawbones, and healthy gums and other mouth tissues.

Study the chart showing the proper foods for a basic, balanced diet. Do you find that there is something important you frequently overlook? If you do, then you should make an effort to remedy the deficiency. For example, do you have Vitamin C every day? It is believed necessary for keeping gums healthy. It is a matter of scientific accuracy that continuous neglect of certain nutrients such as proteins, iron, and certain vitamins can lessen the resistance of mouth tissues to infection.

There is a tendency for many people to take certain daily vitamin pills in the belief that these will ensure one's good health. The vitamin industry has done much advertising to promote this feeling.

Health authorities say that vitamin pills are usually not necessary if one eats a normal variety of the proper nutritional foods. In the United States people rarely get vitamin-deficiency diseases. In most cases the small amounts of vitamins which are needed are found in our daily diets. If a physician or dentist feels that a certain vitamin is necessary he will prescribe it.

GROUP ONE

GROUP SEVEN

GROUP TWO

GREEN AND YELLOW VEGETABLES
some raw, some cooked, frozen or canned

BUTTER AND FORTIFIED MARGARINE
(With added vitamin A)

ORANGES, TOMATOES, GRAPEFRUIT
or raw cabbage or salad greens

EAT THE BASIC SEVEN EVERY DAY

GROUP SIX

BREAD, FLOUR AND CEREALS
natural whole grain or enriched or restored

POTATOES AND OTHER VEGETABLES AND FRUITS
raw, dried, cooked, frozen or canned

GROUP THREE

MEAT, POULTRY FISH OR EGGS
or dried beans, peas, nuts or peanut butter

MILK AND MILK PRODUCTS
fluid, evaporated, dried milk or cheese

GROUP FIVE

GROUP FOUR

147

Dentistry as a Profession

When the time comes for you to choose a career you may wish to consider dentistry. It offers a lifetime of service in the healing arts and sciences. It is a rewarding, lucrative profession, and especially adaptable to the talents of a science-minded man or woman. There is also much opportunity for research and specialization.

More than fifty excellent dental schools are scattered all over the country. The dental-school curriculum is not easy, but students find it very interesting and challenging. It extends over a period of four years. To enter such a school you usually need only two years of predental education in a college or university. How-

ever, it is found that two out of three applicants remain a full four years in college to obtain a bachelor's degree before entering dental school.

Candidates who apply to dental school are required to take a Dental Aptitude test. This is a one-day examination given throughout the country three times a year.

The Dentist's Emblem

The official emblem you see in the illustration may remind you of the one displayed by your physician in which the serpent is entwined around the staff of Asclepius, the Greek god of medicine. However, in the dental design this snake is coiled around an arrow which represents an Arabian cautery, the ancient "branding iron" used to sterilize and sear wounds to stop bleeding.

The triangle is the Greek letter delta, which stands for dentistry. The circle is the Greek letter O and stands for odont, which means tooth. The background has 32 leaves representing the number of teeth in the adult set. There are also 20 berries denoting the number of baby teeth.

History of Dentistry

The practice of dentistry started fairly recently in recorded history. Writings of the early Egyptians between 3500 to 1000 B.C. describe certain conditions of the teeth and mouth. These reports and the evidence found in the jaws of Egyptian mummies show that these people suffered from the same dental diseases as modern man.

149

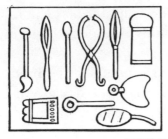

INSCRIPTIONS OF DENTAL INSTRUMENTS FOUND ON
TOMBSTONES OF ANCIENT EGYPTIAN AND GREEK SURGEONS

The records also tell of "physician for the teeth." There is evidence that certain plants and herbs were used to relieve pain of toothaches, either as soothing medicated packings on the cheeks and in the mouth, or when swallowed by the patient to make him insensitive to pain.

Certain forceps and other tools have been found in ruins and some historians believe these were used for dental work. But there is no evidence that the ancient Egyptians ever practiced oral surgery or ever extracted teeth. Some teeth in mummies have been found to contain gold. But it is not certain that this was to cover decayed areas of the teeth, since gold and precious stones were often set into teeth for ornamental reasons.

There is proof that in certain cultures wood, metal, marble and other stones, ivory, and also natural and animal teeth were used to replace lost teeth. These were attached to adjacent sound teeth with wires, bands, or rings made of gold or silver. Plant fibers, animal gut, and leather lacings were probably used for attachments.

Records have also been found in Mesopotamia (modern Iraq) describing dental science. These have led experts to believe that extractions were made here as early as 700 B.C. It is interesting that toothaches were believed to be caused by a "worm." In addition to medical treatment, the usual superstitions, magical rituals, and chants of those days were constantly used.

At about this time in Phoenicia, on the Mediterranean, craftsmen were making dental bridgework and other parts using artificial teeth. In Italy, jewelers were also making delicate false-teeth devices. Some of these have been found by archeologists and have been placed in museums. Another remarkable Italian find was a dental appliance which may have been used to straighten a few teeth by wiring them together. As you know, this is a procedure widely used today.

Through the ages in every civilized country, from the Chinese to the Incas and Aztecs, there was experimentation in dentistry. This was done in order to lessen pain, improve the condition of the teeth, gums, and mouth, or simply to make one's smile brighter. The Arabs learned to use wax, gold foil, and other metals to fill holes in teeth left by decay.

In Greece, dentistry was a distinct vocation beginning around 500 B.C., and was often described by some famous physicians such as Hippocrates and Galen. But

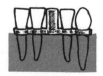

AN ANCIENT SOLID GOLD TOOTH
BANDED TO NEIGHBORING TEETH
WHICH WAS FOUND IN ITALY

this work was mainly done by dental specialists and carried on in dental "shops." Loose teeth were extracted with special forceps. A decayed tooth was "cured" of infection by being cauterized with a red-hot wire inserted into it. Some remedies for toothache were cloves, pepper, and ginger applied to the painful area.

Greeks were proud of their fine white teeth and used to scour and polish them. The Romans, too, utilized this form of dental hygiene. In their literature it is mentioned that wealthy families had their teeth cleaned by slaves using special small sticks—an early form of toothbrush. Toothpowders were made from finely ground pumice, an abrasive volcanic stone. Burnt eggshells were also used.

During the Middle or Dark Ages (400–1400 A.D.), there was hardly any scientific inquiry or attempt to improve dentistry throughout Europe. The dental techniques of the Greeks, Romans, and Italians were known mainly in the monastaries. The monks who lived there, were the chief practitioners of dentistry and they were often assisted by barbers, especially in France. In the 12th century, by edict of the Pope, the monks gave up their practice and the barbers and quacks then took over. Treatment consisted mainly of extraction. In Arabia, however, dentistry was done by physicians.

This was the period in history when the general public knew or cared little about science or critical thinking. They blindly followed illogical and superstitious ideas and behavior as a way of life. For example, it was believed that to cure a toothache, or to regain a lost

152

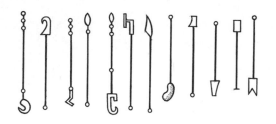

tooth, one had simply to acquire a tooth from another person, preferably from a hanged criminal.

The literature of this period has many tales of graves being illegally opened and the teeth forcibly removed from dead bodies. Another source of human teeth was the sale by poor people of their own permanent teeth. These teeth were sold for pitifully low prices.

The person who acquired the tooth rarely did anything with it. He only held it in his hand or perhaps slept with it. Just possessing it was all that was considered necessary for the magical healing to occur.

After the year 1400 interest in science and medicine was reawakened and many books were written about dentistry. In fact, between 1530 and 1728, 137 publications devoted to the art and science of dentistry appeared in France, Germany, Italy, and England. In France, about 1700, there were qualifying tests for those who wanted to practice dentistry. This was one of the first steps toward the recognition of dentistry as a profession.

In 1728, Pierre Fauchard, an exceptionally talented French dentist, wrote a treatise on teeth called "The Surgeon Dentist." It explained in clear terms the prac-

tice of dentistry. He made no attempt to hide trade secrets as other writers tried to do. He condemned the unqualified people who were practicing dentistry. This book also set the stage for free exchange of ideas among dentists in the true spirit of science. To this day Fauchard is regarded as the founder of the dental profession.

For years there were no colleges for dentists in the United States. People practiced dentistry without any special training. Some physicians would do extractions when absolutely necessary. Many extractions were also done by men who traveled in wagons through the countryside, often setting up tents or booths in carnivals and circuses. Country people would have their teeth pulled in front of gaping audiences, while loud music would be played to drown out the patient's screams. In some sections teeth would be extracted by the town barber or blacksmith.

Dentistry was learned in the same way as any other skilled trade—one became an apprentice to a master practitioner. This meant that one learned while helping a dentist for several years at little or no salary. Food and lodging were usually supplied by the master. This is the way many early dentists in America learned the profession.

You may be interested to know that Paul Revere, the famous American patriot, was a fine silversmith, and although he was not a dentist, he was a practitioner of dental arts.

In those days, sets of false teeth were very uncomfortable. They were crude, mouth-filling and food-catching devices. The upper and lower plates were kept apart, and in place, by large coil springs. It is said that George Washington had four sets of such dentures. They chattered whenever he made a speech. One set of dentures which he owned was made of wood, with each tooth riveted into the correct place. Another set was carved in one piece from the ivory tusks of a hippopotamus.

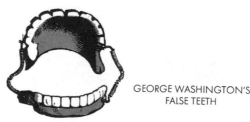

GEORGE WASHINGTON'S
FALSE TEETH

The birth of dentistry as a distinct profession may be dated from the opening of the first dental college in the world in 1840 in Baltimore. It was called the Baltimore College of Dental Surgery. Today there are over 50 first-class dental schools in the United States.

There were outstanding discoveries and inventions which have greatly improved dental science. In 1844 nitrous oxide, called laughing gas, was introduced as a useful pain-killer by Horace Wells, an American dentist. In 1871 the dental engine was first used for drilling and preparing teeth.

In 1895 Roentgen discovered x-rays. Very early in the 20th century there were developed local anesthetics such as Novocain which could be safely used. In 1930 acrylic resin (a plastic) was discovered and began to be used for artificial dentures. Recent developments have come one on the heels of another. They are described in other chapters.

The United States is the leader in dental research. Most Americans receive dental attention at some time in their lives. This is still not true in many other lands.

You should know that it is correct to address your dentist as "Doctor." This title is included in his well-earned degree of D.D.S., Doctor of Dental Surgery or D.M.D., Doctor of Dental Medicine.

BENJAMIN T. MEYER DDS

RING BELL
AND ENTER

Index

159